Silent Conviction

Doug Booth

Silent Conviction

One

1991

Saturday, April 20th, at precisely 10:30, a rare and much talked about event took place.

Freedom was almost never granted to the cons of Battle View Prison, barring the hangman's knot, acute desperation or being stupid enough to piss-off someone who was bigger and meaner.

But this day the biggest and the meanest of them was leaving, and not in a cheaply made coffin.

Anderson ambled unescorted toward the grey steel gates tall and straight, toward unsmiling and indifferent guards. He never hurried. Such was the gait of lesser men, a life-lesson he once taught Billy Rider.

His time was done. He was a free man, with a purpose he never once let falter. He was a man on a mission borne of a promise, despite his real expectation that very soon he would return to Battle View for his eventual execution following the premeditated murder of the woman whom he believed was his wife because, for reasons he could never quite fathom, she had never filed for divorce.

He had promised her that night so long ago that he would kill her for what she had done, and he would. John Anderson was a man of his word. Though first he would honour another vow he had silently sworn years earlier.

His tightly knit society of so many years, the nation's

most dangerous men caged behind rows of wire fencing, stood quietly clapping their hands in a slow and measured rhythm. Some were envious, while others felt troubled. With his departure would come a new age, a new White hierarchy yet to be won, established, and defended.

His cellmate and unlikely friend of twenty years stood with them waiting to exchange a final glance, a final goodbye they alone would comprehend. That did not happen. Anderson was not into laments and sad goodbyes, and for the first time in two decades Billy Rider felt the emptiness of desertion and desperation, a tearless and muted "thank-you" bidding his friend farewell.

Billy knew very well that he would never see Anderson again. Good fortune was not his lot in life. Nor had he ever for a moment believed that John would actually kill his wife. Or believe that he himself would one day walk free through those gates. Easy to say, not so easy to do.

None of which was lost on Anderson whose grim expression didn't change as the huge doors clanged shut behind him. He had forgotten how to laugh years ago, weeks before entering a place where smiles were a hazardous distraction, a frivolous display of weakness.

He combed his fingers through his hair, not yet accustomed to the sensation. The morning air was somehow and suddenly fresher, the sun brighter; its warmth somehow more soothing.

The nondescript minibus was waiting, the kind that would take handicapped or retarded kids to school, or old folks dressed in pink polyester who had lived too long to shopping malls for possibly their last day out. Or an ex-con into ten weeks of freedom. He stopped at the open doors to inhale a deep breath of freedom.

The engine was running; the interior several degrees cooler than the early spring day. The driver ignored him. He was the sole passenger, anxious for the five-mile drive to the armed checkpoint, then five miles further on to the bus station at the edge of some Tennessee jerkwater town that was his gateway to a seventy-one-day journey.

He hadn't travelled that far in twenty-six years, when in another lifetime he had travelled thousands of miles each week to work in Europe dressed in expensive wool suits, silk ties, custom-made shirts with French cuffs and shoes imported from Italy.

Those happy and fulfilling days were long forgotten, the faintest memories made impossible because of her.

Now he was wearing brown laced shoes with rubber soles, beige Dockers, a vinyl belt, and a beige polo shirt. Not much better than prison grey, one rung higher than a homeless person. He had a hundred dollars in his pocket, his birth certificate, a letter from the State of Tennessee, a Statement of Release from the warden, and a bus ticket that would take him anywhere he desired within a 600-mile radius.

He chose Charleston, South Carolina, an easy day's drive south to West Palm Beach, to her, and a mere few hours north to Necessity, North Carolina for long overdue justice, by which time he might have a car. He had until June 30th, determined that, barring any unforeseen events, like the whore being killed crossing the street, ten weeks was all the time he would need.

A job was waiting for him in Charleston if he was willing to sweat out sixty-hour weeks for thirty K a year at a cartage company, full-time if he didn't screw up. Enough for a used car that wasn't built until years after his arrest, a place to flop, nicer clothes and maybe a radio. After half his life in prison he didn't need much, and for the past month or so he had let the thick black hair he remembered grow in streaked with silver without adding a day to his sixty years.

He wasn't hungry; he was fascinated. The bus station where the driver left him was a bench in front of a drugstore where he sat for an hour taking everything in, especially the women passing by. He hadn't seen or touched one in a quarter-century, or heard a woman's voice, realizing he didn't much care. He didn't need the distraction.

He boarded the 12:00 PM Greyhound to Charleston, the driver stopping once for dinner, his first meal in twenty-six years that came with a menu and napkins. He arrived eleven hours later, the meal and the taxi to the halfway house leaving him enough for his meals the next day and a another taxi to the company Monday morning.

He spent seven nights at the halfway house, laundering and pressing his work uniform each evening because he could. The decision was his. The second Saturday of freedom he rented a one-room furnished apartment by the month, the best he could afford and the worst he'd ever lived in.

The place was a hole one notch above Cell 312, a small notch because he had a door he could open and close whenever he wished, where he searched the classifieds in the evenings for cheap cars and toasted Billy Rider with his first cheap scotch since ancient times, reminded by the harsh taste that was foreign to him that he once drank nothing but the finest.

Sunday he slept in.

On the third Saturday he bought a ten-year-old Monte Carlo, unpretentious, co-signed by his boss who believed in second chances and Anderson was already showing himself as a stalwart employee. On the fourth Saturday he drove north to Necessity, North Carolina into a new age with a new-age look.

Once there he grunted, absorbing the skyline, wondering how Miami would seem to him after so many years. Rider had once told him about 90,000. Not quite. Necessity had doubled in population.

He drove around for a while, the addresses long since committed to memory, taking notes. Then he drove to the Necessity Daily News that was open, and that had a reading room where he researched the town's weddings and deaths between June '71 and December '75 until he was satisfied with what he had discovered.

Eager to learn more, he remained until closing to read everything written about the gruesome 1971 murder of Lucy Merriweather, age seventeen, and the murder trial of Billy Rider. Everything Rider had told him over the years, once the barriers had dropped, was true. Just not everything was written, including the peculiarities of small town hillbilly justice.

The coming week Anderson would beg off Friday and work Saturday and Sunday if need be to placate his boss. He needed time at City Hall.

He had confirmed who they were and who they had married, basic data far from good enough for what was required of him. He needed to establish where they lived, though he did suspect where they might work. And what of the women? Were they at home burdened by boredom, or nine-to-fivers striving for equality? He needed to learn about the children, the ages, the workday and their free time.

The Carlton Bank stood precisely where Billy Rider remembered, as was Rigby Automobile, a no-brainer and currently Rigby's Fine Motors.

All in all, not his kind of town. Too small. He couldn't imagine back in the day. Neither was Charleston for that matter, the people somehow too effusively Southern even for the South. If he was never again to see Madrid and Paris, he would at least spend his last few days of cherished freedom in Miami.

As for Billy Rider whom he would never see again, could never see again, the man was on his own. Though no one since his first day had dared to bother the kid, which couldn't quite be described as a miracle, more of a commandment, the true miracle was that Billy had somehow survived his first three years at Battle View to everyone's astonishment.

The punishment he endured was a medieval and barbaric torture, giving him unending respect that would make the remainder of his sentence a ride in the park.

*

The following Friday John Anderson was at the Necessity City Hall at noon.

His first duty was to fulfill a promise, which he did. The Cutters, he discovered, had sold their home and had relocated to the West Coast a few months after Rider's conviction. Most likely, Anderson presumed, to conceal their shame and regain what remained of their shattered lives.

He went to the receptionist, asking how he might contact someone by phone without knowing precisely where they lived. So many things he didn't know, or had forgotten. She told him, directing him to the public phone. A moment later he was connected to the Cutter home in Seattle, a sound he hadn't heard in years ringing in his ears. Then, a gentle voice:

"Hello?"

"Miss Sally Cutter? Do I have the pleasure of addressing Miss Sally Cutter?"

"You do, sir. And who, may I ask, is enquiring?"

"My name, Miss Sally, is not important. More so is that I am calling on behalf of your son Mr. Billy Rider."

The line was quiet. "Sir, my son has been gone from my home twenty years. If I am a source of amusement to you, your thoughtlessness is unkind in the most extreme way."

"Twenty years less six weeks and three days to be more exact, Miss Sally."

"When still he will not be a free man, which is why I consider your call particularly distasteful."

"I gave Billy my word that I would call you. He's never forgotten his family, or stopped loving you. He's simply never been able to tell you himself on the phone, as you well know. And that Battle View forbids all visitors is a blessing in disguise, Miss Sally. You must never believe differently. He spoke of you often with me…most nights."

"Sir, he spoke with you? You know him?"

"I do. Better I would daresay than his own mother."

"Then…"

"Yes, Miss Sally, recently released after a very long time. I was there to greet him if, in fact, not very kindly at first. We shared a cell these many years, managing somehow to become friends which is no small feat in Battle View. So yes, I know your son well. He taught me with great patience what I was required to learn so that I might understand him. We helped each other. Eight years ago Billy achieved a degree in Social Sciences; last year he obtained his master's. Above all that's what he wanted you to hear, so that you might be proud and learn to forgive him. He's a smart man. More importantly, he's strong and he's fit despite your worst fears. He's respected, Miss Sally. That's rare in any prison. In Battle View it's nothing short of a miracle."

"But, sir, for what purpose did he study when he cannot in any way impart his knowledge to others if not with a pen?"

"For *my* purpose, Miss Sally. Once hearing his story, I convinced him over time that he must be ready for a new and different world, that he must always have hope and be prepared. As you must from this day forward."

"For what new world, sir?"

"The world you live in now, that he cannot yet possibly imagine."

"Sir, you are distressing me."

"Do you believe in God, Miss Sally?"

"I do not, sir. No good reason has ever been argued that I care to accept or embrace."

"Then believe in your son, as I do. Believe in what is right, as I do."

"Sir, what must we hope for? What do you know?

Please be frank with me."

"What I know is that Billy did not kill Lucy Merriweather. Suffice it to say that I am once again a free man, a man of my word, despite which I believe Billy has certain reservations."

"Then you will never see him again, to tell him that we spoke?"

Anderson never understood the sense in delaying unfortunate news. "No, Miss Sally. I don't believe I will ever see Billy again. We have different paths best travelled alone. However, believe me when I say that I am a man of my word and he knows we are speaking, if not at this precise moment."

"What hope, sir? What paths?"

"The hope that you will see your son, of course, and that he will tell you himself of his dreams he does not yet know to wish for. I must go now, Miss Sally. Do not give up hope that Billy will one day search for his mother and his father as I have. He's coming home, Miss Sally. You must believe that. Just don't be taken aback by what comes knocking at your door. He is not the shy boy once wrongly taken from you."

Sally Cutter's quiet sobs were difficult to hear. "My husband, sir, passed on some years ago. I believe he died of a despairing heart. His final words were of our Billy. We never once forsook him in our daily thoughts."

"In his heart he is aware of that truth, Miss Sally. I do deeply regret your loneliness and that our speaking will fill your mind with such disquiet without your husband's comfort. Yet I would implore you to be as hopeful and confidant as I am. Your son is a good man, an innocent man. I truly believe that. His conviction twenty years ago resulted from shoddy police work, a deadbeat lawyer, and your son not telling the entire truth at trial. For which he paid dearly. Had he been truthful, less fearful of what he believed might happen had he conveyed the complete truth, he would not have gone to Battle View. Others would have in his place."

"Sir, what truth did he not tell? What others do you mean?"

"Billy knows who killed Lucy Merriweather. However the time of proving his innocence is long past. He has no hope of that, not on his own."

"Then for what possible reason was he afraid of speaking truthfully, incurring such a dreadful and vile punishment?"

"In part, your view of him. The rest will be for Billy to tell you. In my view, at worst, a misdemeanour and not entirely his alone. If guilty of anything, Miss Sally, he was culpable of being innocent in mind and body at a time and in a place when others were not. I assure you that is no longer the case"

The long distance operator cut in. He had a few seconds remaining.

"Thank you, sir, for calling. I will anticipate the very least and be overjoyed by whatever more I receive. When I do see my son, and now I must believe that one day I will, I will tell him with my first breath of the joy of the hope you have brought me this very day. You have strengthened my heart, sir, as I believe you once strengthened my son."

He chuckled.

"Sir?"

"Billy spoke to me often of what a delightful and unpredictable character you are. I truthfully wish I could see for myself, though I can hear clearly in your voice that he did not exaggerate in the least. Good day, Miss Sally."

"As I hear clearly, sir, that you are a good man. I will believe forever in my heart that the transgression which caused your incarceration in such a horrible place, for such an intolerable duration, was not as a result of your premeditation but of an unfortunate event beyond your control. Good day to you, sir."

The line went dead, Anderson wearing a wide smile. He could see in his mind the vivacious seventy-year-old that Billy Rider would certainly hurry to visit one day soon. He hoped.

*

Next he went to the registrar's office where freedom of information was more available than most citizens realized. A good place to spy on neighbours for curious minds too afraid to peer through bedroom windows and the Merriweather's ill-spent hatred of Billy could not possibly be discounted from what was about to take place, to be proven, and, above all things, be forgiven.

Anderson had killed his victim as a reflex action which the court interpreted as second degree murder, when he really should have killed his wife. That lifelong regret occurring to him much too late to avoid a death sentence by virtue of temporary insanity, which he would soon rectify, fully prepared to step upon the gallows so that he might fulfill a dream. Billy Rider, though, was innocent, should never have done time in the nation's septic tank.

The other names were Rigby, Dwight; Carlton, Jake; Rigby, Darlene; and, Carlton, Eleanor. Brothers and sisters he was anxious to secretly discover, to secretly encounter on behalf of a man who had kept Anderson from becoming worse than his loving wife had made him.

What he planned for the four of them would not put him back into Battle View, what he planned for her would.

He scribbled precise notes until closing, crossing the street for dinner, not certain whether to shit himself or die laughing. The latter understandably and necessarily postponed until after he killed his wife.

According to the final judgement and newspaper reports, which were equally important back in the day, Billy Rider had raped and killed young Lucy Merriweather. Anderson knew better, convinced years earlier. Never happened. The then eighteen-year-old Billy Rider was falsely accused.

unable or unwilling to defend himself, which Anderson understood.

Rider, at the beginning of his sentence was, to say the least, reclusive, withdrawn: Dumb, deaf, and stupid…to all except Anderson who'd fought internally with all his strength not to become involved with the kid. He hadn't needed the aggravation. His life in prison had been good, as good as could be since setting the ground rules, his rules, with the Blacks and Latinos.

Now John Anderson was reading that Dwight Rigby had married Eleanor Carlton two years after the trial. The wedding, apparently, was magnificent. The bride, not surprisingly, was blushing and dressed in white. Anderson wanted to piss himself. Compounding the intrigue, Jackson Carlton, Eleanor's brother, Jake to his friends, had married Dwight's sister, Darlene, who was also a blushing bride garbed in white.

He wondered, what the hell! Collusion mixed with social inbreeding, hillbilly cops and a judge too blind to see kangaroos leaping around her court.

Justice, particularly North Carolina good ol' boy justice, was bullshit. Justice wasn't uniform: No uniform code of punishment, everything riding on the sex, mood-swing, and well-being of the magistrate.

Any con would agree that women were the worst on the bench, too often giving in to the temperament of their erratic specie, despite their presumably inadequate training. As in Rider's case, personally enraged, not seeing beyond the matador's red cape.

Two

1951 -1952

The faded signage on Route 2 where the rutted and narrow
road began or ended read:
Charity: Pop: 999
Gas Bar & Diner 23 Miles

Charity wasn't much of a place any time of year. There was
no charm, no quaintness. Century-old weather-worn homes
with uneven roofs and crooked verandas littered more than
lined the Road Out, the town's only road that was never the
Road In; long enough to conceal them from the highway,
too narrow and broken for a dotted line. There were no
fences, no sidewalks and no pretty gardens, numbered
mailboxes telling the townsfolk what they already knew.
Tire tracks carved into the dry grass of front lawns
designated driveways left empty by the menfolk who each
day took the Road Out to wherever their work might require
them.

The school was the town hall and movie house, the
bingo hall, the prayer hall and the men's club, closed to all
save for the Sabbath during the summer weeks when the
town's small squad of teachers would escape elsewhere to
supplement the little they earned. Though the preacher,
being that he was the principal as well, remained to guard
over the key and his flock who would seldom, and never
with purpose, forego their weekly admonishments and self-

recriminations. Not when their neighbours would want to know why, or create the reasons that best suited their misgivings.

The drugstore was in the grocery store, the closest salon for the women and barber for the men were across from the post office twenty-three miles down Route 2. The women's and girls' beauty needs were the domain of Mrs. Bolton who, strictly by appointment, sold Avon products from the catalogue on her coffee table in her front room.

The town had no dentist; he was down the road as well, though the doctor did maintain a private office at the volunteer Fire Hall located at the base of the water tower at the dead-end of the Road Out and would, on occasion, deem the extraction of a painful molar or incisor his responsibility at an additional cost.

As for the police, they were never seen in Charity, never needed where neighbours married neighbours and never locked their doors.

Life was slow with the invisible monotony that insidiously encroaches until it's too late. The single purpose of graduating from high school was to escape the 998 others who already knew too much about you, very few of them ever succeeding. They lived and they died, with nothing much to anticipate or remember in-between, one generation moving in as another was taken out by the undertaker twenty-three miles away.

Winter months in Charity were cold, long and dark, with too little snow to make the town appear crisp and clean and too much to make the season any more bearable than other seasons. Springtime wasn't green with cleansing midday rains or the fresh scents of colourful blossoms. Nor was autumn bright with red and gold leaves rustling against cool breezes, while summer unerringly brought an insufferable heat from a glaring sun made worse by a suffocating thick blanket of stagnant dank air. Seemingly endless days in the valley with little else to do but frolic and splash and tease the girls down at the creek.

Girls were expected to help with household chores, training to become dutiful wives and good mothers, to set good examples for their own daughters. That's what decent girls did, while the boys would search for mischief after school, leaving their education behind to find work in department stores, car lots, or hawk their wares door-to-door like Mr. Bolton who always left early and came home late to his family.

Betsy Bolton had once dreamed of getting out, of running away with Buck, the boy she liked most in Grade Eight. She could work as well as any man in a department store, or perhaps as a typist somewhere she had never been. She was smart enough, and she was very pretty. She was popular with the boys, constantly flirting with them and teasing them. However over the summer of '51 she had developed into more of a woman and none was better in her eyes or in her heart than Buck.

He was bigger than the other boys. He was stronger, more daring, more charming, and he treated her right. Throughout the previous fall and winter he would carry her books home from school, holding her hand, young hearts eager for the coming of spring with their love even now in full bloom, when they would sit on her steps at night and kiss when Mr. Bolton wasn't peering through the parlour curtains.

Then at last came the long-awaited freedom of summer days by the creek, giving vent to his pent-up yearnings and her frail emotions, heated weeks of kisses more passionate, embraces more ardent, and Buck's more daring probes.

Betsy wasn't allowed down by the creek, not alone, not without her girlfriends, which really didn't matter.

Sunday, the last day of September, was muggy, abnormally hot for that time of year, the young couple once again making their way unnoticed to a small patch of coarse grass where dried leaves were falling from trees far away from the more populous and stony expanse that scarcely resembled a beach. They were alone in Shangri-La where the deeper water swirled and babbled and the hot sun warmed their chilled bodies.

They weren't missed by the others. They never were, strolling from sight, his hand clutching hers, Buck carrying her satchel and his. Hers was stuffed with her towel, a blanket, and the sandwiches she had made; his was less full with his towel and the flask of whiskey he had filled from the bottle that his father kept in the kitchen.

The entire day belonged to them, swimming and frolicking in the cool water where Betsy would often cling to him, or kick her feet wildly to keep afloat, waiting until noon to lay out her picnic while adoring Buck who sipped his whiskey and gazed at her with such tenderness. He was so mature, as was she. She was a woman. He told her so often. He loved her. He would never let anyone hurt her or take her away. She was his woman, and she believed him, her first sip of liquor burning her throat, the second warming her chest.

Buck put the flask to his lips, pressing the tip of his tongue against the narrow aperture.

Betsy's third sip was easier, smoother, her fourth and fifth making her drowsy, cradling herself into his protective arms.

With her picnic lunch forgotten, Buck feigned yet another sip, offering Betsy the last few drops as any thoughtful man in love would.

Her eyes closed to the urgency of his lips pressed to hers. She wanted to sleep in his arms forever. She had never felt so consumed, her body tingling with such unfamiliar and exciting sensations, her mind numbed by a torrent of dreams and new expectations. He was taking her away; he promised her so, to anywhere she wanted. In three years they would leave Charity behind without the slightest regret. He would buy her a big house and a convertible, like the one he'd seen in a magazine.

Waking to his touch, Betsy wasn't at all shy seeing Buck laying by her side dressed in his trunks, her damp bathing suit laying in a small heap at the edge of their blanket. She stood unsteadily, taking his hand, and went with him into the water where they bathed the sweat of the afternoon from their bodies and kissed, her body weightless in the water, joined with his in a frantic and heated embrace. Betsy realizing that very afternoon how Buck really loved her and cherished her, hating the whistle of the late day freight train that shattered her wonderful delirium and Buck's victorious forays into her body.

Clothed in her sundress they joined the others and walked home in a crowd, leaving Buck at her doorstep, rushing her dinner to sit with him that night on her steps, on the eve of their fourth week in Grade Nine, so anxious for those three long years to pass, her father's heartless taps on the window erupting too soon.

One day as late fall was once again melding with winter, Betsy left school early feeling unwell and went by herself to the Fire Hall to see the doctor, returning home to help her mother with dinner. That evening she announced to her mother and father that she was having a baby.

Her mother, alarmed by the scandalous news, shrieked and wrung her hands. Her father waited a few moments longer, considering what he had heard. Heaving himself from his seat he went to where she stood, striking his daughter across her face, pushing her from his path.

A few moments later he was at Buck Rider's front door threatening to call the State Police, to have him arrested. The boy was stricken with panic, barely able to speak, insisting that he would never do such a terrible thing. However Mrs. Rider knew her son was a liar; she knew that he stole from her and would often deny doing bad things. She begged her neighbour not to involve the police, certain that she and Mrs. Bolton together could decide on a better solution to shelter Betsy from shame.

From that evening on Mr. Bolton spoke not a word to his daughter until the afternoon she gave birth, nor would he or his wife ever for a moment think to bother with the corrupted infant once born.

As the weeks and months passed Betsy and Buck became more of an item, whispered about and pointed at. They were the envy of everyone at school. Buck by the other boys for his bravado and daring to do it, all of them curious to hear more; Betsy by all the girls who believed she really might leave Charity behind. However, for what little it matters, they were wrong.

Betsy's flirtatious days were at an abrupt end, for the other girls soon learned from their mothers that she was a tramp.

*

When they did leave school, much sooner than planned the following June, Buck and Betsy did not leave Charity. Buck had found part-time work after school months earlier that became full-time stocking shelves in the town's grocery and drugstore, living with his parents until Betsy gave birth alone with a stranger to their son in her girlhood bedroom surrounded by inanimate dolls half its size and school books that would no longer serve a purpose.

Billy Rider was born in his mother's bed and named by her near noon on June 30th, 1952, moments after the doctor arrived from the Fire Hall.

She had so many dreams, dreams of leaving Charity that she and Buck hadn't had time alone to discuss. Though her mother had other more urgent dreams: Getting her promiscuous daughter out of her house.

Betsy didn't realize she was getting married that same day for reasons of propriety, in her bedroom and by her school principal who believed the prayer hall would be inappropriate given the immoral circumstances of the union.

When she learned the truth she cried unstoppable and

copious tears, her body trembling, when not even her mother ventured to comfort her.

It was not what she wanted, she implored. She wanted a white dress, and dancing, and for all her friends to see her and envy her for her new husband and baby. She wanted a nice home and for Buck to have a car. That's what she wanted.

Her father guffawed, retorting that, on such a fine summer's day, the friends she once had were at the creek having fun, being young and being decent. Whereas she was now a mother and a wife with a home of her own to maintain.

When he told her in a punitive tone, which he was confident God would condone, inwardly delighted by the panic and dread which he evoked, where and what her new home was, she told him she wanted to die.

That was God's dominion, Mr. Bolton replied, whenever He might choose to forgive her carnal sin. Then, closing the door between them forever, he declared with cool detachment that he wished never to speak with her again.

Her new home was an unpainted flat over the grocery store, a stairway from Buck's work, furnished with what their parents no longer needed or wanted. Buck's new convertible was Mr. Rider's rusting pick-up truck that he could borrow on occasion until he could afford one of his own. Their honeymoon that evening was a sparse and sober meal at the brightly lit diner twenty-three miles down Route 2, which is all Buck had money for as his son Billy slept tightly-wrapped on the backseat of the truck.

Buck never got his car or his truck, working long six-day weeks stocking shelves and making deliveries to pay the rent, put food on the table and clothes on their backs; while Betsy worked two or three hours in the store after supper each night washing the floors to bring home what little she could for diapers and medicine for Billy and a bottle of whiskey each week for Buck.

Billy Rider never discovered any of that as the years passed. He knew nothing of his early beginnings, his mother's dreams or his father's failure to take her away. Though he would never forget his last night in the window.

Billy didn't speak much then. He had nothing much to say. He'd never been anywhere or done anything to talk about, except play in his sandbox behind the grocery store. He never smiled or giggled. He had no reason. He had no friends, no one to play with. To the neighbours he was a bastard, food for their gossip. They thought he was slow, not quite right in the head, keeping their children away.

At home his mother would call him for his meals, seldom yelling his name twice. That's about all she ever said to him. She would send him to bed early each night to sleep on a full stomach, and seldom bother with him in the morning until she might notice him sitting in the hall quietly waiting for something to eat. Although on Saturdays he would sit in a shallow tub of tepid water until the water made him shiver, while she would sit pensively on the toilet seat to ensure that he didn't drown while secretly wishing that he would.

Those were the nights he liked most, when his mother would briskly rub him dry as though she might love him.

He almost never saw his father, happy when he didn't, frightened when he did. His father was always angry, making his mother afraid, and Billy didn't like the harsh smell that came from his father's mouth. Often his mother would cry, and Billy would cry, his mother never once thinking to comfort him, to make him feel better. So one day Billy stopped crying.

Billy Rider didn't understand what an orphan was, or that he had become one. He sat in his windowsill hugging the worn flannel that covered his knees, mesmerized by the jagged streaks of white light piercing the black night, forcing his eyes not to blink. He didn't want to miss a single one, with each flash searching for faces in the flood of thick and ominous clouds threatening to swamp his safe place, his secret place to hide from the yelling and screaming that was until then so much a part of his young and neglected life.

He wasn't afraid of the dark or the night; he loved the tempest pelting relentlessly and fiercely against his window, the prolonged and cacophonous roars of thunder that rattled the glass, as much as he loved the stars and the moon most summer nights when he should have been sleeping.

But his last night at home was different, the noises were different, nature's violent symphony not enough to cancel out the high-pitched shrieks and terrified shrills. His mother was screaming. So he opened his door, not certain at all that he should, afraid that he might be caught, punished for not being in bed, padding his way as far as he dared to where he could see his mother being killed.

She was a gruesome rag doll pinned to the wall by her throat. Her face was contorted and smeared with blood, the blade disappearing into her dress more times than Billy could count. Her eyes wide open with fright never saw Billy, her arms and her legs flailing, trying to strike back to save her already lost life. She was coughing and chocking, her mouth spewing spittle and blood.

Billy stood in a daze, his shoulders slumped, his arms by his side, watching his mother slide from the wall onto the floor, her white dress drenched in red, tattered and torn. She was convulsing and wailing, her arms crossed against her fatal wounds, pleading, gasping for air, asking Buck why.

His father stepped past her. He was laughing and snivelling, slicing the air, blood from the blade splashing her face, the wall and the floor. He was twirling in half circles, jerking, jabbering, talking gibberish too loud and too fast for Billy to comprehend, kicking whatever was near, a clenched fist pounding his head, his face strained with rage.

Suddenly he jerked sideways, glaring at her. "What!"

"Ya didn't have to kill me, Buck. I gave ya no cause to kill me."

"She got what was coming to her," he screamed into the air, his singlet and trousers drenched with his sweat and her blood "what she's deservin' of for what she done. And that ain't no lie."

His body arched forward, hovering over her. He was sneering and grunting inches from her face, his mouth twisted, his scowl maniacal.

"That's right, Betsy! Ya surely did! Ya finally got what was deservin' of ya for what ya done, for the way that ya always were. Flirtin' and carryin' on!"

He clutched his head. She was to blame, constantly nagging and jeering.

"That's the gospel's truth, what with all your cryin', always carryin' on about this and that, never stoppin', always blamin' me for what ya brought on yourself! Not me, Betsy. Ya'll from the get-go, from the day ya brought the little fucker into my home."

Betsy lay in her blood, sputtering more onto the floor. "I always did love ya, Buck, afore the boy. We could have got Billy gone, Buck, somehow. Found somewhere to leave him and took a bus to somewhere better than here."

"Never did mean to put a life into ya, Betsy. Was just givin' ya what ya wanted the best that I could. Too high a price for a few pokes in the woods. Never should've happened. Ya should've stopped me afore I got started. But ya didn't. Ya kept makin' me want ya. Me thinkin' ya'll would make your hole clean of what I put into ya. The way that ya should. But ya didn't. Ya let it fester. And now see what ya got... a gut full of holes."

Betsy was finished listening.

"That's right. I've gone and killed ya Betsy! Done a good job, too. Ain't no fixin' that. Ain't no tears gonna bring ya back now. Ain't my fault! Ya got what was comin'! Ya got to understand that."

His head was aching. What choice did he have?

"Don't see that I had a choice. Ya know that's the God's truth! Goddammit, Betsy! A man's gotta fix what needs fixin'. Ya went bad on me from the get-go and I don't see why. Can't explain it. Not treatin' me the way the Good Book says, losin' your good looks."

He knelt by her side, grabbing her hair. Her eyes flared open. She was limp, sobbing quietly and rapidly dying.

He twisted her head violently against the tiles, pressing hard, raising his other arm. Betsy Rider whimpered once and died. The thick wooden handle he left in her back scaring Billy the most.

Billy was quite certain his mother was dead. He'd seen a dead cat once before, not certain what that entailed, his body too frozen to move as his father passed him by without saying a word. Moments later, transfixed by his mother laying on the kitchen floor, a rush of air told him his father had not gone.

Buck's one hand pounded the air, his other gripped the half-empty bottle as he strode to his wife's side. He wasn't finished with the blame she deserved for the anguish she'd brought him.

"Ain't right, Betsy, the grief that ya caused!" He spun around, his arms spread wide "All this, cause ya wanted a poke down by the creek. Ya wanted to be a woman and ya hungered for more, not happy enough with my hands on your tits or your bare ass! No! Not Betsy Bolton! And what do I get for treatin' ya so good?" he screamed. "Him, that fuckin' retard that sure as hell ain't of my doin'," he kicked her, "and not one decent poke since."

He kicked her again. She wasn't listening, ignoring him like she always did. "Tell me now, Betsy. Who else? I know others got to feel them tits. Who was the lucky one who poked ya'll better than me close enough to the time? Should've known ya couldn't stop at one, not once ya had a taste of it."

He turned to the boy, stomping his foot into Betsy's warm blood, draining the whiskey into his raw throat, coughing and swearing before hurling the empty bottle into the air and reaching into his belt.

"She was to blame, boy. And ya'll!" he screeched at his son. "Now! See what ya'll have gone and done, ya'll and her!" He kicked the handle. "Ya'll made me do this!"

His head was pounding. What more could he say, or do? He never did like the boy, but the neighbours would think badly enough of him for killing his wife. Instead he raised the gun to his head and died.

Betsy and Buck Rider were barely nineteen. Their son, Billy, was barely four that midsummer evening without the memory of presents, or a cake, or friends at his party to remember.

Billy stood for a while then went to his window to live in the present until discovered the next day by the grocer who thought it curious that Buck hadn't come to work.
*

Three days later Betsy and Buck were buried. No one attended. Nor did the preacher bother reading from the Scriptures. Their souls were too forsaken. What right had he to second guess the Lord?

Not many days later Betsy's father passed away in another town as he worked, many convinced by his own hand; many others not at all surprised given the deep burden of his daughter's sins, though a welcome blessing to each of them for different reasons which Mrs. Bolton welcomed and believed.

At thirty-seven and single Mrs. Bolton sold the house before the coming school year for half its worth. She was eager to take the Road Out for the last time.

She put her husband's clothes along with Buck's and Betsy's into the trash along with her own that wouldn't fit into her single piece of luggage. To the frequent disposals she added her furniture and mementos that meant nothing, preferring to see her life and belongings burned to ashes at the back of her house as she watched from the porch rather than seeing her neighbours benefit in any way from her escape.

The aging car she had never liked she sold for the one-time "take it or leave it" price she was offered, fully aware the salesman had taken unfair advantage of a grieving widow and mother.

She had no reason to stay, wanting out more desperately than her daughter's long-ago girlish dream, far away from the gossip, the stares, and the silent aspersions. With her husband's and daughter's insurances she could live very nicely until once again she could place herself in the care of a good and decent man.

Billy was the problem. Always was, truth be told. The boy would spoil her future and, after so many years, she had no desire to raise a second family. Let alone care for the son of her promiscuous daughter's killer. Like father, like son; she could see the truth in his eyes. The boy would come to no good and the Riders certainly wanted no part of him. Not even offering to drive her and the boy to the bus station down the road. That was the kindness of the preacher who felt as God's messenger that his duty was to preach one last sermon as they turned onto the Road Out.

Her younger sister, Sally, lived in Necessity, North Carolina, a two-day bus ride to the East as far away as the young girl could then afford. They hadn't spoken very often in the seventeen years since her sister's often promised and successful escape beyond the Road Out.

At first forgetting Christmases, then birthdays, all other occasions became more of a nuisance than a pleasure. Nor had the girl waited very long to marry, eager for a family, disheartened to discover she was barren, calling soon after with news of the two boys the couple had adopted.

Older boys no one else wanted, Mrs. Bolton presumed. Delinquent boys, no doubt. She was always flighty that way, unpredictable, never restrained by good judgement or reason, though the boys were now boarding at college most of the year and the summer of '56 was coming to an end. The timing was ideal for Billy to bring her sister renewed purpose, bring new meaning to her life.

Betsy's mother, however, did not stay a moment longer with her sister than she needed to leave the boy, explaining that she would miss her bus to Charlotte where her first flight would take her to New York. She was relocating to the West Coast to begin a new life, where with a bit of sun and personal attention she hoped one day soon to once again at least resemble her age.

The truth was, she was increasingly unnerved by Billy. He hadn't spoken a single word since the murder-suicide; he hadn't cried a single tear. He simply followed her every move, devoid of expression, his blue eyes that now seldom blinked always shadowed and dull.

She left them without tearful goodbyes, without a warm and final sisterly embrace, disappearing into the waiting cab without thinking to wave; neither Sally nor Billy aware of how widely the woman was smiling.

Billy never again saw his grandmother. He quickly forgot her with nothing to remember her by and never once thought to care, through the first difficult years coming to believe that his great aunt Sally was the loving mother he was meant to have and deserved.

Three

1971

The months of May and June were a total nightmare. Endless days of unceasing rain and oppressive humidity made the air inside dank, heavy with smoke and foul with the habits of agitated men caged, their daily yard time cancelled. Angry and frustrated men searching for any diversion.

July 01st was not that way, and they hadn't much longer to wait. The sky was clear blue, a gentle breeze cleansing the late morning air, cons from all three blocks breathing relief in the walled and gated yard. Blacks and Latinos and Whites, all pumping iron, jogging the perimeter, or doing push-ups inches from the frail carpet of steam gradually wafting away from the grey concrete floor which was as close as they would get to soft grass under their feet for much of what remained of their lives.

Others slumped into corners, despondent or troubled, while others sought out allies or kept their distance from any trouble that might become their own.

Everyone except John Anderson. He wasn't in the yard; his yard, shared by Black Boss and the Latino's El Jefe. Three men who might not oversee Battle View Prison, yet unquestionably kept order in the nation's hell…when doing so was in their best or mutual interests. And what was about to happen was decidedly not in his best interest. Black Boss and El Jefe commiserating…sincerely.

He wasn't in the yard on the first beautiful day in weeks because he was royally pissed and moody, which was seldom a good thing for anyone.

Not a chance that he would be. He was alone in Cellblock Three, on his bunk, waiting, his legs dangling over the side, waiting, asking himself why. Why in the hell was he getting stuck with a pink-skinned newbie, a mommy's boy? Some punk kid who'd put his eager dick into where it didn't belong, freaking out when he was finished with her and killing the poor girl.

The entire place was waiting for this kid. As was Anderson who, the day before, had wanted to kick the warden's balls through his throat when the obnoxious shit came to his cell not merely to confirm the kid's arrival. He wanted to explain in detail what the kid had done, to gloat over the extent of the sentence, and tell Anderson that he would have his new cellmate for the next twenty years.

Anderson gave the kid three days, tops, before he'd be spread apart like a Christmas turkey, stuffed at each end in some dark corner by some white guy turned homo out of necessity or by natural proclivity. Either way, the Blacks and the Latinos would simply and often kick the shit out of him: Entertainment, something to pass the time bro, amigo.

That inevitable first night the kid would piss into his mattress, his mind and body too filled with terror to move. He would sob through the night, smothering spastic coughs into his pillow. Or curl onto the floor by the shitter, wanting to puke.

The second night he would whimper. He would dribble spittle from the corners of quivering lips, suck spurts of air through a runny nose and, perhaps like the young girl he raped, huddle into a tight ball to block out the raucous jeers that would inevitably penetrate the coarse pillow pressed tightly against his head.

They always cried, the young and tender newbies. The third night, the third of many more, wouldn't be as bad and by the fourth night he would know what to expect until someone else arrived to take his place. By which time he might even miss the attention, or the protection. Or be dead.

Whatever way, Anderson was truly pissed. He had no intention of transforming his cell into a nursery. Cell 312 had rules. He had rules.

He'd known about the kid for a while, a few days, since tapping into the rumours of the White grapevine. Everyone knew, some eagerly waiting. Although he alone was privy to the full extent of what was coming his way.

The warden had blind-sided him twenty-four hours earlier, leaving Anderson with no time to create the perfect scenario. That said, time was money and, in Battle View, the primary currency was survival.

First Anderson would wait for the guards to leave, waiting a moment longer before sliding quietly from his thin perch to eye the boy without saying word-one before circling him, grabbing his throat and beating him senseless. That way the kid would learn where not to beg for help. That's what he would do. Welcome to Battle View Prison, boy. Welcome to 312.

He thought of the story he'd been told from back in the day, whatever that meant, whenever that was. Everyone knew the story; some even believed it. The Whites did at least. The Latinos from the squalor of rundown barrios and ghetto-hardened Blacks, they didn't give a good shit about white boys or their tales.

Some other kid, some smartass kid, should have been sent to Juvie for what he had done. No big deal. Instead they sent him to prison for stealing a car or breaking into some old lady's house.

He was also a punk, then, a big man with the young girls at school. Thing is, they put the kid into a 9 X 12 cell and left him alone to soil his pants with a lifer, a mean son of a bitch ten times bigger, older and meaner...the kind of mean nurtured by the most elemental of prison instincts: Survival.

And then, only if you were the biggest and meanest son of a bitch in-house. And John Anderson, inmate 7319, was all of that and more.

The kid, he was told, didn't see the huge fist smashing into his face. Nor the second, nor the many punches and slaps that followed. When he was finally able to open his eyes, blinded by blood and tears, the con towering over him ordered him in a guttural wheeze to stop blubbering, to get used to his new life, to strip off his pants, or get on his knees. Whatever. Just do it.

Which would happen first? Which might be worse? Which might be the least worst? None of that mattered to a hysterical young mind. That kid was living his new life, what society had said he deserved, what he could expect for the next five years because his daddy wasn't rich. Boohoo.

The boy cowered into a corner. He brought up his knees and locked his hands together, wailing for his mommy.

Instead a couple of guards came, snickering and leaning unconcerned into the steel bars. Guards rushing in and ringing alarms was the stuff of B-rate movies. In real life that never happened. They didn't much give a shit about the human trash they watched over.

What they saw was the boy held high in the air by the neck, dangling, his feet flailing, his body dropping to the concrete floor in a sobbing heap when the guards and the con agreed that he'd had enough...for the time being.

The con simply said, "This is prison life, boy. Your life now... with me, not your mommy. This me and you, real cozy like. This is it, what happens every day, and then some." He stooped over the boy, chortling. "Better me than someone who won't treat you right."

Then the con sprang onto his bunk. Propped onto a thick arm, his eyes fixed on the boy's that were too blurred to see, he licked his lips. His grin was wide, a meaty hand patting the mattress.

Instead the terrified boy was jolted violently backward

past the bars. He was rudely dragged to an office by one guard, prodded with a baton across his back and shoulders by the other inches from outstretched arms restrained by more grey steel bars.

Eager fingers wanted to touch him, to feel him. High and low voices screeched at him and taunted him, each man declaring his lewd anticipation of something new, something smooth and fresh to reawaken and sustain them. None caring that the kid was convulsing and snivelling, barely able to walk.

All newbies whimpered. No one was ever coddled or cuddled in prison, unless…and then never openly.

Shoved through the door, the kid collapsed. Waiting for him were the judge, the warden, the tearful mother, and maybe the old lady or the guy whose car he'd stolen. Long story short, the boy was sent home. The lesson was learned, engrained for a lifetime, and the big-ass con probably got an extra hour of fresh air alone in the yard for his kindness.

That wouldn't happen to Anderson's boy. Not Billy Rider. He wasn't going home with a bloody face and a sore jaw, otherwise intact.

No. The Rider boy was coming to the nation's worst hell to spend his days and nights on the lower bunk because the upper bunk mattered in prison. At least once he was housebroken.

That way the kid's piss wouldn't seep through onto Anderson who always slept soundly to dream of his beautiful, young and adoring wife. The whore he couldn't wait to see once more and kill because she's the one who put him there, because he'd become the biggest and the meanest son of bitch in Battle View Prison through no intended fault of his own.

Six years earlier he hadn't known the story, and wouldn't have cared. He knew then what waited for him, arriving in the dark, soaked with rain, the shaving, the shower, the de-licing, the strip search, the firm admonishments from the warden before spending his first night on the lower bunk, though convincing his cellmate towards more equitable terms one month later.

His first full day after a sleepless and worrisome night he skipped breakfast with good reason. He strode into the yard, into a chaotic circle of tattooed and pumped-up Blacks, his bowels a conduit of gurgling shit. They let him pass, all of them smirking, unblinking eyes amused, thinking the white boy was lost or just plain stupid.

The man he would come to know as Black Boss was as huge as he was arrogant. His coal-black skin glistened with sweat. His bright white teeth were framed in gaudy strips of gold behind bright pink lips that curled into a conceited grin as Anderson came purposely closer. An instant later his head snapped to the side, his cue-ball eyes bulging impossibly wide as his bulk was flung backwards, his jaw smashed into shards an instant before Anderson transformed his vulnerable nuts into a useless decoration.

Anderson stood sneering a moment longer, victorious, wanting to scream from the searing pain pulsating in his fist, jerking on his heels to get the hell away.

The unflinching Mexican who stood out amongst his cronies was next. Or so Anderson thought, hoped for, believed. All or nothing. Die then or die later. Get the shit beat out of him then or later. No difference. Get things done. That's what he remembered his dad always saying, though what he got was open palms and "hombre, no problema. Not today anyway. Your point, it is made hombre. See for yourself."

He nodded, inching his way backwards. The Mexicans, whatever they were, weren't smiling or smirking. They were backing away, Anderson resisting the urge to tremble as a dozen guards came at him with a mission, twisting him, tripping him, slamming his head and chest to the concrete ground.

He spent the next thirty days in solitary, not

complaining about the extra year added to his sentence, thankful he hadn't messed himself that day in the yard. When he got out he had respect from the Latinos, not many Black friends, and the Whites from Cellblock Three knew to stay away.

He was a loner, had been for most of his life. Never much into making friends, more interested in connections, contacts and upward mobility which now extended to the upper bunk.

He wasn't interested in becoming The Boss, White Boss, or anyone's boss by challenging the current kingpin of the White block. Nor did he recognize or pay homage to the self-appointed potentate who had more air in his head than grey matter. Anderson was apolitical. He always had been. Prison would not change that. Nor did he need some tattooed bubba's protection, which was pretty clear to everyone.

He had zero interest in the other cons, the block, or their petty prison squabbles and grievances. He was dealing with sufficient issues of his own; he didn't need or want the hassles.

Yet in very short order, despite his resolve, the cons of CB-3 were increasingly drawn to him They saw that he was genuinely unafraid of the ham-fisted bubba whose influence over them waned with proportionate speed towards a complete cessation, which the lifer wisely chose not to oppose. By which time Inmate 7319 simply became Anderson.

He didn't speak prison talk; he didn't talk much at all. He was too educated to regress. He was erudite and well-travelled, an up-and-coming marketing executive. He was Mr. John Anderson with a bright future and a beautiful wife. Or he had been until the last night he arrived home early with a dozen red roses from a business trip cut short.

Yeah, his wife was beautiful then, which he supposed hadn't changed much. She'd be thirty-five in a few weeks and probably looking ten years younger. No doubt no longer lamenting her dead lover with so many more to console her.

He'd done six of the twenty-five plus one for killing the guy, his first blow stunning the man. His second snapped the Frenchman's neck, though not once since had he considered himself as a murderer. Spontaneous? Sure. Vindictive? He suspected possibly so, being that the memory of her sprawled on his bed, screaming, squirming her nude body from under the dead weight, the Frenchman's contorted mask somehow no longer appealing to her, remained unblemished as a precious Kodak moment. That recurring image was the single most important element of the driving force that would see him through.

Once free he would find her and he would keep his promise to her.

He was forty, trim and athletic, forbidding prison life to prematurely age him with twenty years remaining to plan a single event in a preordained future indelibly tainted by his past and present.

He'd gone through two cellmates in six years, men without much reason to live, men scarred by life and prison who no longer cared much about anything. Neither was his mentor. They knew to keep a distance, each of them content to spend their time on the lower bunk before the first guy managed somehow to die in his sleep and the second more recently passed away as the result of an anticipated and unfortunate circumstance concluded in the showers.

And now the newbie was coming in: a white boy, pink and squeaky clean. Good.

Anderson was anxious to once again teach a lesson, to teach respect, to teach the need for quiet in Cell 312. The kid had no idea what hell was. He wasn't hours away from a schoolyard brawl. The cons, they loved two things, two diversions from an otherwise grey existence: rapists and paedophiles. The younger the better. Absolute terror for a newbie.

The Cat was another matter, a cruel remnant from the Dark Ages and something else for the kid to whine about. Anderson snorted, strumming the tips of his fingers against his knee. Five times two times three. Five searing strokes twice each year for three years, each stroke meant to break the soul as much as the back.

The kid had no idea.

He slouched against the cold wall, staring into his open book at the bookmark, the pristine photo taken of the reason he would survive prison for something he didn't mean to do, something that wasn't his fault. Because of her his life was prison. At sixty his degrees would be worthless. He'd be worthless, condemned to a life of washing dishes or to the streets to beg for nickels and dimes. Sure as hell the paltry few dollars she couldn't steal from his 401K wouldn't do much for him. At least in prison he had meals and respect.

Prison, he had come to accept, was not simply his present or his future. Prison was his destiny forged by her. A destiny he would interrupt for a short while, for however long he needed to find her, to reunite with her. All he wanted, all he needed, was to see her one last time. That was her destiny as well as his. How pretty would she be then? He suspected not very. Such was the just desert of even the prettiest whore.

He'd learned from his lawyer that his wife was never quite the loving and devoted woman he'd fallen in love with, courted and married. Never what she claimed. Despite which, that fact had no bearing on his sentence.

For years she had been a successful whore earning an enviable living in Miami throughout his frequent and solitary business trips, admitting to the court, to his utter disbelief, that she would also and often entertain other men during the business trips she would occasionally share with him to Europe. At the same time denying her prostitution, claiming instead that she was very simply as insatiable as she was desirable, that what she did was part of her nature for which she never once received or expected payment.

The Frenchman was a favourite, she told the court; a man she loved and might have married had she not met John Anderson first, the one man she had ever allowed into their home, in *her* bed. Or so she repeatedly and shamelessly professed.

The court believed her, seeing no relevance in the defence attorney's assertion that, in fact, she was not then, nor had she ever been, a professor. That she had for years misled her husband while plying her trade behind his back. She was, in fact, a whore.

The lawyer was at once reproved, the gavel declaring him out of order. Brenda Anderson was a troubled woman, a fraud within her marriage and arguably of indecent and dubious character, the judge agreed. She was not, however, on trial for her actions. She had committed no crime other than the blatant treachery perpetrated against her husband, which was for him to pass judgement on her with his court's blessing, not the court itself.

No shit he would pass judgement. And he did, that day and many times before.

He declared her guilty, her sentence delayed for reasons beyond his control as his was read aloud. But one day she would hear the verdict and sentence read aloud by him, without appeal, the due punishment swift and true.

Prison wasn't so bad. He chuckled. Besides, he had the court's permission.

Four

1971

The 400 miles from Raleigh, North Carolina to Battle View in an armoured van, his wrists and ankles shackled together and secured to a belt of steel links, lasted five hours in the express lane of the I-40 with an escort of Federal Marshals.

Billy Rider didn't care about the fine weather; he cared about never again being with his family. They were his sole focus. He didn't see the need of taking in the countryside one last time, which would mean staring past the marshal facing him, when he could close his eyes and enjoy his mother, father and brothers who believed in him and remained with him until the checkpoint.

Those last five miles were the worst of his life, worse than his arrest, worse than the judge's gavel arcing swiftly and silently through the air.

He remembered her grim expression, her words chilling him. Not the lash, which he didn't understand at all. He remembered reading that her single disappointment throughout his trial was that premeditation could not be established. He was a despicable being, for which she truly would have delighted in pronouncing his death sentence. However, left with no other choice, she was content to impose the cruelest and most appropriate penalty available to her under the law which she sincerely wished would quickly prove fatal. She couldn't imagine a more appropriate birthday gift.

That was the previous day, the last day of a three-week trial, a precious few moments with his family forbidden by the judge who caustically reminded him in a rant that he hadn't given the Merriweathers any such opportunity.

Battle View Prison was a windowless, concrete fortress with a mile-wide belt of denuded land encircling the structure, the perimeter sealed off by a fifty-foot fence buried in a ten-foot deep concrete trench. This was not the holding facility at Necessity's police station, or the state capital's detention centre, Billy Rider believing he would be killed there one day soon if his heart didn't explode first.

The van slowed to a stop, the marshal guarding him standing to join the driver and another uniformed man who had boarded and was armed with a shotgun.

Billy Rider sat wedged in a corner, deciding that staring at his knees was the best thing to do. He was too afraid to watch the marshal and the guard coming towards him to unshackle his feet that were chained to the floor.

Neither man spoke, the marshal hammering the steel frame of the seat with his club, jerking his head towards the door, the vibration as startling as the muted and violent clangs.

Billy wiggled his way to the edge of his seat, standing, staring at his feet. His face was flushed, his shoulders slumped, his fingers laced together. Defeat: His first big mistake.

The armed guard jolted him forward and past the marshal with a forceful shove: His indoctrination: Battle View Prison's well-deserved reputation was not one of kindness. The worst of the worst lived out their lives behind those high walls ten miles from anywhere in any direction, cut off, escape impossible with nowhere on the arid field to hide, armed sentries preventing unwanted access to the private and unmarked road.

The driver ignored him; the guard urging him abruptly with the stock of his gun to hop, jump or fall from the bus to the ground where a second unsmiling and armed guard was waiting. He didn't care. Just get it done. Quick like, and the exchange was made. Billy Rider was officially a lifetime resident of Battle View, Tennessee.

Billy didn't see the blue sky; he didn't feel the gentle breeze. He saw his shackled wrists and the chain that connected to his manacled feet and the rolled-up legs of his county-issued orange coveralls drooping over his county-issued white sneakers.

He felt fear; he felt abandoned. He didn't hear the clanking of the heavy steel doors slamming shut behind him, welcoming him. Sound was foreign to him, forgotten by him since the epiphany of his childhood that silence was the safest sound.

He saw them, all of them, the men in the grey denim coveralls gawking at him from behind a double row of wire fences. He didn't see the dogs between them or the coils of barbed wire strung between the spiked tops; he saw them. He saw their eyes. He saw their mouths pursed and twisted into shapes that made him afraid when, until that moment, he'd felt the less fearful dread of uncertainty. He was afraid because he knew what they were saying, the closest ones.

He felt an urgent need to cry, but he didn't know how, his eyes refusing to even glaze over.

If only he hadn't killed the girl, his lawyer had chastised him even before the trial began. He might have served as little as fifteen years. The townspeople knew he wasn't right in the head; but the girl was dead, viciously murdered, her skull crushed by the rock found smeared with her matted hair and blood. The thing is, the guy never once spoke about Battle View for Billy's entire life, and never once did he mention the lash. That would have changed everything.

He realized they had been expecting him, waiting for him, though he hadn't a clue about what would happen to a young rapist and murderer in such a threatening place.

He thought he might have his own room, where they

would bring his meals, like at the detention centre. He hoped so and, if so, he would never leave. No one had brought him face to face with his reality. His grieving mother, who fifteen years earlier had received him as her own, for fear she would frighten him more than he was. Nor his father whose mind could not endure the reality. Nor his lacklustre attorney who practically wiped out the family's resources, because doing so would have meant more involvement with them when public opinion was wholly solidified against the boy and those proclaiming his innocence.

Now he was at the threshold of his atonement, a day of first discovery, one day past his nineteenth birthday, a day of learning what was right and what was wrong, of what was yet to come.

Crippling images festered in his mind, his chest throbbing all the more fiercely with fresh and reasonable fears. The whippings troubled him the most. He hadn't once been strapped at school like the other boys, made to lean over the principal's desk or extend their unsteady hands. He didn't want his hands to hurt.

He had no sense of prayer. His parents had never gone with him to church; they had never owned a bible. Sundays were family days for car rides to new and different places and walks in the park, TV and popcorn, and a mother's warm embraces. Besides, as he would soon discover, despite some believing that God might possibly be benevolent and loving, He had wisely chosen long ago never to enter Battle View Prison.

Billy had never seen a prison. The worst he ever knew was the state detention centre, which wasn't terribly bad, and the daily visits from his mother who would bring him fresh fruit and milk that he would drink right away were always comforting.

He loved his parents deeply, loathing himself for having ruined their lives, hating that he would never see them or his brothers again. Once, at the beginning, in the detention centre, a preacher came by thinking to redeem his soul. The self-made cleric never returned to sit with Billy who naturally assumed that God had more patience with His children who were not deaf and dumb. And everyone knew Billy was a dimwit, dumber than a doorknob most would agree.

Hurried through more steel doors, some sliding, others unlocked, the inside was colourless and bleak, quiet, foreboding to an innocent mind.

Made to waddle in his chains through the windowless corridors of the administration offices housed on the first floor of the main block, the rubber soles of his sneakers didn't squeak against the granite floor. The walls were bare, the lighting high and bright.

The guards halted Billy abruptly at the mahogany door, Warden Prescott's private door, yanking his collar, gagging him. They made him wait, one guard knocking, disappearing into the office where Billy was about to discover how bad life could and would indeed be.

The warden was by no means a gentle sort. His mannerisms daunting to a scared kid. He didn't stand. He had no reason to for an inmate, especially one that was deaf and dumb. Instead he reached across his desk for a file that he had briefly studied that morning.

There was no point in talking, wasting his breath and his goodwill. The kid was too stupid to understand. Instead he pointed with a commanding finger to a chalkboard, impatiently instructing Billy Rider with his other hand and farcical signs to read what he had written, waiting a moment before slamming an open palm against his desktop several times for attention.

He pointed again at Billy with the same finger, then to his own wide-open eyes before smacking the back of his head, needing to ascertain whether Billy had understood the words and their meaning. Billy nodded that he did, accustomed to what his father often referred to as "the laughable antics of prejudice," wanting to scream, remaining silent.

Naturally, he understood.

He would first be showered and his head shaven. His head and body would be powdered with disinfectant, and he would be issued new clothes. He would meet with the doctor. He would be examined to ensure that he was fit, and be escorted to Cell 312.

He would adapt. He would follow the rules. He would expect no special treatment because of his impaired mind and, in thirty days, as was the law, he would again be examined by the doctor to ensure that he was sufficiently fit to undergo the punishment of five lashes to his back. The second five to be inflicted at the discretion of the warden during the second six months of his first year.

Prescott shook his head. What *he* didn't understand, what *he* wanted to know, asking his guards, was why the hillbilly kid from Jerkwater, North Carolina was sentenced to the Whipping Room in a month's time and not the gallows.

They agreed. Why was that?

Sort of an easy one, though, the warden suggested. Goddamn. Get rid of a sicko child killer, get rid of a social freak no good to himself or anyone else. "Damned if I wouldn't hang the little shit myself."

Yep. Sure as hell they would too.

"Too bad this little fucker didn't kill the poor girl here, is all I can say."

They agreed, nodding their synchronized and empty heads that belonged on a dashboard. Tennessee was an unforgiving place to kill people, lessen, of course, they was any shade of black.

What they didn't know was that Billy agreed with them, firmly convinced that he would be better off dead.

Shoved once again into the hallway, Billy barely made

his way to the showers where he knew to strip, his legs failing him with each step, not liking that the guards hadn't gone away. Happy at least that his hands and feet were at last free.

He stood naked, his body cold, his eyes squeezed shut. He turned blindly on command, the tip of the baton jabbing at his shoulder, his body stiffening at the loud buzzing reverberating through his head as clumps of his hair fell at his feet.

Shaven, prodded into an open stall, he stood under the steaming water thankful for the heat, one guard tossing a bar of soap onto the floor, smirking. He felt sick washing his body in front of them, rinsing the suds away. He wanted to vomit standing there dripping, searching for a towel, stooping for the one flung at his feet.

They ordered him closer, one guard ripping the towel from his waist. The other, his hand gloved, threw fistfuls of powder at him from head to toe, signalling him to turn until Billy was fully coated in white.

His new underwear and coveralls were coarse, tagged with his new name: 8314. Two of each with two pairs of socks and one pair of new sneakers. The single sheet and blanket in Battle View grey for his bed were coarse as well; the plastic on his pillow crackled inside the grey case.

At the infirmary he stripped once again The examination was thorough. Billy was poked, prodded, thumped, squeezed, weighed and measured, at the end of which the doctor's signature approved him for Cell 312.

Cellblock Three was deserted, the thick smell of smoke and men lingering. The grilled stairs and railed walkway made him uneasy. He felt dizzy. He could see through them to the main floor, more afraid of what he would see if he raised his head.

Three-twelve was open. All the cells were open. He wanted more time. He needed more time. He wasn't ready.

He saw the grey concrete floor, the grey foot lockers, the

shiny steel toilet, the steel sink, the bunks and the man's legs hanging over the edge. The man was enormous, grim-faced; his eyes were cold and empty. Billy knew a lot about eyes. The man was dangerous.

"Anderson," one guard said, "this here is your new boy. He won't be much trouble. He don't talk, can't. Not right in the head. All the same, he's yours. You keep him in line. It's on you."

Anderson ignored them, his eyes drilling into Rider's. He had quickly learned, as would Rider, that the Battle View line separating the criminals from the guards was very thin, if not invisible. In other words, they weren't worth yesterday's shit once outside the high walls or their uniforms.

They nodded, grinning, and left.

Billy stared at his new shoes, hugging himself, rubbing warmth into his arms.

Anderson dropped to the floor. This, he could not believe. Apart from his obvious attributes, which Anderson assumed was the case since Battle View Prison wasn't co-ed, Billy Rider could easily be mistaken for a timid girl amongst the thick-skinned and hardened, sinewy or pumped-up cons.

Not a good thing in any prison, but deaf and dumb to boot. Shit. And lots of it. The kid was truly in the deepest shit. Everything about him would scream "be my daddy tonight" to any deprived con with that particular proclivity. Why not prance in wearing a frigging pink party dress?

What's worse, for him, he was white, too white. His eyes were too blue, his scalp smoother and cleaner than a shaven head should be. He was 5'7", a possible five-eight, and slim, too slim. His lips were too pink, his arms and chest as bare as his head. His hands were delicate, girlish, his fingers long and slender. A matter of time, and not much time, before he'd be hanging from a railing or shanked in the showers. In a word, he was pretty. Too pretty.

Anderson was 6'3". He was masculine, his torso and arms tanned and chiselled from hours in the yard, his once charming manner a remnant of his past. He was toughened and cynical, devoid of trust and emotions not linked to his survival, dreaming each night of killing once more.

His current plan evaporated, pent-up anger melding with disappointment. Teaching Rider any lesson would be tantamount to harming a defenseless girl, Anderson snorting at the irony, still royally pissed. He knew very well the cons who wouldn't want him as a diversion would want him dead. Not 7319's problem. Just not in his cell.

He jabbed an erect forefinger at the lower bunk and walked out.

Five

1971

What was left of his day Anderson spent bench-pressing in his own space.

No con ever thought to spot for him, nor did Anderson ever think to ask. He had no friends, no one he trusted enough to expose his throat. Prison was not a fraternity, not for him. Never would be. They were not his brothers, unlike his frat brothers who had turned against him for the second-degree murder of his wife's john du jour.

All he shared in common with the cons was time. They all came in the same way, chained and shuffling. Most were stoic, not showing fear, all except a rare few condemned to what remained of their natural lives. The very worst of them, without question the most fortunate, were also the most penitent...once blinded by hoods, waiting for the trap to open and the precision knot to snap their necks.

Very few ever survived to leave Battle View behind as their worst nightmare, as he would. Those who did were guaranteed to return, as he would.

Though despite Battle View housing the worst, not all were strong, not all the dead followed in a state of peace behind the hangman. Many entered into their new eternities unannounced, desperately by their own hands or not, their newly discovered souls deprived of a detached cleric's final and dubious absolution. Departing from one hell to enter another.

Anderson had missed his breakfast, choosing to remain in his cell. That was bad enough. He didn't need the smirks or the snide chuckles of the other cons at his table who already knew about Rider, or thought they did. Not that he ever stayed longer than needed to eat his meals, keeping conversation to a minimum. He spoke when needed, which was seldom, when his intervention was required to maintain order in Cellblock Three when minor crises might arise, or in the yard with Black Boss and El Jefe to settle larger disputes with potentially more disastrous repercussions. Otherwise he had nothing much to say.

This day he had even less to say, and now because of Rider he would go without lunch. The mess hall at that hour of the day was off-limits to all but Latinos.

Instead he went straight to the yard frustrated, musing that the Cat was the least of the kid's worries.

A deaf mute, and simple. Quite possibly, Anderson thought, simple enough not to hang himself. Most of the youngest ones did at some point, or tried. Rider would, or should, if the Cat didn't kill him first. He clenched his right hand into a tight fist, each knuckle scarred. Battle View wasn't a place for the weak or the timid and Rider was both.

Not his problem.

He snorted. In six years he'd seen cons, mostly young, methodically crawl over the railings of each tier and fall, their necks wrapped in strips of bedding, believing that was sufficient attention to detail, never thinking to seek advice from more experienced cons who knew better than to stand directly under the entertainment.

Death was seldom instant, though always dramatic and often lasting several minutes. Once over the rail, misgivings and regrets were futile. The face would discolour to a deep purple and distort, the mouth would gnaw the air gasping for elusive breath, the feet and arms would thrash the air until desperate fingers would too late claw at constricted throats.

Cheap theatre with the eagerly awaited encore of indifferent guards who inevitably arrived too late to reclaim the corpse, most often letting it free-fall to the main floor.

He'd seen other cons beaten unconscious to silence their screams, and flung over. No one caring, no one interfering. Everyone blind to the shocking suicide.

Either way, once over, the spectacles were forgotten.

He'd seen men stabbed in the showers for whatever insult or infraction, all young, all of them dead. No keen sense of survival. Though not one face could he remember. Nor would he remember Rider's.

He scarcely saw the sun begin to set, startled, the 6:00 PM siren evacuating the yard, guards impassively herding the cons inside to their cells for the day's second count. And there was Rider, cringed impossibly small into the corner of his bunk, his knees wrapped tightly in his arms, his eyes squeezed shut, ignoring his name.

A guard went in, his baton smacking against Billy's shoulder. He pointed to his watch, then to the corridor, telling Billy to get his ass out. Billy did, making his formal debut, stepping into a row of fifty-nine other men, staring across a void to 180 others.

All eyes were fixated on him, all mouths whispered about him.

Anderson ignored him and, once accounted for, went to the mess hall to fill an empty stomach.

Billy Rider went to his bunk. He didn't know where else to go. Waiting until he supposed all the men were gone he went to the toilet and faced into the wall.
*

Anderson sat facing the entrance, eating in a private world amidst the roar of collective murmurs, the clatter of trays, shuffling feet, belches, gulping and coughing. Unlike the others he wasn't hunched over; he didn't tear at his food or fill his mouth beyond capacity. He would leave Battle View for a short while one day with the behaviours of a civilized human being intact, intent on taking care of business without the indelible imprint of the country's worst prison. He wasn't planning revenge, he was dreaming of equality, equalizing an unjust imbalance.

He didn't bother to ask. Not his problem. Besides, food was forbidden in the block. Most everything was forbidden in the block.

The prison had rules; the block had rules. So did the cells, enforced by the keepers of the upper bunks. Anderson had rules.

He stood, emptied his tray of scraps and left. No time like the present to set the kid straight while the block was free of the bored and the curious, most cons usually preferring their full thirty-minutes of relative freedom in the mess hall before returning to the block to wait for the 8:00 PM lockdown.

Billy Rider was on his bunk, his head down like a pouty schoolgirl hugging her knees, Anderson wondering where a vacant mind might wander. He kicked the bunk once, really wanting to grab the kid and smack him, ordering Billy with a curt nod onto the railed walkway where they stood facing each other, Anderson leering down, Billy searching everywhere to avoid eye contact.

A second less demanding nod told Billy to follow, the indifferent shrug telling him…or not. Anderson didn't look back.

They circled the block, Anderson pointing over to 312 then to Billy, thinking any effort to speak somewhat futile. At the stairway they stopped on the second tier, Anderson warning as best he could with open palms and shaking his head for Billy to stay away. The first tier brought the same warning. The main floor was scattered with benches bolted to the floor, each one off limits for any newbie. Billy followed to the showers, uncertain, his face devoid of expression, inwardly grimacing.

This was a first for Anderson. He was fluent in three languages, something the Latinos hadn't yet discovered. Nor would they. Now he was stumped by silence. He took a moment to think things out.

Finding a bar of soap he drew a calendar on a tin mirror bolted to the wall: The first ten days of July.

He put a fingertip hard against the 1, then the 3, the 5, the 7 and 9 with approving nods, pointing to the rows of showers. He smeared the even numbers warning Billy with open palms fanning the air. Before walking away he pointed to the latrines, the open stalls lining the opposite wall, scrawling1-30 on the mirror and pointing sternly with both forefingers at Billy, his eyebrows arched.

When the kid might take his showers or do his business wasn't his problem. The question of where was another matter.

Billy hurried to catch up, ignoring the toilets, fairly certain he should shower on odd-number days, wondering why the man hadn't pointed to his wrist or drawn a clock on the mirror, wondering why he hadn't spoken a word. Perhaps he was deaf and dumb also.

They went to the library, which Anderson believed was an absurd waste of his time and effort, despite which he opened the door to let Billy peer inside. Moments later, Billy trailing, Anderson pointed to another door, the Commissary for smokes, gum and chocolate bars and not much else. He didn't bother with the Infirmary. Every newbie had seen behind that door and Rider would again too soon.

Lastly Anderson pointed to one guard, then to another, and a third, then to his mouth, waving a finger. The warning was clear, if not completely pointless.

At the mess hall Anderson spoke to a guard. Permission denied. The Blacks were chowing down. That Anderson had chosen to leave after his meal wasn't the guard's problem. Rules. Anderson walked away, smirking at the thought of twenty years of relative silence. Showtime was over.

Billy followed, uncertain, wondering about the man who seemed annoyed. Yet behind the man's dark eyes he could see silent questions, the same curiosity he'd seen countless times since his childhood.

At their cell Anderson leaped onto his bunk. He reached for a book, stretched out, faced the wall, and began reading from where he had inserted his wife the day before. At 8:00 PM precisely, 312 and the 179 other cells in the White Block were sealed; at 10:00 the lights went out, save for the eerie grey-green hue illuminating the block and the menacing spectres whose patrolling footsteps Billy didn't hear.

As for a tired John Anderson, July 02nd would come all too quickly.

Six

1956

Sally Cutter did not look or act like Billy's grandmother or her niece, Betsy Rider. She had washed away any visible family resemblance and traces of Charity years earlier. In fact she didn't look like anyone's grandmother. She was modern. She was eye-catching by any standard, free in body and mind, and didn't give a hoot about Southern Bible Belt hypocrisy.

She had never previously seen Billy. She scarcely remembered one-year-old Betsy laying in her crib. Neither was she invited to Betsy's wedding, hearing instead of the less than blessed event some months later when Mrs. Bolton had at last felt compelled to explain the baby, though the inexcusable slight was not what kept Sally from Betsy's funeral. Had she known, had her sister called her in time, she would have attended the service out of respect and quickly left, despite her intrinsic belief that the Road Out was One Way.

She was thirty-five, youthful and fun. She was the talk of Baptist Necessity.

She didn't believe in God; she believed in accepting those who did, if not the historic narrow-mindedness of the South. She didn't believe that wearing skirts below her knees made her a better person, or that wearing tight sweaters and silk blouses made her a worse one. So she wore shorter, more alluring fashions to the distraction of neighbourhood men and the two-faced envy of their unimpassioned women.

Her husband whole-heartedly approved. That's what truly mattered, not that she cared, and her two sons absolutely adored her.

She sunbathed in the backyard wearing scandalously small swimwear that post-war Parisians had ten years earlier begun modelling on beaches and calling 'bikinis'. This in spite of the pope at the time declaring them 'sinful' as though she might care. She didn't, particularly given the Sistine's famed in-your-face works of art. Nor did she care about the neighbours gossiping.

Don't like, don't look.

Each new summer brought more daring designs fashioned on her Singer that she copied from magazines that others wouldn't dare to peruse while sitting in the shade wearing paisley sundresses and wide-brimmed hats. Often with the strings undone across her back for a more unblemished tan.

She sipped Margaritas on her porch in sneakers and bobby socks, flared shorts cut daringly high, knotting her unbuttoned blouses for affect. She wore her husband's tee-shirts cinched with a belt to take out the garbage in heels, the baker's man and milkman often treated to baby dolls or silk chemises if they walked into her kitchen at the right time to replenish her fridge and pantry.

No one locked their doors in Necessity in 1956.

She was a teacher ahead of her time, and popular. Students never arrived late for her classes, many eager with questions to ask her after the bell had rung, presumably wanting to learn more.

Boys of all ages drooled over her, though the girls would never openly confess to wanting to emulate her. At dances she would let them discreetly kiss and hold hands, while other chaperons would report the sordid misdemeanours to the principal who knew better than to reproach her for fear of losing her to another school.

That was Sally Cutter.

Necessity was home to 90,000 middle class souls. Most of them, for appearances, more self-righteous than God-fearing.

Homes were marked off with white picket fences and housewives hung their laundry on the line near or after dusk for the sake of propriety. Not Sally. Daytime any day was fine with her. She didn't want anyone thinking for a moment that she might wear sensible cotton briefs that came six to a box from some heap in a bargain basement. Not that anyone did.

On Saturdays men mowed their lawns. They did household repairs and washed their cars while their women baked for the Sunday Gospel Clubs. Boys rode their bikes and girls played house with dolls; while teenagers, like their co-conspirators anywhere, would shamelessly lie about where they went and what they did.

Sunday was a day of prayer and reflection, a day of sharing the bounty of one's table with friends and neighbours, of goodwill towards all, barring certain colours not found in a rainbow, homosexuals and whores and fornicators, and those who would willfully harm their children.

A chorus of church bells sounded each Sunday morning across the entire city to greet the preachers' flocks, and everyone knew someone who knew someone. Necessity was not a place abounding in secrets.

Sally Cutter worked on her tan throughout her days of rest. The only teachings of interest to her were her own. She had no need of lectures, her husband equally without fear of Satan's demonic grasp. This Sunday, however, was different. Little did they realize as Sam answered the phone's loud rings disturbing their day of rest that he was setting the stage for a murder that would one day obliterate what would then remain of their lives.

Two days later Billy arrived, spared, as one might suppose, from the next fifteen years of his life in an orphanage, which was Mrs. Bolton's backup plan calculated to make Sally's and Sam's decision that much easier. Though Billy would not believe or care throughout those many years to come that Buck Rider should have shot him dead that fateful night.

*

Sally Cutter taught the final year at Necessity High. Sam Cutter made his living as the Chief Columnist for the Necessity Daily News as well as the midday host at the paper's sister AM radio station, 580 on the dial, where his office adjoined the studio.

They were good and honest people, untainted by bigotry and gossip. They took to Billy immediately, undeterred by his quiet demeanour, though not once would his new parents ever hear him speak a single word.

During their first week together Sally remained at home with him, understanding his moods, his mannerisms, his likes and dislikes. They went shopping for clothes and shoes, the likes of which Betsy and Buck could never afford; she took him to a restaurant one day for lunch, and to a park where she rented a rowboat and watched his amazement at the geese, the ducks, and dogs splashing at the shore. He played on the swings and the monkey bars, neither happy nor sad when they left. All in complete silence.

The second week Billy learned about nursery school, and throughout that school year all went well. The children were too young to care or to hate. They hadn't yet learned to be cruel, though their parents and the town soon began to understand and agree that Billy Rider was peculiar.

Kindergarten the next year was less forgiving. Other boys would punch Billy from behind when he wouldn't answer them; the girls would stick out their tongues and make faces at him when he couldn't understand them.

He didn't hear the words, he saw in their eyes that he was stupid, a crazy weirdo. He was nutsy and a dummy. However, through all that torment, Billy never cried. Nor did he ever smile or giggle with glee. He played quietly and watched, often alone, passively content when his mother came each day to find him.

His new and more comfortable home was his world. His language was clapping: A simple vocabulary of gestures developed untiringly over time by Sally. Until his second Christmas when his older brothers came home for a short while with a single and special gift they expected would excite Sally and Sam.

Sally, of course, scolded them. They had dreams, ambitions beyond Necessity, what Sally called their Road Out. She understood. Their future was in medicine, each of them accepted into Med School that was mere months away. Nevertheless, they were not wealthy doctors yet. They were impoverished students. All the more reason they should not squander their hard-earned money on frivolous gifts when mom and dad and Billy were more wanting of their company.

The young men agreed, in a flippant tone that she knew from experience was hopeless to pursue.

They arrived Christmas Eve, Sally at once speculating what special gift could be hidden in such small suitcases. She would not accept any foolishness, threatening in her mind to refuse any gift her sons could not afford. Though not a word was mentioned, nor did she venture to ask.

She began Christmas Day in the kitchen preparing hot toddies for them and a cup of warm milk sweetened with sugar for Billy. Outside the best they could hope for was a thick layer of frost. The snowman would have to wait. Snow seldom whitened the streets and lawns of Necessity, North Carolina.

Billy had a few weeks earlier sat with Santa Claus at the mall for the first time in his life, not much liking the event, not knowing what to ask for or even that he should. Santa Sam who was sitting by the glittering tree dressed in a red robe and a white tuque was much more entertaining to him.

He'd never opened so many gifts, mostly socks and underwear and sweaters. But they were his. Though his best gifts were the red truck from Santa and the model airplane kit from his brothers.

Sally went again to the kitchen to fill three orders for more toddies. Billy was too busy playing with his truck and flying the box that the pieces of plane were stored in.

When she returned with the drinks she opened her gift, proffered by one son, a beautiful doily crafted by his girlfriend. Girlfriend? Really? Then Sam opened his, a linen hanky embroidered with a stylistic S for a stylish man, the other brother made clear...and, yes, embroidered by his girlfriend.

Sally was greatly relieved, hugging them both. She loved her gift. She had been so worried they would be rash. Now, about these girls...?

The two boys exchanged glances, confused.

One brother said, seemingly shocked, "Mom, those are not our special gift to you and dad."

His brother said, "I should say not. Mom, we met a man. He's an expert in his field."

"Yes, he is. And we spoke with him at length about Billy. He is your special gift."

The brothers had met a man who was a leading speech therapist performing clinical research at the university and who badly wanted to assist in awakening Billy's world at no cost to the family. Merry Christmas to all. That is, if Billy could possibly spend the coming year away from his loving mother and father.

Together they handed Sally an envelope tied with a ribbon. Inside was a handwritten letter from the good doctor, inviting Mrs. Cutter to contact him at her earliest convenience so that they might discuss her son.

Sally didn't hesitate. She spoke with the good doctor that very afternoon, her hopes spiralling upward as she listened to his expectations and successes.

He and his wife would bring Billy into their home and, he promised, the Cutter family's next Christmas would bring untold joy.

In the meantime Billy would be close to his brothers. He would see them often and the Cutters were invited to visit without restriction, particularly Sally whom he entreated to join Billy throughout that coming summer. The boy would require all possible sources of support and encouragement.

Four days into 1958, at age five, Billy left kindergarten behind to join his brothers at university where he would remain for twelve months.

Seven

1971

July 02 came as expected. As did 7:00 AM with a din of cell doors sliding back, waking those not already eager to step out.

Anderson slipped into his coveralls. He lay still, listening, his fingers laced together at the nape of his neck. No sobbing. No sound at all. That was a good thing. More incredibly, he mused, no impromptu encounters either. A peculiar reprieve. That would happen soon enough.

Then came the sound of water dribbling into water, Anderson too slow to staunch the flow. The kid was standing at the toilet facing the wall in violation of cell rules. Cell 312 was clean space, Anderson's space, not a frigging outhouse. No exceptions.

So the kid *was* simple. Not Anderson's problem. Not a good enough excuse. Like Anderson, he would have thirteen hours to shit, shower and shave at the latrines. Shave? Good one, he thought. The kid couldn't even piss right. How he ever raped a girl was impossible to imagine.

He jumped down, not convinced that Rider was smart enough to flush. Shoving Billy aside he flushed with his foot, pointing to the unused roll of tissue and making circles in the air, pointing at the sink and the stainless steel seat. Billy took the paper.

Most cons were impervious to the usual human frailties of bashfulness and its pursuant shame. They were hard-core, the worst, most of them doing time for brutal murders. Others, few in number, would hang their bed sheets across their bars for privacy. Either way no one cared, including the guards. Nevertheless, doing so was also a clear indication that other less natural urgencies for privacy were taking place.

Again no one cared except those who pissed like girls, like this kid Billy Rider, Anderson thought. That was the big problem. Once assigned to a cell, that's how things were till death do we part. No discussion.

Anderson massaged his brow. Rider was the youngest in Battle View by five, maybe six years. He was jailbait, recently netted. He was pink and he was fresh, standing in the corner with his shoulders slumped, sulking like the proverbial geek at the prom without a date.

Anderson understood clearly that his previous prediction was way off; the kid's first day was here and now. He'd be basted like a turkey dinner and whimpering on his bunk for his mommy by noon. Bad enough that in a month they would tear his back to shreds. This whole thing was truly deep shit.

Why him? Why now? Anderson had never once thought of having kids, had never wanted the hassle, especially a daughter. Way too much effort and sacrifice for far too little appreciation and zero return on investment. Not to mention the whore's spawn might not have been his. Now he had a daughter with a dick. Not good.

They faced each other: Savvy vs. trepidation. Anderson's mind raced. For Billy Rider, time stood still.

Breakfast for Cellblock Three was at 8:00, each head counted before the door closed. Failing that, lunch was at 12:30. No one cared who ate and who didn't. Three meals a day and the commissary. That was it.

The cons had no special privileges. Radios were not allowed, nor were televisions. Personal clothing wasn't allowed, nor were personal items of any description. The sole luxuries were smoking and one phone call a week, which meant doing menial tasks for fifty cents a day. Cigarettes were 40 cents a pack and Battle View was a place, not a town, not found on any map. Any outgoing call was long distance, more costly than smoking.

Reading was free, the library lined with books donated from libraries, though most who could read couldn't be bothered. For Anderson the room was a retreat where he was seldom bothered.

Anderson chose not to work. He didn't smoke and had no one to call. Besides, once free he would be given a new pair of shoes, pants, a shirt, and bus fare to the whore who had closed their joint savings account during his trial before moving to another city to avoid a probable inquiry into her prostitution. Instead he spent his days staying fit, while at night he maintained his mind.

He'd be damned before washing other men's clothes, floors, shower stalls or toilets, baffled by those who constantly bitched about not being able to clean county highways of debris and road kill while guarded by Tennessee hillbillies on horseback with long guns. Never a chance in hell that would happen.

He wasn't like them; nor was he guilty by association. He hadn't spent his life in and out of jail, killing, stealing and raping. He was there because of her, the wife who hadn't once thought to lie for him, to save face. No. Not her. She had preferred being judged by their neighbours and their few friends for what she was. A whore. She didn't care. Not to mention selling their beautiful high-rise oceanfront home he had paid for with his parents' insurance money, moving north to West Palm Beach to re-establish herself without so much as a day of lost revenue. No wonder she hadn't once cried about his lack of interest in children. Life was too good.

He jerked his head, signalling Rider to follow.

The mess was grey, stark and cold any time of year.

Bright ceiling lights glared, reflecting off thirty-six steel tables and a polished floor, making the place functional and uninviting, making the new white boy stand out like a beacon.

Anderson took a tray, a plastic fork and knife, a plastic glass and cup. Billy did the same. Two eggs, two strips of bacon, two slices of toast, a juice and coffee. That was it. No custom orders, no refusals. Take what's on the tray and keep moving.

Anderson had his table, sitting over the etching on the bench indicating 112, 212, and 312 signalling for Rider to sit facing him over his same numbers. Cellblock Three was White. Blacks were housed in CB-One, the Latinos and various others in CB-Two. They would mix in the yard from a judicious distance, and in the showers. Crossing lines any other time was to invite trouble.

The eight others at the table were all six-foot something, scarred, tattooed, and streetwise.

Anderson sipped his juice, the others gulped or guzzled. He took up his knife and fork; the others were hunched over, slicing and jabbing with their forks with one hand, clutching their toast with the other. The heads turned in unison, first to Rider, then to Anderson. Their expressions were grim, their jaws articulating behind open mouths twisted into permanent sneers.

Anderson was clear in his mind.

"The kid's name is Billy Rider. I don't know much about him, just what I see. Like you. He's in for rape and murder...and doing serious time." He stopped talking, filling his mouth, drafting thoughts as he chewed. No one spoke. He sipped his coffee. "Here's the thing, so pay attention. He's deaf and mute, that means dumb. He doesn't hear and he doesn't speak. So let's not have him pissing his pants each time he turns around. The block has nothing to prove by beating on him. You can see that plainly enough. So spread the word. Rider gets hurt, I get hurt. If, and more likely when, he does something stupid, you come to me first. Do not cause me grief. I do not need this kid messing himself in my cell." He thumbed the air, gesturing behind him. "As for the homos, anyone who touches him goes to the infirmary, and they'll hear it directly from me today. As for you and the others, you see something, you get in the way. You get involved and you come to me. Besides that, he's on his own. No better or worse than the rest of us." He scanned the table, eye to eye with each man. "We understand each other, gentlemen?"

Each man agreed in turn, ignoring Billy. They remembered Anderson's first day and he was a shitload meaner six years later.

With his breakfast finished he snapped his fingers under Rider's nose, standing. Billy did the same. He fingered the number 312 on the bench, jerking his thumb, telling the kid to get lost.

Anderson went to the latrines.

Later, on each tier, Anderson went to the cells he would often see cloaked with bed sheets any time of day. As a rule the homos were easily distinguishable by their scars. They were the most loathed and abused in prison, more so than rapists. Many were outright paedophiles, others adopting the behaviour for reasons of survival, others for the dubious attention in an otherwise hostile environment from those who made no secret of their natural proclivity.

The latter two were almost always smaller men, boyish, if not plainly effeminate: Billy Rider.

They understood. Hands off, literally. The Rider kid was a remote dream, a fantasy, like getting out of prison alive or living out their sentences if they chanced to believe otherwise.

Anderson spent the remainder of the morning in the yard doing his thing. At lunch Billy Rider joined the table on his own, avoiding eye contact. The nine men ignored him, each one more interested in his ham and cheese sandwich, field berry pie and ice tea.

In the yard that afternoon Anderson went to the Latinos' jefe.

They had no issue. They had no interest in El Tonto Blanco. "The loco ones, man? You cannot ever tell with them, you know?"

He did.

The Blacks' boss expressed his sentiments somewhat more succinctly. "Like you, John-boy. We don't think about no women. Too troublin'. Sure as hell we don't think about no white boy. You and me, we don't got no issues, man."

Anderson walked away with nothing more to say or do, wondering why he had even bothered. The first and last time, he promised. No more interference. The Rider kid was on his own.

Nothing good ever came from doing good, not in Battle View. Not unless someone else died, and you didn't. He'd done what was necessary for himself, for his own peace of mind, not Rider.

All that mattered was getting out and a bus ticket to somewhere.

Eight

1953

Brenda Peters left her Nebraska home at the beginning of August to begin her studies at Florida State University in Tallahassee that September, by which time she would be eighteen.

The month would scarcely allow her sufficient time to complete everything she had to do. That's what her proud parents believed. She was the smartest of all the Peters past and present, and by far the shrewdest, certain to achieve her goals.

She had 300 dollars in her jeans, a small fortune, which is all they could afford. She was so grateful. And they were not to worry, she insisted. She would work part-time on weekends and after class.

She was smart, but in the 50s smart girls became librarians, teachers, or deteriorated into not so smart housewives and mothers. She wanted more. She wanted to live, to meet important people, to become noticed and sought after. Any random thought of brats sucking on her perfect breasts, her lithe body stretched and misshapen, and diaper pails made her ill.

She was 5'10", brunette, shapely and slim. She wasn't the beautiful girl next door, not simply attractive. She was stunningly beautiful, despite the fact that until then she was forbidden by her father to wear make-up that would entice the boys and give rise to immoral thoughts and wicked behaviour.

Her face was flawless, highlighted with dark chocolate-brown eyes, full lips and a perfectly symmetrical nose. Her breasts were her focal point, though not strictly private. She had often made them readily available on short-term loans throughout her high school years to the best looking boys as a means of combatting boredom. Her tight blue jeans revealed as much about the rest of her, the access to which was permanently denied to any and all aspirants. They were diversions, not her future.

She had promised herself from the first eager grope of a calloused hand that no hayseed farm boy would ever get that far despite her irrepressible curiosity which she intensified each evening with her ardent and practiced fingertips. The last thing she needed or wanted was to end up like her mama.

She arrived in Tallahassee on a Sunday, calling her anxious mama and papa to say that she loved them. Then she had supper and boarded an all-nighter to Miami where she would fulfill what she knew was her destiny.

Monday, too restless to think of breakfast, she went shopping for skirts and blouses, silk underpants, elegant sandals and a purse handcrafted from real leather.

By noon she also had a revealing two-piece bathing suit that would shock her mother and a sundress that was daringly flimsy and strapless, with scarcely enough left in her new purse for a cheap hotel room since the dorm room in Tallahassee knew nothing about her. What was left she spent on lunch, completely confident she would succeed.

Soon after, refreshed and eager, the first restaurant refused her. She was too young. At the second she was too Midwest: A taint she would soon remove. At the third restaurant the owner eagerly agreed to give her a chance.

Seeing dollar signs he welcomed her at once with little formality, taking her into the back. He gave her a new pair of linen short shorts and a silk halter top in the restaurant's red and green colours, telling her not to detract from the outfit's sensual allure with her underwear.

She couldn't think of a single objection. No point wearing what the patrons could not see.

Although, as lovely as she was, her face needed some final touches. He called in another girl to help her with make-up she'd never worn, to help gloss her lips, to paint her fingernails and the tips of her toes the way her father had never allowed. As well, the ponytail belonged back in Nebraska, a classic French braid the ideal solution until her first paycheque.

An hour later she was twenty-one, and legal, her boss agreeing to pay her in cash each night for a week to help her get by.

Her script was short, made compelling by her sweet voice, the contours of her scantily clad body impossible to ignore. She wore her own shoes and by midnight she had brought in a few hundred guests. Her cut was thirty dollars. The hotel she found, with a barman that didn't ask her age, cost eight. She was on her way.

She kept her room for a month, by which time she was newly coiffed and almost perfectly tanned from lazy mornings on the beach, moving into her unfurnished apartment before the first of October. By Christmas her fourth-floor ocean view domain boasted all the modern amenities she could have imagined. Sadly though, despite knowing her parents would be heartbroken, what with her studying so hard, and working whenever and wherever she could, she had no choice except to remain in Tallahassee for the holidays and study every waking moment.

Their gifts were wonderful, far too extravagant for them to afford, she scolded. And theirs, she assured them, would arrive very soon. More importantly, she loved them very much.

On the twenty-fourth she had driven to the Tallahassee Post Office in her new Chevrolet convertible, arriving an hour before closing.

Near the end of her first month she had invited the barman to her room on her night off with a dual purpose. Her time had come to discover whether or not she had what it takes, if she had the guts to launch her career. She was also unabashedly eager to assuage her curiosity.

Strangely, she mused, she felt no shame at all earlier in the evening while explaining her business plan to him. She was comfortable with him.

He was the one taken aback discovering that he was chosen as her first, her teacher who would become her willing mentor.

She was excited, visibly too eager, undressing herself without seduction as though she were alone. She wanted badly for him to see her naked, to judge his initial assessment of her as she spun in a tight circle for him by the bed before throwing back the sheets.

Boys seeing her breasts was not a new experience or sensation. Dozens had seen them, groped and sucked them as though expecting an endless flow of cider to squirt into their mouths. Nebraska farm boys would fondle and grope anything with a nipple.

Alejandro Garcia, however, was the first real man to view her, to study her nudity and exquisite beauty. The first man whose erection was both telling and hypnotic. She hadn't once before seen a man fully undressed, and certainly not one so manifestly aroused by her with no way to determine to what degree he was endowed. However she couldn't imagine that he could possibly enter her without some cooperative effort.

She lay first on her front, easing onto her side before laying back with her feet together and her arms by her side.

"Do you like what you see, Alejandro? I think you do."

"Yes, I do very much."

"Just don't forget what I told you. This is my first time ever."

He chuckled. "I am deeply honoured." He knelt by her feet, parting her legs, edging his way closer, blowing a stream of air through his lips. This he would cherish. "As special as this evening is for you, Brenda, this most wonderful time together is equally so for me." He hovered over her. "Do not be nervous. We will begin gently."

"I'm not nervous. I've waited years for this moment." She wasn't. "This is what I really want to do. I know that. What I don't know is whether I can, whether I'll be good enough."

"Then we should discover this truth without more talk. Talking will come after."

He kissed one breast, leisurely, guiding her hands to his back. He kissed her other breast with equal attention and pleasure. He eased backward, slowly, masterfully trailing kisses to her tiny V of soft and dark brown hair, inhaling deeply, her scent urgently telling him that she was ready

He was not. He teasingly parted her lips, his tongue exploring, pushing deeper, his thumb's expert touch evoking a sudden yelp, Brenda willing herself not to squirm, thinking she shouldn't.

Alejandro eased forward, kissing her breasts, pressing his mouth to hers, the familiar flavour exotic to her as he slid one hand under her buttocks to gently raise her. She had no other option. She surrendered, a second unexpected squeal escaping her mouth, followed by another when he reached maximum depth with a jolt.

He luxuriated there for an instant until she was ready for more, her body gradually rocking with his more deliberately with each intense thrust, her hands firmly grasping his buttocks, her mind reeling as their ardour mounted to a feverish climax.

She wasn't thinking of what might come next; she wasn't thinking at all. Her mind was too flooded with new and electric sensations, her body racked with spasms and glistening with thick sweat.

Quite by accident she glanced at the little clock on her table. She was on the verge of delirium, her body twisting, her violent thrusts meeting each of his with equal abandon.

In her wildest expectations she hadn't expected to convulse as she did, or to scream as loudly, or that her body would continue shuddering as he retreated to between her knees.

She wanted more, begging him. Alejandro, however, fell back. He needed to re-equip his body. He needed a drink, standing from the bed to fill their glasses with a passable Merlot he'd brought to her room.

"An evening of good lovemaking, Brenda, requires intermissions." He passed her a tumbler half full. "This is one way in which women are without question superior to men, even to a Latino."

"The best thirty minutes of my life, Alejandro."

"And of mine. Again, without question. You are divine." He saluted her, sipping his wine. "You have spoiled me for the future, chica. This wine, it is bitter after tasting your body's rich flavours."

"So, I was good?"

"Incredible is the better word." He sat beside her. "However, Brenda, if this is truly how you wish to live your life, to become the best, there are things you must learn and things you must consider."

She rolled onto her side. "Like what?"

"To begin with, most men are particular about their women's pasts. Finding a man to marry you will be difficult once you begin this life and, possibly, your life after much more so. You must be aware of this. Your future may be one of loneliness, chica."

She gulped a mouthful of wine. "I don't want to marry. I've seen the end results. And babies are out of the question. What I want is this. This is who I am. I'm certain of that, Alejandro."

"Then you must take precautions."

"I have, a while ago. No babies or aprons for this Miami girl."

He nodded, pursing his lips. "In this case you have made your future men very happy. They will not be burdened by thoughts of prevention. These things, they inhibit our passion; they make us feel silly and prevent further possible pleasures. And regarding these particular activities that some may request of you, you must never put anything into your mouth that has not come from your pantry and you must never put your lips to these foreign mouths."

"You mean like your cock?"

"Do not use such words. They are not required. They are the words of street girls."

"But I kissed you." She glossed her lips with the tip of her tongue, smiling.

"Because I am your first and I am your friend. These men, some will be my age, while many others will be younger. However many will be older. These will be your most faithful clients. This is what you want, to spend your nights with older men?"

"Yes, I know I do. But not men…gentlemen, Alejandro. Gentlemen who can afford me."

"If such is the case you must be as exquisite as your body. You must not encourage any man who is not complete, or beneath you, men who are not clean or whom you believe to be vulgar or unkind. The girls on the streets are for these men. Not you, and not more than one man each evening."

Brenda Peters shook her head, tousling her dampened hair. "No, Alejandro. I won't ever be a whore. That is not what I want."

"I say this because no one will pay you a high price if you do not appear as pure and pristine as you are this evening for me. Yet educated and travelled men will pay well to experience such a beautiful body for as long as you allow them. And for this you must be familiar with the finest places, until they come to you when your knowledge and skills are more complete. As well, of much greater importance, as you become the best and remain so, your body must also remain yours. You must only share those parts of you which we have enjoyed together this evening. No other part of you. To do so would quickly damage you and put you on the street. You must care for your body and for your mind as well. These men will want to speak with you of many things. You must be aware of the world and speak well."

"At home I listened to the radio in my room each night, copying how they said what they did."

"This is not good enough. You must return to your schooling. You must lose the little of you that remains in Nebraska."

She pouted. "I thought I had."

"You must be first class. You must dress yourself and appear in a first class way. This you will only achieve by being with such people." He glanced at the floor, at the tee-shirt, her cut-off jean shorts and penny loafers strewn beneath her silk undies and satin bra. "I, too, was anxious to see your body, chica. Yet sadly you undressed for me too quickly. This is not the way. Men will prefer helping you, enjoying their seduction of you, cupping your breasts, sweeping away your hair and kissing your neck." He gestured with the glass in his hand. "This is what prostitutes will do, Brenda. They are always anxious to arrive, even more anxious to leave. This is not you. These clothes, they are not you. If you want, I will tomorrow show you the best stores. You must wear what is feminine and be appealing to men of good taste. You must learn to be an exquisite and deliciously inviting woman, not a country girl without her pitchfork lacking instruction."

"I have more clothes. I do."

"I have seen these clothes. You must learn to dress as the woman you wish to be, not a young imposter. As you must learn the patience of undressing, chica."

"I learn quickly."

"This is good, because I see that I have much to teach you and not much time."

She gazed at his penis. "Alejandro, since you are my first, telling me I should refuse the others, shouldn't I at least try once? How else will I know? Besides, fair is fair." She slid a hand between her legs. "This didn't come from *your* pantry."

He swallowed the Merlot not moment too soon. "Perhaps I will let you convince me, this one time before we resume your lessons."

She put down her glass, easing onto her knees, enclosing him in her free hand. "How many men will pay me well for too much conversation?"

"You are right. We must continue. And you remind me that they will not always want to strain their arms or gaze into your eyes."

He put his glass by hers. Her plan had come to fruition. Nothing would stop her.

Alejandro proved himself an excellent teacher, neither of them thinking to sleep. He was ten years older, familiar with the intimate needs of a woman's body; Brenda was impatient to learn, greeting her new day exhausted and naked, ready for breakfast and shopping.

Over the next few days between breakfasts and their respective shifts he worked with her constantly and persistently. He took her to luncheons in fine restaurants; he taught her about place settings, the priorities of flatware and stemware and their proper uses. He introduced her to good wine and the difference between appreciative sips and drinking. He taught her that, once in her mouth, the food she consumed was a private matter. He taught her about silk camisoles and tap pants, garters and stockings, and how best to wear them.

She wore her best new dresses, skirts and blouses,

practicing not sitting in either as though mounted in a saddle or any other stirrup. Above all he taught her the art of seduction and being seduced, each night returning late to her room to test her and grade her.

Their last morning together he left her once again depleted, though this time fifty dollars richer. Fair was fair, he reminded her. His work was done. She was now a businesswoman, not his lover, not any man's lover, worth that much and more. She must never be taken for granted.

She refused.

"Alejandro, you have taught me so much. This is too much money, half your week's pay. I should be paying you."

He insisted.

"My parting lessen to you, chica. I am not the poorest of men, although a much happier man since meeting you I am also the last average man you will engage in this way. You will never achieve what you most desire with men like me. You must seek out gentlemen of distinction, as I have shown you. They will not worry about so little a part of what they earn in a year, not once their eyes transmit to their hearts what they must do. Nor have I."

He kissed her cheek and left.

Until then, she had been too preoccupied with other matters and felt strangely deserted in the room alone.

Over the next few weeks on her nights off, and from her new apartment, she went to uptown bars, never leaving alone, each evening gaining sophistication while learning more and varied techniques. Not at all surprised by the extent of her pleasure.

She realized that Alejandro Garcia was right. Erudite and sophisticated men would indeed pay her well, and they did. Her first client, a doctor, happily rewarded her with twice what Alejandro had given her, a sum she immediately adopted as her current worth. He was also right about what they would expect of her,

She hadn't waited long before enrolling in a community college to study history and literature and by her second Christmas her own upscale, out-of-town patrons at the restaurant were increasingly parking at the curb waiting for her as a delectable end to their evenings.

Her life was by far better than any Nebraska dream. Her future was bright, closing her first full year with two grand in the bank, ten grand more tucked into her mattress, and a wardrobe of beautiful clothes.

Ironically, her single frustration was Nebraska. She loathed the Midwest, when she could easily afford the trips to Paris or London or Madrid that she wanted so badly. Instead her two summer weeks' vacation each year were spent with her parents, mostly spent driving the nearly 1500 miles into dust, tumbleweed and cow shit.

The first summer she explained to her parents that she had learned to drive and that the Chevrolet was borrowed from her roommate whose parents lived in Tallahassee. The second summer she didn't bother, committed from then on to flying…to anywhere far from Nebraska.

Her single source of satisfaction were the boys she had left behind, the ones with memories of her half-naked body, if they even remembered the warmth of her soft flesh. They were ploughing fields, dressed in work boots thick with mud, sagging coveralls and the same sweat-stained baseball caps they'd worn at school. All of them reduced to the country bubbas they had once scorned. They had no idea who she was when she first walked alone into the general store, their mouths gaping as she sauntered out calling their names.

Subsequent Christmases were no better. Not since her mother thought to surprise her in Tallahassee where Brenda had hurried to rent a furnished apartment and perforce went to the university bookstore each year for the books she required.

By April of '57, then twenty-one, Brenda Peters had a

regular clientele and a net worth nearing 42,000 dollars cached in a safety deposit box. An impossible amount. She had also reduced her restaurant hours, finishing earlier while convincing her boss to double her salary.

She was spending a thousand dollars or more each month with not much left over, occasionally dipping into her secret play money, which alone was four or five times what any other girl her age might hope to earn in a week. Her problem, however, was two-fold: Her parents and her graduation.

Mrs. Peters had scrimped and saved from the house money each week since Christmas to witness her daughter's grandest day, though graduations were expensive. She had no idea until her daughter called.

Brenda was devastated. She needed a gown and cap, a new dress and shoes with not enough money left over after all her other expenses. What choice did she have other than to forego the ceremony altogether? She was beside herself, crying, all the while aware that, despite her mother's heartrending disappointment at not attending, Polly Peters would not hear another word. She mailed her daughter in Tallahassee that very day the money she had saved.

A month later Brenda journeyed for the last time to Nebraska, this time by air from Tallahassee where she stayed for a day, stopping into the post office for her money before searching for a stationary and printing store.

At first the young man refused her, shocked by the request, although before she left a few hours later as a graduate of Florida State he was paid for his work and delighted by a secret he could never share with his wife. Despite not being a man of means, he was gentleman enough to assist a lady in need, he justified as she strutted from sight.

An early morning flight the next day brought her to the Lincoln Airport near noon, where she hailed a cab that took her to the bus station, where a travel-weary daughter waited outside on a hard bench in the heat for her first glimpse of the loving parents she longed to see.

At the farm Mr. and Mrs. Peters were thrilled, snapping pictures of the gold-embossed document to show their friends. They could not believe their little girl was now a professor at the University of Miami, or that she had graduated first in her class. To celebrate they took her to the town's diner for dinner and a glass of the finest house wine.

When she departed a week later to take up her new post, she left with fresh apple pies, jars of preserves, and a box of childhood memories which she discarded at the bus station before taking a taxi to the airport for a direct flight to Miami.

She was at the convergence of several dilemmas with a good deal to contemplate. She truly enjoyed her sexuality. She enjoyed the variety, the arousal, their admiration of her exquisite body and the intrigue of continued newness. She had achieved her goal.

She wasn't a whore or a prostitute or a cheating wife. She was simply doing what other girls willingly did in payment for fancy dinners or what they believed was love.

That wasn't her. Not only did she not care about love, she wasn't screwing in the backseat of cars or in Nebraska barns. Her clientele were all gentlemen, professionals. As was she, receiving what she believed was lucrative compensation for excellent services rendered. However, to the State of Florida, she was indeed a prostitute and a tax fraud.

Not having friends didn't bother her. From a distance she liked the girls at the restaurant and her boss. That was enough. She had no time for close friends. She worked six days a week between three and 9:00 PM, using her free night for two college classes while very reluctantly limiting herself to entertaining three men at most each week, usually until three or four in the morning. Her other nights she dedicated to studying as her heavy workload began catching up with her.

In her best world, she would quit. And then what? She was uncertain.

Her boss was now paying her twenty cents for each person or couple she lured into his restaurant for dinner or drinks, constantly surpassing 300 each night. Truth be told, she didn't have to supplement her income. Even without her gentlemen her income surpassed that of many of her doctor and lawyer acquaintances.

Quitting would allow her more free time to herself, allow her to develop her career full-time, to satiate her almost narcotic obsession while maintaining her lifestyle and allow her to vacation in a manner she deserved.

Best of all, she could take her work with her and gain European experience. Yet she could not deny that the restaurant did afford her an endless source and selection, and, more importantly, exemption. No state law existed against sudden attractions between the restaurant's patrons and its employees. Or where the attractions might lead. Nor was she the only girl making extra money. Miami girls were in high demand and the boss didn't care. Not with his Cadillac and gold rings, and he also knew better than to ask.

Without the restaurant she might be more visible, vulnerable to vice cops and dirty cops bartering freebies, pimps wanting a cut, and sight unseen clients. None of which was good. Her workplace gave her protection against those perils, while bluntly reminding her each night that she was better than standing on a South Beach sidewalk handing out menus and that one day soon her safety deposit box would not suffice.

She didn't want the complications of a boyfriend or a husband, having made certain of never having children in spite the doctor's first reluctant words and his final lecture on how she might well have ruined her life, her chance for motherhood and true happiness. A pre-emptive measure serving dual purposes: Her eternal peace of mind and her clients' freedom, for the hundred dollars they paid, to recapture whatever they had lost or had never found.

Alejandro had been right about that also. Being with Brenda Peters was easy, and relaxed, like being with their wives or girlfriends, except more expensive and worth every penny.

That said, a man in her life would be convenient. She was constantly disappointing unaware men her age, refusing invitations from the other girls to double date at the beach or bar-hop on her day off.

Her fear was that someone might one day suspect her duality. Enjoying her youth by joining a customer for drinks after work was not the same as being labelled a whore.

Nine

1957

In early September, dressed for the occasion in silk and satin, garters and lace, high heels and a designer clutch, unrecognizable to anyone as the girl who hours earlier was handing out menus, Brenda Peters went to her favourite French café where she was known for her excellent taste in wine and her generous gratuities. The place was also her safe haven where she always arrived and departed alone, eating leisurely meals at a corner table that looked out over the Atlantic while dreaming of Europe.

She was celebrating her twenty-first birthday, determined that very soon she would vacation in Paris or London. She never sat at the bar, and she never accepted a gentleman's invitation to join his table.

The sea was calm, black, sparsely lit by the party and cabin lights of departing cruise ships she wondered about, letting her imagination get the better of her, her thoughts drifting, unaware the gentleman had halted her waiter with a genteel smile and a convincing sleight of hand.

"Excuse me, mademoiselle. If I may introduce myself, my name is Jean-François du Valois and for the past hour and more I have been captivated by what must be the most beautiful woman in all of America. I would be inconsolably crushed were I not permitted to join you for a desert and possibly a digestif that would make my evening truly the most memorable."

She was accustomed to well-dressed men. Her clients were doctors and lawyers, bankers and a senator or two, her list of referrals growing monthly to the point where her serious concerns were becoming imponderable.

She had outgrown her day job as she had outgrown Nebraska, reminded of the annoyance with each weekly deposit to her safety deposit box. She really had no choice. Quitting was absolutely requisite to her larger plan.

He wasn't much taller than her, dressed in shades of blue: a dark blue suit, a Mediterranean blue shirt cuffed with sapphire links, and a pale blue tie clasped with a sapphire clip. She gave him mid-forties. He was trim, his face and hands lightly bronzed by the sun; his nails were manicured, his hair the colour of hers that he wore loosely swept back.

His brown eyes sparkled, a thin smile more genuinely hopeful than arrogant, the waiter's menu was framed in his hands. Different, she thought, if not a bit showy.

"I'm sorry. My meal is finished. I was about to leave."

"Such a fine meal without a desert? This is not at all possible." He held the leather folder closer. "I believe, mademoiselle, that you would devastate your waiter…and most certainly me. Clearly a callous destruction of two innocent men."

She hesitated, remembering Alejandro, glancing at her watch. She wanted to laugh, resisting the urge. "That would be terrible of me, wouldn't it? I suppose I could stay a while longer, since you seem so determined."

He pulled out his chair noiselessly, signalling the waiter. "At your service, mademoiselle, and with your permission…" He ordered two Rèmy Martins, the waiter noting Brenda's and his selections from the menu.

"My name is Brenda Peters. I teach at the University of Miami."

"I am delighted, Brenda, and please call me Jean-François. I arrived today from France to negotiate the importation of machinery for your state's air and seaports which will numb our minds to discuss."

"This your first time in America?"

He shook his head. "Once each month, to Miami once each season, this trip thus far being my most pleasing."

"But you just arrived."

"Indeed."

"Such a travel schedule must be very difficult on your wife, Jean-François."

He chuckled. "*Was* difficult, I do suppose, since she chose to replace me with another more to her liking." He raised his right hand. "You see, no ring, and no mark."

"I'm so sorry."

"I am not. She is happier now, as am I. And Brenda, what of you? In which areas do you specialize?"

"Literature and History. I'm beginning my first year."

The waiter came with their flan, cerises-jubilées and their cognacs, Jean-François raising his glass to her.

"The history of France I do hope. Where you must surely visit one day, if you have not yet done so."

"The seventeenth and eighteenth centuries are my favourites. Such an elegant era. So, yes, the history of France. And, yes, I will visit one day soon."

"An elegant period indeed, for the very few and the very fortunate. Otherwise, quite terrible."

They spoke for an hour, unhurried, Brenda enchanted by the man; du Valois intrigued by such a desirable young woman he had discovered sitting alone, curious as to why that might be.

Brenda signalled the waiter for the bill, du Valois redirecting him. He insisted that he pay for her dinner as well, warning that further objections would go unheeded. Et voilà! With little choice she graciously accepted.

"May I escort you to your home, or to your car, Brenda? Please allow me this pleasure."

"Jean-François, thank you. I'm very flattered.

Unfortunately I come here quite often, alone. I don't want them thinking badly of me."

"Ah, I understand your concern entirely. Yet sadly, for me, with the night air so inviting, perfect for a few quiet moments by the sea, I must walk alone to savour our short time together as I attempt in vain to dispel my deep sadness."

He couldn't be real. She knew what would come next once outside. Not at all certain, her mind opposing, her body very willing and very ready. "I suppose you could follow me out in a few moments. I would enjoy a peaceful few minutes at the ocean."

She stood. He stood, taking her hand in his, slightly tilting his head, grateful for her company. And she was gone.

Not long after they were strolling along the meandering seaside boardwalk with her arm in his. Not long after that, he kissed her without warning.

"Brenda, will you sleep with me tonight? I must be honest with myself and with you. We feel a certain electricity, do we not? And not for one ephemeral night that will fade in time from our memories. This is not what I desire for you, or from you. I will be your ardent lover and faithful companion for as many nights this week as you will want me."

She was unashamed of her body, unashamed of how she lived her life, yet for no reason she could fathom she suddenly felt consumed by the guilt of treachery.

"Jean-François, I am a professor, or I'm beginning a career as one. However to put myself through school, because my parents were too poor, I…well, I slept with men. I still do, very selectively and with professional men, men like you…and they pay me. What I need you to understand is that I am not a prostitute. I'm not. I am as professional as the men I entertain. I enjoy what I do and I'm very well-paid for my work. Well-paid. Jean-François.

I'm sorry if I'm shocking you, however "lover" is not a word I use and I haven't kissed a man in four years. Nor will you kiss me again this evening."

"I am not shocked, Brenda. Nor am I surprised. What I am is French. We are well acquainted with such matters. For a Frenchman to have a mistress, this is not an unusual circumstance. Not at all. We call this our cinq à sept, what you Americans for some reason call your happy hour." He brought her hand to his lips, kissing her palms. "So, Brenda, tell me, will we negotiate our terms for the week where we stand…or in the morning?"

She loved his accent. She loved the way he spoke her name, emphasizing the 'a' as though he was whispering her name, casting a spell upon her. He was without question more refined than her American clients, despite their affluence and social standing. She searched his eyes. He wasn't the least bit taken aback as they sometimes were at first. Nor did he appear eager.

She cleared her throat. "Negotiate? I don't think so, particularly while we're standing on a street corner. What you get is a fixed price, a fixed menu, and customer satisfaction. You can decide for yourself in the morning whether we see each other again. Those are the terms."

He agreed. And when she told him her fee he coughed a quietly polite laugh. She was well within his means.

Du Valois was so captivated by her naked beauty and her voracious appetite, and Brenda so gripped by his relentless and expert devotion to every detail of her body and pleasure, that she could no more let him go than would a desperate drug addict scatter his white dust into the wind. Forever lost.

Throughout the week they shared sumptuous dinners at his expense without a moment's lull in their conversations, nevertheless ending their heated evenings and greeting intense mornings without the distraction of meaningless words, from which she walked away with more than a very substantial compensation when she might well have paid him.

She told him about her life, as she saw fit, her doubts about a lifetime of teaching, fearing she would soon tire of the routine, and of Alejandro who, du Valois concurred, had been right.

In his view as well she had the choice of one career or the other. The Frenchman adding that continuing her professorial duties was fine, however three late nights each week, and wanting more, would eventually harm her, ruin one career if not both, and turn her beautiful face into a mask, her divine body into a common resource for less cultivated men.

She was superb, he imagined at Literature and History as well. However he strongly encouraged her to make a decision to her advantage and to her contentment, which he personally believed, in a cavalier tone, should be in the interest of modern mankind and not those souls reawakened by her from their violent deaths in centuries long past. She was too young, vibrant and vital.

As for her fees, her sisters in France, Les Hôtesses, the very best ones, were the highest paid in Europe, the most respected and sought after. As well, 100 dollars was a laughable affront.

Outstanding women such as she were a welcomed and pleasant diversion for men of means such as he, yet merely an infrequent extravagance for men such as she was then entertaining. In his mind no explicable reason existed as to why she would place such an inexcusably paltry value on her body and her intrinsic charms.

She didn't reply; she couldn't, feeling frustration.

Nor would they think to practice their profession six nights each week. Such a schedule was insane. They would work four, possibly a fifth for a particularly favoured gentleman, the good ones, taking requisite time to sooth and condition their bodies in spas and with frequent retreats to the Côte d'Azur and the Costa del Sol. In his opinion, given his intimate knowledge of her, of her unyielding proclivity and her ceaseless hunger for her body's arousal, what choice did she have other than to abandon teaching forever?

She was becoming overwhelmed. If he thought that of teaching, she wondered, she would never dare to tell him the truth and risk losing all that he might bring her.

Through him she discovered Switzerland and the peculiarities of that country's banking system. He assisted her with the money transfer, reiterating in the strongest terms while adding another 250 to cover their last evening together that she was greatly underpriced for her skill and her commitment to her clients' pleasure. The fee was what any man of means would expect to contribute to a woman in Paris who would delight him so thoroughly throughout the entire evening. That said, in future, whether in Paris or Miami, he would expect her exclusivity throughout the length of his stay or hers. In return for which he would pay her in full and in advance without the monotony of demeaning financial concerns.

How could she not accept? She was stunned, and by week's end her safety deposit box was empty.

In October she flew to Paris for ten days with her parents who saw the City of Lights from a bus, lodged in a four-star hotel not far from du Valois' rented château. Brenda viewed the city through the windows of his chauffeured limousine and slept with him each night, excusing herself on two occasions to dine with her parents before returning to his bed. Not that she wanted to. He wanted her to, her European fee of 2500 USD paying for much of her family vacation.

For the next several years du Valois would go to her once each season, as would several of his close French associates from time to time, some married, some not. She would see him in Paris once each summer, their days spent in rapture, du Valois accepting that on those particular occasions, save the first, her evenings would be otherwise committed.

She went without him to the airport the second Sunday, strangely disappointed by the revelation which he explained with cavalier insouciance. His wife, apparently returned to him, had invited guests for an afternoon. Du Valois, naturally, was equally disheartened and no less eager to see her again in December.

Seated in First Class, her parents belted-in a few rows behind her in Coach and nervous about take-off, she stared into the mesmerizing effervescence exploding in her fluted glass.

"Excuse me, miss," he glanced at the overhead bin, "2B. I apologize for interrupting your thoughts, however I believe you are occupying my seat."

He was disturbing her. Jerk. "And I believe that I was keeping it warm for you," she retorted too curtly.

He put up a hand. "In that case, miss, please stay as you are. I no longer have the slightest interest in white, fluffy clouds, the curvature of the earth, and the cities of Paris and Miami are sufficiently familiar to me from any direction or altitude. I'm fine by the aisle, unless you would rather. In fact I'll be quite happily closer to the stewardesses and service carts."

"Good for you. Then we'll both be fine, won't we?"

He sat, without the slightest adjustment to his comfort.

He was a cliché, she mused. He was tall, dark and handsome, very handsome, his drawl a dead giveaway. By no means a country hick, not by a country mile. He was expensively dressed with not a hair out of place; his nails were neatly trimmed, his fingers free of gold. He was young, up and coming, a junior something or other, or working for his daddy for more money than he deserved.

She felt closed in, trapped. She had been undeniably rude to him because she was frustrated with herself, Jean-François and Alejandro haunting her thoughts. The guy was simply being polite, an integral part of Southern nature she often found annoyingly effusive.

He was in his own world. Or was he purposely ignoring her? Men often shied away from her because of her stunning good looks, often too insecure, which she believed was a good thing as in "don't waste my time." Anyway, he didn't strike her as the timid type. Besides, he had disturbed her first.

"That was rude of me, sir. Please let me apologize."

He faced her, leisurely, his manner relaxed. "Not at all, miss. I assure you. I was at fault for disrupting your thoughts. We should never intrude upon those we find gazing through windows or into a glass of champagne." His smile was real. "Or so they say."

"My name is Brenda Peters." She held out her hand.

"A pleasure to meet you, Miss Brenda. My name is John Anderson."

Miss Brenda, a cute aspect of Southern gentility, and a little thick for a Northern girl. "Brenda will do fine, John."

"Thank you, Brenda. Were you in Paris on vacation or business, may I ask?"

"A little of both. I was doing research on the French Revolution, to share a sense of realism with my students. I have a particular interest in Marie-Antoinette."

"Was your research in French? Are you fluent?"

"I'm embarrassed to say that I am not. I relied on a distinguished French counterpart whom I met this past summer. He took an interest in me, and I suppose I took advantage of his kindness…absolutely privileged to work with him. He's extremely renowned in his field, Professor Jean-François du Valois." She sipped her champagne. "I suppose I should make an effort to learn."

"You would open a new world."

"Are you… fluent?"

"I am. My mother was French. She and my father passed on a few year ago, a car accident."

Her lips parted effectively. "That's awful. I'm so sorry for you."

"Thank you. Victims of sad coincidences. An oncoming trucker suffered a heart attack. Dead before the collision. No one's fault."

She nodded compassionately. Too much personal information. Not interested. "Was that your purpose for being in France, family?"

"Not quite. I am decidedly not the family type." He chuckled. "My Christmases and Thanksgivings are always peaceful events, and I save a fortune on gifts."

Brenda snorted. "I understand. I do. I know everything I have to about Christmases: Fun until you're ten…if you think socks and underwear are fun."

She accepted a refill from the stewardess, smiling; John asked for a double Johnnie Walker Black. He had a hunch that underwear with her could be fun, lots of fun.

"So you were here on business?" she went on.

"I'm a marketing specialist with high-profile clients in Paris and Madrid. When I'm not here developing their strategies, I'm there. Or on the West Coast. I moved to South Miami from Georgia after the deaths a few years ago, where I'm actually not home very often."

"Better Georgia than Nebraska. That place takes a long time to wear off."

"Which seems to have occurred rather successfully in your case. And your parents, Brenda?"

"Back there, farming. They joined me here for a few unsuccessful days. They weren't comfortable and went home early. Fish out of water. More comfortable with pork and beans than Bordeaux and vichyssoise."

"Each one an acquired taste."

He liked her. He believed he did very much. Something about her stirred him. And he knew precisely what.

She began liking him as well. He was twenty-six, soft-spoken, courteous and single. The epitome of a Southern gentleman. He was eager to arrive home, to Coral Gables, twelve miles from the restaurant, to a week's vacation with nothing planned other than sprawling on the beach.

He had a warm smile, making her laugh when he lamented during their final approach into Miami that the flight was ending too soon. He took the leap, thinking what the hell. His chances were as good as anyone else's.

"Brenda, I would very much like to call you this week. I see an evening of dinner and dancing in our futures, under a canopy of stars. Is Saturday good for you? I will gladly provide you with credentials and a full list of reliable and credible references who will vouch for my honourable intentions."

She giggled, hesitating, though she felt the same impulse. She felt good with him.

He waited.

She squeezed his arm. "I wouldn't dream of ever being so cruel to such a delightfully charming man, not twice in so few hours anyway. Dinner and dancing sound wonderful, if a week from Tuesday is good for you. I teach class most evenings as well, John, when I'm not tutoring. Not so much for the extra money, more for the gratification I derive, despite very recently deciding to double my fees. The work is very demanding at times and I'll need the time to find a substitute professor."

She made no mention of her Saturdays, and neither did he. Tuesday was fine, John noting her phone number and address. Saturdays would happen later, he thought, if they were meant to be.

Brenda was first off the plane, walking quickly with him through Customs and Baggage Claim, ignoring her parents until she was certain he was gone.

Reunited with them, she walked with Polly and Walter to the gate where their flight to Lincoln was scheduled to leave a few hours later. She hugged and she kissed them, saddened.

She wanted to stay longer with them, regretting that her students had adamantly volunteered to meet her at Arrivals, always so anxious to learn from her, to one day be like her.

Polly and Walter were so proud.

Ten

1971

Anderson could not for a moment picture in his mind how Rider's back might look after five lashes, let alone thirty, despite the other less severe casualties of the Cat he'd seen. Cruel and unusual punishment, unthinkably uncivilized for modern times, albeit deserving and not cruel enough for what the kid had done to the girl.

Anderson had asked the warden how often, not that he cared. He was curious, concerned more about the sobbing and snivelling that would inevitably postscript the legal torture.

No one much cared about the hangings. They were something to talk about, a novelty the day of. Those cons were simply gone, walked or dragged out and never seen again. Conversely, those who went to the Cat, released from the infirmary two, three days later, would invariably return to their cells wretched and broken, unpitied by all, the objects of prison scorn.

They were all older, the ones he'd seen, most of them stronger than Rider. So what was in store for a kid as weak as a prepubescent girl?

Murderers understood murderers, professional or amateur, premeditated or passionate, most of them lifers. The same way repeaters understood repeaters. They were losers, society's unwanted refuse. Their destiny. Paedophiles and rapists were another matter. They were twisted predators, preying on the most vulnerable, sick-minded perverts and the lepers of Battle View, their deserving punishments raucously applauded each time with howling jeers by straights and homos alike. And now he had one in his cell.

He'd seen the backs of those men, the flesh deeply sliced into red and jagged strips, painfully healing over time into raised and purple welts branding them for life as diseased and degenerate fiends. All of them defiantly smug on their first walk to the Whipping Room, each one terrified each time thereafter, their weak legs failing.

As for Anderson, he was increasingly convinced that Rider would shit himself into a pine box before the first stroke.

The kid's back? He shook his head. He couldn't imagine. Luck of the draw. Another judge might have sentenced him to the strap, a strip of perforated flat leather inflicted across his bare buttocks while bound to a table. Bad enough, and yeah, fucking humiliating, but the lash was truly vicious. Anderson correctly assuming the judge must have been a mother and who could blame her?

Rider had a month of leisure and three years of dread coming his way, unstoppable unless he had sufficient will not to survive. Common sense dictated that suicide was likely the lesser of two equally ironic evils since Anderson, for reasons he had yet to justify unto himself, had precluded other possible eventualities.

Failing that Anderson had a predicament of his own: The kid was frigging spooky. He had no expression. He had no light in his eyes, not a single reaction and he could stare for minutes at a time without blinking when he wasn't fixated on his own feet, only opening his mouth to eat.

Quiet in the cell was one thing, twenty years with a muted and unresponsive simpleton was an unreasonable expectation. They should have put him in a mental institution with other zombie-like creatures, his own kind, not Battle View. Or have done him a favour and execute him outright.

The kid was obviously not right in the head. Anyone could see that. Should never have been born, probably making his way through school on sympathy grades for no good reason, taking up space, time and money. The Riders of the world brought nothing of value to the table. They were takers. They had nothing to offer, no real reason to exist beyond a society's holier than thou righteous sense of itself: Deadweight living off welfare, society's tax dollars ill-spent by the nation's do-gooders.

Irrespective of high school or murder, the kid's future was a dead-end. The sad part was, if Rider had dropped out, or had never been born, that girl would be alive.

He despised himself for thinking that way, the tiniest fragments of humanity prevailing, struggling each day to keep him sane.

Before Battle View, before his hell, such soured thinking would never have pervaded his mind. Disallowed by his good nature, his decency and goodwill.

He inhaled a deep breath, most of what John Anderson once was, was now gone, shadows of his past forever lost in the dark netherworld of Battle View Prison. A humph blurted through his nose. Hard for a man to keep his pants neatly pressed and his shirt cuffs white when he's knee-deep in shit.

Fate, he supposed, like walking in on a whoring wife. She's the one who needed thirty lashes.

Anderson ambled into the block, to his cell for the day's second count. After his dinner he went to the library for space. The next morning before breakfast he stomped his foot several times onto the bottom edge of Billy Rider's mattress. Shower time, mimed as best he could to the amusement of those nearby.

Billy at first hesitated, getting the message more succinctly, reminded by Anderson kicking his footlocker to take a change of underwear with him. He did, walking out, turning to see that Anderson was not behind him. Nor would Anderson be with him at the table for breakfast; the kid had to learn and Anderson was too agitated to eat.

Sure Rider was off limits, which Anderson was aware would not extend to accidental hard knocks, accidental tripping, accidentally dropped trays, or verbal abuse, not until he grew a pair and stood-up for himself, which Anderson was inclined to believe would never happen. Not with this boy.

He skipped breakfast, his emotions too pumped, in the yard his body and heart-rate working at maximum effort to keep up, to clear his mind. Futile. Not working. He dropped the weighted bar into its cradle, sitting, slumping forward, the day's heat soothing to his back. As though he needed a reminder.

The kid had probably never been punched, never had his nose bloodied in a schoolyard brawl or been kicked in the balls. Now he was in for mankind's worst shit-kicking, his flesh ripped open.

He punched an open palm. Damn! The kid was *not* his problem. First off, Rider *would* be better off dead. No question, not with what he was facing. The boy was weak, defenseless, close to brain-dead already. A few minutes of terror on a trap door. So what? Then snap, then peace everlasting. Not a bad deal when considering the coming three years. Anderson didn't know, never had to think about it. Could Rider even scream?

He should never have interfered, arresting the natural order of things against his better judgement and sense of survival. Had he minded his own business, the kid might already be dead, or thinking of ways to tear his bunk sheet into strips that wouldn't give way or tear into his throat under his weight.

No. Not bright enough. No way.

Anderson stood, for the time being he was alone in the

yard. Most cons, they needed their food. He didn't, not that day. The entire situation was perverse, not his concern. Screw perverse. That the warden had dropped Rider on him like a shit-bomb was an absolute brain-fuck.

The country didn't whip females, just men. The common consensus amongst states claiming that women and girls, who might commit crimes so punishable, were too weak mentally and physically to endure. The State of Tennessee, in this case, and a North Carolina judge, wrongly assuming that Rider was a man.

Anderson had twenty years remaining. What he was considering could easily add three to five, and for what? A kid who deserved each stroke? The one good thing Anderson could foresee in what he was formulating was that, if anything, the kid would definitely know how to keep his mouth shut.

His mind gave him the go-ahead, his body reluctantly waiting until moments before Rider might tippy toe into the mess hall for lunch.

July 03rd of that year was pleasant. A clear sky was layered with streaks of feathery white clouds, the air warm and fresh for a midsummer day. From what Anderson could determine from the yard, the block would be practically empty, save for a few homos doing their thing. They didn't much care about tans or keeping their bodies resistant to the next threat.

He walked out, ignoring the guard, muttering, cursing himself.

He noticed a single sheet hung on the second tier. Good for them, they were buddies. Very contented buddies apparently because when the block was still, which was seldom, a pin dropping would wake the dead. A single guard on the main floor sat on a bench, enjoying an otherwise peaceful time-out and a smoke before his break.

Billy was on his bunk, sulking with his eyes closed. John was instantly and irrationally more pissed with him, not kicking this time. He grabbed the kid's sleeve instead, yanking Rider to his feet, slamming him hard against the wall and glaring...though not entirely for affect. He needed the kid to understand, if that was remotely possible.

No reaction. Not a single twist to escape the hand gripping his throat. Absolute defeat. Anderson had never been a man of half measures, always committed once the decision was made, always ready to share praise or accept sole responsibility for failure. No different now. He would go forth, for better or worse, fully aware that he had forever been justly and sorely reduced to the lowest common denominator of Battle View Prison.

Redemption denied.

"Do you have any idea at all?" he demanded, his voice guttural. "You answer me, boy. You answer me now, somehow, any way you can. Do not *fuck* with me. Do you have any clue whatsoever?"

Billy didn't answer, staring, not blinking. He was waiting, trying to swallow behind Anderson's grip. A clue about what?

Anderson let go, threatening with a firm finger pressed hard against Rider's forehead.

He tore at his own singlet, plunging the limp material into the sink. He waited for the water to rise, braiding a tight, thin band and knotting one end. He motioned for Billy to strip to the waist and to bare his back. He forced the kid to face the wall with his arms outstretched, Anderson kicking his feet far apart and causing Billy's knees to buckle.

He flushed all guilt, all shame from his mind. He was doing a good thing, possibly saving the kid's life. What more reason did he need? He was doing the kid a favour.

He stepped back, raising an arm, holding the other out for balance and momentum, twisting his torso to a full ninety degrees, his muscles taut. Drawing in a breath he released his pent-up tension and the rage he felt with a fierce rush of adrenalin, saving the life of a killer.

He beat Billy five times with equal force, the first unexpected blow evoking a spastic twitch. After that, nothing, Billy standing stoically as he was, unmoving and unblinking.

Twirling Billy around, Anderson said, "That, kid, was playtime. Not even close to a mediocre rehearsal. On the first, four weeks from now, you'll feel as though razor blades are slicing you apart and you are going to seriously bleed." He jabbed his forehead with the tip of his forefinger. "Do you understand? Tell me something. Tell me somehow that you understand."

Apparently not. Then again, Billy had been told all his life that he was too stupid to understand, terrified at the moment that the man towering over him was crazier than he was.

Minutes later they were in the mess hall, Anderson eating quickly, motioning for Rider to do likewise. When he was done he put half his sandwich and what was left of his milk on Billy's tray, threatening him again with a stiff finger. Billy nodded that he understood, when really he didn't. The man had to be crazy.

Not long after, and throughout the afternoon, Billy pumped iron for the first time in his life.
He bench-pressed ten pounds until his arms gave out, Anderson then forcing him into sit-ups and push-ups with little reprieve. The Blacks and Latinos standing around were all curious about the previously remote Anderson and his new protégé. Even Black Boss and El Jefe were scratching their heads.

That night Billy Rider went to bed in a state of flux, his mind a confused and swirling kaleidoscope of Sally and Sam, his brothers, Lucy Merriweather, the judge and Anderson.

His body ached, his back stung. He was scarcely able to open and close his hands and the coming day would be no less exerting, Anderson had promised as though he couldn't wait to inflict more pain.

Billy fell asleep not certain what to think. Not certain he could live very long in such a bad place with such a cruel man. Yet in the morning he awoke to see Anderson standing facing his lower bunk. The day had begun.

The routine became a daily event, full mornings and full afternoons, each day more demanding on Billy as Anderson continued giving up his own bench time, part of his lunches and suppers. All in absolute silence other than Anderson talking to himself, his temperament affected for the sake of the other cons who might be thinking that he was beginning to soften.

By the last week of July Billy Rider was pressing fifty; his arms were becoming toned, his abdominals harder, his back stronger. He had also gained fifteen pounds that warranted a new set of coveralls which had not done much to please the warden who Anderson asked to meet with the afternoon of the thirty-first. He'd done all he could, leaving Billy alone in the yard.

"You're causing quite a bit of chatter, Anderson. You and your playmate."

"Not my problem, Warden. More self-interest than anything. Trying to toughen the kid for tomorrow, save myself some misery when he comes back. He may be deaf, I'm not."

"We should've hung the little shit, truth be told. The judge must have been in one bitch of mood that day. Good thing is, for him, he'll pass out after the first or second blow."

"Then you stop?" Anderson tried.

Prescott belched a cough, smoke exploding from his mouth. "You keep thinking that. No. Fact is, then he doesn't feel a thing, not till he wakes. Happens most times. A few weeks in the yard pumping iron won't do much for him." He lit another cigarette. "Generous of you though. Hear you share your food, too. You found religion, Anderson?"

Anderson shrugged. "Did what I could. Like I said, for me. What's the timing tomorrow?"

"Early, before breakfast. Can't have him regurgitating on the floor."

Anderson pursed his lips, nodding.

"The thing is, Warden, the kid's here for the rest of my term. The three blocks know he can't speak, can't hear, and that's fine. His lot in life, no one else's problem. However, in the mess hall, at the table, the other cons they don't much like being with him. They're a little spooked, and that's not a good thing."

Prescott didn't like cons in his office. "Get to your point."

"These past weeks in the yard I began wondering how he got to do what he did, at a graduation of all places. Maybe he can't talk, or maybe he won't. Who's to say? Maybe he can hear just fine, playacting for whatever reason. Or not. You said yourself he was deaf and dumb at his trial. Your words, which makes you wonder. How did he graduate? Seems to me he must be able to read and write, if marginally. Twenty years, Warden, a long time to spend with someone who doesn't speak, hear or blink. Which I'm thinking might cause me to reconsider the rock pile thing or to join the uproar about the road gang."

"Goddammit, Anderson. I gave him a goddamn new suit because of you. What else you in here sniffing for?"

"A writing pad and a pencil."

"A writing pad and a pencil." Prescott guffawed, coughing more smoke, wiping his mouth, blue veins streaking his face. He paused, catching his breath. "With a desk and comfy chair, I suppose? Sure. Why not?" He leaned forward onto his elbows. "And whose eye do you suppose he'll take out first with his new pencil?"

Anderson glanced at the warden's desk. "No one's eye, Warden. Not if it's felt. One pad, one felt pen. Could solve a few potential issues: The guards and the mess hall, the doctors after his whipping. You tomorrow, when you've got to tell him things."

Warden Prescott waited, feigning deep thought, albeit not very well, at last acknowledging the good sense before reaching into a drawer. "One pad and one crayon each week, if need be. That's it. And we're done here, Anderson."

Anderson turned on his heels, walking ahead of his escort to Cellblock Three. He went to the library first, then to the mess hall near the end of the allotted half-hour. Then he went to 312 where Billy was sitting in the corner of his bunk, not cringing, his legs outstretched, his arms crossed.

"Tomorrow's the big day, kid. Good luck. Sorry I couldn't do more to make you ready." He sighed. "At least they won't rape you and crush your skull." He tossed the notepad and felt pen onto the bunk. "Don't know about you. Something's not right in that head of yours. In any event you are now on your own. Nothing else I can do. I'm done. My opinion, for the little it's worth? Get stronger...and stay that way."

He sprang onto his bunk, facing the wall, opening his book, caressing her photograph with his fingertips.

Not long before lights out Anderson heard a rustling, turning to see what Rider was up to, thinking the kid might be pissing into the toilet instead of his coveralls.

His surprise was clear. Billy was standing facing him, his face expressionless, seemingly unafraid or oblivious to the morning fast approaching. He held out a sheet of folded paper pinched between his thumb and forefinger. He was waiting.

Anderson took the note.

Thank you, John. I think I am ready because of you. I understand that now.

I will get stronger and I will stay that way because of you.

But I did not rape Lucy and I did not crush her skull.

She was my friend.
Billy Rider

Eleven

1971

August 01st was a Sunday, in a place where days didn't matter, where the only visitors allowed any day of the year were the hangman and a cleric of choice to see the miserable penitent on their deserved way, most cons declining God's forgiveness despite trembling knees, soiled clothing, and tear-streaked faces beneath a black hood.

As expected, Billy Rider's sentence came a day late. Warden Prescott's Saturday was ironically taken up with his wife, his children, and other God-fearing white folk at the annual church picnic, singing His praise with hands held high when they weren't stuffing their faces with His blessed bounty.

Billy Rider spent a wakeful night dispelling frightful images from his mind, images of the warden grossly oversized, towering over him, forcing him hard against the wall while beating him time and time again with a knotted rope the way John Anderson had made him suffer.

The cold wall felt damp on his skin, making him shiver, keeping him awake, each strike stinging.

He didn't know not to expect breakfast, no one had thought to tell him. He had no idea when to expect his punishment, though he did hope it would happen soon so that he could take a shower and spend his day in the yard making himself stronger for the next time. He couldn't understand why John seemed to believe he would spend so many days in the infirmary when the kids at school had always returned to class once punished.

In fact his day began at 06:45. Billy Rider saw them arrive and stop at his door. Four of them, three guards and the warden. Then he saw Anderson leap to the floor, leaning into the far wall a few feet from their bunks with his arms crossed. The man's expression was solemn, his eyes giving hope.

Billy was tired, beleaguered. He pulled himself out from his bunk and stood straight facing out, appearing calm, forcing all dread from his mind. He was acting for John, scared shitless as Cell 312's barred door slid open with a harsh scraping sound that woke the entire block.

Prescott, impatient, barked at the guards to "get in there and let's get this thing done!"

The three guards squeezed in, Billy turning once to see Anderson's cold expression as he was handcuffed, his feet shackled, hauled from the cell and marched out of sight past rows of silently grim faces peering out from behind their own bars. Not a single con jeered, and not because of Anderson's dictum the previous day, each man feeling for the kid not yet out of his teens.

Anderson's cell door slid closed, for the ten minutes that mattered. Rules.

The escort went first to the infirmary where the doctor was mandated to declare Billy Rider fit for his whipping, Billy reading that he should touch his toes, turn to the left and the right, and then touch his nose with the forefinger of one hand and the other. The doctor examined one eye, then the other, and inspected his mouth. He was asked with another two printed words and question marks whether he needed to void himself in either way. He shook his head that he did not and the doctor signed his consent.

The Whipping Room was located in a separate area between a row of Solitary Confinement cells sealed off behind windowless doors and the more imposing door leading to a small and restricted yard beneath the warden's office where the wooden gallows stood. Inside the walls were bare, the ceiling glaring with bright 100-watt bulbs.

The two wooden chairs were for the comfort of the warden and the attending physician.

Against one wall was a narrow table to facilitate strapping, thought by an ignorant judicial system to be worse than the lash. The table was secured to the floor with bolts, thick leather belts affixed to the bottom of two sturdy front legs, two more fastened permanently to the top edges for the unfortunate inmate's hands.

The table was bolted because in past times many bigger and stronger inmates would often lift the table high off the floor during the administering of punishment thus endangering their well-being as well as that of the guards present who would be instructed to sit precariously at the farthest edges to prevent further displays of unrest.

Laying perfectly centred on the steel top was a leather strap attached to a wooden handle, which was not lying in wait for Billy.

On the other side stood a wooden frame made of dependable and worn oak. The edges were rounded, the surfaces smooth with the sheen of recently applied oil, slightly angled forward and forming a tall and wide X.

On each cross member near the top, separated by the length of a man's reach, were buckled restraints hanging limp from years of use. At each base, separated by an equal distance, were foot-traps with identical restraints. Hanging from the centre of the intersecting beams was the Cat, Battle View's horrid version of the lash no less wicked than the tools of any medieval oubliette.

The Cat was attached to a foot-long handle crafted from oak; the nine slim thongs were thirty inches in length, tightly knotted at each end, each crude tip meant to inflict the deepest possible and most merciless lacerations.

Punishment enough, though in Battle View's case, with

no state law in place to specifically prevent a warden who preferred and enjoyed the sight of men dangling from a rope, the thongs were treated with oil days before to keep them soft while the tips were soaked in water and left to dry, keeping them all the more effective.

On the floor by the frame lay a canvas stretcher.

They motioned for Billy to remain still. One guard released his hands, while the other freed his ankles and untied his laces, tugging away one sneaker then the other. All the while Billy Rider stared from one archaic apparatus to the other.

Prescott gave his approval to continue, foregoing the last-minute and state-required communication with the prisoner who couldn't speak anyway. He saw no reason for further delay. He was in somewhat of a hurry. He had been asked by his pastor the day before to lead the congregation in early Morning Prayer.

Billy was prodded towards the Cat. They undid his buttons and stripped away his singlet, belting his coveralls at his waist by the sleeves. They secured his wrists at once, tightly in place before shoving each foot in turn rudely into the slots at the base a few inches from the floor. The buckles pinched painfully through his socks, his body pressed by its own new weight against the slanted frame.

Though Billy's mind was too occupied with what they were doing to feel afraid, forgetting his mother and father until he saw the warden to one side acting like a clown.

Prescott held out an open palm, his stubby fingers stretched wide, mouthing one through five as he closed each one into a fist before pointing to Billy and making the sign for Time Out as though signalling the end of a game before he disappeared from sight to sit with the doctor.

Then the guards disappeared, Billy's head drooping from his shoulders to between the arms of the Cat, remembering John, thinking of John, thanking John for what he had done. John was his friend. Because of John none of the others had harmed him. Billy knew that much. He knew what they were saying.

He closed his eyes. Soon he would be in the yard, working out, pumping, getting stronger.

Billy Rider didn't scream when the first nine claws tore through the clear skin of his back. He blurted a single and ghoulish groan instead, the miserable cry resounding in his head louder than any blast of thunder, his face instantly contorted into a macabre and gruesome mask, his jaws stretched wide apart, his quivering lips stretched tight, choking on gulps of dry air, his slim body twisting violently once.

He thought then that he might not go to the yard, that John had told him the truth, the anticipation of what was yet to come terrifying him, forcing his mind to focus on John.

John would stand tall, and so would he for as long as he possibly could. John had tried to make him ready for this. He was no longer a boy. He was a man, a con in Battle View Prison. He would stand tall for as long as he could and, above all, he would not cry. He would never cry.

Billy Rider soon believed he was dying, strangely thankful, anxious for once in his young and unfulfilled life to feel completely at peace.

His final thought was of his first father, Buck Rider. He saw clearly the barrel of the gun close to his face, wavering: he saw his father's twitching finger on the trigger, the fear in his father's eyes, his father's head exploding onto the wall. Better that his father had killed him as a little boy that day, so that he might now be at rest in a far better place.

But Billy wasn't dying. No. His tortured mind was simply and mercifully sparing him further anguish, freeing him from the arms of the Cat, returning him into the loving arms of his mother.

Twelve

1959 - 1970

Billy went to where he felt loved. His pain and suffering mercifully held in abeyance for a short while.

*

Sally Cutter was first at the front door, her warm hands pressing gently against her son's cool cheeks, her soft lips pressing lightly against his forehead. She was smiling, squeezing him hard with a mother's love as only a mother can.

Billy came home to his family from his year-long sabbatical at the university that ended on December 23rd, 1958. His father and brothers competed selfishly with Sally for his attention, each of them anxious to speak with him, to see with their own eyes what he had to tell them in either of his two new idioms.

Since her long summer of learning away from her husband when Sally had become fluent in signing, studying long hours each day by her son's side, practicing faithfully each day thereafter, she had also taught her husband to sign which was somewhat more frustrating and certainly no less challenging than teaching her day students.

Sam had no talent for language, firmly of the belief, and often reminding her that, wherever he might travel, the charm of his Southern drawl and his genteel presence would see him through his journey. That's when she would smack his cheek and make him work all the harder.

Notwithstanding those best efforts he continued missing a word or two, making them laugh with the occasional and impolite faux-pas. As for Billy, he had also mastered the art of lipreading which, for most of his life, he would keep to himself.

The speech therapist had foretold the future correctly. Christmas that year was indeed filled with indescribable joy.

Lacking his history, uncertain whether Billy was born with the defect, the man and his staff were unable to determine with certainty why Billy could not hear or speak. The most common opinion was that of a possible complication during his birth, since Billy was born at home without the proper assistance of a midwife. Or a catastrophic event which paralyzed in some way his mind, something decidedly more dramatic than being told of the loss of his parents, memory of which for a child of his then four years would soon fade.

Hence, for Billy, they entertained no further expectation of a cure; they would instead treat his condition and his parents' malaise with a new language skill. To which they added lipreading when Billy surpassed their wildest hopes of success, giving him free rein at a better life.

However in January the state board decided that Billy had missed too much preliminary schooling to possibly be ready by year-end for Grade Two, which required Sally to take a leave of absence throughout what remained of the winter, the spring and into the summer. She was enraged, disparaging them in the strongest terms before converting her wasted anger into Billy's advantage, teaching her son throughout those months to read and to write well beyond the minimal skills of his age group.

In spite of which September '59 did come quickly, Billy meeting his first day of higher learning in the First Grade with new shoes, grey flannel shorts, a new chequered shirt and a brand new schoolbag with new schoolbooks to carry slung over his shoulder. He was excited. He would meet other children his age and make friends.

Though at that tender age he was a year older than his classmates and a few inches taller.

He was different, he stuck out. And, just like the parents of the other kids had warned, he was simple in the head and they should stay away.

Grade Two was no better, Billy nodding his agreement one day when another boy made him aware that he would be better off dead than stupid. It was true. It was, the boy taunted, because his father had told him so.

And so his life went throughout seven long years and much longer summers spent alone without friends to play with, his world and his education silent, the town of Necessity largely believing that Billy Rider was that way by God's will and design. The Lord had in His mercy vacated a malicious mind, forestalling the blasphemies of impure declarations by depriving the boy of speech. That's what the older kids told him, from what they had learned from their parents at home. There wasn't a soul in Necessity that hadn't heard of young Billy Rider.

They openly mocked him, pointed and stared. Much easier was their ignorance than compassion, their hatefulness than caring to understand. He learned then that people were cruel, asking Sally one day as church bells echoed across the town whether that was the reason she didn't believe in God or attend church, because God had made those people so cruel.

Sally responded, as though expecting the question, that they were unwell, their minds diseased because there was no God anywhere who could make them better despite their weekly atonements, their futile prayers, and the desperate ringing of church bells announcing that they were all clustered together and anxiously awaiting His divine touch.

Would high school be better, he wanted to know?

She never lied to her son, or sweetened the truth. She

had no reason to believe that anything would change for the better, which worried Billy throughout that entire summer.

In September he went to Necessity High on his own, not with his mother who left an hour earlier to prepare her day.

He knew where to go and what he must do, arriving at his homeroom before the rush of those who resented their summers ending too quickly. When they did come, he understood at once by their unsmiling faces and caustic whispers that his life would not soon improve. He knew each of their faces by name, and by their hurtful remarks from the seven years past.

 Billy sat at the back of the class so that he might read whatever his teacher might say when she wasn't facing the board. He did likewise in each of his classes, earning marks that were amongst the highest on any exam, not that he cared, excused by virtue of his doctor's insistence from any sort of activity in the gym, spending his time instead in the library.

He attended no dances, nor was he ever invited to parties at the other kids' homes. He had no little gifts at Christmas to open except the one he found in his desk from a secret admirer whom he knew had wrapped it the night before after he went to sleep. He had no Valentine's card to exchange and no way to take part in the school's Easter parade. He was completely forgotten, and in June Sally and Sam discovered he had failed the year to such an extent that remedial summer lessons were out of the question.

When his parents, understandably distraught, asked why he would have intentionally done such a terrible thing, he replied with a smirk that he needed to make some essential changes in his life and would start by leaving those kids behind, since he couldn't very well leap into Grade Ten.

Sam burst into laughter, slapping his knees. No sign required. Whereas Sally threatened each of her men with separate scowls and went to her kitchen so proud of her son for not giving in.

The following year began well, his mother exacting a sacred oath and promising strict reprisal if he for a moment thought to disappoint her once more.

Again he sat at the back, this time beside a girl he'd never seen before. Her family was new to Necessity, the entire school knew. His mother had told him a few days before, adding that she might like a friend to help her adjust.

He promised to consider the matter.

She was shy, sitting at her desk the first morning before the class filled with her head down, her long hair draping over much of her face. Billy wondering whether his mother had told her to sit there. And, if so, he would scold her that evening.

He waited, watching her sit there quietly staring at her hands. He felt uneasy and suspicious. The situation was awkward, Billy thinking he should be unhappy with his mother.

He took up his pencil and wrote her a note, reaching across to her desk. What choice did he have, thanking his mother?

Hi, my name is Billy.

She shook her head, making a face, pushing the paper away.

He wrote her another. *Yes, it is. What's yours?*

She glanced his way. "I'm Lucy."

He wrote, *Hi, Lucy. I think you're very pretty.*

"Why don't you talk before you run out of paper? All this is very silly, and very annoying."

He scribbled the answer. *I can't talk and I can't hear. I'm reading your lips. That's what I do.*

She scrunched her face. "What a terrible thing to say. I don't believe you at all. You're a very bad liar."

This time *he* shook his head as he wrote. *You'll hear about me soon enough. I'm hearing-impaired and mute. But you can call me deaf and dumb. That's okay. They all do. They all think I'm a freak.*

114

"Is that true?"

Billy nodded, smiling. *They think I care.*

Lucy Merriweather was suddenly sad, frowning as she crumpled the note. Her face was drawn as she studied the boy beside her. She would never call anyone dumb. She would never.

She knew about hate. He wasn't the only one. She sat straight, running her fingers through her mousy brown hair. The jagged and purple scar ran from her ear to her neckline. Why not, she thought? Let him stare, get the hurt over with. Then he could run and tell everyone.

"You're not the only freak. Want to laugh? Want to be the first? Go ahead. I won't mind."

He didn't think what to write. *No. I don't. I told you. I think you're pretty. We should be each other's friend. Friendly freaks.*

She giggled at that and they were friends from that moment on, close friends. Though Billy was never allowed in her home and Lucy was forbidden by her mother to ever visit in his. She had heard all she needed to know about him from the other mothers, dismissing Lucy's accusation that she should stop listening to ignorant housewife gossip.

Billy passed that year with high marks. At Christmas he received a real gift to open in class, and a Valentine's card, though neither he nor Lucy ever went to school dances or to the movies. Billy knew he would never dance with Lucy or any other girl, as much as Lucy would never be crowned home-coming queen. Not with nicknames like Dumbo and Lucy Scarface.

The absolute worst were Darlene and her friend Eleanor, the heads of state in each grade as they progressed towards graduation, never once thinking to invite Lucy into the fashionable clique of the prettiest girls.

That summer was Billy's happiest. Often he would take his lunch to the Riverside Watch not far from school and not far from Lucy's home to spend his afternoons reading, and often Lucy would think to do the same when her mother was gone.

The next year Billy left Grade Nine at the top of the class as well, quietly accepting the teachers' praises and Lucy's rewarding bright smile.

That summer again they spent secret afternoons by the river whenever they could.

Darlene's and Eleanor's rat pack often passed by giggling and teasing with childish made-up jingles, threatening to tell Lucy's mother that she was always sitting so close to "the dummy, the dummy, Lucy's favourite dummy."

Lucy yelling at them "to just go away." Which they did, making silly gestures with their fingers and hands.

Lucy had to ask, she couldn't tell. *Did that mean anything, Billy, what they were doing with their hands?*

He answered quite seriously. *Can't you tell? They're jealous. They wish they could be as pretty as you.*

She punched his arm.

Billy believed summertime was much worse for Lucy. His nemeses were working. He was free of them. Dwight for his father, learning about cars, and Jake for his father, learning about banking. For Billy the summer was a reprieve from their constant and surreptitious ridiculing, though Septembers were never far off.

But something else happened that summer of '69 that was their very special secret. Lucy no longer needed to read Billy's scribbled words. Unbeknownst to her parents and his, Lucy was quickly achieving Billy's level of fluency in signing. She was a quick study.

However throughout Grade Ten Billy and Lucy didn't see each other as often outside their homeroom where they began and ended their days. Nevertheless, until the chill of winter, anxious for the warmth of spring days ahead, they would meet when they could by the river.

The River Watch was Lucy's favourite part of

Necessity, angry with her parents, despite loving them, for caring more about their neighbours' opinions of them than Billy.

They would think differently if they would once meet with him, she implored, invite him into their home. A plea which they constantly refused, her parents more worried each day that she was developing into a young woman and that Billy Rider would one day soon think to harm her in so dreadful a way.

She knew what they were thinking, telling them they were being ridiculous and needlessly unkind. Billy would never think to treat her that way. He wasn't that kind of friend. They hadn't even kissed or held hands, she told them. Which cast her mother into a severe state of flux and her father into a tirade of threats of violence against the Rider boy and promises of the unkindest castigations for her.

The following summer, the last they might have spent together, Lucy was hurried off to England on her first day of vacation to live with her aunt. She was sixteen.

She wrote Billy each day, describing her days and what she had seen, mentioning once or twice her evenings of polite incarceration, her last letter suggesting they meet at the Watch on the seventh of September, Labour Day, when she would bring him a slice of her birthday cake that she was preserving in the icebox especially for him.

She had the biggest surprise for him, such wonderful news that she was so excited to share with her dearest and best friend, which she wasn't telling. He would have to remain curious until then. She would not tell him anything more.

He kept each letter in a drawer close to his bed, reading them each night. He hadn't seen her for ten weeks, his curiosity peaked. That was the last letter she wrote that would reach him in time, Billy not in the least prepared for what he would see despite his most fanciful thoughts.

He couldn't help walking quickly to meet her, stopping so abruptly that he thought he might stumble, first noticing her breasts and her silk blouse, lowering his gawking eyes to the sheen of her beautiful bare legs between her new high-heeled shoes and her short, pleated skirt. The best of Britain had come to the worst of North Carolina, which is not quite how Billy interpreted the vision before him.

You can close your mouth now, Billy. It's not very becoming of a gentleman to stare at a young lady.

Wow, Lucy! You aren't pretty anymore. You're beautiful! I can't believe how much you've changed. What a wonderful surprise.

Thank you, Billy. She kissed his cheek. *I missed you terribly. But this is not my big surprise.*

I missed you too. He smirked, stepping back. *Wow! What has happened to you?*

Do you like the new me?

Yes. I do very much. He gave her a little box, gift-wrapped in red, her favourite colour. *Happy birthday, Lucy.*

The delicate locket was inscribed with her name on the front, his on the back. Inside was his picture.

She wrapped her arms around him, kissing his lips more like a sister than a newly created woman. *I won't ever take it off, Billy. I won't. I swear.* She paused. *I'll tell them it was bought while I was in London, which won't be a lie.*

So, Lucy, what is this big surprise? Tell me. I've been waiting all week. Please tell me.

When I arrived over there my aunt and uncle made a big deal of me coming home from America. I was so embarrassed. They had all the neighbours over for brunch the first week. One of them was a surgeon, Billy. He wanted to see my face and, when he did, he had no expression at all. I thought I would die. Then he smiled and said that I shouldn't worry, that I would soon require the greatest selection of hairpins. He called my parents straightaway from the kitchen for their permission and I went with him the next day to his surgery. Lucy pulled back her newly coiffed hair that she had purposely let drape across her face. *What do you think, Billy? I'm so happy now that I went. I didn't want to at first. I wanted all my summer with you. Don't you think they'll all be so surprised tomorrow to see that Lucy Scarface is now so much prettier than them?*

Thirteen

1970

The guards freed Billy's trembling hands first, grabbing him roughly by the arms. Neither guard caring much about his head that flopped loosely backwards and sideways as they jerked his limp body upright and half dropped him to the floor before releasing his feet.

They left his feet as they were, in his socks, dragging him parallel on his damaged back by a hand and a foot across the concrete floor to the stretcher. He was too insentient to care. He was with Sally and Sam.

They used their feet to align him, kicking his legs together, his arms to his sides before rolling him onto his front to carry him irreverently away as they would a corpse or the spoiled carcass of some dead beast, his arms dangling over the sides, his head twisted to one side.

The doctor preceded them. The devout Warden Prescott went to bow his head in prayer.

*

No one had happened by the River Watch all that afternoon as Lucy and Billy shared her cake, revelling in the quiet privacy, interrupting each other endlessly with their summers' events that they hadn't fit into their daily correspondences.

Not surprisingly, Lucy had more to say, Billy very content to listen while his gawking wide-eyes paid appropriate attention to his newly discovered tops of her legs and the frilly thing under her blouse which he was well aware was not a tee-shirt. He saw his mother often enough at home wearing fine silk and satin. But that was his mom, this was Lucy and he was with her. Wow!

She was animated in her room that night before school, so happy that Billy would walk to school with her in the morning. She laid out her clothes by her dresser, eager to show them off, more eager to show off her brand new face. And Billy was as willingly and wickedly mischievous, impatient to conspire with her.

She had been so terrified that first week in London, not of the windfall surgery that no one except her aunt and uncle had known to hope for, rather of the doctor misleading her, possibly telling her horrible lies.

In fact he had not. Her young face revealed not the slightest trace of the ugly and purple scar once caused by a band of steel strapping recoiling, streaking free from a large crate her father had opened, slicing into her cheek and her neck. She was reborn that day. That's what the attending physician had said, missing death by the width of a finger. Easy for him to say. However this time she truly did feel reborn, too much so to sleep.

She was anxious for her first day at school, impatient for her final year to end, eager to leave Necessity in a year's time to rediscover herself at college. Her life was just beginning, though she was no less eager the next morning to see Billy as she waited for him at the corner of her street where her mother couldn't see her.

They strode through the doors together; Billy in his new slacks, sweater and tie not to be outdone. For the special occasion Sam had advanced him a week's allowance to buy her an elegant and shiny plastic barrette.

Lucy was wearing another set of the latest fashions from London, and would again the next day. Her blouse was of silk, the other girls wore polyester and cotton; her skirt was shorter and pleated, mid-thigh when she was walking or standing, their hems came to their knees whether they were sitting or not; they wore flats, Lucy wore low-heeled leather pumps. The other girls wore their hair in girlish ponytails tied with rubber bands or ordinary kerchiefs from the mall, Lucy wore hers in a current European updo held in place with her best friend's gift.

She wore a rich leather handbag on her shoulder, their wallets and compacts were stuck in their vinyl schoolbags.

And so the school year began.

She had practiced being haughty all summer long, which she found easy to do in London, culminating her performance the previous day with Billy as her captive audience at the River Watch.

Sauntering past Darlene Rigby and Eleanor Carlton that morning, ignoring their gaping mouths and the shared disbelief pouring out from their bulging eyes, was the absolute highpoint of her summer vacation. For Billy, being with her, seeing the girls' brothers doing double takes was more than he wished for, signing with Lucy that *you are the most beautiful girl in the entire school, Lucy. You always were. Best of all, none of them have any idea at all what we're saying.*

But you know what they're saying, don't you, Billy? And you promised me. You did.

That's our best secret ever, and yes, I do. Apparently, Lucy, you are a complete little bitch...and, yeah, I'm still a freak. Nothing new there. Those two want to know where you got everything, and what happened to your face. Rigby and Carlton are checking out your legs and your chest. They think you're...you know, hot.

How hot, Billy...Billy...how hot?

Well...fucking hot!

He was hesitating. He wasn't telling her everything.

What, Billy? Tell me.

It's nothing. They're jerks, Lucy. It's just that, well, this time, I do sort of have to agree with them.

Which was far from a lie, even farther from the entire truth.

She giggled at that. At their homeroom they stopped, Lucy squeezing him hard before they stepped in to spite everyone staring and give them something to talk about.

Her day could not be any better.

As for Billy, his day couldn't be worse. He was worried. He despised Rigby and Carlton for what they had said. He would never let anyone hurt Lucy that way.

*

When Darlene Rigby and Eleanor Carlton did finally succeeded in finding outfits as enticing as Lucy's, in Charleston, near Christmas, their Baptist fathers at once forbade them to wear such indecent apparel. Their mothers agreed, as did the mothers of all the girls. If the Merriweathers thought so little of their daughter's reputation, that they would let her flaunt her body so unabashedly in public, particularly with that Billy Rider boy whose mother was no better, well, they must certainly be the worst kind of parents.

Lucy, on the other hand, much to their ever-mounting envy and its proportionately festering and hurtful spawn, continued buying her British labels, often from upscale stores in London with her aunt's enthusiastic support and keen sense of fashion.

Then came Christmas and 1971, the year she would be eighteen and possibly leave home forever.

Most school days Billy walked Lucy as late as they could manage to the corner near her home, meeting her weekend afternoons at the River Watch where she enjoyed spending her time "studying."

She liked Billy a lot. She had ever since that first day, and she always would. He hadn't once thought to kiss her, or try anything else like groping her breasts or putting his hands under her skirts. Lucy, quite frankly, often wondering why not. So he was more like an older brother. So what?

She didn't think she would mind, not with Billy. She was, after all, drop-dead gorgeous and a little curious about what he would think and how she would feel. It's not as though they would go all the way.

Since her operation all the Grade Eleven boys had asked her out, about three years too late. Even Dwight Rigby and Jake Carlton had tried hitting on Lucy, formerly Lucy Scarface. All of them bluntly refused. She was a contest, each one hopeful of being the first to get into her pants, to wave the victory flag. Her lips curled into sneer, to fuck the stuck-up bitch. She didn't need Billy to tell her that.

She knew most of the other girls were sexually active, often with more than one boy at once, which she couldn't imagine. All those boys knowing so much about their bodies. And they didn't seem to mind, though they might if they knew what the boys were saying about them, the way Billy did, describing the girls' bodies to all their friends and what they had done.

They were using horrible words, Lucy quite certain that Billy was not telling her everything. And the girls were no better. Every day they talked about the boys they'd been with in the boys' cars or their basements, comparing their bodies and prowess, or the lack thereof, ridiculing those while hoping to soon try out the ones that either came highly praised or drove the best cars.

How she wished she could read lips like Billy, like being invisible in someone else's bedroom...or basement.

Almost every day they would eat their lunches on the front yard of the school and Billy would tell her what the others were saying.

Anyway, if she did have sex with anyone, Billy would be her first and no one else would ever know.

Fourteen

1971

Billy Rider was unresponsive to the doctor's efforts, yet breathing well enough with a temperature not unexpectedly high considering the current demand on his body to heal. He couldn't imagine and didn't care about the whirlwind of demons and dreads swirling behind Billy Rider's twitching eyes.

He layered Billy's shoulders and back with salve, leaving the ripped skin exposed, leaving him handcuffed to the bed to prevent him from turning. He posted a guard and went home to become what he wasn't, the MD on his licence plate misleading his neighbours and friends.

Unlike the warden, his office in Battle View was a stigma, a hideous blot he might conceal though never erase, a constant reminder of failure that led to his divorce and his drinking, in no way a symbol attesting to the rank and authority he wanted others to believe.

Billy Rider understood why he should be in prison, and who by quirk of fate had put him there. He also understood that he justifiably refused to testify in his own defence to spare his mother and father the shame of the crime he did commit with no ill intent.

He was swayed in a moment of weakness, with only himself to blame. He believed deeply that, had he gone earlier to the Watch that night, Lucy would be alive and he would be with her. That neglect alone was sufficiently good

reason to endure a life sentence and torture.
*

Rigby Automobile was Necessity's one-stop shopping plaza for all your motoring needs. Mr. Rigby owned three car dealerships, one motorcycle dealership, four garages and one used car lot all in a row. The plaza was open five nights a week and Saturdays until noon.

His wife stayed home managing the household, caring for their children and doing light chores not worth paying outsiders for. His dream was to one day sell European luxury models and bring his son into the business; her dream was for Darlene to marry and raise a family as beautiful and enviable as her own.

Rigby had the best prices in town, the best value and after-sales service in town. In fact he had the only prices in town. If you didn't buy his cars, you took the bus or shopped in another city.

That was his son's future after university, and his daughter's after high school, whom he believed mustn't wait too long to find a suitable man and start her family. After all, what was good for her mother was a perfectly reasonable expectation of her.

Dwight and Darlene were twins with distinct features and traits that set them apart. They were seventeen. Her hair was a deep red, the colour of glimmering embers, his was blond. He was 5'9", she was shorter by five inches. He was handsome; she was attractive, emulating her mother when she really wanted to be and act and dress like Sally Cutter.

What they had most in common was the flawlessness they shared in their parents' eyes. They could do nothing wrong. They were Rigbys, the town's elite, their social circle selective and small.

He was the best in any sport at school, a golden-haired jock, a big man with the prettiest girls and most willing girls who vied to be his steady and be seen at school in his Buick convertible. After all, it was only sex. No big deal.

Absolutely everyone was doing it and being with Dwight Rigby, even for a week or two, meant everything.

Darlene Rigby was a tease, and Necessity High's best kept secret along with Eleanor Carlton. She was good at music, often entertaining her parents' guests who would endure the recitals and applaud her politely.

Dwight, however, was the brighter of the two with an enviable future ahead of him.

Father and son had agreed that spending his college years in a frat house would encourage detrimental behavior. Or at the very least inhibit his academic success, Dwight concurring with his father that he and Jackson Carlton should make use of the family beach house in Wilmington throughout the coming years where they could study with each other without interruption. This, of course, with the strictest prohibition against carousing.

Mr. Carlton gave his blessing as well and would naturally meet Rigby's upkeep expenses dollar for dollar. They were lifelong friends and associates, wishing for their sons, and one day their grandsons, to maintain that cherished bond.

Darlene, on the other hand, was a girl, a pretty girl who would one day attract a wonderful man. She would consent at the proper time, and with her father's approbation, to become his wife, to become a mother and, not long after, a grandmother.

She couldn't wait, often asking her mother what she should expect…"You know, mother, being with a man?"

Her mother would explain in different ways. not wanting to offend or scare her naïve young daughter, that women were intended by God's greater plan to become mothers and that any decent man who would truly love her would not thereafter satiate his selfish carnal hunger at her expense when not for the sake of thereby bringing into the world another beautiful Rigby child.

In fact, Darlene hated her life. She hated her father, and

she hated her mother even more. She hated being dragged to church each Sunday morning, smiling at the preacher, shaking his always moist hands.

They were such hypocrites. As though her father wasn't fucking his secretary those nights he worked an hour later than closing time. She'd seen the side glances more than once, the nods, the cute little smiles. She wasn't stupid; her father was. And her stupid mother said nothing.

She hated Lucy Merriweather the most, and her idiot friend who was always with her. She thought herself so superior with her stupid accent, her slutty British clothes and her repaired face. She was a complete bitch. She was because Eleanor thought exactly the same.

*

Mr. Carlton was the president and CFO of Carlton Bank, founded by his grandfather, the seat of Necessity's old money and much of what was new.

Very much like Mrs. Rigby, Mrs. Carlton concerned herself primarily with spending her husband's money while being a dutiful wife and a good mother, attending to their home and planning events with which to fill their calendar.

Their first child was Jackson, who somehow had managed to ruin her body at the time of his reluctant birth to the extent that Eleanor was adopted some years later when they determined that Jackson should have a playmate more in keeping with their social values and elevated station. They were seventeen and best friends with Darlene and Dwight.

Jackson's sole ambition was to please his father and to one day take over the bank, believing he had very little need to further his education since he was apprenticing each summer and considered himself already very capable. Which is not what his father believed.

He would first earn his stripes. He would become his own man, a worthy component of the family's name and of the bank, not merely depend on his name or their resources for his future.

He was an average student, with average looks and average success with average girls, envious of Dwight who always attracted the most attractive, which Jake attributed to his friend's Buick convertible.

He followed Dwight wherever he went and did whatever Dwight thought was best.

The two of them together would often at night peer through each sister's window as the girls prepared for their sleep. That's when Dwight got the brilliant idea of inviting the girls to the beach house for the coming summers and long weekends once he and Jake moved to the coast for their studies.

Why not? Making good use of the girls made sense on so many levels, not the least of which was keeping any and all college girls from getting too attached.

He was certain he wouldn't have much trouble convincing Eleanor into his bed. And he could see the way Jake drooled over Darlene each time he saw her, pretty certain the girls were virgins. Not that virginity mattered. All the girls in his class were regularly putting out, getting laid, wanting to be the most popular, many of them achieving their goal at least once in the back of a Buick.

Except Lucy Merriweather who pranced around like she was so special. What he wouldn't give to get into her one time?

Jake agreed and they shook hands. He was certain Eleanor would come across with not too much effort, and he believed he had a good chance with Darlene. They should do it, without telling the girls, as though nothing was planned. Let them believe whatever would make them ready and willing.

He agreed with Dwight about Lucy, since being shot down in flames before he'd even opened his mouth. One time, he mused. Just once and "I would tell the entire fucking school."

*

Eleanor Carlton was equally in awe of her friend who made the best decisions and also drove a Buick. She liked what Darlene liked and hated what the Rigby girl hated, which meant she hated her mother and thought very little of her father.

They were the prettiest girls at school, dressing like old maids when Lucy Merriweather got all the boys' attention by dressing like such a slut. Something they could only do on weekends at the mall in their new stylish outfits before changing back into jeans and sweaters in the public toilet stalls before driving home.

They practically never went to the River Watch to spend time alone when the mothers were at home. Billy Rider was too creepy and was always there with *her*. Besides, there was nowhere to lay except in the grass that wasn't secluded at all and would ruin their clothes. The one place they could think of nearby to possibly be alone and unseen was in the grove and, even then, some people walked their dogs during the day and the place was too dark and scary at night.

They would drive instead to the end of the long and unused cul-de-sac behind Necessity High with blankets and beers their fathers would never miss. Despite their secret and evolving feelings, they were increasingly eager for their senior year. They had loved each other for some time, Darlene increasingly of the opinion that they were missing out, that they could have that much more fun if they included a few boys.

Eleanor agreed, the two girls heading into their final year with a plan. They would wisely restrict themselves to the younger boys in Grade Ten, depriving their final-year peers with good reason.

The elite Grade Elevens would never think to speak with kids they considered inferior. Hence the brothers would remain unaware, Darlene and Eleanor threatening each new and ever-hungry adherent with immediate cessation of privileges if word ever got out. Which never happened for obvious reasons of self-interest, the girls frequently arriving home scarcely in time for dinner as ever before with their skirts and their blouses no worse for wear.

One day early in April, driving past Billy and Lucy late in the day on their way home from school, Darlene burst into irrepressible giggles and laughter.

"What?"

"What if we did, Eleanor? I mean really, what if we let that freak fuck us?"

"Don't be ridiculous. I'd rather let my dog fuck me."

"I think we should. I have the perfect way and the ideal time. It'll be so much fun. And then we'll tell her absolutely everything."

"No way, Darlene. I mean, look at the guy. Do you think he even has a cock?"

"Let's find out. How bad can it be?"

"You're making me ill."

"Then you can sit in the car and watch me. And after that he can watch us. We haven't done that yet, and I want to. I want a guy see us playing. I want to see what happens to him. And so do you. I know you'll change your mind, Eleanor. You always do."

Eleanor wasn't certain. The other guys were different. She loved teasing them, she loved them seeing her and touching her. She guessed that getting the idiot to fuck her might be okay, if she didn't have to see him or touch it. Anyway, Darlene was right. She always gave in, but letting him see her with Darlene, giving the creep something to jack off with…She wasn't sure at all about that.

"Okay, Darlene. We'll let him fuck us, one time. That's the deal and he is not touching our mouths. I swear, Darlene, if you do anything with yours I will never kiss you again. Personally, I think I'll barf."

Darlene always got her way, the two girls agreeing with wide smirks that even if he did kiss them he certainly wouldn't tell.

Fifteen

1971

Late in the day Monday Billy Rider stirred, gradually aware of the searing stinging across his back. He clenched his fists, gritting his teeth, pushing his face into the hard mattress to muffle his groans.

How could he possibly survive five more beatings? He couldn't. He would rather be dead, very certain he would be if not for John's intervention. Yet, as horrifying as the whipping was, the skin of his back shredded into thin strips, he would gratefully endure the torture each week if what happened to Lucy could be undone.

He had disappointed her in the worst possible way. His friend. He had made her a silent promise to himself and he had let her down.

With all the times he had known what they were saying and thinking, why hadn't he even once caught the slightest hint of what Rigby and Carlton were planning? He couldn't fathom, and never would, how sick their minds were to overpower, rape and kill such a little and defenseless girl. Their own classmate.

Or their malicious sisters? The girls he understood. They used their bodies shamelessly to make fun of him, which was fine. He didn't mind. He was getting laid. Why would he have cared? He knew exactly what they were planning the moment they turned onto the dirt road. He knew absolutely everything about the tenth graders. Everything.

Including that Darlene and Eleanor were easy and eager to fuck. Besides, feigning idiocy is so easy when everyone believes you are an idiot.

Billy Rider's ten-week living nightmare had gone quickly. How could it be that Lucy was dead, that he had spoken with her, laughed with her just hours before? Now he was condemned to Battle View Prison so few weeks later for the next ninety-five years of his life.

How would he survive? How would his life be then if he did survive? He didn't care. Or would he find them and kill them as soon as he was released? He didn't think so, not at 114 years of age. He was a bit late for that, and would suffer the guilt, knowing full well that he would not have hesitated to kill either of them had he suspected. Something he would beg Lucy to believe with each breath until he could no longer breathe and be with her once again.

But what would she think of him now, squirming and wincing with pain? What kind of man would do that, act weak? John wouldn't. John would be strong.

He tugged at the steel numbing his hands, calling out for the doctor. He wanted to go to his cell. He was hungry and he wanted to eat something.

The doctor shrugged. He had no opinion. However Billy would eat before leaving. Food was forbidden in the blocks and Billy would collapse in his weakened state before making his way to the mess hall. A few hours would make no difference.

After Billy's meal, after applying more salve to his patient's field of scars, this time applying bandages, the doctor summoned a guard and returned to his work as Billy was escorted out.

The day was over, all cons accounted for before supper; heads turning one by one until all eyes were focused on Billy climbing unassisted past the first and second tiers, the cons on their bunks coming out to see what the fuss was about.

Anderson clapped once, the sharp report resounding across the quiet void, then twice, a third and fourth time more quickly, giving rise to a thunderous applause.

They all thought he was dead. They believed he was done for, if not crippled for life. To a man they supposed that at best the kid would spend a week with the doc before being able to stand, let alone making his way straight and tall up three seemingly endless flights of stairs.

If they didn't know, Billy did. John did that for him. And Billy summoned all the strength he could to not let John down.

Reaching the third tier, the cacophony subsiding, the grim faces and cold eyes of hardened and heartless criminals greeted him as they watched him pass by, each man inwardly flinching at the extent of the carnage seeping through the white bandages in red blotches across the width of Rider's back.

At 312 Anderson stepped aside. His supper could wait. He wanted to know before the kid passed out or dropped dead. He needed to know, to be certain. And he wasn't ready for any bullshit.

Billy eased onto his bunk.

"A day and a half. That's impressive, kid. Got to say. Seems like there's some hope for you after all."

Billy nodded, thinking he was smiling. He wasn't. He reached for his pad. His hands were trembling, yet he felt compelled to write. He had to tell John.

Thank you, John.

Anderson hunched his shoulders in a cavalier shrug. "Now, I'm thinking, tell me if I'm wrong here, that you have understood every word I've said over the past month. And everyone else in here for that matter. Am I about right with that? You read lips, kid?"

Billy nodded, scribbling. *Of course I do, and I sign. You should learn. I think you're probably smart enough.*

Anderson's head bobbed like a dashboard puppet in

sync with a metronome, a ridge of bright teeth beaming behind a dark tan. He was right. Damn straight he was right. "Perhaps I will, kid. In the meantime you make damn sure to keep that lip thing to yourself. Don't do anything stupid. Those guys out there, they like their privacy. So be smart about what you do. Understand that. It could be a lifesaver…or very much the sad inverse. You got that? You understand?"

Billy signed that he did, that and more, leaving Anderson to figure things out.

He believed that soon he and John would come to terms, if they hadn't already. Which wasn't a critical issue at the moment. Right then he wanted to sleep. He wanted to escape once more into his dreams of Lucy. He needed to spend time with her, desperately hoping she would somehow sense that he would forever miss her.

His dreams were the only way for him to tell her how he felt, that he loved her and that he should never have gone to the dance and left her alone.

*

Saturday May 22nd had arrived, heralding the last week of school and summer's freedom.

The Graduation Dance had been months in the planning, Darlene and Eleanor serving on the committee. Those with passing grades were supplied with tickets, most with their prom dates of choice set up, the rest resorting to second best pickings with desperate pleas and promises of having their fathers' cars to make-out in. No one daring for an instant to approach Lucy Merriweather who was every boy's first choice in his wet dreams.

Darlene and Eleanor had gone shopping with their mothers for the new prom gowns and sandals they would wear, as far as the cul-de-sac where they would change into their mini-dresses, their new lingerie and open-toed stilettos. Reversing the process after the dance in the girls' locker room when everyone else had gone and no one would be the wiser.

Everything was set. Even Mrs. Cutter convinced her son Billy to act as coat monitor and verify tickets at the door, especially since Lucy Merriweather wasn't going.
*

I wish you were going, Billy told her.

My mother is so angry that I won't go unless you take me, Billy. She's embarrassed because her daughter is the one girl in school who doesn't have a date. That's her fault, not mine. She doesn't understand. She really believes you're a bad influence, that you made friends with me when other boys wouldn't because of my scar, because you thought I was vulnerable and easy. She thinks one day we'll do something bad together and my life will be ruined. She really needs to get a life and stop poking her nose into mine.

Billy agreed. Her mother was a little bigoted, not at all like his mother.

We should, he replied.

We should what?

We should take off all our clothes and ruin your life.

She smacked his shoulder, not that she hadn't been thinking increasingly about him that way, and she was on the pill since leaving for London. Not that her mother didn't trust her, though what she really didn't like, more than her mother's blind attitude, was Darlene and Eleanor beginning to treat Billy almost as a human. She didn't trust them at all.

You can't be friends with a girl once you have sex with her, Billy. Remember what all the kids at school are saying about each other. I would die if someone talked like that about me.

You're forgetting that I can't speak. We should be okay.

She hit him again. *Anyway, I'll wait for you at the Watch tonight. My parents are going to a party. They'll be home late. Then you can tell me all about it.*

It's all my mother's fault. She's even giving me dance

lessons.

Your mother's the best. Lucy noted the time on her watch. Four o'clock. *I should go, Billy. You have to get ready and my mother wants me home early for dinner. I can't believe she thinks I'm here all the time by myself. And my father isn't any better.* She made a face. *Daddy's little girl. Get real.* She leaned over, clutching the sides of his head, kissing his mouth hard. *What would daddy think of that?*

Billy didn't care.

*

Sally Cutter stained her son's cheek with an imprint of her lips, which he promptly removed. His father gave him twenty dollars in case he wanted to take a girl for an after-dance soda or a hamburger, which is exactly what Billy had in mind. He also planned to kiss her again. Wow!

He left home as the sun began sinking into the horizon. Darlene was the evening's hostess and she wanted him at school thirty minutes early, when she would explain what was required of him. Not aware that she had previously written her instructions for the idiot.

When he arrived Eleanor was with her, greeting him with unusually warm smiles.

They were wearing their hair the way Lucy did, their dresses displaying almost all of their legs, the way Lucy wore hers, which recently, he believed, she often made shorter for him when no one else was around to see. He had to admit the girls were hot, though he did think that dancing in their shoes would prove impossible.

As students began filing in, served their first glasses of punch, Darlene went in search of Jake eager to open the evening with the first dance. Eleanor went to find Dwight who, like Jake, had begun the evening a while earlier with a full bottle of bourbon stashed in the trunk of his car.

They understood nothing would happen that night, Jake agreeing with Dwight that the girls would give them a better first experience together at the beach house. Besides, neither boy, despite often watching each sister undress through her window, wanted to see his sister getting laid.

There were plenty of others to take for a ride in the meantime.

As part of the planning committee the girls were also members of the clean-up crew. They would need time after the dance to restore some semblance of order to the gymnasium before recreating themselves as decent and good daughters for their parents.

The dance went as planned and expected, Darlene and Eleanor taking turns to bring Billy a glass of punch until, not far from 10:30, once Dwight and Jake had sneaked out, they offered to drive him home. He thought that was okay. Why not? He had nothing more to do, Darlene telling him with a brief note that first they would make one quick stop which the girls believed he would enjoy.

He smiled and agreed, following them to the car and sliding into the back.

*

The cul-de-sac was deserted, never used, a dark strip between tall grass under a starry sky as the car proceeded covertly without its lights to the very end.

The night air was stagnant and warm, ideal for strolling in a park, holding hands, or watching a movie at a drive-in, or dreamily swinging on a home-made pendulum hanging from the branch of a huge oak tree…or not.

Darlene cut the engine, silence flooding in; the night air seemingly darker and heavier.

The three sat for a moment without saying a word. Darlene was elated and eager; Eleanor wasn't. Her stomach was agitated and churning. She had never done this before, sharing her physical attraction towards Darlene with a boy, especially him when any of a dozen or more others would think they had died and gone to heaven. Anyway it's what Darlene wanted, the serene scene abruptly igniting into a pastoral stage when Darlene's foot tripped the high-beam toggle.

"This will be so much fun. I promise. Our brothers would shit if they had any idea what we're doing with him."

"Weird, that he can't tell what we're saying. It's creepy, Darlene."

"He will soon enough He can't be that stupid."

"Think he'll tell his little bitch girlfriend?"

"Think I care?" Darlene drank from the bottle of vodka they'd opened earlier while changing their clothes and filling small plastic vials that would help set the mood with each sip of punch. "Give him some more. He should already be a little high."

Billy reached between them for the bottle, smiling. He took one sip, then another before Darlene swung open her door and slid out.

"Get out, Billy." She waved at him from between the lights.

He followed behind Eleanor as Darlene stood the bottle on the hood, reaching for a few notes she'd trapped under the wipers.

"We're really nice girls," Billy, she said. That's what one note read.

Eleanor added, wanting to choke, that "we hate that we treated you so badly. We are really very sorry."

He didn't mind, with no way to tell them, feeling more than a little light-headed.

"But saying we're sorry doesn't mean anything. So we thought of this way to show you."

Billy dropped that note to the ground, taking the bottle from the hood.

Losing herself for a moment in the darkness, going to the trunk for their thick blankets, Eleanor hoped he would empty the entire bottle and drop dead. Returning she said, "Billy, you stand here between the lights," signalling what she meant. "We don't want you to miss a thing."

Billy obeyed, curious

They didn't have much time. The idea was to teach that bitch Lucy a lesson, not to give her creepy boyfriend the best ride of his life.

Darlene unstrapped her stilettos, padding to behind her friend. She unzipped Eleanor's dress, pushing it to the blankets. Eleanor in turn did the same for Darlene who immediately tore away her camisole and pushed her panties past her knees and her ankles as deliberately as she could, not for a moment taking her eyes off spell-bound Billy.

She was naked and twirling. The deep red of her pubic and not so private hair against a backdrop of white skin, made whiter by the heated glare of the lights, where her open legs were posed wide apart, was a compelling sight, Billy wishing as she stood there that he was staring at Lucy.

She went to him, removing his tie, tossing it to the ground as Eleanor came in closer to ease away her bra shoulder by shoulder, dropping it at his feet, cupping her breasts before cupping Darlene's and kissing her, letting Darlene push her panties past one raised foot, then the other.

Billy was lost, his mind in a daze. His shirt was gone, Darlene working at his belt while Eleanor sank to her knees to remove his shoes and his socks.

"We always do this, Billy, the two of us," Darlene said, not caring that he couldn't hear, fairly certain that he didn't care either. "So much safer than fucking a boy and so much more fun."

She pushed his slacks to his ankles in a single motion, letting Billy kick them away, which he did in a hurry. He was getting the hang of things.

Eleanor tugged once at his shorts, gasping at what sprang out from under the band.

"Holy shit, Darlene. I mean, holy good shit. If he fucks us with that he'll kill us."

Darlene didn't hesitate. She gripped Billy with both

hands, gaping at Eleanor with wild-eyed anticipation. "If we had known about this thing we would have fucked him already." She squeezed him hard, releasing him, grabbing the bottle, swallowing once, handing it back to Billy who stood waiting for something, anything.

"You watch us, Billy."

"Yes, you watch. This is for you. This is our way of saying we're sorry." She wanted to gag.

For the next several minutes the two girls went into a world of their own, each tender touch unrehearsed. Their bodies had become an integral part of their friendship since the first curious weeks of high school, a requisite and private prelude and sequel to the boys of Grade Ten who were never a sufficient release. This evening was different, neither girl forgetting for a moment why they were there, about to share their bodies with the village idiot for no better reason than another girl's wardrobe and pure spite.

When they were finished Darlene lay back on the blankets, propped onto her elbows. Eleanor reached out for Billy's hand, pulling him down, guiding him between her girlfriend's legs.

"Do you know what to do with me, Billy?" Darlene asked. "Have you ever done this before with that little bitch?"

Eleanor tapped his shoulder. He wasn't listening. She took his hand again, pressing his fingers into Darlene's soft crimson hair, feeling violated. She loathed touching him more than she hated seeing him touch Darlene. "He needs your help, Darlene. I told you, I am not touching it."

Darlene raised her knees, grabbing his buttocks, bringing him forwards, thrusting slightly until she was aligned. She was breathing hard on purpose, at first. She wanted to make him crazier than he was. Her heart was racing with excitement at seeing the three of them naked in the car's high beams.

Eleanor lay close beside them, the way Darlene always

wanted her to, supporting her head in one hand, fondling her breasts with the other. The freak was losing his mind.

His face was inches from Darlene's. "Push the thing into me, Billy. Push hard." Yet she couldn't wait all night. She took him in her hand, her hurtfulness instantly turning to urgent obsession.

Billy thought his head would explode. She was wet and warm, her breath sweet, not at all what he had ever thought to expect whenever he went to bed thinking of Lucy, her body smelling of sweat and perfume.

He kissed her mouth, the sting from her slap exciting him.

He was grinding, pushing hard, the way she was saying. He wanted to press his hands onto her breasts, not certain how, raising his body to try. What was happening? Darlene's face was twisting in agony, yet she was yelling at him not to stop. He squeezed one gently at first, then the other, her flesh soft to his touch. Then he groped harder. He didn't care if he hurt her. She wanted him to. Her mouth opened wide, her body jolting and bucking, sinking into the ground, telling Billy to stop, Eleanor intervening to push him away.

"Holy shit, Eleanor! I mean, holy shit. You won't believe this. I swear, if not for the stupid dance we'd stay here all night fucking him."

She wiggled backwards for space.

Billy was kneeling. He was fixated by the matted hair, by her parted lips that were glistening and inviting, by the sweat drizzling from her belly. He was amazed by what he had done, at what he was seeing. His breathing was erratic, his chest heaving, not at all embarrassed that they were gawking at his erection.

Eleanor had no intention of touching his mouth with hers, the thought made her ill. She could see what he had waiting for her, what he had done to Darlene, with no desire to touch that either. That was not part of the deal.

Yet she was quickly on her knees in front of him, squirming, resting on her arms and rocking to and fro. She wanted to get it over with, thinking he would get the idea. He didn't, Darlene rushing in to help her, crawling between her calves, wildly bumping and grinding herself into the back of her girlfriend's thighs, digging her fingers into the smooth flesh of Eleanor's buttocks to show Billy the way.

As excited as Billy, Darlene hobbled to one side; Billy moved in without thinking, his mind too muddled with sensations, emotions, vodka and punch.

He went into her without any resistance, grabbing her the way Darlene had, his breathing out of control, his body dripping with sweat from his work, the night air and the lights. He hadn't once in his life dreamed he would see a girl this way, particularly with him pushing his way inside her. Her body, he thought, was perfect, her breasts much easier to fondle than Darlene's.

The scene was surreal. Darlene was kneeling beside them, naked, her knees far apart, lifting and lowering her body, keeping perfect and hectic time with their mounting and zealous rhythm.

Billy was focused on her, then on Eleanor. Then on Darlene, then on what was at hand, in his hands, massaging and squeezing. Eleanor's lips were glistening; the delicate folds pushed in and pulled out, each thrust smoother and deeper. Her ass was flawless and white, a tiny splash of pink on her right cheek doing nothing to distract him, his curious fingers too anxious to probe and explore.

Eleanor was doing nothing to heighten the moment. She was jerking involuntarily with each thrust, pushed and pulled, keeping her promise, her forehead close to the ground.

She was counting each one, despising him for seeing her that way. Then she began losing count, his thrusts bolder and deeper, his hold on her hips and her ass tighter. She raised her head, glancing under her body at his hands clutching her breasts, their skin glaring under the bright lights. She heard herself grunting, saw herself starting to jam each of his thrusts, their bodies colliding.

She was gasping under the full force, reaching for Darlene's hand, beginning to believe he wouldn't stop until morning, beginning to accept that she might be having a very good time.

The only sounds Billy could hear came from inside his head, not Eleanor's abrupt screech. His busy fingers were sensing something recently discovered, something learned from inside Darlene, her coming eruption. He secured her tightly in place, pulling her backward, her knees just then jerking from the blanket, his body slamming harder against hers, raising her.

Eleanor's hands flailed in the air. Her balance was gone. Her entire body was in his control. She was shrieking and gasping. She was convulsing, her face contorting in shock. Billy was grasping her breasts, squeezing hard, her mouth exploding in a loud wail as the two bodies collapsed.

Bent forward they were motionless for a moment as Eleanor regained her senses, squirming away, dragging herself to her feet.

She was done. Her body was soaked.

Darlene stood with her, reaching for the vodka, sipping a little, saving some for her friend before passing the rest to Billy who hadn't yet thought to dress, too preoccupied with the attributes of two naked girls glistening with sweat in the middle of a field.

"I cannot believe I let that creep fuck me or that I'm standing here naked and smelling like shit. God! His hands were all over my ass and my tits. Shit, Darlene, I can barely stand. Look at me." She cupped a hand between her legs, groaning. "How's yours?"

"You put it in the air for him. At least he didn't kiss you. Want to talk about shit?"

"He's got a dick like a horse."

"More like a donkey. Either way, don't complain. He gave you a lot better ride than me."

"I'm not complaining." Eleanor glanced at her breasts, pressing her palms against them. "Shit, I think he was trying to milk me."

Darlene checked the time on her wrist. "We have time, Eleanor. Once more."

"The freak's staring. Let's get out of here before he rapes us."

Darlene smirked. "We should stay, and screw the dance. Tell them we got sick. We won't get another chance, not with the donkey. Come on, Eleanor. And your pussy's never been so...like mine. He may be stupid, but he did give us the best fuck ever. So let's do it again. We really have to, Eleanor."

"No! That was not part of the deal."

"You sure? I mean, shit, look at it."

"No, Darlene. We are going back. That was the deal. He's seen us naked, he's seen us make-out and got his big dick wet by wrecking the school's two best pussies. I think he's done alright. Don't you?"

They turned to face him, Darlene a little annoyed at leaving too soon. He hadn't moved, and he hadn't weakened at all. If Eleanor didn't want more, he did standing there ready.

She sauntered to the trunk, determined that Billy's show wasn't over.

She returned with a bottle of water, a facecloth and a towel to wash the class clown away. Billy stood gawking in amazement, watching them clean each part of their bodies as though in slow motion, draining the water across their bellies and between their legs. The effect was overwhelming.

He watched them kiss and slide into their panties, tugging their dresses to their hips, fondling each other once more as though he had gone before helping each other with

146

the zippers.

Darlene tossed her camisole onto the backseat; she couldn't be bothered. Eleanor tossed her bra with it; her breasts were beginning to bruise.

"That was really fun, Billy. But we don't think you should tell Lucy."

"We can do that for you."

"And we will. We know once we tell her all that you did…"

"And how well you did it…"

"Yeah, she'll want to fuck you herself."

"We really do want to stay, but we can't."

"So you can put your big thing away now, Billy, while I turn the car around." She made a shooing gesture. "And get off the blanket."

The two girls slipped into their shoes and climbed into the car. Darlene did a four-point turn, waving, leaving Billy in the dark to gather his clothes and finish the vodka.

He didn't hear their laughter, though he suspected as much. Not that he cared. He knew what they thought and most of what they had said. He could fill in the blanks. So what? He finally got laid, and was apparently better than all the other guys. Not bad for a donkey.

That's what really mattered.

He scanned the ground. The bottle of water was empty. His clothes were a shambles and the sweat on his body was beginning to cool. He stank. He brought a moist hand to his nose. The girls' scent was pungent, making him wonder whether Lucy would smell that way too, or whether she would know what he had done and hate him forever.

Sixteen

The Same Night

Anderson stood outside 312, leaning against the railing. He was staring in, mystified while the hemispheres of his brain did battle.

The kid had proven he had guts, enough anyway to stand tall and make a statement. A good beginning. Cons respected that. He watched Billy lying face down on his bunk, sleeping, teetering at the edge of unconsciousness, his body once in a while twitching.

So Rider *was* deaf and mute, and far from dumb. The kid was able to converse in two silent idioms, which pretty much made Anderson feel dumb. He'd never travelled to any country where he couldn't make himself understood, satisfied with the several dozen where he could, never wanting to lose that control or feel that helpless. Now in a very real sense he did.

The kid would know everything that he and everyone else was saying, excepting the Latinos. Maybe. He didn't know. There was a lot about Rider that didn't make sense, in spite of which that peculiarity could get him killed. Or, for that matter, make Anderson more aware of what was going on in the yard and the block. He had to admit, reading the future in prison had certain practical benefits and longevity was at the top of the list.

He couldn't imagine what was in the kid's head, or what Rider had overheard throughout the past month. Perhaps he would learn to sign. He had the time, and how hard could it be? He snorted. The kid did have something in common with everyone in Battle View after all, everyone except Anderson.

He was innocent. Anderson believed that. He believed the note and he believed what he had seen in Rider's eyes. The kid was more fearful of Anderson not believing him than he was of the Cat.

Nothing about him made sense. If he didn't kill the girl why was he paying for it with the worst shit-kicking possible? No one takes a hit like that without a good reason. So, yeah, Anderson would learn. What better way to find out what really happened, or what would?
*

Lucy Merriweather didn't think one way or the other about Billy being at the dance. She was happy for him, yet his mother should have known better than to put him in that situation. She had to at least suspect how cruelly her son was treated at school, even though Billy would never think to hurt her by telling her.

She waited until her parents had gone out before taking her shower and doing her make-up, her body tingling and titillated by caressing hands and probing touches she imagined were his.

Almost hating to spoil her reverie she dressed in front of the mirror into her finest lingerie that she hadn't yet worn, nor had Billy ever seen her skirt and her blouse imported from London. She wondered whether she would be nervous. She believed she would be, in a nice way, certain he would be pleased with her body and not make her feel silly.

She had made up her mind. Her parents wouldn't be home until very late and, at the very worst, they would never think to come into her bedroom and Billy could always leave through the window. Which she thought would be very romantic.

Then she undressed, first her blouse and her skirt,

intently, the way she had practiced and performed alone the last several nights. Then her camisole and panties lay on her chair and she stood staring into the mirror. She was proud of what she was seeing, certain she was doing the right thing.

She wouldn't wear stockings because her skirt was too short. In any event her aunt the summer before had taught her that well-dressed ladies never wear stockings or pantyhose with opened-toed sandals. Instead she would wear silk tap pants and a camisole because her blouse was too sheer and her bra would show through, making her appear cheap.

That's not the way she wanted Billy to see her.

She studied herself closely. She was pleased with her work and he would be too, reaching out for his hand, guiding him to her bed once more before dressing and leaving.

Billy was taking her for a soda and something to eat to begin their last summer together for a very long time, possibly forever. She was moving to Boston, leaving her parents, Necessity, and her best friend behind.

She would be gone four years, more convinced each day that she would never return. She knew she would soon make new friends with others her age, kids less vicious than those in Nowhere, North Carolina and very possibly become somebody's lover. That day would have to happen sooner or later.

But that night she was dressing as a sophisticated young woman for Billy. Her mind was made up. Mr. Billy Rider would be her first, which she believed was a much better idea than a soda.
*

Dwight Rigby and Jake Carlton were in front of her house. They had no interest in the dance. Their entire focus was on Lucy Merriweather.

They knew Rider was at the school, which didn't make

any sense at all. Not even the ugliest girl would want to be seen dancing with the ghoul, their sisters saying simply that they wanted to get back at Lucy for being such a stuck-up bitch. She was the only girl not going to the dance, and *he* was.

They didn't get the connection.

Everyone at school knew that if Lucy wasn't at home studying, she would be at the Watch with her face buried in a book or wasting her time with Billy Rider.

Rigby and Carlton had already gone there and waited a good while before driving the most direct route to her home where they parked and had another swallow or two of bourbon while they waited, their senses aroused by the unexpected sight of Lucy's parents driving away.

An unexpected bonus. And, better yet, the night sky had darkened.

Rigby was first from the car reacting on impulse; Carlton followed, one twisted mind reading the other.

The bungalow was a cookie cutter home, distinguished mostly by the address and Mrs. Merriweather's garden. Not much else. The open spaces between neighbours was planted with trees and shrubs acting as a privacy wall.

Diffused lighting came from the living room window, the rest of the house was dark, Rigby and Carlton hoping and praying that Lucy was inside. The decision was a no-brainer, Rigby and Carlton scanning the street and the unlit porches as they made their way unhurried to the backyard.

The room at the closest corner was Lucy's. The light was on, though the room was empty, Carlton jabbing Rigby when the shadows and diffused lighting through the bathroom's glazed window went suddenly black.

Lucy padded into her room, neither smiling nor sad, her brow furrowed in thought. Her head was wrapped in a turban, her body wrapped in a towel; neither Rigby nor Carlton believing their incredible good fortune, confident the evening would end well.

They stood breathless as she laid out her clothes on the bed, inspecting each piece. She sat at her vanity to blow-dry her hair, working the tresses into a braid, enhancing her eyes, her lips and painting her nails, oblivious to the sick minds a foot from her window, Carlton shaking Rigby's shoulders like an excited child as her towel fell away and she stood reaching for lotion.

They stared wide-eyed as she caressed her body with cream from her shoulders to her toes, bending and stretching this way and that, stopping to set down the bottle, planting one foot on her chair and painting her toes, pleased, raising the other.

She stood poised for a moment in front of her mirror, swaying her hips in small circles, pausing, her hands cupping her breasts, and pausing, pirouetting with her hands in the air. She stepped in closer to the mirror, facing away, craning her neck over her shoulder to see how she looked from behind, running a hand over her smooth curves and squeezing.

She turned into the glass, cupping her breasts once again, her brow furrowing.

She paused, gazing at her reflection, pressing her fingers into the velvety strip of light-coloured hair, softly at first, smiling at herself, smiling at him. She pressed harder, letting her mind wander, telling Billy how she loved him, how she loved him arousing her body.

Her evening would be the most wonderful of her life.

Rigby and Carlton were determined and dumbstruck. Lucy was dressing in front of the mirror, intently, into lingerie their sisters would envy.

They wanted the show to go on forever, thinking her skirt and her blouse would end their time at the window. It didn't. The show began anew as Lucy unbuttoned her blouse, laying it across her chair. She unzipped her skirt, gazing into her eyes in the mirror, letting it fall to her feet, bending to place it with her blouse. She stood staring at herself, nodding, pulling at her silk top, hesitating at her breasts, pulling it over her head, right away pushing her panties to the floor and stepping away, reaching for both, studying her body closely and smiling, reaching out as though taking a hand, walking to her bed where she sat for a while to ponder before dressing again as enticingly as she could.

Shit. The evening had begun too well to end so abruptly. That couldn't happen. They'd put too much effort into her.

They hurried with a purpose to the car, stirring their minds and bodies into a frenzy. Things had to go right. They waited and watched. She wasn't staying at home, not after all that. No way. Which meant she would have to leave soon or they were screwed.

"What the fuck was all that?"

"That was fucking fantastic," Carlton said, reaching under the seat for the bottle. "Shit, Lucy Merriweather, stripping and getting herself off in the mirror."

"Something like that wasted on Rider. She definitely needs to get seriously fucked. I need to get seriously fucked. She's primed, man."

"I've never seen anything like that. Got to say, I wasn't thinking much of Darlene."

"Not with those tits. I've never seen tits that perfect. I thought I'd lose it." Rigby blew a stream of air past his lips, taking the bottle. "Her ass belongs in a magazine, with her pussy on page two. Shit, did you see that? Fucking perfect."

Carlton brought up his hands, clenching them half open into rigid claws. "Not tonight they don't. Those cheeks and those tits belong right here, fucking ASAP."

"Yeah, after I get out from between those legs. Shit, I came close to jumping through the fucking window when she got herself off. "

"When was the last time you fucked a virgin?"

"Your sister, next September."

"Damn straight, and yours with her."

"They'd freak if they knew about this."

"Let them freak in September. Pussy is pussy. Take what you can, when you can. Life's too short."

Laughter erupted, Rigby capping the bottle, abruptly ordering Carlton to shut the fuck up. Lucy was stepping out.

"I swear, if she doesn't turn left I'll drag her into the back and do her right there. Her pussy is definitely getting it somewhere tonight. The least she can do after fucking with our brains."

"Damn straight. Yeah."

Lucy did turn left, twice, Rigby waiting until she disappeared around the corner to follow her. Lucy turning the next corner made Carlton bounce up and down, reaching into the back for what they would need. Lucy was going to the River Watch and Rigby chose a more direct route. Timing was everything.

Lucy went to her favourite bench, the one closest to the water where she could hear the river flowing against the concrete wall. The other benches and tables were empty. The pathway was deserted and dimly lit with Victorian-styled lamps, the small cluster of trees to one side taking on the appearance of a setting from a grim fairy-tale.

Her musings ran rampant. Her parents competing with Billy for time and space.

She was no longer in high school. She was leaving her home and going to college where she would live on her own as a woman. Who would she meet, and when? Would she ever have sex, and when? Or why? Because she might love him or because she would soon be the last virgin on earth?

She was proud of her body, and what was the big deal anyway? Her mother going ballistic whenever her father might see her in baby dolls or a slip, but not in a skimpy string bikini that showed absolutely everything at the beach to everyone except Billy.

This summer would be different, she decided, with special days to remember. There were so many places to hide and be private at the lake where they had never gone, where most kids never stayed longer than when the time came to run home for supper. Why had they never done that? Besides, someone would have to see her naked one day. So why not Billy, that night, in her bedroom, and then why not at the lake all summer long whenever they could?

And if he was too shy he could take his trunks off in the water. She definitely would not.

A hand clamped over her mouth, snapping her head violently backwards, a second at her throat, her body instantly yanked into the air. Two other hands anchored her legs in a tight grip.

All she could see was the sky, men in dark coats and hoods.

She was squirming and twisting, jerking, trying to kick and to bite her way free. They were taking her into the grove, away from the lights.

She strained to hear a voice, a name, a single word, struggling against them to catch the faintest glimpse of who they might be.

One man dropped her legs, the other released her throat. One arm was locked over her breasts, his other hand sealing her mouth.

The man in front of her tore away her skirt with both hands, tossing it onto the ground. He tore at her tap pants, pulling them past her ankle before trapping her feet. He tugged one shoe away, and the other, punching her in the stomach to help calm her. He ripped open the front of her blouse, scraping and bruising her skin as he tore it rudely from her body, shredding her camisole in two, breaking the thin straps at her shoulders before stooping to reach for her panties.

The man behind her released her mouth, choking her with both hands, stifling a scream. The other man stuffed her mouth with the silk, her face soaked and stained with tears, her eyes searching through a viscous film for any clue they might give her.

Carlton was behind her. He kicked out her feet, dropping her to the ground, forcing her onto her back, pulling her arms over her head, locking her hands tightly into his; her knees were parted wide and pinned under Rigby's.

She struggled to breathe through her nose. Her temples were pounding. She wanted to scream under his crushing weight, her face purple from strain. He punched her again, putting a finger to his mouth framed by a tattered hole in a hood that she thought must be home-made.

He groped each of her breasts. He squeezed hard, kissing them roughly, his tongue leaving a moist trail from one pale crown to the other, pinching them. He wanted to see her reaction. He wanted her to remember her first, arching backward to probe her labia with his thumbs, pinching them between his fingers before ripping at his own belt and slacks.

Lucy lay as motionless as she could, smelling his breath. She'd never felt such excruciating pain as Rigby forced his way in, his black mask hovering over her face. She didn't care about being naked or raped; she wanted to live, to find her way home and, with no way to plead, she lost track of time.

Rigby was done, squirming backward to between her feet, signalling Carlton for help and together they flipped her over.

Carlton was delirious, his adrenalin surging. He sank his fingers into her buttocks, squeezing, probing the soft flesh, slapping and kissing and biting, leaving her chafed and bruised. He didn't know what to touch or do first. He wanted as much of her as he could, for her to feel his excitement while he ignored her guttural moans.

Rigby stood, staring down, panting, adjusting his slacks, leaving Lucy as she was. He knew his friend liked his women on their knees. He snorted, wondering whether

Darlene would.

Carlton wasted no time raising her buttocks to meet him, cleansing her with a fresh can of beer, one hand caressing and smacking her flesh, the other washing her, making her ready with the foam and the liquid cascading between her clefts and her legs.

He went in easily, slowly and deliberately, taking his time, relishing the sensation, enjoying the moment, etching the sight of her into his mind as he probed and caressed every part of her. He'd waited too long to be with her to care that her knees and her elbows were bleeding.

When he was done, they flipped her over again, inching his way to her knees. He wanted to kiss her mouth, to kiss and fondle her breasts, to have her once more while she was there.

She was no longer a threat, her body depleted and still. Rigby stood to lean on a tree, enjoying the view.

Carlton found her mouth squeezed shut, her lips so tightly pursed that her head quivered under the tension. He slapped her once, twice, to no avail, Lucy yelping when he grabbed her two breasts at once, digging his nails into the tender flesh. He pushed down hard, jerking her body. He was incensed, pushing her legs so far apart that she gasped, the next few minutes blocked from her mind as her delicate body was repeatedly crushed against the hard ground.

She was thinking of Billy, escaping somewhere with Billy.

Why was he so late? Or was he at their bench waiting? She had to run to see Billy.

Carlton rolled onto his side, breathing hard, arranging his slacks.

Rigby lit a smoke. He plucked the silk gag from her mouth and went about gathering the rest of her clothes they would take with them. She wouldn't be as quick to run home in the nude. She would squat behind parked cars or hide behind trees where she would most likely piss them away before taking another shower.

Carlton reached for the beer can. Lucy's arm shot out, scrambling to her feet.

"Jake!" was all she could blurt before she began running as fast as she could to the river, to the light and to Billy. She had to reach Billy.

Dwight Rigby twirled on his heels, dropping her clothes. Carlton was much slower.

The river was close. What terrified her more with each long stride was that she couldn't see Billy, hysterically screaming his name. Why wasn't he there? She was resolved. She had nothing to lose. At the very worst she would jump into the fast-flowing water and be safe.

Rigby was gaining, sweeping a rock into his hands as he ran, stumbling.

She was seconds from the light, and then she would be free. She was an arm's length ahead, her nudity and the sight of her frantically running was strangely erotic, arousing him, his body and his mind raging with renewed and feverish urgency. The rock launched from his hands, targeting her back; he wanted her once more, aiming too high, and then Lucy fell.

She lay inert on the ground when Carlton caught up.

"What the fuck! Her head's bleeding."

Rigby was keeled over, catching his breath. "I aimed for her back, to stop her," cried Rigby. "I swear."

"Are you insane, and then what? Fuck her again? We are in deep shit, Dwight. She saw me, man!"

Then a choking whisper, dark blood mixing with plaintive tears: "Jake, Dwight, please don't hurt me anymore. Please don't. Please, I want to go home."

"We are so fucked. Why did she have to do something so stupid? This is on you, Dwight.

"Suck it in, asshole" Rigby hissed, scanning the pathway. "And you've got that wrong. This is all on you, for *you* being so fucking stupid. Not me. You. I've got no intention of ruining my life and my future for a piece of fresh pussy. Not going to happen. And I'm sure as hell not hanging around waiting to be arrested because *she* did something that dumb and *you* let her. Shit. And I am not going to prison for this, Carlton. Neither are you. It's not like we hurt her. Not until now. This is her fault. She should have stayed quiet, let things be. This was her choice. Now, get me that fucking rock."

Lucy was sobbing, trying to understand what had happened, what was happening, pleading in desperate whispers.

Carlton obeyed the command, not hesitating. He found the rock that he needed both hands to hold, passing it to Rigby who raised his hands high and let the thing fall.

The whimpering ceased, the rock tumbling to one side as Carlton stood quietly by, clenching his mouth against the sight and sound of her imploding skull.

"Shit, Dwight..."

"We did this together. You and me because we had to, because of you. That's what friends do. Anyway, it's done."

"Shit," was all Carlton could manage to cry.

They hurried back for her clothes that they tied into a tight ball with their masks and hurled into the river with the can and her shoes.

Rigby flung her purse as far out as he could, neither one bothering again with the body. She had nothing more to give them.

Lucy was half in the dim light of the River Watch pathway, her body left broken, bruised and bleeding.
*

Billy arrived not many minutes later, his head filled with excuses, the first lies he had ever thought to tell Lucy.

She wasn't there, Billy assuming she would come later. She must have felt nervous about being alone in the park so late at night.

He waited a while, not yet recovered from the shock of

his evening. Two girls at once, not half bad for a deaf and dumb freak who was suddenly very curious about how Lucy would look naked, how her body would smell beside his. Not that he would ever see her that way or be with her that way.

He shrugged. He was pretty certain his memories of Darlene and Eleanor would stay with him a very long time, at the same time hoping their thick smell lingering on most of him would fade before he met Lucy. He was pretty certain all girls smelled the same, since Darlene and Eleanor seemed to, and that she would realize what he had done and why he was late.

He didn't want Lucy to ever hate him.

He couldn't say the evening hadn't turned out well. He would tell his mother that he had a wonderful time and thank her for convincing him to go. He began meandering, remembering their bodies so exposed under the car's brilliant lights. Wow! He didn't think he could ever be with Lucy again without imagining her that way.

Something was laying there at the edge of the grove, a dog or one of the city's homeless bums. He went a few steps closer, waited, and crept nearer.

He froze where he stood. The naked and sprawled body, Billy was certain, was that of a girl. His legs and his arms were trembling. He was afraid.

He inched closer. What if she needed help? What would he do? What could he do? That's when a rush of dry air gushed from his throat and he ran as fast as he could to save Lucy.

He crumpled by her side, wanting to scream out her name, touching her body, scanning her body, afraid to touch the cuts and the bruises. He was afraid he would hurt her, putting his hand to her damaged skull that was thick with her blood.

Gently he turned her over, cradling her head in his lap, closing her eyes. He twisted out from his shirt, cloaking her body. His tears splashed into the blood coating her smudged and damp face. He needed to comfort her, somehow knowing she would want the warmth of his hand lightly cupping her breast.

He sat there until three in the morning caressing and kissing her face, staring into her locket. Until Lucy's parents and his came running frantically with the police, Mr. and Mrs. Merriweather fearing the worst, Lucy's mother fainting, sparing her mind the horror as she came nearer, her father held to the ground so that he would not kill Billy.

Billy was dragged to his feet and pushed into a tree. He was handcuffed and dragged by his arms to the cruiser.

Sally and Sam Cutter would never again hold their son in their arms, the judge caustically forbidding to them what Billy Rider had callously and with purpose stolen from Lucy.

Seventeen

1991

Saturday evening, May 18th, the grime of his double shift rinsed away, Anderson sat on his threadbare sofa with enough gut rot left in the bottle for another hit before lights out. He snorted. No grating cell doors and no deafening 10:00 PM siren; nevertheless, lights out at ten.

Twenty-eight days were gone, somewhere, somehow so quickly, a mere forty-three remaining. Not much time with much yet to accomplish. Not the least of which was the ever-vivacious and talented Miss Brenda, Anderson increasingly cognizant that outside the walls of Battle View time did not stand still.

Sunday he would discover their addresses, the same way he had found Sally Cutter. Then he would wait impatiently to track the Rigbys the following Saturday. He would put faces to names and stay over to discover as much as he could about Mr. and Mrs. Carlton on the Sunday, to begin doing in earnest what he had once done better than most others: Design a strategy that would guarantee mutual success.

Sunday he rose early. Force of habit. He had never allowed himself to doze in airports or sleep onboard planes, somehow believing those who did were not very good at whatever they did. And he sure as hell never slept past his time in his cell, despite the occasional temptation, viewing the practice as not the best survival technique.

Breakfast was grits and brown sugar, fried eggs and bacon, figuring he wouldn't be enjoying his freedom long enough to justify rethinking how to cook fine meals.

He made the call with his third coffee.

The long-distance operator had no listings for a Rigby, Dwight on Hickory Road, or a Carlton, Jackson on Emery Street. Were they the correct spellings, was he certain?

He hadn't seen them in a while, he confessed. He was hoping his friends hadn't moved out of state, that they still lived in Necessity.

Well, she did have a listing with such a spelling on Meadowbrook Drive for Rigby, and for Carlton as well. Could they be the ones?

He was pretty certain. Yes.

Would he like the numbers, would he like the addresses as well?

"Miss, thank you so kindly for your help and your patience. I am entirely grateful to you."

"And you are entirely welcome, sir. May I assist you with anything else?"

He hesitated. "I do hate to impose. However, trying to get my former classmates together is proving an almost insurmountable task. I do have another name, though… Anderson, Brenda. She may also have married under Peters. Brenda Peters. I believe she lived in Miami at one time."

He was to stay on the line, she apologized. She would do her best as quickly as possible, Anderson on the verge of disconnecting after five minutes just as…

"Sir, are you ready with your paper and pencil?" She asked. "I have two listings for a Brenda Peters. One in Miami, the other in West Palm Beach. I also have a West Palm Beach listing for a Brenda Anderson. And would you believe she lives on Peters Lane? Isn't that unusual."

Maybe not so much for a whore. "At the very least an unexpected coincidence, miss."

"Would you like the numbers?"

"Very much." His pencil scribbled each one. "And the addresses, miss, might I possibly have those?"

The Southern charm he had earlier in life inherently exuded was difficult for non-Southerners to resist, downright impossible for Southern belles to dismiss.

He thanked the woman with more Southern profusion, cradling the receiver, curious as to why the Anderson home on Peters Lane would not have a civic address. He wondered whether that would be a problem. Time would tell.

He left his apartment to purchase another bottle at the corner package store. He didn't need a drink, he wanted one. Or perhaps he did need one. The cheating bitch lived on a street designated with her name. Probably servicing the entire city council.

Necessity could wait a week. He couldn't.

*

The week seemed interminably longer than his first month spent in solitary licking his wounds, once again begging off Friday.

He departed early, his first destination the First National Bank of Georgia in Savannah to possibly claim what was rightfully his. He didn't know. Being king of the heap in White prison didn't mean squat anywhere else. Though he did have his letters and his ancient ID which included a paper driver's permit issued in 1962.

The teller, as was expected, wasn't certain. When are they ever? Anderson thinking she might wet herself when she saw the Battle View Prison letterhead. Without moving, possibly because she was standing in a puddle, she called the manager who summoned Anderson into his office.

The man was stiff. He was decked out in a grey three-piece with his tie perfectly knotted, the shine on his shoes blinding. His cuffs, Anderson wanted to correct, were an extra and errant inch past his suit sleeves. Not to mention that no man since the last century familiar with proper dress would ever for a moment consider displaying a tie clip above his buttoned vest.

Anderson was wearing jeans and a sweatshirt, repressing a growing urge to scream "boo!" The man had obviously never sat face to face with a crazed killer.

Anderson wanted his money, in full, the five thousand left untouched in his 401K since 1965, potentially six or seven with compound interest. He didn't know. When he was convicted he didn't much care. He hadn't bothered to enquire about his account's future growth potential and a trip to Battle View did not include financial planning. Nor had he kept current with newspapers following his conviction since Battle View was neither a newsstand.

The man made a show of his authority in the matter. He called his assistant, demanding this file and that, during which time he studied Anderson's documents, twice, and a third time, a better choice than banal conversation with a dangerous indigent.

Within a few minutes the assistant returned with a single file, the manager leaning into it as though ready to devour the few pages. The entire affair was most unusual.

Not Anderson's problem.

The man wanted to clear his throat. He didn't. "Mr. Anderson, your account opened here in 1952 with intermittent deposits until 1965 when apparently all activity abruptly ceased."

"Abruptly, yes. That is indeed true, sir. Until that year when I was convicted for a brutal yet gratifying murder. I was sentenced to Battle View, where I then nearly killed some other guy for jerking me around." He dragged his seat a few inches closer. "So might we possibly accelerate this meeting somewhat, sir? I am quite pressed for time."

"Yes, most certainly. The amount that final year was five thousand. Your memory serves you well. However, with accrued interest, particularly throughout the early eighties, your current worth in this account, Mr. Anderson, is 45,000 dollars. That value, understandably, will be lessened by taxes and certain banking fees."

Disguising his incredulity was difficult. "To what extent?"

The manager fiddled with his calculator. "I would estimate by some forty percent in total."

Anderson nodded. "In fifties and hundreds, if you would be so kind. I'll wait."

The man put up his hands defensively, bordering on a spastic cough. "That is quite frankly impossible. We will require twenty-four hours to finalize such a large transaction. I would suggest noon tomorrow at the latest."

Anderson glanced at his watch. Nine-thirty. "You mean to suggest noon on Monday, seventy-five hours. Can we agree on end-of-business today? Shall we say three, because I really can't see the difference?"

"You're right, of course. I simply had your best interests in mind. Further fees would apply, however. Possibly as high as a hundred dollars, which I believed might inconvenience you."

"It will not, sir." He stood and walked out.

Anderson spent the day until three touring his personal landmarks in Savannah, feeling no sense of history. His parents' home was scarcely recognizable, their gravesite manicured and maintained. He remained a while to spend time with them, leaning casually against their stone, not bothering to speak. He assumed they were informed, that they knew everything about him and that they understood, waiting as long as he could to say a final goodbye.

The bank manager greeted him precisely on the hour, a small stack of fifties, a larger bundle of hundred-dollar bills laying on the edge of his desk, Anderson accepting the manager's offer of a canvas bag.

He stayed the night in Savannah, paying cash for a five-star room on the Riverfront, a fine meal in his room, and a good night's sleep in a quilt-covered bed.

He woke early, virtually alone on the I-95 through to West Palm Beach where he arrived Saturday, May 25ᵗʰ, well before noon, feeling renewed and invigorated.

The narrow side streets feeding onto the beach were jammed with cars. Pampered and giddy bikini-clad girls paraded along sidewalks with that air of teen-age self-importance that hadn't changed since his time. Their faces and eyes were meticulously painted, their hair braided to perfection for the sole purpose of snaring any worthwhile male of the species too dumb to escape the snapping jaws. What had changed, however, was their skin, how much of it they were casually displaying.

Punk-ass boys, pussies really, tanned and as pretty as the girls, fancying themselves invincible, God's gift, trailed behind them, boosting each other's already inflated egos. Anderson snorted derisively. In his day no Georgia boy would possibly have presumed to be so vulgar.

Not his problem.

Peters Lane wasn't hard to locate a few minutes beyond the edge of town, a road marked PRIVATE * NO ENTRY crowning a crescent of expensive, sprawling and gated homes. Not the best place for an ex-con to be discovered amidst the Jaguars, Mercedes and her own Bentley convertible parked by her front entrance.

He retreated several blocks, where he paid for parking. He expected to be a while.

He found a beach shop where he bought a swimsuit, a tee-shirt, sandals, a beach hat, a tube of zinc oxide and a straw shoulder bag. He bought a chilled six-pack, a couple of Michigan red hots, and found a spot for the day behind her home that was wide open to view inside a gated and wrought iron fence. Not a problem, not his anyway, not with 500 feet or more of hot, white sand separating her Shangri-La from the pale blue sea.

His Bushnells brought the place in close. He judged the white stucco side walls framing her single-story villa at twelve feet, the narrow tops lined with nasty double rows of V-shaped iron spikes which he presumed were in place to discourage miscreant seagulls from replastering the surface and ex-husbands recently freed from Battle View Prison intent on killing her.

She was clearly talented. A whore and a clairvoyant, although strangely he felt less emotion than he had anticipated, which he decided was a good thing. Passion was for the bedroom, *was* being the keyword, once upon a time, for a short while, certainly not for the meting out of long-awaited justice whether poetic or otherwise.

Behind her gate was an expansive stone patio highlighted by a glittering pool. The lounge furniture was draped in white and shaded with white canopies. He saw a wet bar lined with stools and bottles, and something else he knew nothing about filled with swirling water. A setting straight from the movies, like Ginger Rogers and Fred Astaire, when he didn't even own a television and hadn't seen a movie since…He couldn't remember. Though one day very soon he *would* discover her spa's stress relieving qualities, luxuriating in the heated and agitated water while savouring a fine scotch from her bar, savouring his life's finest moment before terminating his freedom.

Not seeing her that early in the day didn't trouble him. Besides, she had two other homes and most whores would work their wonders late into the night or early morning. Only the bargain basement girls plied their trade during the day from inside dark and dingy bars. Despite which, by one o'clock he began to worry that he might be sitting in the wrong place, three empty cans laying in a row by a damp depression in the sand. He wondered whether she might have two cars, one for work, one for pleasure, and had gone somewhere for the weekend. He wondered about a lot of things.

She came into view a little past two.

He recognized her instantly, her strut, her confidence,

the way she pivoted her head from side to side in a way that he once thought was cute, as though she wanted to see everything happening around her. This, however, he was having a hard time with. She was practically naked. She was naked, completely at ease and visible to anyone passing by.

Anderson slid onto his front, lowering his profile and raising the Bushnells. He refocused, his brow creasing in disbelief as she came to him up close and personal.

Her ass and her breasts were entirely bare. Her ass was tight, though he had not the slightest recollection of how that bare flesh once felt in his hands; her breasts were as firm as he remembered them, though not their soft warmth; the thin, orange patch barely secreting the main tool of her trade and as brilliant in the sun as a roadside flare. Her skin was flawless with not a speck of white marring her contours. She was toned and shapely, all woman. She always was, and decidedly well-off.

He sensed an unequivocal and irrepressible rage mounting, commandeering his mind, distorting rational thoughts. He breathed deeply several times. He had been hoping for so much worse, a haggard face, a scar or two, sagging breasts. He didn't know what. Something. Anything that would demean her and please him. At least a rounder shape, a liver spot or two. He brought her in closer.

She was fifty-four, appearing more like early-forties through his lenses. Outside and shamefully naked. Not that he couldn't adjust given adequate time. What else had he missed in life because of her? She was beautiful, her brunette hair lustrous and thick. Her face was smooth, her lips glossy with the colour of mahogany, her eyes masked by dark tortoiseshell glasses. She carried herself with grace; classy, he had to admit, from a stranger's perspective. From his, she was a whore. A rose by any other name.

He coughed a laugh. Throughout his trial, which began when he immediately stood to freely declare his guilt to the jury, to his horror-stricken defence counsel and the apoplectic judge, his mind was consumed with a single and persistent question. How could she so easily strut into a stranger's hotel room, matter-of-factly strip off her clothes, fuck him once, twice or all night, gather up her clothes, take his money, and leave to degrease herself in *his* shower night after night? He had to ask her. He would ask her.

Her orange hat was wide-brimmed and droopy. She was wearing high-heeled sandals, the same shade, and a matching wide-band watch. She didn't seem the slightest bit like an aging whore, Anderson curious how any woman could manage that profession for close to forty years when most roadways that well-travelled would be impassible were they not repaved every ten years. Too bad she wouldn't see fifty-five in a few short months.

She came to the gate, peering past him, or leering at him, sipping her drink without bothering to cover herself.

He wasn't stirred. Not by her, not by any woman. The good ones wouldn't want him, the others, well... Mr. John Anderson had never shopped in bargain basements.

He was good for a while. She wasn't going anywhere, not like that. At least he didn't think she would.

He pushed himself to his feet, leaving his new and used cans in his hat. He strolled to the shoreline, continuing north for a while ankle-deep in the water. He'd been free for a month, not once thinking of paying for the service of a much younger woman to reawaken long-dead urges and long-forgotten ecstasies.

He wouldn't know where to begin, how to touch her or where, whether to arouse her, or even whether he could, even if he did now have the money.

And what would he say to her beyond the occasional grunt with no past or future between them? For which reason he declined a night on the town with the men from work, not believing for an instant that young and desirable women, and lots of them, would dance for him or sit on his legs in the nude for a measly ten dollars. Or that for a hundred dollars he could do whatever to them, except that, in a private salon for an hour.

He didn't believe them. Besides, they had wives. He had one room and a radio.

A hundred or more for an hour, for what was once free, discounting his ruined career and portfolio, his home and his life? That was not a good deal. Not when he was earning fourteen. All he wanted was for Billy Rider to live a good life, to start over with Sally Cutter and his brothers, and that the men of 312 would not cross paths on Billy's way out.

He returned ninety minutes later, surprised that his hat and the three full cans weren't gone.

Mrs. Anderson or Miss Peters, which he assumed had a lot to do with whether she was on her feet or on her back, was doing easy laps in her pool, wearing her hat.

He sat cross-legged by the empties, watching until she was done. He was intrigued watching her step onto her deck, naked, tanned and dripping. He saw her tug at the orange strings, first one, then the other, dropping the patch to the deck. He watched her towel herself dry, stretching and bending before slipping into a robe. At the bar she mixed a fresh drink. She glanced once toward the ocean and disappeared into her home.

He finished his three hot and bitter beers, inducing a light sleep, waking near six. He felt good, rejuvenated by the persistent warmth of the sun, its glow more golden than midday.

He wanted to stay longer, debating at length, deciding at last that he couldn't. As it was he wouldn't arrive home until 3:00 or four in the morning, expected at the office by seven on a Sunday.

Reluctantly he left her, doubtful he would see her again before mid-June with so much to do. The timing was crucial and June 30th was fast-approaching.

Eighteen

1971

Billy whimpered in restless sleep throughout the night, Anderson wishing he could rent a cell by the hour. He'd learned not to care about the anguish of others.

The next morning the doctor chose to let Rider sleep, though most likely he was still hung-over. Anderson went to the yard for the day, breaking for lunch and supper in the mess and the library until eight that night to give Rider space and to give himself respite.

*

Realizing he was deaf and dumb the police had foregone the Miranda. What was the point?

His ribs ached from the cop's heavily booted-foot that kicked him over once Lucy was taken from him, a gun pressed to his head. His face scratched and bruised from being forced onto the ground and manhandled into handcuffs.

The cold steel on his wrists was tight, his feet scarcely touching the ground as the two cops first on the scene carried him swiftly into the kaleidoscope of the electric blues and reds of dome lights and away from his mother.

This was the most horrific crime ever in Necessity, on their watch. They left him shirtless and alone in the cruiser until the ambulance arrived, until detectives came to take over the scene, his wrists shackled at his back. His shoulders were slumped, his demeanour wretched and pitiable. His imploring eyes peered from the window, his parents forbidden to approach the car. The flustered cops uncertain how to react when Sally and Sam stood in the distance telling their son to be brave.

They believed in him and loved him. He could not and did not do such terrible things to his Lucy. They would hire a lawyer immediately and everything would be fine. They promised him, instructing him firmly not to write a single word until his lawyer arrived, translating while issuing the same warning to the detectives. Sam supposing correctly that the officers first to arrive on the scene weren't bright enough to read Billy his rights.

Thirty minutes later he was at the police station.

Billy Rider was charged with grievous assault, battery, rape, and the murder of Lucy Merriweather. He was fingerprinted, his ruined clothes and his watch stripped away. They photographed his naked body, scraping his face and his genitals without telling him why, shoving him into a small room where he was trapped behind a windowless door without his mother and father.

He was terrified, too terrified to feel the dull buzz of his receding hangover. He had no sense of time, no sense of what he had done wrong, yet puzzled by why he felt guilty.

He had no idea what was happening, or what had happened over those previous five hours.

He would not let himself believe that he had found his best friend murdered and raped. That could never be true. He was dreaming. He was living a horrible nightmare, unable to wake up.

Frightful images of her nude body and her blood made more hideous by the dark assailed his mind, confused with flashing images of Darlene and Eleanor standing naked in glaring light. The residual stink on his body was real, making him ill; the sight of his mother's hysterical shrill and her desperate pleas repeating over and over again no matter how tightly he squeezed his eyes shut.

With no way to communicate with him, Billy refusing to lift the pencil, the detectives left the dumb boy alone until midday when Sally and Sam were at last able to recruit a willing attorney who did not reside in Necessity and was free of emotional conflicts.

The arraignment was delayed until the following Wednesday.

Judge Allison Stillsworth denied bail, setting a tentative trial date of June 08th that would allow the police ample time to investigate, establish a motive and show that Billy Rider should be tried for the crimes. During which time the Cutter home was legally ransacked by motivated cops probing for clues, producing Lucy's letters, interrogating a distraught Sally and Sam, and questioning their neighbours.

In stark contrast, they respectfully searched Lucy's bedroom, interviewed the parents, discovered Billy's letters and what clothes were missing from her closet that night.

They interviewed the principal, his teachers and classmates. They also interviewed Darlene Rigby and Eleanor Carlton.

They alone knew the real truth. Billy did rape her. That was a no-brainer. He had roused himself into such a feverish state while he was with them, so desperate for more when they left, that he went searching for Lucy and he raped her.

Together they confirmed that, "Yes. Billy did leave the dance early, about ten-thirty. He had a serious thing for Lucy. He was really upset when she wouldn't be his date for the dance. He was demented. He did weird things. Ask anyone."

*

When the detectives left, the girls went to Darlene's room. When they finished their affectionate addiction to each other, they sat against their pillows and sipped vodka from shot glasses.

"Billy actually killed Lucy. He raped her and he killed

her. I can't believe it."

"We're in shit, Darlene."

"No, we are not."

"I'm not so sure. If our parents ever find out…."

"What, that we're fucking? Think your mother never fucked around before your father? Get real. And my father cheats all the time," she sneered, "with all that Love Thy Neighbour bullshit. Anyway, how would they? Those cops have no reason to question Grade Tens."

"The freak's going to tell them. He'll tell them about us, you and me…this"

"We'll say he raped us, like he did to her. And how do you think he's going to prove our girl thing?" Darlene drained the full two ounces. "Go home right now if you're afraid. I don't care."

"Yeah, sure. We drove him a mile down a dirt road late at night so he could rape you while I sat in the car waiting for my turn. Then we went back to the dance and didn't tell anyone. Good plan, Darlene. And I'm not afraid."

"Don't be snide. We're minors and he's a year older. So yeah, we could yell rape if that's what we need. Which we don't because he hasn't told them anything. And he won't. Besides, there's no law against fucking a freak. So what if our parents find out? They're hypocrites. Who do they imagine will marry us anytime soon without fucking us first to check us out and approve the goods? I mean, really." She refilled their glasses." Anyway they have no proof. We'll say he's a liar, that he's always bothering girls. He's a freak, Eleanor."

Eleanor startled. "No. You're wrong. There is proof. We have to get dressed and get out of here." She flung herself from the bed, reaching for her shorts and sweater. "We didn't take the empties."

Soon after the girls were at the cul-de-sac. They found the two empty bottles, crushing one and smashing the other into tiny shards inside a grocery bag with the tire iron, disposing of their possible undoing in a trashcan at the mall.

Let Billy Rider tell the cops whatever he wanted.

*

The crime scene produced nothing. The rock was the sole piece of evidence found by the body.

The cops had cordoned off the entire area finding nothing more than a cigarette butt and Rider didn't smoke, confirming to the DA that they were stalemated. They combed along river's shorelines, and again they found nothing. The investigation went nowhere, what little they did have pointing indisputably to Billy Rider, a deaf and dumb kid with the hots for an attractive young girl who wore provocative clothing that night and was leaving him behind in a few months to meet other boys. Go figure.

They kissed, and maybe they didn't, the kid wanting more than she was willing to give out. Look but don't touch, after she got him all hot and bothered. Her classmates interviewed were all in agreement that she was a tease, always taunting the boys with her skirts too short and her blouses too revealing. She thought she was so high and mighty because she'd gone to Europe.

She went inviting trouble to where she wasn't supposed to be, her parents believing she was at home. She dressed that way to get a reaction, and she did, meeting a boy alone in the dark, scantily dressed. What was she thinking? Or, what was she expecting before things went too far out of control?

The coroner's report indicated that this was her first sexual episode. So she said "stop" after a rough grope or two, and he either didn't or he couldn't. Her upper thighs and breasts were badly bruised. Something a horny and excited kid would do.

She suddenly felt terrified, and began to struggle. So he punched her, apparently viciously, and then he stripped her, the lesions and bruises on her upper body and legs consistent with clothing violently torn away. That's when he raped her, repeatedly, lesions to her back, buttocks and legs indicating she was unclothed at the time. The internal damage she suffered was too extensive to consider that a single event had occurred. She was defenseless, at his mercy for a considerable time, the chafed condition of the alleged perpetrator's private parts supporting that conclusion.

She was screaming for anyone to help her. So he told her to stop, slapping her. But she didn't stop. He began choking her. The terrible bruising on her neck consistent with a ferocious struggle. And somehow she got free. She fled, panicking. She was desperately trying to escape. which he couldn't let happen, her badly scraped knees and palms proving that she fell forward, hard, her damaged occipital bone indicating without doubt that he was chasing her, that he first attacked her from behind with the same rock.

Maybe she passed out, which they all hoped was the case, when he possibly raped her again, raging out of his mind, thinking he must punish her, going shitty when he stopped at seeing the blood. He knew she would tell, that he would go to prison for a very long time. And that's when he killed her with a second merciless blow while she lay whimpering, her last breath cut short.

He killed her and threw her clothes and purse into the water that coursed around the River Watch at four or five knots. Or he dug a hole somewhere, since the trashcans within a square mile turned up nothing. They didn't know, and Billy Rider was not cooperating.

In view of the evidence against him, the official police report recommended to the prosecutor's office that the murder trial of Billy Rider should take place as scheduled.
*

Not until his arraignment in criminal court midway through his first week, when he was transferred from the Necessity Police Station to the County Detention Facility in the state capital, did Sally get to see her son. However Sam would

177

have to wait until Billy's first day in court.

The defence attorney had appealed each of those first days to a dismissive DA to no avail, Judge Allison Stillsworth finally giving her consent at the arraignment for Sally Cutter to act on the defendant's behalf as translator. Until then Billy had been as unwilling to communicate with him as with the police.

She was heartbroken at the sight of him dressed in ill-fitting coveralls and sneakers, his wrists and his feet shackled together. She held him close, consoling herself as much as her son without telling him why, fearing that news of Lucy's funeral that afternoon would cause him insufferable anguish.

Enduring his mother's severe admonishments Billy began telling the truth. He did leave the dance early. No one would dance with him and he felt awkward standing alone at the coat check because no one had arrived wearing coats.

He was supposed to meet Lucy at eleven, arriving at the Watch closer to quarter-after. She was already dead, the way everyone found her. Her clothes were gone, that's why he covered her.

"The police report says you were molesting her body when they arrived. That true?"

Sally replied, "I wanted to comfort her…and I knew she wanted me to. I did nothing wrong. I wasn't hurting her."

"Is that why you were meeting her, to play touchy? The police found semen on your shorts and a whole whack of it in her. Things get a little bit out of hand? Seems you have the same blood type as the assailant. Care to talk about that?"

Billy shrugged. Sally replied, I'm eighteen. Things happen, which doesn't mean I raped Lucy. I did not."

"They found traces of her lipstick on you."

Sally answered, "When I found her, her body was warm. I wanted to kiss her. I never did before. I was saying goodbye. I wanted her to know how I felt. She was the only friend I have."

"Did you intend to have consensual sex with her? Is that why she dressed that way, to get things started?"

"No. She dressed that way because she's seventeen and pretty. Why do you dress *that* way?"

"Did you kill her?"

Sally answered for him. "Those two kids adored each other, as friends. He did not kill her and neither one was expecting or thinking to have sex. They went to be together, because her parents are narrow-minded bigots. He wasn't welcomed into their home and the single reason she was never in our home is that this racist town has too many eyes and too many loose tongues and her parents threatened Lucy with her final year in a private school. So, Counselor, let's be clear. No murder. No rape. "

Lawyers are like undertakers. They're actors feigning compassion when they don't give a good shit.

"How did the two of you communicate, if you can't speak?"

Sally answered for before Billy. "He taught Lucy to sign."

The entire room went quiet, Sally squeezing her son's hand.

"You left the school alone, at ten-thirty, you're sure about that? You went straight to her, you didn't go somewhere first, perhaps with another girl? Because if you did, this all goes away and you go home right now…tonight. All we need is a name and, if she's eighteen, and that's how you got your shorts wet, that's going to be unquestionably fine with everyone."

"I don't have a girlfriend and no one wants to…," Sally interrupted herself to scold him, "have sex with a deaf and dumb freak. That's what they call me."

She wanted to cry. She wanted her husband with her. She asked, "What will happen? How long will all this last? How long must Billy be in here?"

"He's here until he's no longer a suspect, which is unlikely at this point since he's the only suspect. Or until he's sentenced. This Judge Stillsworth, she doesn't waste time. We'll know very soon after the jury delivers the verdict what the sentence will be. The same day."

"What are we facing?"

"We've got a dead girl with her head in his lap, his hand on her breast, and an engraved locket on her neck with Billy inside. We have her blood on his shirt, on his pants, his face, and on a rock that also shows an imprint of his hands. She was dressed from what I've read a little provocatively and in all their letters they write about their upcoming "special" times together at the River Watch. And, Mrs. Cutter, the boy reeked of sex. The medical report indicates that his penis underwent some very aggressive contact consistent with Lucy's damaged tissues. So the boy is either lying about another girl, or he did in fact rape and kill Lucy, or he stood behind some tree and thought about her with some pretty intense feelings. If you get my point, which doesn't explain the distinctive body odour. And that thing about comforting her, to the DA, that's gross sexual misconduct perpetrated on a deceased person which, I promise you, will delight Judge Stillsworth to no end."

"Billy, darling, was there another girl?" Sally asked.

"No, like I told you." Billy glared at the lawyer. "And I don't jack off behind trees. Screw the report. And screw you."

Sally believed him. "My son is innocent."

"Mrs. Cutter, the one thing Billy has on his side is that Lucy wasn't a promiscuous girl and nothing was found in your son's room that would indicate past or present deviant behaviour, the types of things found in those out-of-town-limits adult stores or in girlie magazines. That's it. And unless he tells us the name of the girl, any girl, he's facing hard time." The lawyer dropped his chin into his chest, lacing his hands, shaking his head forlornly for affect. "If only he hadn't killed her, Mrs. Cutter. Then we wouldn't be here, not unless he got her pregnant, got the parents involved. Even then we could have talked to the DA, pleaded with the judge for a lesser sentence, fifteen, at the very worst twenty. Thing is, who bashes in the head of his girlfriend twice? And if the DA can prove intercourse with a deceased person he'll spend his life in a padded cell, which we will not let happen. We'll argue that they had consensual sex that went bad. She ran and he panicked, bringing her down with no intention of hurting her. Not until seeing what he had done did he panic and kill her."

Sally was furious. "He didn't kill her! Damn you!"

"Then he was in the wrong place at the wrong time. So tell him to help us. Because right now he's not doing squat to help himself."

Billy sat calmly reading their lips, tapping the table. Sally conveyed the question, "What will I get if they say I'm guilty of murder, and what will I get for raping a girl?"

Sally's expression went blank. She tilted her head, turning to Billy, not believing what he was asking.

"So you did have sex with her?"

"No. I did not, which doesn't matter because you think I did and so will they."

The lawyer glanced at Sally before answering. "She experienced more than one rape, sustaining grievous injuries prior to her death. That's first-degree rape, a Class B1 felony. So twenty years. No discussion. No parole. The murder was second-degree, a Class C felony. The DA can't prove with any certainty that you went there for the express purpose of killing her. Up to fifty years, though probably much less. You have no history. My best guess is more like fifteen. As for your need to comfort her, who knows? Stillsworth could be in a rare good mood. If not, you can expect another five. That's the maximum, and I don't expect any of this to run concurrently. You'll see your mother again in forty years." He gave his attention to Sally.

"And, quite frankly Mrs. Cutter, I would seriously think about leaving town when all this is over."

Sally was sobbing, overcome with fear.

Billy knew his mother's heart was aching.

Darlene and Eleanor would scream rape. He had no doubt whatsoever. They were younger than him by a year and a half. They would say he stole liquor from somewhere and got them drunk. Their parents were important and had lots of money and no one would believe him about the Grade Ten students they had always gloated about fucking. So forty years for two counts of rape or forty years for being innocent of hurting and killing Lucy, which his mother believed in her heart he did not do. He didn't care what anyone else thought.

Sally's voice was breaking, Billy's fingers more difficult to read through her wet eyes.

"Mom, I didn't kill Lucy and I didn't hurt her. She was my friend. I would never do such a terrible thing to anyone. I would never hurt my mother that way. I'm innocent and if I can't convince you I won't convince them. There was no other girl and there was no tree. Those doctors saw what they wanted to see. And my smell could only have come from holding Lucy so closely." He faced the lawyer for an instant. "And tell him this. You're the frigging lawyer, so do something to help my mother."
*

Sally and Sam had only been to Court once before, to attend Billy's arraignment.

They had early on been forewarned by the school and the newspaper that, in the event Billy was found guilty and convicted, their positions would be terminated immediately.

Sam was wasting no time job-hunting. Despite his belief in Billy, he had a wife and two other sons drowning in tuition debt, whereas Sally's entire focus was on Billy. She insisted that the lawyer visit with Billy each day, otherwise she would not be allowed. Each day she travelled to the state capital, explaining to Billy that she, and not his distressed brothers, was the reason they had not come to support him. She had ordered them to stay away, which did not mean they believed him guilty. They did not.

On Friday, June 05th, Sally embraced her son for the last time. The shock of what was about to come would one day soon after kill Sam Cutter and devastate Sally for the rest of her life.

The courtroom in Raleigh, the state capital, was filled to capacity. None of the ten young women on the jury came from Necessity, nor the two much older men.

Judge Allison Stillsworth sat on the bench, presiding, known by many to be as strict with her nineteen-year-old daughter as she was in her courtroom.

The trial lasted three weeks, during which time Sally retained her right to translate on behalf of her son, albeit through glass partitions, their lawyer increasingly less enthusiastic about his client's chances. His office and his home were receiving hate mail, as were the Cutters. Nobody wanted them or their son back in Baptist Necessity.

Closing arguments began on the 29th, defence counsel standing first with very little to say that hadn't been said before so many times. He sat by Billy, dejected, appearing visibly defeated to all in the court.

The DA's summation tore through him like a bullet. Sally's body froze, her blood ice-cold; Sam pressed a hand against his heart. Billy sat calmly, his face devoid of all expression, instantly reliving the brutal murder of one Betsy Rider.

"Ladies and gentlemen of the jury, with all the clear evidence before us, and against this very evil man, you must in good conscience return a verdict of guilty. This man did, without any question, willfully, and for his own gratification, rape and then kill little Lucy Merriweather, an innocent girl who in no way precipitated this heinous crime. Billy Rider is guilty, as was his father of raping a girl barely fifteen, escaping the law solely by wedlock, holy matrimony, then butchering her repeatedly to death with a kitchen carving knife when she wasn't much older than Lucy."

"Billy Rider is the regrettable issue of that rape. He is not the village idiot as the town of Necessity, his school and his neighbours perceive him; he is genetically inclined towards violence, towards rape and towards murder. You must not be deceived. You must remove him from our society, lest one of yours or your neighbours' be his next innocent victim. For he has nought else to do in this life but to descend into much greater depths of despicable wickedness until, like his father, he takes his own evil life. I ask you, who amongst you would think to give him employment or desire him as a neighbour amongst your vulnerable children?"

The sequestered jury adjourned to deliberate with cautions from the judge. The next day, moments before noon, they re-entered the courtroom.

One the first count of rape in the first-degree: Guilty. On the second count of murder in the second-degree: Guilty. On the third count of necrophilia: Innocent. On the fourth count of sexual misconduct with a deceased person: Guilty.

The room exploded into loud claps and cheers, until the gavel and the furious "silence!" cut short the elation.

Sally and Sam Cutter stopped breathing. They imagined the worst for their son, invaded by panic as Billy was marched from the courtroom and the judge adjourned for a lunch break.

The session resumed two hours later. Neither Sally nor Sam had budged an inch in their first row seats, seated behind their son. Before Judge Allison Stillsworth began, Billy turned to face them. *They found me guilty, which is not the same as proving me guilty because I am not. I love you both.*

Then Billy paled, staring past them at Dwight Rigby

and Jake Carlton whom he had seen throughout each day of the trial, each of those days and nights wishing their sisters would come to testify on his behalf. No one would have to have known about their pasts, or what actually happened that night. They could have told any number of lies to help defend him.

The two were smiling, practically giddy, their faces absurd amongst so many dozens more solemn expressions waiting to hear the sentence delivered, Billy wondering whether they knew what their sisters had done.

Rigby leaned into Carlton's ear. "Word has it he was mercy fucking some tenth grade double-bagger?"

"No shit. Who?"

Rigby snorted. "Who knows? She ran away with the bag. Anyway, who cares as long as he finished her in time to make things right for us? We would have been in serious shit."

Billy's brow furrowed. What did they mean "make things right for us?"

His lawyer put a hand on his shoulder, the room was standing for Judge Allison Stillsworth. As they resumed their seats, he and Billy remained standing, the judge asking the Merriweathers whether they might have a victim's statement to present before sentencing.

Mrs. Merriweather stood, aided by her husband They did not. All had been said, except that Billy Rider should never once for the rest of his life be allowed to see the light of day or walk again amongst God-loving and decent people who should never have to fear deviant predators such as Billy Rider.

The judge's preamble lasted a brief few minutes, mostly for the benefit of Mr. and Mrs. Merriweather who sat opposite Sally and Sam. Within her power to do so, she would apply the full impact of the law to, in a very small way, compensate for their grievous loss and bring them closure.

"On the first count, that of first-degree rape, with clinical evidence of two separate incidents, Billy Rider you are hereby sentenced consecutively to a prison term of twenty years for each offence. On the second count, that of second-degree murder, the District Attorney failing to establish premeditated intent, and in accordance with the Fair Sentencing Act of North Carolina, you are hereby sentenced to an additional term of fifty years. On the third count of necrophilia, I reluctantly accept the jury's decision and implore the Merriweathers to free their minds of such vile imagery. On the fourth count, that of sexual misconduct with a deceased person, that deceased person being a minor, and lacking sufficient evidence to prove necrophilia, I hereby add an additional five years to your existing term of ninety years without benefit of early parole in Battle View prison, Tennessee, constructed for the incarceration of the nation's most loathsome and repugnant criminals."

"In addition to which, and in accordance with this state's fullest measure of the law for the crime of rape in the first-degree, you shall be subjected, in the first three years of your incarceration, to the lash. That punishment to be carried out twice yearly and with no more than five strikes across your back on each occasion. The first of these six punishments to be inflicted on the thirty-first of the coming month. Your incarceration effective immediately." Before smashing her gavel onto its oak base, she added. "Happy birthday, Mr. Rider. My single disappointment in this trial is that I am unable to impose the death penalty since premeditation could not clearly be established. More's the pity. You are a despicable being and I profoundly wish that the earliest stages of your physical punishment at Battle View will prove as effective as any noose."

The gavel resounded.

Sally Cutter wailed, her screech piercing the air, reaching with Sam to touch their son, held back by bailiffs as their defence counsel begged the court to allow his clients a few private moments together.

The judge's denial was scathing. Why would he care to presume for a moment that she would allow *them* what Billy Rider had so callously, in a moment of panic and fear, after so viciously tormenting and injuring the girl, stolen from Lucy and her parents?

The entire courtroom was suddenly distracted.

Sally pulled away from Sam's hand. "My son is *not* despicable," she hissed, her voice strong, venomous with hate, "My son did not do any of these horrible things. You, Judge Stillsworth, have made a grave and careless error in judgement. This miscarriage of justice you see fit to condone is despicable. You are despicable. The police did not do their job. They have allowed a killer to go free. From this day the town of Necessity has no reason to feel safe. Shame on you; shame on everyone. If I could curse you with any effect, I would see you all destroyed for what you have done here. As for you, Mrs. Merriweather, our children were together almost each day of the week at the Watch for over three years, each other's best friend. They were dear to each other. Lucy was fluent in signing, yet you never cared to know. They wrote each other letters, and you never knew. What kind of mother knows so little about her child? Shame on you for blaming my son and keeping Lucy from her devoted friend."

Billy was facing her, standing stoically for his mother and father. He smiled, feeling the need to comfort them, the little colour he had in his face draining instantly at seeing Rigby and Carlton. They were chuckling, mocking him, amused by his mother's sorrowful outburst.

Rigby was shaking his head. "Holy shit, Battle View," he said. "That could have been us. I've heard about that place. It's a bitch and he's got you to thank for it."

"Hey, I'm not the one who smashed in her head. Let's not get too righteous."

"Can't say I even remember how she felt. Can't say I'll

do it again. Too much like work."

"Anyway, what's he got to lose? We've probably done him a favour."

Sally was threatened by the judge, ordered to sit and be still. She remained standing.

Billy was led away. He would never see either parent or his brothers again. The privileged few ever allowed into Battle View Prison were the ones seldom if ever allowed out.

*

When Anderson returned to 312 Billy was awake, though the kid hadn't eaten since the previous evening and wouldn't until morning, which bothered Anderson not at all.

Nineteen

1991

Twenty years later Billy Rider's memories of that night, of how he lay awake obliterating the pain with memories of his times with Lucy, and that next morning, were as vivid as though he had lived them the previous day.

He remembered the doctor coming to his cell with his kit, removing the bandages, making some wounds worse and not asking any doctor's questions. He remembered the pain, the stinging salve that tortured before healing, the other cons peering transfixed through the bars of his cell. Though what he remembered most was that August 03rd, foregoing his shower, treading weakly to the mess hall as all the others passed him by. He remembered how the cons at his table stopped eating as he sat; he remembered barely managing to hold his tray steady; he remembered no one helping.

The breakfast, he remembered, was delicious, or seemed to be after not eating for sixty hours. Lunch and supper not so much. He remembered how shocked he was, and grateful, when, before they left him, the cons at his table put their cups of juice in front of his tray, at lunch their milk, and at supper their desserts.

When he was finished he went to the yard, as he would for the remainder of his life, quite certain at the time that he wouldn't live another ninety-five years.

The evening of April 20th, hours after John's release,

Billy sat in the dark on the top bunk spread out. He was pensive, recounting those first days and more. Who would think that in prison a man would have such a great deal to remember? Yet he did.

In that first year he grew stronger, bidding farewell by his second encounter with the Cat six months later to his pretty boy mien and timid manner. That time he fought not to pass out, fully awake for breakfast the next morning when the cons once again gave him what they could to help rebuild his strength.

The second and third years he spent his time exclusively in the yard, his torso darker and sculpted. His face had hardened and his eyes were more alert. His single purpose was beating the Cat, driven to never again collapse on the floor or whimper in his sleep.

Which is precisely what he did, the last time stepping from the Cat on his own with a weak smile to shake the stunned warden's hand and wish him a very Happy Valentine's. John did that, watching each day as Billy became more of a con and less of whatever else he might have become.

By that time John was signing fluently, while often learning in advance of someone else's stabbing, beating, or hearing what the guards whispered under their breaths. He was also increasingly convinced that Billy was innocent, thinking that one day he might actually help the kid clear his name. Anything was possible. The thing was to never give up hope.

On February 15th, 1974, the day after his final whipping, as Billy lingered over the last of ten cups of juice that had become a bi-annual tradition that was thankfully at an end, John stayed seated as the other cons went their separate ways.

Billy Rider had assumed the believable appearance of a con. He acted like a con, separated from the others by speech unless John condescended to translate, his newly acquired skill from then on obsoleting the once scribbled notes. That was John's doing. Survival: 101.

Look like one, act like one, kid. Just remember you are not one of them. That's what he would say, over and over again.

*

You're probably the first accused rapist in here who hasn't been stabbed, beaten or killed. I really thought you'd be dead by now, kid.

You're not the only one, and I sort of think the Cat is a beating, John. You should try it. I'm pretty sure you'll agree.

Don't be a smartass. What I want to try is lipreading. I see it as a useful tool.

Billy was learning to conceal what he was thinking. Even happy cons rarely smiled or joked. *Why, when you're the only one I speak to?*

Because I see it as a useful tool, because this hand thing is too one-sided. And because I asked you.

It will take a few years, way more difficult than signing. Think you're up to it? You've only got seventeen left.

John let that one go, partly responsible for the attitude that had become second nature. *Yeah, I think I can manage. So let's do it. And, at the same time, let's get you educated. If you ever do get out of here no one's going to hire a dummy.* He paused, grinning. *Sorry, no offense.*

I'm not getting out. Earth to John. Life sentence, and a bonus. Free funeral.

You know what? John shook his head. *No, you don't. So listen up. Do not ever give up that hope. The same way I know that one day I'll find her, I kill her, eat a good meal, and come back here to 312. And there's another reason, your brain. These other men have nothing to think about all day except their past glories that put them here. They don't think about getting out because they all come back if they do. They don't have to worry about futures. I believe you do. I believe one day you'll be out of here and you must be ready, Billy. The third reason is that I'm an educated man and have shit in common with someone's empty head. So let's change that. It'll give you hope, the same way you beat the Cat. Good for you. But why do you think you did that? Because somewhere in that high school head of yours you hope or believe you'll get out, that someone will do something decent, and for that you must do more to be ready.*

Billy thought a long while, John waited.

Educated in what? Breaking out? Think the warden will let me practice pole vaulting?

More silence.

John shrugged. *I don't know*, though he continued speaking in unison with his hands out of habit. *Ask him. Personally, I'd prefer walking out. The difference is, you won't come back.*

Billy Rider knew when to stop being Billy. Anderson didn't have too many buttons to push. *Then, social work. I guess. I think I could like that, if you care to tell me how. I don't have books and I don't have a work pass. You got that figured out?*

Actually you do. Before you pissed off the warden with your handshake, I lined you up as Battle View's newest barber. So don't be a smart-ass. Not a big deal. No one in here's got hair. So you can't really fuck up. Either way, I need you out of my cell a few hours each day for some private time. And you're welcome.

You really think someone out there is that decent, like the two girls who fucked me, laughed at me, and really fucked me over by not helping to defend me? They could have made all this someone else's problem, John...like their brothers.

Yes, them. And so must you.

Anderson stood, muttering something as he left.

I didn't catch that.

That's right, you didn't.

*

The warden couldn't care less than he did, approving the home-study once Rider had earned sufficient money to buy his own books, telling Anderson he was wasting his time. The kid was not getting out.

But now, approaching his twenty-first year in 312, one very long row of books in the library was his alone, books he had paid for as Battle View's barber longest standing barber. Education set men apart. Yes indeed, he mused, being that, since John's freedom, he no longer had anyone to talk with.

All that seemed so blurred into one timeframe, a seamless lifetime. So much studying, their last night dissolving into lights out with incredible and unwanted speed.

Billy didn't believe him. He didn't believe Anderson would kill her and didn't believe he would ever see his mother again. Sometimes John could be a real shithead.

You won't really kill her, John. He signed. *You and I know that. You're free. You're not coming back.*

Leaving here doesn't make anyone free, Billy, except you. John glanced out at other cons milling around, some of them with thumbs up, others nodding a con's version of "goodbye." They only ever read each other's words in the library or in complete privacy. *You're the exception, and you are getting out. You must believe that, and when your day does come do not mess up. You get that job you believe you will never have. You find your family and you forget about who and what put you in here. By the way, refresh my memory, they were who again... Rigby and Carlton?*

Dwight and Jackson... Jake. The lesbian sisters were Darlene and Eleanor. Thanks for stirring up memories.

Think they're still in Necessity?

The guys, probably. The girls, who knows? Who cares? They probably got married to guys who didn't mind fucking pink sewers. They were pretty busy back then.

I remember the stories.

John, you don't forget your promise. Please find my mom. Please. You call her. You tell her I'm good in here, and brag about me a little. Let her know I'm sorry, you know, for fucking up so badly. He chuckled quietly. *Just don't tell her who with.*

You didn't. They fucked you. Big time. And I don't forget promises. So yeah, the whore is very dead...after I take care of your mom. She comes first.

Anderson held out his hand. *This is it, kid. Glad we met. That said, let's not get all kissy and wet-eyed tomorrow. I'm walking out and I am not looking back. You got that?* The men shook hands. *Have hope, Billy. And that's what I'll be telling your mother. Your day is coming and you make damn sure you're ready. Because you are leaving this place.*

Sally Cutter, John. Necessity, North Carolina. Sally and Sam Cutter. Don't let me down.

What, kid? You think I'm deaf and dumb or something? He slapped Billy's shoulder. *Goodbye, Billy. Been good knowing you.*

So many weeks, months and years of signing and talking abruptly ended that last the night when John leapt onto his bunk for the last time, stretching out, facing into the wall without showing the slightest excitement about the coming day.

Not a day or night had passed in his twenty years that Billy hadn't thought about his mom and dad, imagining his brothers as successful surgeons. And Lucy, missing her. Beyond that he never dwelled on the passage of time, passing one day at a time in the mess hall, the yard, or in the library the days that rain interfered with his workouts.

Birthdays hadn't for years crept into his thoughts, too closely linked to what remained of his life. Nor did he dwell on Rigby and Carlton. Not since the last time six, seven, however many years earlier, when he silently spoke to John in detail about them, about how they'd laughed at him in court, about what they had said. Until, out of the blue, John mentioned their names again the previous night, reminding him to have hope, reminding him who put him in Battle View.

Yeah, John could sure as hell stir up shit sometimes.

So he was educated, certified by the state to teach, so what? The very state that convicted him of a murder he did not commit. That one night in Necessity destroyed his life. What was John thinking with all his talk about hope? What hope? What did John ever imagine freedom would bring to a convicted rapist and killer, a future indelibly stained in narrow minds by a past impossible to explain and even more impossible for anyone to believe?

Who would dare to hire him with that lingering doubt, to teach children otherwise preordained by fate to live in silent misery?

And women, a woman, any woman? Who would want him, believing that he'd murdered poor Lucy, not to mention the undeniable proof of his guilt etched permanently onto his back that would eclipse any state pardon? No. The question was academic. His life was Battle View, the raw company of rude men whose idea of good manners was flushing before they stood. Some of them.

As for women, he scarcely remembered how one might look naked, having completely forgotten how he had felt that moonlit night at the end of a dirt road watching them strip away their short dresses, their underwear and shoes as they taunted him, urging him to play with them, standing so close as one pulled at his shirt and tie and the other pushed his pants to the ground.

He remembered John long ago commiserating with him, telling him where one day, once he was free, he might find a good whore at a good price if he needed to reacquaint himself with the process that badly and not be worried about banal conversation.

John had always talked about freedom, about never giving up hope. Almost as often as he spoke about finding his wife, about killing the whore who was so beautiful in the photo that John never let fade. Billy didn't think he ever knew the woman's name.

He wasn't jealous of John. He missed the man already, remembering the terror of his first night. How frightened he was of John, and with good reason, his second day of learning, and the beating that helped save his life.

He was disappointed though, that John hadn't turned to wave farewell after they had become so close, particularly since they would never again see each other. He hadn't even gone to the mess for breakfast.

At 7:00 AM sharp he left the cell as though nothing had changed, speaking with no one. He spent time alone in the yard with Black Boss, was taken to the warden's office, and was gone.

John had promised him that he would be back, a man of his word, adding with a bizarre smirk on his face, "in time to pass each other at the gate, Billy, on your way out," though Billy didn't believe for a moment that his friend would kill his wife. Or that he would ever see John again.

Even the other cons noticed the snub, Billy not believing for a moment that his life would change for the better in John's benevolent dream of his freedom. That was John's way, never pessimistic, never counting down to the day that had come to him at last.

Anyway, in the morning he would show the new guy around. Cells had rules, his rules, and one of them was pissing somewhere else. Not his problem.

Twenty

1957 - 58

Returning to Charleston from West Palm Beach into his sixth week of freedom was monotonous. The highway was dark with nothing to see. Together with the reflective streaks of silver lane dividers, the glow from his dashboard was hypnotic, the hours spent stretching and yawning, shaking his head and talking to the vacant seat beside him in an effort to forego the thrill of crashing into a ditch, an abutment or wherever else his brain might choose to fall asleep.

Twenty years was a long time to spend with another being in close quarters, closer than any wife or girlfriend. His once precious free time was when Billy was shaving heads, and even then men were always crammed into the yard or milling around outside his cell. Yet, now, in a way, his nighttime hours were lonely, almost too quiet.

"I had the strongest urge to jump the gate and drown her, Billy. Upside down. Not too deep, mind you, so I could see her face. Or, more to the point, that she could see mine. She has to see my face, Billy. She has to share my joy, my dream. She has to know that I'm the one. Otherwise what is the point?"

"She could have screamed rape. Would have solved a lot of problems. Would have been a kind gesture. Don't you think? We'd be divorced, she'd be the rich whore she is today, and I'd be the hero husband. I'd be retired and gazing out from *my* private beachfront patio instead of spying into hers. I should have killed her that night, Billy. Big mistake. I have to say, she was quite a sight stamping her feet, all naked and sweaty, her face soaked with tears, her running back and forth holding her head, ranting, asking what I had done, what I was doing. Well, I was calling the cops. Someone had to deal with the mess."

"Never run from a problem, Billy. Face it straight on. Serious shit doesn't go away. I stood there, watching her tantrum, watching her naked, the sirens getting louder. I didn't care if she didn't. I mean, what the hell! Though I did suggest that she get into her panties to answer the door. Which she did, I would have to say, very eagerly. Go figure. Come on in, boys. That's when I realized I'd messed up. That's when I told her."

"I'd become a public enemy the way she'd made herself public property. All that "get down!" shit, Billy, that's real. A little dramatic, though, and when you don't they don't know what to do. I turned. Simple as that. Game over."

"I can't imagine those six and a half years; me thinking I had the prettiest wife in the world, the sexiest, while she mocked and scorned me each night, telling me she loved me, that she missed me, that she wanted me home in her arms and in our bed. Then leaving each night to fuck total strangers. Never did find out where all that money went. She got paid, Billy; I know she did."

"I still have time though. Five weeks and a day. That's your day, Billy. No need to rush, no need to spoil things. I kept my promise about Sally, and I'm sorry about Sam. I suspect you'll know yourself in a short while. I hope so, Billy, since I really do not want to see you again. Battle View is my destiny, not yours, kid."

"What I need to know, what I was never told by her or anyone else, is why the whore married me in the first place. I mean, goddamn, what was she thinking?"

"Fate, Billy. Destiny. I was meant to kill du Valois the

same way I was meant to meet you, to get you educated and set you free. Five weeks and a day, Billy. That's your destiny, and I do mean to set you free."

"What was she thinking, Billy?" What the hell was she thinking?"

*

John Anderson experienced no awkward moment at Baggage Claim in Miami. He kissed her cheek and hugged her. He wanted to set the mood for the Tuesday, promising to call her Friday to confirm.

Monday morning he called his West Coast clients, rescheduling their appointments to early November. The rest of his week he spent clearing his desk of recurring and delinquent paperwork, welcoming the relative reprieve, calling Brenda early Friday evening before she left for class.

Yes, Tuesday was most definitely good. She wouldn't think of cancelling. Excellent. He'd made reservations at the Stork Club for an unforgettable evening of elegant dining and dancing, he promised her. She couldn't wait. She was certainly anxious to see him again.

Tuesday, October 22, 1957 was a beautiful, warm, and moonlit night on Miami's South Beach. He arrived at her building on time, at 7:00, holding a delicate corsage for her wrist, a white boutonnière enhancing his lapel.

Brenda strutted from the elevator with a smile, allowing a kiss on her cheek, letting him decorate her wrist. To anyone passing by they were the quintessential couple. To John they were perfect together, he believed. And Brenda had thought all week that he might have a chance. She hoped.

However first dates then were the forerunners to a future, to more important and long-lasting testing, or an immediate closure to failure.

How would she sit, how would she talk, and about what? How would she eat? Would she jab at her succulent meal with weapons scooped from the setting, or decide on each morsel as though selecting a unique experience she would savour? Or would she eat with her elbows on the table, waving her weapons in the air, a mannerism of the day considered by many as urbane and quite chic, one he considered quite impolite and foretelling of closure.

Despite first-night jitters, John Anderson was certain the evening would bode well.

Or would he drink too much and embarrass her? He hadn't on the plane, so what? He could be a complete fake, a genteel exterior while drunk and disorderly on the inside, an intoxicated and stupefied mind bent on manipulating his woman, her...once she became his woman?

She didn't know. How could she? Yet she didn't believe so. What she saw in John was the ideal man, ideal for her, more convinced as he held open the door of his car.

The Stork Club was alive with couples dancing, couples sitting at linen covered tables; the ladies in elegant eveningwear sipping their tall drinks through straws, the men in formal attire swirling the ice in their scotches and whiskeys.

Brenda's black-blue satin dress showed as much of her breasts as she wanted him to see, the soft swells scented and creamed, the hem a daring hand-width above her knees for the times. Yet natural for her, intended to ensure his distraction. His black suit, snow-white shirt, silk tie and good looks ensured hers. He was much taller and more muscular, no less effusive and no less attentive than Jean-François, and every bit as handsome.

He ordered for her, eloquently, speaking casually with the Latin waiter in Spanish, not once referring to the menu. She was impressed. The same way she had loved the grace and the elegance of dining with Jean-François in Paris. The best of both possible worlds, she mused, her own linguistic skill limited to at long last erasing the dust of Nebraska from her speech.

Though she did suspect that he was a good deal less wealthy, despite First-Class travel, which was fine. If she would, in fact, require a husband one day, which she increasingly believed she might, she would want and she would need one with a demanding and lucrative job…and his was ideal.

From then on they saw each other on Saturdays and the occasional Sunday, excepting the week leading up to Christmas when she and her colleagues attended a two-day weekend conference for which the distinguished historian, le Professeur du Valois, had travelled from Paris earlier in the week to present his findings.

Still, they bought each other Christmas gifts and spent the day together in Coral Gables, Brenda not yet comfortable with staying over, the temptation of giving her body to him too great. What if they didn't work out? She didn't know. She needed more time, and he gave it to her. He could wait; he was infatuated with her.

They spent New Year's together dancing at the Stork Club and he bought her a pendant on Valentine's. In April he wanted to fly her to New York to see the Easter Parade and attend a Broadway show; she refused. She couldn't possibly spare the time, what with her daytime and evening classes so near to her year-end. Her workload was simply too crushing. He understood.

Yet Brenda changed her mind not many days later, surrendering to her feelings. Her growing affection for him was now an undeniable love, fearing that he might soon lose interest her if she didn't act soon upon her true feelings. She called him, to his heart's delight, saying "yes, yes, sweetheart, let's go. And sweetheart…I love you," she gulped, "I do, and I'm trusting you not to hurt me."

That's what John knew, not for an instant thinking he should get the hell away or run for his life. Or that his countdown had begun, that a Manhattan hotel room would very soon seal his fate…and hers.

She had never uttered those words, not to John, not to anyone. She felt that letting his lips touch hers when saying goodnight was enough, fully aware that her time was drawing near. He was twenty-six, primed, and exceedingly eligible. He wouldn't wait forever and, when he asked why she sounded upset, she replied that she was upset with herself for being incredibly silly, for being afraid, and for making excuses when she really did love him.

The next day a dozen red roses arrived at her door. The note simply read: *We love each other.*

What he didn't know was that the previous day, strutting her way to the restaurant, late again for work, a young woman dressed in a green halter top and red flared shorts held out a restaurant menu to Brenda. She was smiling, she was sexy, telling Brenda that from four to six ladies' drinks were half price.

Her boss had reached the melting point, fed up with her antics and demands. She wasn't the only girl with long legs, a tight ass and tanned knockers on the street. As she might have noticed on her way in, or would on her way out. He didn't give two hoots what she did on her time off, with whom or how often. If she wanted to die young that was her business. What he needed, all he cared about, was a girl who wanted to work in his restaurant and do a better job than the girl across the street.

He wished her luck and never saw her again.

She was delighted, once the intense and foreign shock of rejection wore off, before which she wanted to stab him, miffed for a few days that she hadn't shocked him instead. She no longer needed the restaurant. She hadn't for months. Her client list was extensive, many of them regulars, never-ending referrals constantly adding to her inventory of men. What she truly lacked was time.

After her first experience with Jean-François she put her notepads aside, destroying them. She replaced them with date books, those times and identities transcribed meticulously into beautifully leather-bound agendas where she elaborated on their penchants, their descriptions, their professions, their frequency and her fees. She also began keeping ledgers.

Truth be told, he did her a favour. He'd made her independent. Now her most important quest was to become John Anderson's devoted and loving wife.

*

Brenda had always dreamed of seeing New York City, the iconic statue, scanning the streets of Manhattan from atop the Empire State Building and shopping at Macy's.

Easter 1958 was all that and more. She saw Broadway and sailed across to Staten Island in her latest spring wardrobe. She made love for the first time with the man whom she adored, his face beaming with pride, his first and subtle probes and kisses urging bashful squeals, her flushed face buried into his chest.

His touch was gentle, unhurried; Brenda uncertain what he might expect of *her* hands. She didn't know. She flinched ever so slightly as he drew back the blankets, making her vulnerable, pulling her tenderly and without any effort fully onto his body, guiding her knees, letting her rest there until she was ready.

Brenda wanted to hide under her lustrous hair cascading between them. He wouldn't let her. He needed to see her, to see her chocolate-brown eyes open wide or squeeze shut, to hear her first telling gasp, the theft of her breath that could never happen twice in her lifetime.

Brenda closed her eyes, leaning forward, nodding as she placed her hands on his shoulders, letting him guide her. She was holding her breath, sensing his pressure on her hips, sinking deliberately into place, the sensation so foreign to her, suddenly so eager, sinking suddenly deeper, her body jolting, her eyes flaring open, surprising him with the sweet air rushing from her mouth warming his face.

Her full weight was on him, slowly rocking, following

his lead to a crescendo of groans, an urgent crushing of bodies, her intensity mounting, matching his, her explosion wild and unbridled. She lost all control, her body convulsing, coming too close to launching herself from their epicentre, sinking John deeper into the mattress before she collapsed onto him securely locked in place and depleted.

"John, wow!"

"Yeah, wow. You're beautiful, Brenda. I mean, you are really beautiful. I meant what I wrote in those flowers."

She wiggled her hips, giggling. "I suppose I'm officially stuck on you too, so to speak. I love you, and not merely because I'm feeling ripped apart."

She smiled coquettishly.

"What?"

"Nothing. All I'm saying is that I'm glad that I waited for you, that I could give you something so special to me." She kissed him, pulling away, squirming and bouncing from the bed. "I love the way you smell, but I'm taking a shower. I think Chanel is a better choice for dinner. Don't you?"

He didn't.

She padded from sight, locking the door out of habit, John thought. That would soon change.

When she stepped out she was wrapped in a towel, for all the good it did.

He was next, taking with him fresh clothes, not locking the door.

When he came out she was dressed and ready for dinner. She couldn't imagine a better catch. Absolutely all her girlfriends would be envious of her, once she met them. Until then she would make do.

John had arranged with the hotel's concierge for reservations at Le Bâfreur for the occasion about to change Brenda's life, the maître d' himself taking charge of their evening.

As a prelude to dinner they celebrated her coming out

with a bottle of Mumm Cordon Rouge Brut '49. The creamed celery potage was complemented with a chilled Pouilly-Fuissé, their shared Chateaubriand accompanied by a full-bodied Margaux '51 as they danced between courses.

Brenda could still feel the pulsating sensation he'd created inside her. She believed she couldn't possibly adore him anymore than she did at that moment, her head nestled against his chest, her body held captive in the warmth of his arms, each passing moment proving her wrong.

She purred. She could imagine her entire life with him, groaning in misery at the end of the song.

He had to ask her, and he would. Or she would shut him down hard that evening, give him a reality check and possibly a double bill for her services and wasting her time.

He pulled out her chair, signalling the waiter as he sat.

"Sweetheart, I feel...I don't know, dizzy, wonderful, so much in love."

"Then marry me, Miss Brenda. Be Mrs. John Anderson, if only for a lifetime."

"What?" She brought a delicate curtain of mahogany-tipped fingers to her mouth. "Sweetheart, please, don't be rash. We haven't even slept together."

He chortled. "Short-term memory loss at your tender age? I sort of think we have."

"No. Not a euphemism. That was absolutely fantastic. I meant literally. You have no idea how I'll look in the morning without my make-up. I'm not a morning person, sweetheart. I can be very grumpy. I'm afraid you might hate me."

"That is impossible. I could never hate you, or hurt you that way. At least think about it over dessert. Promise me?"

She gazed into her lap, demurely, then into his eyes. "Yes, sweetheart. I promise. I do."

"Good. Then I won't say another word. No pressure."

The white-gloved maître d' came with his cart, addressing John in French.

Brenda was entranced, fascinated as he worked his magic preparing their cerises-jubilées, striking his match, Brenda's mouth opening wide into an animated smile at the blue flame spreading across the platter of deep-purple cherries and ice cream, flickering.

"Sweetheart, I've never seen such an exquisite dessert." Not since my last night in Paris with Jean-François. "How delightful." She clapped her palms together in gleeful praise.

The maître d' acknowledged her tribute to his presentation with a bow, serving Brenda, then John, bowing once more before walking away.

The couple devoured the decadent indulgence in silence, Brenda once in a while looking up to see John entirely unperturbed by her quiet composure. When she placed her spoon onto her plate he signalled his co-conspirator, the two men excluding Brenda from their brief exchange.

The maître d' returned again with his trolley, his demeanor solemn, serving Brenda a Rèmy Martin, and John, placing a silver plate draped with a white linen serviette between them. The two men nodded, the maître d' bowing to Brenda before stepping away.

"Sweetheart, the evening couldn't be any lovelier. I'm delirious."

"Or you, Brenda." He raised his snifter. "To beauty."

"Thank you, sweetheart."

John reached for the linen, letting the small blue velvet box beneath catch her eye. He paused, teasing her, sipping his cognac, reaching once more for the serviette, this time opening the box.

Brenda stared at the titanium band crowned with a diamond. "Sweetheart…"

"So, Professor Peters, how exactly will we change your name on your diploma, or do we?"

"Sweetheart, it's too extravagant. Are you sure about this? Shouldn't we …?"

"I couldn't be more certain, or more in love. The question is Brenda…are you certain?"

She gulped, bringing her snifter to her lips. The amber liquid burned her throat. The time was right. Now, or possibly never. He couldn't be a more ideal and timely solution. She would soon need a means of substantiating her lifestyle, her home, her car and her wardrobe. When might the next time be that Mr. Right would happen along, and why had she spent six months grooming him? "Yes, sweetheart, I'm sure. I want to become Professor Brenda Anderson. I want you in my life forever." Yes! Yes!

"And we agree that kids are on the backburner?"

"As previously and theoretically discussed, yes we do. Besides, sweetheart, I've just today learned to enjoy what can go into me; I'm in no hurry whatsoever, if ever, to see what can come out. God, no!"

She held out her hand. The ring was a perfect fit as a parade of tuxedoed men circled the table, the gloved hands applauding the future Professor Brenda Anderson, alias Mrs. John Anderson.

Twenty-One

1958 - 59

Charleston was thirty minutes away, Brenda managing to keep him awake. That one night in Paris was more than reason enough to kill her, he mused.

"The whore had the audacity to tell the court she'd been with another man throughout our entire honeymoon, Billy. Him. Du Valois."

"What kind of man does that, Billy, fucks another man's bride? A wife? Things happen. That I can understand. But a bride, what kind of woman does that? And I'm the one who goes to prison?"

"Can't get over it, not after all these years. That dreamy look on her face, her open arms each night, me thinking I married the last virgin left in the entire country, all the while making heated love to a public gutter for seven years. Seven years, Billy, dipping and soaking in other men's shit."

"I'm thinking I'll shoot her, Billy. Something fast and easy. Or stab her first. Then I'd have her attention for what, ten, fifteen minutes? Get the best bang for my buck. Think that's long enough? Thing is, if I choke her, which has certain merit, she might talk me out of it. She has a voice like honey, Billy."

"Anyway, first things first, like getting the right tools for the job. Black Boss, his cousin's got things ready in The Swamp. I just have to get there, two days I don't have. I'm tired, Billy. I haven't been this tired since they arrested me, when they kept me up all night asking the same damn stupid questions. Why did I kill him? Why didn't I just leave?"

"I don't know, John."

"That's not cool, Billy. Answering? That's not good. I need to know I'm not losing my mind."

"What was the mystery about a naked man in *my* bed fucking *my* wife that was so difficult to understand? Sort of a no-brainer, don't you think?"

"She was good. I'll admit that. On the other hand, given the choice, I've got to believe the Frenchman, if he had had the slightest suspicion, would have left early or stayed home. Talk about the wrong place at the wrong time."

"Destiny, Billy, like her floating upside-down in a pool. Peaceful for her, quiet for me. She never did like the sight of blood. A win-win, really. Don't you think, Billy?
*

When John suggested during the flight home that they one day soon fly to Nebraska to meet Polly and Walter, since he was marrying their daughter, Brenda flat out refused. She would absolutely never again step foot in Nebraska…"sweetheart."

Calling her mother as soon as she arrived home in Miami, before meeting her client for dinner, was painful enough. However Mrs. Peters was certain her daughter would soon change her mind about raising a family of her own.

Brenda was heartbroken. She wouldn't see her fiancé until the weekend, when he was invited for dinner Saturday evening and stayed over. Sunday dinner was in suburbia when she drove home before dark, leaving John to pack for an early Monday flight.

They agreed. They would live together as soon as possible and to hell with public opinion. Her parents wouldn't have to know and neither one of them had close friends. She found her collegiate peers boring, and he was seldom at home long enough to make friends.

She would not live in suburbia behind a white picket fence, she insisted. Then what, aprons and a clothesline? He understood. And he couldn't live in a one bedroom apartment no matter how spacious, no matter how spectacular or private the view might be. She agreed, insisting that the view and her access to the beach were non-negotiable.

The following weekend the search began in earnest, lasting through to mid-June when John put his home up for sale and Brenda advised her landlord not to renew the lease.

Their home was now a fourteenth-floor, seaside penthouse which they purchased, well beyond budget yet doable with a down payment financed with John's inheritance and the sale of his house. They moved in almost immediately, each agreeing to start their new life together with new furnishings. No history. No questions or lingering doubts.

Her quandary in recent weeks, however, was twofold. The first was John. She couldn't possibly come home to him dressed as someone's seductive mistress the week nights he chose not to travel. The other were her numerous venues. She was increasingly too familiar to the reception staff and concierges at many or most of the five-star hotels since her clients were uniquely men of distinction. She needed her own place which would give her the anonymity and the freedom to increase her clientele and her fees in line with European rates since du Valois had sent her a good number of new clients.

A week later, when John was in Madrid, Brenda located another beachfront condo in South Beach within an easy walk to her spa and by his return she had the place furnished with a flair that would appeal to her male clientele and, in particular, Jean-François du Valois.

No longer restrained by the restaurant she was free and

able to increase her flow of traffic, making better use of her afternoons while keeping her mornings for her treatments at the spa and her weekends free for herself and her future husband.

The upscale and more intimate ambiance with a feeling of home would afford her clients so many extra benefits. She could now offer them complimentary and premium bar service. She would no longer arrive with them from dinner, or knock on their doors to simply undress for them. She would greet them fashionably in fine dresses, costumes or lingerie or nothing at all. She could extend her services to satisfying their appetites on her private balcony or in her designer bathroom, and they would be the ones to leave.

She was excited, by Christmas entertaining some nine or ten gentlemen each week, her monthly transfers from her safety deposit box to Switzerland approaching eight grand after two thousand in rent, wardrobe expenses and booze. her car and her household contribution to John who had a better sense of finance. More than John earned in a year. promising him that after the wedding she would no longer teach evening classes, with the understanding however that she would continue with her summer classes and might occasionally be required as a substitute.

John thought she was pouting, disappointed by his intrusion into her life's work. He wasn't wrong. She wasn't at all pleased at the prospect of a twenty-five percent decrease in her revenues, from then on speaking with du Valois a few weeks in advance of his tentative travels to the US to coordinate his schedule with John's.
*

The wedding was days away, the couple arriving in Paris on December 27th to hotel suites on different floors. She was adamant. The groom could plead all he wanted, he would not see her naked again or touch her until her wedding night.

Her parents arrived a day later, anxious to meet their

211

son-in-law. They had done what Brenda had asked of them when, weeks earlier, she sent them a money order with specific instructions of where to go and what to buy in order to minimize her embarrassment.

She wanted a simple French wedding on New Year's Eve, nothing extravagant; John once venturing to ask what was so simple about flying to Paris and finding a protestant cleric at that time of year.

She ignored him. All he had to do was buy a new suit, be there on time, and say "I do."

She would take care of the rest. She wanted to drink champagne on the Eiffel Tower at midnight with her husband, and she would. In fact, she had called her friend and colleague in Paris, whom John had never met, who had immediately volunteered to assist her with the planning. Unfortunately Jean-François would be skiing with his family in the Pyrenees, he and his wife naturally devastated that they would miss their dear friend's finest moment.

When du Valois left her South Beach hideaway a month earlier he promised to fulfill her entire list of wishes. He thought her plan was magnificent, far superior to demeaning herself, wasting her life and her natural skills on students who would amount to nothing. As for John, he told her, for a woman to have a single ardent lover, or to bathe in the pleasure of a different and devoted lover each night, what was the real difference? The body and the heart would forever work at cross-purposes. Such was the nature of man and of woman. N'est pas, petite chérie?

On their second evening John invited her parents to dinner, the conversations seamless. He found them delightful. On the third day he introduced them to a Paris they hadn't seen a year earlier, ending the evening at the Folies Bergères where Brenda thought she might quite possibly die when her father commented that he hadn't thought to see that many attractive female bottoms in his lifetime.

On the thirtieth the men were left to their own devices. Brenda needed breathing room. She was suffocating. She sent her mother to the hotel's hair salon and she escaped, returning late in the day to her private suite, ordering room service and spending a quiet evening alone.

Jean-François had happily and eagerly taken the day off work, reassuring her that nothing would change. He adored her entirely. He and certain of his associates would most certainly continue to require her charming company and delightful services, reassuring her further and more concretely when he reserved her for the week of the twelfth and paid her in advance before quickly and expertly taking her mind off the following day.

Married women, he told her, "are the most desirable companions of any man."

December 31st was brilliant and crisp, their feet crunching the packed and pristine snow as the bride walked with her father to the open doors of the chapel as the sun was setting over the ancient steeple. The bride's mother went earlier with the groom.

He was dashing and such a gentleman. He paid attention to her, listened to her. Since meeting him she didn't feel at all like "mother" or "the missus" or "the wife over there." She was Miss Polly and more than a little envious of her daughter whom she was learning to dislike.

Brenda wore dark green suede winter boots, a woollen cape and a close-fitting woollen cloche in the same shade of green. Her wedding dress wasn't a dress at all, and she wasn't wearing white, which immediately shocked her mother. She wore pale green satin shorts that were flared with cuffs and a sheer green blouse with three-quarter sleeves that served no purpose whatsoever other than its colour over a darker green three-quarter bra.

Mrs. Peters was speechless. She didn't know which was worse, the fact that her daughter was exposing her undergarments meant for her new husband's eyes alone, or her entirely exposed thighs, standing before them in a House of God so scandalously naked.

Brenda replied, "Mother, get real. We're in Paris. You know, the fashion capital, and these are not scandalous. They're pantyhose and I'm one of the first to wear them, me, your daughter. You might even see them in Nebraska in fifty years. They're new and they're chic and, the best part, I never have to wear panties again."

That piece of news caused her father's mouth to drop open, wisely agreeing with the wife, as one would expect; the groom agreed with the bride. The minister had no comment.

Minutes later he pronounced them "man and wife, for better or worse, till death do you part," and they went for dinner.

John ordered champagne, refusing to let the father of the bride pay. The two couples later strolled to the Eiffel Tower to welcome in the New Year with a second bottle; the old folks retiring early to the hotel. They were going home, Polly without a gift from her daughter a week from her forty-sixth birthday, Walter anxious for fresh air and a thick steak that actually looked like one and wasn't buried under what he could only describe as bull's cream.

Mr. and Professor Anderson began their honeymoon dancing and kissing their way into 1959. He could not have been prouder of his new wife. Nor could Brenda have been more pleased by other men's candid appreciation of her, and their women's open envy of her avant-garde ensemble, the adoring couple's cloud nine evaporating on the twelfth when his honeymoon ended and hers began anew.

"Sweetheart, don't worry. Go to work, I've got plenty of things to keep me busy."

"Be careful. These Frenchmen, they're a pretty smooth bunch."

"And they also help to pay our bills, sweetheart. So go, please. I'll be fine."

He did, promising no later than 6:00 when he would devote his evening entirely to her.

She kissed him goodbye, already missing him.

Closing the door she waited a moment before dialling. "Jean-François, it's me. He's gone. I'll be ready in an hour. And, Jean-François, we have to talk. I really need your advice."

*

John pulled into his building's parking lot at 3:35 AM Sunday. "Man and wife, my ass. Man and whore more like it, Billy. She gets the better and I get Battle View with a bonus for kicking Cleaver's ass. No justice there, kid, at least not till death do we part. Payback."

John stared at the passenger seat covered with wrappers, snorting. "Goodnight, Billy. We'll talk again soon. when it's time for you to come home."

Twenty-Two

1991

John managed to arrive at work on time, dead asleep in his bed by 8:00 Sunday evening.

He was one of the company's top performers, one of the strongest men. He was the most charming to the clients' wives and mothers without the slightest false claim of being a gentleman. Because he was one. He hadn't once let himself forget what was once so integral to him.

Still, he was a mover. He was faceless, viewed as an unskilled worker, a bottom-feeder on the social ladder and he didn't much enjoy the feeling. He didn't enjoy sweat running down his face and his back. He didn't like that his shirt was always damp, a brown shirt with his name decaled in yellow on one pocket so that no one need bother to ask him, the company logo on the other, clinging to his back when once he wore fine suits and ties.

In particular he didn't like working twelve-hour days and sleeping ten.

He didn't think himself better than the others, even though he was. He had a bachelor's in commerce and a master's in marketing with international experience. Their experience was pretty much limited to the inside of banks or the homes of innocent victims and, most obviously, jail cells. How they ended their days in taverns or strip bars, he had no idea. Nor did he care.

Throughout the week he became increasingly agitated

with himself. What was he doing, and why? He had no one to answer to. He had no parole officer because he wasn't on parole. He was free. And that was the problem.

Hidden in his apartment and car he had as much cash as he would bring home in two years, with considerably less time left to him in which to keep his promises and make things right. So why not in the meantime rekindle Mr. John Anderson as well? Why the hell not? Why was he wasting his short-lived liberty with ex-cons inevitably working their way back to prison or jail when he was better than that?

He had no good answer, when once countless barons of industry would seek his sage advice.

He resigned Friday at the end of his shift, thanking the man sincerely for all that he'd done. He didn't have to explain. His boss understood. Anderson had to reshape his life, somehow find the man he once was, and he wouldn't succeed at thirty K a year plus five-dollar tips. He had to find a better way, leaving signed proof with the man of payment in full for the Monte Carlo.

That night he donned boots, jeans, his best sweater, and went for dinner to a finer restaurant. He passed a spa, stopping to reserve time and services on Saturday.

Saturday, refreshed after a massage, facial and manicure, he went to a haberdasher where he was fitted with dress shoes to match his two new suits, a half-dozen shirts and ties. He bought more slacks, sweaters and casual sports jackets. That evening again finding his way to a fine meal, pleased with the day, though amazed that the cost of dressing like a gentleman had quadrupled. Money well-spent.

Sunday he went to the beach to strategize, to probe all possible liabilities, create practical solutions and solidify a course of action which he would update as required.

He was two days into June, worried. His fault for wanting to see the whore. Change of plans. He would do The Swamp Monday through Thursday, providing him with

217

inadequate rest in Charleston on Friday, putting him in Necessity Friday night with not much choice.

He needed what Black Boss had done for him, but doing Charleston to New Orleans in two days was impossible, if not outright stupid, counterproductive, and he didn't want to die on the road trying. Too far. He didn't want to fuck up. Not now. He wasn't thirty anymore. Besides, Cleaver's cousin might have a different timetable, be out of town, unreachable. He didn't know. He hadn't yet spoken with the man.

He did that evening, the timing convenient for both men. Once properly outfitted he would be good to go. Do some catching up. Not have to run himself ragged by jamming everything into weekends. With his weeks free he could breathe a little. Time was on his side.

He departed Charleston Monday morning at 9:30, first renting a safety deposit box at his bank to secure what he didn't require for the trip. He didn't have a credit card and hadn't known what that was until the bank refused him the day he went with his ex-boss to open an account. He was all about cash. The other reason was that he had no reason to trust Cleaver's cousin. He and Cleaver were good, in prison, evenly matched. But who was to say his jaw wasn't a persistent sore memory.

Maybe he was being set up.

He stayed Monday night in Tallahassee, Tuesday night in New Orleans on the periphery of The French Quarter which wasn't French at all.

He stayed in his room, ordering room service. He never did like The Quarter, assailed by jazz worse than a jet engine, the crowds, the smell of urine at the edge of most lanes, Midwest housewives who once they arrived felt the inexplicable and urgent desire to transform their cheap tee-shirts and often not-so-nice titties into excited and beaded peepshows.

He didn't get the attraction and the only set of Midwest

tits he needed to see belonged to a Florida whore.

Wednesday morning "the man from Battle View' called Cleaver's cousin to confirm, agreeing they should meet on the corner of Canal Street and Bourbon.

When that Cleaver asked what he was wearing, Anderson said, "red sweater, blue slacks, blue shoes." When Anderson asked Cleaver, he replied, "a black Cadillac."

Anderson was to park his car wherever and stand on the southeast corner. An hour later the men met, John visibly taken aback as he eased into the front passenger side.

The Battle View Cleaver matched Anderson in height; now maybe fifteen, twenty pounds heavier. He was scarred, bald and ugly. He spoke AAVE, Black street slang, his arms and hands moving in spastic concert, shuffling along wherever he went as though one leg was shorter than the other, and you were either a "boy," or a "mothafucka," unless you once shattered his face and were from then on hyphenated with respect.

This Cleaver was the complete antithesis of the Black Block's boss. He greeted Anderson with an open hand. No gaudy jewellery cluttered his fingers, no gold held his teeth together. His suit didn't show a single crease; his shirt was crisp, his tie expertly knotted. The understated stainless steel Rolex was his single accessory. He spoke with a Southern drawl and was clearly educated, light-years from Battle View. The car was pristine, not a speck of dust and the radio was muted. They were meeting to do business.

The two men shared obviously failed first impressions.

"You are not what I was expecting, Mr. Fellows, and somewhat later than I anticipated. I was beginning to suspect you might have entertained second thoughts."

"Right man, wrong name. John Anderson."

"I'm afraid not, Mr. Fellows. You see, calls from Battle View are monitored. So when my cousin called on your behalf asking me to prepare your kit, he couldn't very well tell the entire world what precisely ex-con John Anderson required of me. So, with that in mind, welcome to New Orleans, Mr. Patrick Fellows. Pat to your friends, I'm sure. A solid name for a man of your persuasion, since no black man out of Battle View would have required my services."

"I don't understand. I asked for a gun and a pick set. That's it."

"My cousin thought otherwise."

"He gave me a price. Five grand. Part of the reason I was holding off. Cons don't get relocation expenses. I needed a while to regroup. That's all I've got on me."

"Which you naturally believed was expensive for a used gun. Am I correct?"

"Sort of."

"The price of your package stands, Mr. Fellows."

Anderson was silent, trying to make sense of what he was hearing. "He told me as I was leaving him, minutes before I walked out, 'Don't be no dumbass, John-boy. You out, you stay out. You got respect in here, hard-earned. You come back, you got to start over.' His exact words. What did he tell you?"

"Simply that I should expect a friend, that, yes, you were respected, a man of your word interested in chrome and pearl, some toothpicks, nose spray, the name of a good man and all that implies. That's all. I suspect you realize I'm paraphrasing."

"I got that impression. Do you accept cash?"

"As long as the ink's dry." Cleaver slowed to a red light.

Anderson reached into his pocket counting out fifty bills, placing the payment on the centre console. "Five grand, and what does one expect for five thousand, Mr. Cleaver? In English, please."

"The box is on the seat behind me, Mr. Fellows. No need for undue curiosity at this time, if you don't mind. I assure you, the quality of each piece is excellent. You have a clean chrome-plated nine mm complete with suppressor. Italian-made. Brand new with two clips and fifty rounds, tested by me. You have a ten-inch stainless steel stiletto with white pearl, a German-made precision lock pick set and a can of mace. The rest will be yours in approximately ninety minutes: Birth certificate and driver's permit. The real thing, not simply well-done, which will be duly registered this afternoon. Nor should you hesitate to obtain a passport whenever you might require one. You are now Patrick Fellows in a red sweater for the next five years, residing at any address of your choice…whenever he is in your best interest, including whenever your behavior behind the wheel might occasionally be perceived as conflicting with the State Highway Code."

"Patrick, thanks for that. I'm impressed." Anderson paused. "Mr. Cleaver, do you speak often with your cousin?"

"I'm a legitimate businessman, Mr. Fellows. You might say this part of me is a hobby, a lingering remnant of my past. When he went to prison I should have gone with him. I didn't. I found work cleaning toilets and floors and went to school most nights, the way he told me, trying to figure out my future while remaining somewhat incongruous at the back of the class for many years. My journey was long and difficult, though incredibly smooth compared to Battle View. You see, I had intended to join in the fray with him the night he killed those people. It was a gang thing. I was younger by many years and suitably impressed. I wanted to emulate him, to follow in his footsteps. That was the last time I laid eyes on him. Before leaving home he gave me a stern lecture. He hugged me. Then he struck me with such violent force that he knocked me unconscious for several hours. Because of him I now own several fine restaurants."

"You know, I always did suspect your cousin had a sensitive side."

Cleaver faced his passenger, smiling. "Which would

require a very liberal definition of the word. And, yes, I speak with him often."

"May I impose upon you, Mr. Cleaver, with another favour? Would you thank him for me? I am most deeply grateful for this…for Patrick Fellows. That was above and beyond, big time. Please tell him that in case, for some reason, I'm unable to. And would you ask him to tell the one who matters that I am well, that freedom day is fast approaching, and that I did keep my promise. He'll understand. Will you do that for me?"

"I will, rest assured. That said, Mr. Fellows, I sense an unnecessary conflict between my cousin's interpretation of your future and the one held by you. You are aware, are you not, of my other services?"

"I am."

"I would encourage you to bear that in mind. The cost is a good deal more. However we guarantee results and Patrick Fellows need never have existed. Nor would he require the tools of a new and intimidating trade, if I may presume that much. My associates are extremely expert in their field and in good conscience I must concur with my cousin's final words to you. We still have time to implement changes."

"My business is personal, Mr. Cleaver, a collision of destinies if you will. And very irreversible. Besides, my days would never be the same without your cousin's charming disposition. That connection alone should tell you that I'm far from intimidated."

"Then what of Mr. Fellows?"

"Patrick, thanks for that." He chuckled. "If he can assist me in some way, so much the better."

Cleaver nodded. "I wish you luck, Mr. Fellows, in whatever direction your journey takes you and for however long. In spite of which you have my number."

They drove on to a building Anderson cared not to remember, parting company not long after. He spent another night in Tallahassee, testing Patrick Fellows for the hell of it, deciding what, if anything, to do with the guy.

He arrived home late on Thursday, fully committed to living a more leisurely few weeks, to pacing himself and enjoying the time left to him. He wasn't unemployed, he was on vacation with no plans for Friday AM that didn't include sand, sun, a few cold beers and a myriad of unresolved questions before departing late in the day for dinner in Necessity.

Twenty-Three

1991

Friday, June 07th he slept in, rising at 9:00.

At the beach he didn't drink much. The truth was, after so many socially dry years, he was learning to drink all over again. Pacing himself. He'd begun drinking at eighteen, in college, the occasional one too many sky-rocketing to his head, moderation persevering prior to any exam and his fast-approaching eleventh hour was no different.

He spent much of the afternoon watching girls in bikinis pass by. Many snubbing him, or thinking they were. In fact he was maintaining a skill set, watching them talk, watching their lips berate other girls, their parents, or the popular hate of the day. They were important, walking too quickly, going nowhere, their make-up thick as pancakes on a sunny, 30° day in June on a white sandy beach.

And they were adults, important adults; smoking cigarettes and blowing blue smoke from between lips that were too pink or too red. They were experts, fashionable experts, holding them between two fingers in the heated air in a Boy Scout salute, dropping the butts into the sand and walking away.

He forgot them. He had his own snotty females to deal with. Twenty-three days remaining, one day more for Billy whom he chatted with on and off while driving north on the I-95.

Not many hours later Patrick Fellows checked-in to

Necessity's best four-star. The only one in town. He ambled around the town square killing time before dinner. Hotel rooms now seemed too much like cells, because they were, albeit somewhat more accommodating.

They always would be, he supposed.

Saturday, the eighth, he woke early, his adrenalin pumping. He was eager, so close. At the very worst he could find the whore again and pop her at his leisure, poof, poof, face to face, as long as she recognized who was pulling the trigger. He didn't have to be creative. What mattered more than saying goodbye to her in a pool was getting Billy out.

Again he strolled the town, asking questions that he, Rigby, might ask. He had lunch and went for a city tour zigzagging his way along the highlighted lines on his map past shopping malls, churches, schools and Rigby car lots brimming with activity en route to Meadowbrook Drive that wasn't much different than how he remembered the Savannah of his youth.

Huge oaks canopied the avenue-wide roadway without the eeriness of Spanish moss clinging to branches and leaves like sticky and self-perpetuating green webs. The street was lined with impressively large homes, modern, lacking the detailed craftsmanship and stateliness of Georgian manors. Not old money, not for generations to come. These homes were financial statements, proof of new money and lots of it. Or plain evidence of submissive and apprehensive husbands maintaining extravagant wives and obnoxious broods. Not his problem.

What he cared about was that the homes in Rigby's and Carlton's neighbourhood weren't glued together the way he'd expected. Since *they* seemed to be by their homes and their women.

Their homes were definitely upscale, identical after sunset, temples to the Joneses, the car salesman keeping up with the money-man, or the inverse, clearly each man maintaining expensive wives and likely as not assuming more debt.

The Rigby façade was white brick with white shutters framing wrought iron bars and tinted glass. The door was white with glossy black trim with white Georgian lamps on either side. The meandering walkway was delineated by manicured cedars seemingly too perfect, too formal, and more Georgian lamps. The top floor boasted five windows, the main floor displaying the door and four windows, the entire structure sitting in a platter of roses and other vibrant florae Anderson had no idea about.

The Carlton home boasted blue shutters, a blue door, and lack of originality, one home separated from the other by lush grass, fountains, and blue cedars carved into unnatural shapes filling a space sufficiently wide to allow for a third home. That was a good thing.

Getting into either would be an easy matter for any graduate of the U of BV.

At 4:05 a Mercedes sedan drove into the Rigby driveway. Through Anderson's Bushnells the man stepping out was dressed more like a yachtsman in his preppy blue blazer, blue shirt, tan Dockers and tasseled loafers than the heir to the throne of Rigby's Fine Motors with whom he would meet one day soon. Perhaps for a test drive. He had to work on that.

Rigby seemed not to have a care in the world, springing along like a teenager after his first piece of tail, not a hair out of place, his face beaming as the door opened wide.

She, whom he supposed was Eleanor, greeted him with a toothy smile, no less preppy in her coiffed hair, A-line skirt and high-collar blouse. Anderson wasn't seeing a rapist killer and teenage slut, he was watching The Donna Reed Show live and in colour. All that was missing was for her to raise a foot submissively behind her and kiss him.

No way! A loud burst of air burst through his nose. Miss Donna Reed, in person, the whole nine yards including "dear."

He held his imagination in check. The best strategies were borne of planning and incremental steps, not irrational dreams or the temptation to shoot them where they stood. No real satisfaction there. He was a strategist, and a good one. His plan was a living thing, a vital organism taking on a discernable shape that he would nurture and make flawless.

Anderson waited a few minutes before driving off. Bankers didn't work Saturdays. No need to waste time.

Sunday morning he arrived early in front of Carlton's, wondering why all church bells sounded the same. Weddings, funerals, or Sunday gatherings suited to individual needs or purposes, whether holy or wholly superficial, they all sounded the same.

The women stepped out from their white and blue doors first, Rigby and Carlton sealing their respective façades behind them. The couples waved at one another, smiling; the men doing what men do, opening doors. Anderson not at all surprised when Rigby pulled out first, slowing, waiting for Carlton to fall into formation. Each man entitled to demonstrate their individual successes to all who might see them and be filled with wonder.

No. He wasn't surprised. Big fish, small pond. Billy had that perfectly right.

A few street corners later the best friends were shaking hands and slapping backs, brothers were hugging sisters, and girlfriends were kissing. God must indeed be love, just not in Battle View. Love thy neighbour, ladies, which was what really peaked Anderson's curiosity.

Carlton had status in the community, family prestige. He was important. Rigby, he wasn't so sure. An inflated ego was more the case. Whatever the case might be church was an excellent venue for shaking hands and a few minutes later both men were with God's right-hand man in Necessity. Anderson agreed with them, the day was indeed glorious. Praise the Lord. Each man securing another hand to shake and back to slap before stepping inside.

The service ended at noon. More bells while the two men got a head start on the business week.

Carlton had a preppy stick up his ass. He was stiff, his smile disappearing each time the person he acknowledged disappeared, always glancing over his shoulder to see who was next in line: A client, maybe the cops. Like Rigby, probably constantly proving himself to daddy before taking over the reins. Or proving to himself that he was as good as Rigby.

They were the last to leave, Rigby shaking Carlton's hand; Darlene kissing Eleanor, each one hugging her brother.

Déjà vu. He thought, makes a man sad not having a family.

Anderson followed Carlton who trailed Rigby, the imports identical with matching high-gloss titanium glints. No surprise there from what Billy had told him, the lead car continuing on to the next driveway as Carlton slowed into his. Then a wave, and they were gone.

Anderson went for lunch, wondering if he'd toss his salad after witnessing the freak show whose final curtain he was about to draw closed.

He passed each home once an hour until five, twice ambling by for a slower, more studied surveillance. No signs of cameras. Nothing had changed, and nothing was worrisome. Each driveway had a Mercedes parked alongside a BMW. Bright red for the redhead, bright yellow for the blonde. Very Cute. Nor had anything changed after dinner. Every possible exterior light illuminated the Rigby, Carlton homes and their gardens, subdued lighting from each of the windows and doors assuring that any passer-by would take notice of the adjoining seats of self-adoration. And he did.

With Monday fixed in his mind, he drove an hour out of

town to the airport where he rented a late-model two-door before returning the hotel.

Monday morning, early, Rigby was the obvious first choice. Husband and wife came out together, 9:00 AM, Anderson more interested in him. Then a kiss, nodding heads and synchronized watches. They were meeting for lunch. How romantic. Anderson a little curious when soon after both imports veered into the car lot and parked.

Carlton was next. He and his wife leaving home at 9:50 in separate cars, arriving at the bank by 10:00 in a little family convoy.

Each hour on the hour the cars remained parked, the Rigbys leaving together for lunch.

Later in the day the women arrived home alone near 5:00, minutes apart, Anderson assuming to begin their familial duties before Carlton arrived for dinner at 6:00 and Rigby two hours later.

Good. Keeps a woman level.

*

Tuesday he began again with Rigby. The same boring routine, Anderson stopping into a diner after Carlton for a light breakfast and a phone call before his appointment early that afternoon at Rigby's Fine Motors. Mr. Patrick Fellows, president and CEO of Fellows Marketing Group, currently in the process of relocating his firm to Necessity, North Carolina required a few upscale vehicles for his people in keeping with his firm's sophisticated image.

No need to put things off.

"Good afternoon, Mr. Fellows. So pleased to meet you. Dwight Rigby. And thank you for choosing Rigby's."

"The owner himself, I feel honoured."

"Not quite the owner, not yet. The owner's son."

"Pleased to meet you. Pat Fellows. I must say your receptionist was very accommodating this morning, which I appreciate being that I'm on a very tight schedule. May I also comment on how lovely she is? Your HR man has an appreciative eye."

"You may indeed, and thank you. Eleanor is my wife, actually. She'll be flattered, as I am."

Rigby offered coffee, Fellows declined. He got straight to the point. He instantly despised the man. He was too smooth, Anderson assuming that Rigby senior was the in-house mentor and guru.

He explained the situation. Currently established in New York and Miami, he was creating a North Carolina branch office to minimize costs and be more available to his mid-Atlantic clients. He had visited Necessity several times, amongst other towns, and he saw a good fit. He was in the process of hiring three Account Managers who would require vehicles on a two-year basis, as would he. Three mid-range, one slightly more upscale though not too pretentious. His firm's reputation and clientele were somewhat conservative in nature, though discerning.

Rigby understood entirely, dedicating his afternoon to test drives and talking too much.

"Must be hard on your wife, Dwight, working while keeping your home, your family. She must be quite a woman."

"She's the best, though not much of a housekeeper. That's between us. And the boys are off to school, which lightens the female load somewhat. Fortunately we can afford starting them in the right direction, teaching them the values that matter. Home for the summer, though, end of June. Then back to it in September."

"Still, that's a big home you have there. Very nice. The deserved reward of a successful man."

"Thank you. I like to think so. The maid comes in," he chuckled, "Mondays AM to clean up, Fridays AM to get things ready. Eleanor's second job is mostly playing weekend hostess and cooking dinners. Not really rocket science, and she's never worked a Friday afternoon that I can remember. In fact she won't. What a man has to put up with to maintain a peaceful home."

They chuckled together, bobbing their heads.

"I like what I've seen, Dwight. And thank you. So here's what I see happening. You take your time, figure out something that'll make each of us happy. We'll see each other,' he paused, "let' say Monday next." Anderson opened his agenda to June 17th, scribbling. "So keep that pencil sharp. And tell me, while I've got you. Any recommendations for a good local bank? I like to keep my business partners local, make myself part of the community."

"There's a few. Carlton's the best in my view. A Necessity cornerstone. Good friend of mine, Jackson Carlton. I'll give him a heads-up."

"Good man. Let's pencil in nine AM, your office. Eleven AM with your Mr. Carlton and I'd like you to introduce us. In fact I'll be in town with my wife, so would you please join us for lunch with your lovely wife. Naturally I would expect you to invite Mr. Carlton on our behalf," he paused for affect, "and his wife if that's at all possible. I assume he is married, stable? My wife likes to get involved, put faces to names. She's big into stability, the natural order of things."

"He is, Pat. Darlene. She keeps the same schedule as my wife. Something about Friday traffic they don't like. They're best friends, have been for years."

Yeah, really good friends, big time, and your sister. "Brenda, *my* wife, finally made a decision on her dream apartment. Took her a few months. What can I say?" He opened his raised palms in a plea for mercy, "a day before her first refusal expired. She travels with me quite often. Hates hotels. Likes her own bed. You know how they are. They get to an age…"

"Got your back on that one. We'll all be delighted to meet her, Pat. Your invitation is gracious and I happily accept on their behalf."

"I have no doubt you'll adore her. Everyone loves Brenda. Puts me in the background. She fits right in, a real people person. In the meantime work on this model for me, Dwight, three of the black and…"

Silence.

"Problem, Pat? That's what I'm here for."

Fellows pointed. "That red one, over there…expensive?"

"Entry model, fully equipped. Came in a few days ago. I think it's in budget at twenty-eight."

No hesitation.

"Add it into the equation. Two year leases. Doesn't hurt to keep the little woman happy." Fellows reached for the release lever. "Been a pleasure, Dwight. I'll keep in touch and you keep that pencil sharp. I'm looking forward to meeting Mr. Carlton and your ladies."

They shook hands.

"As do we, Pat. You have a good week. Anything at all, you call."

Rigby waved from a distance; Anderson nodded, pleased to know that some things never change. Bullshit baffles brains, always would. Not that he was giving undue credit.

*

Tuesday evening, with nineteen days remaining until Billy's birthday and the eve of his twenty-first year in captivity, John remained in his room practicing with his pick kit on the half dozen locks he'd purchased once home from New Orleans. All top grade, all expensive.

He was also aware, once he was told, to beware of security alarms, which few people had. All the same, "don't be stupid, John-boy." He'd learned about ring and tip wires, where to sever them, where likely to locate and disarm the interior panel and siren that would alert neighbours.

He was set. At 1:00 AM Wednesday he parked two blocks down on Meadowbrook dressed in black from head to toe, with black gloves and a hood in a black satchel clutched in steady hands. He was invisible on the dimly lit street, feeling more exhilarated than exposed.

The homes were dark, only the porch lights were lit. The entire street was sleeping. No time like the present.

Nineteen days seemed like a long time; it wasn't. Not with so much to do. He had begun to accept with a difficult mind shift that the whore *could* wait a while. She wasn't going anywhere. Still, his destiny once he was finished with her was Battle View and the sooner the better, before his windfall funding ran out. Though not before Billy Rider was free.

He walked casually between the properties as either Rigby or Carlton might on any bright afternoon, surprised by his composure, not entirely thrilled that the patio of each home was brighter than a frigging tennis court. He took a moment, slouching against a corner wall. Time was his. He selected a hiding place behind a convenient oak where he could stand or sit, yet be concealed in the morning light in the event of any intrusion and made himself comfortable.

Closer to Rigby's, his line of vision made each window and door personal through his Bushnells. Both grounds were as professionally groomed as the frontages, the patios cluttered with furniture and barbeques, each open to the other's view. Though what surprised him was that neither home boasted a pool. The obvious centre-piece of each home were the matching garden doors, mirrors in the moonlight telling him nothing.

He stretched out and waited, remaining alert with chocolate bars and Coke, checking the luminous face of his watch not for the hour, because the thing was new and belonged to him. He was eager. More so than Rigby who anticipated the sale of five high-end cars. How happy would that make his daddy?

The interior lights never went on. Nor did he see any movement through his Bushnells, not until 8:05 when

Eleanor Rigby threw open her curtains to a pre-focused lens. Not bad at all, he thought. Perky, firm, every bit as good as the whore's.

Darlene's windows remained shaded against the early sun, her kitchen or dining room at wrong angles for intimate viewing and he wasn't budging. His focus was Rigby, their garden doors transitioning from a secrecy shield to an animated screen of unaware thespians acting out their mundane roles, themselves transitioning from naked, to half-dressed to ready for the day when they disappeared and Anderson's day became all about sound.

The previous two days the car peddler and his wife left their home near 9:00, the banker and his woman closer to ten: Bankers' hours. They didn't have to worry about sucking-up to clients. Those muffled sounds happened about on schedule, Anderson waiting thirty minutes before concealing his entire head and his hands, walking to Rigby's patio. He was told: Never run. Peripheral vision is sensitive to flashes and blurs. Never run. "Not unless you fuck up real bad, John-boy."

He hurried to the farthest side of each home, hugging the stone walls, hoping not to see two cars. He didn't. Neither the sides nor backs of either house indicating security issues. He was good to go.

Rigby was first; Dwight would want it that way.

High-end bolt locks.

He chose the proper pick, equal to the task, working with the precision of a dentist picking at a microscopic cavity. The driver and bottom pins separated, the shear line clicked, the tumbler turned. A lifetime of seconds. A sigh of relief. The door opened and he was in.

The kit went into the bag, the Berretta came out. He wasn't about to screw up, not certain whether Billy would get his birthday present earlier than planned. He called out their names, nothing.

The house was pristine, though he expected nothing

less. The upstairs was first, nicely furnished if not slightly overstated. Seemed as though the four front-facing rooms were for the kids and guests, each with an en suite bathroom. The corner door led into a more elaborate powder room.

The entire back of the top floor was the master bedroom, his and her walk-ins, an en suite bathroom and a private reading area. The toys were in her beside drawer, and many of them, making the curious boy in him all the more so. Half her wardrobe was dedicated to the who's who of lingerie and things which he was certain the pastor would never see. The videos, now that he knew what videos were, were in Rigby's drawer.

He couldn't wait, hurrying out, pushing through the front corner door, being careful. Another sigh of relief, fairly certain Eleanor wouldn't mind.

Downstairs he ignored the dining room, and foyer. He went into the parlour. He wasn't impressed. Nice, at best. His whore most certainly had better taste.

Two other doors were closed. The office was an office, nothing exceptional: Fax machine, photocopier, and two desks with a phone and crystal old-fashioned siting on each. The top drawer of one was all about cars, the lower drawer home to well-read girlie magazines and a scotch bottle standing at the ready. The filing cabinets behind them were brimming with the names of clients dating back to the fifties. The agenda on the desk was filled with names, dates and times including Pat Fellows and wife Brenda.

He coughed a laugh, pausing for a moment, smirking.

The other desk was decidedly hers, the lady of the house. Thin folders for each of her household duties hung in the top drawer, a vodka bottle stood in the bottom, her desktop too clean to be anything other than a show piece. Female equality. The blotter was unmarked, a pencil and pen neatly arranged to one side, her agenda centred to her leather seat. So much for the time-honoured concept of

Busy Woman, Happy Woman.

He sat, leafing through the pages, taking care not to smudge or tear them.

They had quite the social calendar. Weekends were busy. So were lunches apparently.

*

MONDAY, 17TH, LUNCHEON:
FELLOWS, PAT AND BRENDA. (ELEANOR AND JAKE INVITED)
 CALL ELEANOR

*

 Interesting. That he was aware, he had never been an entry in a social calendar, with the exception of the court's invitation years earlier by way of his lawyer. He was flattered.

Things were getting better, his mind brimming with all manner of images and concepts.

*

SATURDAY, 22ND, DINNER AT HOME
ELEANOR & JAKE, CONFIRMED
COCKTAILS AT 7:00

*

Saturday. Excellent. Perfect timing. As luck would have it, he was free that evening.

He wondered whether casual or formal would be appropriate and whether his hosts would prefer red or white.

Then five empty pages, a boring week ahead, not that they would care.

*

FRIDAY, 28TH, WELCOME HOME (AT ELEANOR'S)
THE CHILDREN
COCKTAILS IN GARDEN AT 7:00
GIFTS REQUIRED

*

Welcome home, not quite, more like a send-off, a fond farewell. She'd put her frigging kids into a calendar with a reminder to buy them gifts. Nice mom. He was pretty damn sure Donna Reed would never have done that. Then again, Donna probably never had a drawer full of ten-inch motorized dildos with pistol grips. He didn't think so.

The kids weren't an issue, weren't a thought. If they were to soon discover that life was cruel, they would at the same time discover the depraved minds of their parents. Or, if like-minded, which he believed likely, think twice.

At last he had a timeline. Ten days to plan for dinner with critical questions to ponder of greater importance than what to wear or what to bring. Then eight days more to complete his journey on schedule. Time management was everything, always had been. He was doing the math, his mind in a whirlwind. Too much information too soon, though thankfully not too late.

The thing was not to panic. Don' panic. Just get it done.

He left, securing the house. He had to get out. He wasn't interested in the basement; he wasn't buying the place and sneaking into Carlton's house was pointless. He knew what he would find: More toys, more videos, more booze in office drawers. Yeah, sick puppies.

Walking, not running, is fine in the dark, or in a backyard. Emerging from between two half-million dollar homes in broad daylight, that's something else. His stomach was churning, his mind racing and, once at the car, he wasted no time getting out of Dodge.

Everything was coming together. So what if he might have to kill her a few days behind schedule. Better late than never.

He gathered his clothes, checked-out early from the hotel, returned the car and went with Pat Fellows to book a flight to Palm Beach International.

Twenty-Four

1991

He apologized for being neglectful. He hadn't been giving her much consideration of late. He wouldn't let that happen again. She was, after all, the centre of his universe.

He had four days of free time that he would dedicate strictly to her everlasting peace, Carlton and Rigby having thoughtfully scheduled the timing and the location of their untimely passing.

First thing Thursday morning he bought a beach tent, a tripod, an 80 - 40X scope, more beer, sandwiches, and this time a cooler. He was set for the day, establishing base camp closer to the shoreline, comfortable and private, not required to extricate himself inconspicuously from his trunks or make requisite and obvious dips into the ocean.

Scoping her would be easier and better with no lens jitter, safer with no idle curiosity. He'd be able to see the fine hairs on her arms, read every word from her cheating mouth.

She came out at 1:00 wrapped in some sort of pinky silk thing knotted between her tits and hiding nothing at all between them and her knees.

Okay, so he was curious. He stayed focused. Apparently the hairs on her arms were the only fine hairs she cared to maintain. Different, he mused. He supposed the style, if one could call nothing a style, had certain appeal. No wonder she could wear such tiny bikinis. He would ask her about that. He would. Was that her preference? Was that an easier way of cleansing the sewer of vermin and pests? Or their preference perhaps, imposed upon her, allowing for their visual inspections of any possible contamination that might unduly affect their virility, their marriages or the healthy births of their children? Or did she in that way thoughtfully facilitate their ease of entry? Or did she in that way hope to heighten their olfactory pleasures, thereby achieving the fulfillment of their diseased minds?

He wondered whether she ever thought of him, laughed at him, or saw his face when she was fucking her never-ending horde. Probably not. She couldn't possibly imagine what the nation's hell would do to a man so quickly and indelibly.

Turn him into an animal for one thing, a survivor. Better a hunter than easy prey. He was so pleased that Cleaver in The Swamp hadn't killed him. Or that the Battle View Cleaver hadn't held a grudge for so many years. He examined his fist, each knuckle. He could have died that day. What saved him, the only thing that saved him, was the absolute shockwave paralyzing his Black contingent.

He snickered. Why had he asked one Cleaver to thank the other when, in a few weeks, he could thank the man himself? Anderson, Rider, 312, four dead in Necessity, and a dead whore to boot. Yeah, he was going back. Even the dumbest cop could figure out that one.

He didn't really know. There was so much he didn't know because of her. Sometimes he felt completely out of it, as though falling into a deep sleep that long-ago evening of April 20th to awaken exhausted in a foreign and distant future. Everything was so different.

And turn him into a killer, for another. He had no qualms about killing her; he had qualms about not killing her, in time and soon. Nor did he feel any emotion whatsoever in turning four boys into orphans. What was an orphan anyway? A four-year-old who watched his father butcher his mother? And who was more the orphan now, Billy Rider or Miss Sally whose soft voice was so broken with sorrow yet so sweet? Or the Merriweathers who soon would redirect their hatred and grieve anew? They were as much the facilitators of their daughter's death as anyone. The breed of parents: Bigots.

No. Those men deserved to die and their sons deserved to discover the truth. Better to hear of their parents' deaths than to endure the humiliation of their families' names; or to await the dates of their fathers' executions for the premeditated murder and rape of an innocent child; or to comprehend the depth of their mothers' self-serving devastation of a man's life and the sordid reasons why.

He followed her every move, her completely useless cover-up fluttering in the wind.

He had once loved her so deeply, adored her, so eager to arrive home that last evening as though they hadn't been married six years and more. Then to see what he did.

He smirked quietly. She was quite a sight. Hell, if she hadn't done all that hysterical jumping and skipping, hopping around naked and screaming before running into the hall in her panties and bra as though the cops were also bringing her a dozen red roses, he might very well have taken a moment to kill her.

He wondered about Brend*a*'s, her front that was no different from the sleazy parlours and brothels of the twenties and thirties.

He closed his eyes, pondering for a moment in darkness. He had so much to think about, too much for a man who, for so many years, had no reason to think at all. Do this, do that, go here, go there; his mind and his body now strangely impatient for his freedom to end, for the relative repose and rigidity of prison. He was tired. He hadn't expected such a twisted and drawn out expedition into Billy's freedom. Shit! What was he doing? He knew where they lived, that they were guilty. What was his problem? Knock, knock. Poof,

poof. What the hell was he doing waiting to crash a dinner party? And the whore. Really. What the hell! He could take her out from where he was sitting, drain a beer to her good health and no one would be the wiser. No one would give a shit. No one ever cried over a dead whore.

He punched his private sand. He would. Damn straight. He would dress for dinner, stopping first at Brenda's that evening for a drink. Why not? Why not indeed? Though for the time being he was drawn to the scope. Not a single blemish anywhere on her, which by no means precluded an eventual hole or two more. And, sure as hell, very soon.

She unknotted the silk, stepping into the pool, oblivious to whomever might see her, her ankles and knees and hips disappearing into the crystal water. Her arms and hands raised into a spearhead, her body slicing the water, disappearing beneath the surface. Reappearing. Her beautiful face glistened, her painted lips were smiling, her dark brown eyes as liquid as ever before, her dark matted hair defining the shape of her skull that he might soon cause to explode.

She swam for an hour, wading between laps.

He would have bought her anything, and he did. Yet his young and promising life ended in Battle View, his single cause for joy at such a horrific crossroads was that his parents were dead, their lives untainted by what he had done. Even though in his heart, the heart that God had thought best not to touch for whatever reason, he believed that his mother and father were by his side, that they understood what he did then and what he must do now. No worse than taking out the trash.

She stepped out. She never hurried. She never had, always measured. He remembered the first time he saw her naked, padding to the bathroom, locking the door. He was mesmerized. Now all he wanted, needed, was to see her dead.

She strutted to the bar, the cheeks of her ass, he had to

give credit, were the probable envy of most body-conscious females littering or strolling the beach. Her tits were monuments to eternal youth; her pussy, he had to choke on that one, or what he had always thought was a pristine pussy, his alone to love, honour and obey, in the blinding sunlight was a thin and delicate stroke of an artist's brush. Fine art: Perfection to the eye and filled with so much history.

He watched her concoct a cocktail. Who better than a bar-owner/whore? A cheating wife? He didn't know. She sipped, smiling with approval, strutting her way naked to a chaise-longue draped in white where she lay gazing past her gated fence toward the blue sea and her killer.

A cheating wife he could have accepted. He would have understood, once, even blamed himself for being away from home so frequently. But a blatant and self-confessed whore on his dime was another matter.

An hour later she went again to the bar, this time facing away to laze in the sun, tanning her back, the occasional blur disrupting his view, no one thinking to stop and stare. He supposed that with so many undressed women on the beach, many of them laying without their tops, most of their asses bare, she wasn't much of a celebrity laying naked and beyond reach.

He maintained his vigil with frequent intervals to stretch, to enjoy a beer and the sea, paying homage with reciprocal smiles to women strolling by, pleased that his legs were no longer white posts labelling him as a common labourer or a convict. They were smiling at him, not John in yellow, not 7319. Him.

Divorced? He assumed so. Why else would forties, young and fit fifties, glance over their shoulders and smile? Unless they wanted out, unless whatshisname no longer saw in them what he was seeing, which was pretty well everything.

Maybe once, he mused, while he could afford to buy

some woman a fine dinner. Buy her dinner or buy her body, the difference wasn't clear in his mind. What was becoming clear since his release is that he was seeing more bare flesh than he could have hoped for and self-denial was an increasingly conscious issue. So maybe he would. Maybe once she was dead he would feel like a man and not an ex-con. Maybe.

At 4:00 he followed her into the pool, and from the pool to the shower.

Only when he gasped for air did he realize he'd stopped breathing. She was spectacular, completely absorbed. She wasn't washing her body, she was caressing every inch of herself, intent, adoring herself in a muted and erotic ballet, a cloak of white froth gliding teasingly from her shoulders across each glistening contour. His mind raced into the past. When would that stop? Why had he never suspected? How could he ever have believed that one man alone could satisfy or even please her?

The cascading water stopped. She stood dripping, combing out her hair, staring in a daze straight at him. Unnerving. He coughed a sharp breath, imagining for a moment the torrent of fetid water gushing out from between her legs if she had the slightest inkling. And she would.

She was parading around the pool, drying, returning her glass to the bar, Anderson thinking she must have a maid. Or more likely a spare man, a spare phallus on retainer. And then she was gone. As was he, taking time to dismantle his Egyptian cotton habitat, content with what he had seen, arriving this time in front of her home in a less conspicuous rental with Florida plates, waiting anxiously to see when she might leave.

He wanted into that house. He needed to discover as much as he could. He wasn't delaying her murder; he was enhancing his just cause, creating a mood, a delightful memory to see him through his coming drab years, or to fill his mind with more pleasant thoughts on the steps of the gallows. Though ladies first. Always ladies first.

He didn't wait long. She stepped from her front door at 6:00, Anderson keeping an open mind.

Her dress was more modest than he expected, with sufficient breast and leg hanging out to ensure the attention she craved… or more likely a repeat customer.

He was always so proud of her. Now all he saw was a faceless body for hire. He trailed her to North Ocean Boulevard where she again disappeared, this time into the underground parking when Anderson stepped out. The name on the panel was B. Peters, her suite number unlisted, Anderson wondering why she hadn't thought to put By Appointment Only.

He returned to the beach feeling like a pro, not waiting for dark. He didn't have to; he was through the gate in a blink and into her home with equal ease. The place was massive, sprawling, larger than Rigby's entire house on a single level, definitely more modern and definitely all female. The walls were plastered with images of the nude female form and abstract oils which did nothing for him. Ceramic and bronze nude sculptures of the male physique and couples entwined stood everywhere, the entire place seething with sensuality.

He went into each of the twelve rooms. The bedroom was definitely for her alone, where she would sleep devoid of emotion, confusing peaceful slumber with escape until noon most days, he assumed. He was in her quiet place, her retreat from the nightly forays into her ravenous body that had paved her way to riches well beyond any dream he might conjure.

The woman lived well. She had sophisticated taste. Nothing was lewd or vulgar, except the woman herself. She would most definitely rank amongst the finest of history's whores.

Nowhere did he see the slightest hint that she might entertain men, women, neighbours, or anyone. Her closets were filled with extravagant yet simple designs, hers alone. Her bathrooms were decidedly feminine, her fridge and pantry filled with foods that would make any man run to the nearest fast-food chain. He saw where she worked-out with equipment he'd never before seen, where she paid to have her body massaged, and where she might keep records of Brenda's and very possibly of her less seemly clientele.

That's what he wanted.

He didn't care about her downtown bars. He cared about who she fucked and when. He already knew where.

He took an old-fashioned from her living room cabinet, choosing a Johnnie Walker Blue. Blue, when all he could ever afford for special occasions was Silver. Yeah, he could kill her. Not a problem at all.

Her office walls were lined with an array of books covering all manner of subjects, Anderson supposing that she might even converse with her customers, though what caught his eye was her credenza and the neat row of mismatched leather-bound agendas with filigreed pages decorating the tops. He had no need to count them, or to wonder what they were. He was too stunned, horrified by the dates.

The first thirty-eight were tagged from '53 to '91; the last five were equally mismatched and stood nameless. He reached for '91 first, opening the book to the page bookmarked with a silk tassel.

He read: *Thursday, June 13th, Alexandre, WPB, 8:00, Straight. 750$*

He turned the page: *Friday, June 14th, Dirk, WPB, 7:00, Dinner First (Reservation). 750$*

Saturday, Sunday, June 15th, 16th, Brenda's, WPB.

Busy woman.

He turned page after page, stopping often to fully appreciate the smooth scotch. The coming week was all about West Palm Beach, North Ocean Boulevard. Welcome to Whoreland, Florida

He flipped back several weeks. Little Brenda Peters kept her weekends free to meet with her boys at Brenda's, either in West Palm Beach or Miami. He remembered Alejandro Garcia. He remembered the man's expression as he strode from the courtroom, the sheriffs hurrying to keep up. He never did quite figure out whether Garcia was claiming innocence or ignorance, expressing shame or guilt. He knew. Damn right he knew and he kept his mouth shut. Guilty.

Saturday, Sunday, June 22nd, 23rd, Brenda's South Beach.

Monday, June 24th, Val, South Beach, 9:00, Drinks First. 750$

Tuesday, June 25th, South Beach, Preston, 8:30, Dinner First (Reservation). 750$

Wednesday, June 26th, South Beach, Jordan, 10:00, Drinks, Out By Eleven. 750$

Thursday, June 27th, South Beach, Frasier, 5:00, Order In. Pizza, Bordeaux. 750$

Friday, June 28th, South Beach, Denise, All Day, Lunch, Early Evening Flight Out. 1000$

Denise? All day? The whore was branching out. That he would definitely have to ask her about.

He replaced Denise and the others, scanning the richly bound histories, reaching for '65.

He skimmed through the pages wanting to vomit, seeing the ten volumes to the left of the slim void. All those years before him. What was the reason? Why did she even bother?

Thursday, April 01st, J-F, All Week, At Home, (Renovations), Margaux '49. 1250$

Bon voyage to the Frenchman.

The Monday and Tuesday, Thursday and Friday were inscribed with the same notations.

That week he had gone to the West Coast and wasn't expected home until Friday and, if not for a bizarre stream of circumstances, he might never have known. His business trip had turned into a funeral, leaving Anderson to mourn that he had ever left home. The CEO of a client company had passed on to a better and more peaceful existence the Sunday evening preceding Anderson's arrival, the week deteriorating from bad to worse until he said "screw it" and flew home early.

Renovations? What renovations? Where? The Miami whorehouse, of course. Where else?

Her home away from home where she continued earning two-fifty each night throughout his entire three-week trial while shamelessly convincing the court she was simply addicted to men, not a whore. How does a woman do that? How that was even possible he couldn't imagine, fucking strangers for money while he was sitting in a cell and being tried for murder.

So much for the Frenchman, almost as though…

Enough. He replaced the book, reaching again for '91. He photocopied the last week of June, still curious about Denise. Maybe *he* would like Denise. Maybe Denise would like him since they had so much in common. He drained his glass, taking it with him through the garden doors that he secured, testing them.

The sun wasn't yet ready to retire. He filled his glass at the wet bar, making his way to the Jacuzzi, wondering at all the switches and toggles, trying each one, watching with amazement as the water erupted into vibrant life, one submerged pastel colour evolving into another, flickering in the swirling water, the gentle purr of hidden motors calming more than alarming.

He stripped, stepping in, placing the Berretta within easy reach. After all, they were legally married. Or he believed that they must be. However if divorce had to happen that evening, which he seriously doubted, if she happened home earlier than expected while he was decidedly indisposed, Pat Fellows would shoot the bitch, finish his scotch and leave.

In the meantime the water was warm and the scotch was warm, infusing his body and mind with unfamiliar tranquility. He was drifting, a forgotten pleasure, wondering whether he could convince Prescott to have one in each cellblock as a reward for the best behaved cons. Or not.

He laid his head against the contoured edge, letting the water take control of his legs and his feet. He couldn't remember ever feeling so free from worry and woe. In fact he felt nothing at all. He was floating, his mind wandering inevitably and irresistibly to her. He was all about her. He always had been, until then, until those fateful few moments outside his bedroom door when his mind went blank.

He realized what he was seeing, resentment creeping into his mind: the pool, the spa, the luxury, the golden sun. All she possessed at his cost, condemning him to Battle View when one simple word would have set him free...or free sooner.

He believed the incredible discovery of her library dedicated to her entire life of whoring that put him there would haunt him forever. He wasn't angry. He was too relaxed to feel anger. He simply wanted to kill her all the more, unless she were to find him dead the next morning in her swirling warm water.

He shook his head clear of her and sat straight. He put his glass aside, his head deep into the water, and screamed with as much ferocity as he possibly could.

Twenty-Five

1991

The downtown core was not exactly South Beach, more sedate, more middle-age.

Miami's Brend*a*'s in '65 was a watering hole, a meeting place to toss a few back before going home to a cheating wife.

The dress code was come-as-you-are. No pretentions. No restrictions. An easy and quiet place to drink, to meet a compliant young lady, or to make one compliant with cheap Happy Hour drinks before crossing the street with her to a six-dollar hotel room before going home to the wife whose neglect of herself would make any man hunger for something younger and prettier.

At his hotel Anderson changed into Dockers, dock shoes and a polo shirt, thinking he might meet someone and cross the street with her. Or not. Brend*a*'s was certainly the ideal place to ensure success, a winning evening, except at that late hour the selection would be limited and the quality somewhat questionable.

What he was not expecting was the queue of well-dressed women patiently waiting arm in arm with men in jackets and ties corralled by a cordon rouge, or the framed poster announcing Reservations Required & Proper Attire.

He informed the tuxedoed gentleman at the entrance that he was personally acquainted with Brenda Peters, that he had met her in Miami and that her invitation to visit West

Palm Beach was open. The man was very sympathetic, taking note of Pat Fellows' name for Saturday evening when Miss Brenda was herself expected at the restaurant.

That would be exceptional, Fellows agreed. Unfortunately his timetable did not allow. Nor did Friday, particularly since he had no idea where she would be dining with insert-your-seven-fifty-then-your-dick-Dirk.

So, Mrs. Brenda Anderson wasn't simply a cheating wife and wealthy men's receptacle of choice, she was an astute businesswoman and owner of two elegant restaurants.
*

Friday morning he trashed the pizza box and wine bottle. He never did enjoy eating alone in restaurants, not that he in any way cherished the company of 379 others from Cellblock Three stuffing their faces.

Breakfast was a Danish and a five-dollar coffee, base camp once again established by 11:00.

The soon-to-be late Mrs. Anderson strutted onto her patio at 3:30 undressed in an open silk robe that she let fall to the deck before spearing the water with barely a ripple.

She swam for thirty minutes, stepping out to perform another exotic ballet of twists and turns, deep bends and caresses to help ensure that by sixty she wouldn't resemble a worn out hag with skin the texture of a sun-dried prune. Leaving John to wonder why she hadn't placed a mirror anywhere on the deck since she was clearly infatuated with what she saw mimicking her every move in her garden doors.

He assumed she did her office work in the mornings, making her afternoons private, since her evenings seemed fairly well-booked. Not that he cared, not that it mattered. He merely hoped she remained healthy a few more days.

Strangely, despite her body inches from his face, he didn't see her as a very naked and very desirable woman. She wasn't sexual or sensual. She was Brenda Anderson, a compulsive liar, a cheat, a prostitute, and the one responsible for du Valois' murder. He was simply the perpetrator.

He had so many unanswered questions, eager for her evening of debauchery with her man Dirk to take precedence over her self-adoring hedonism. He wasn't finished with her or her history books. He wanted to learn about January 12th, 1959 and April 1958, questions he had no time to ask about during his trial. He wanted to feel good about killing her. He'd waited such a long time for closure.

At 4:30 she went in, choosing to deprive him of her exotic shower. He felt cheated. An hour later she stepped into the Bentley wearing shorts and a sweater, prompting more questions. Was the outfit a costume? Was good old Dirk into the girl-next-door thing? A bit of a stretch at fifty-four. He trailed her to North Ocean Boulevard, doing a one-eighty after the red and white barrier barred the entrance behind her.

At her home he was inside the gate within seconds, taking his time at the garden doors, his hands gloved. No rush, his new watch telling him 7:05.

In her office he went straight to the agendas, pulling out '59 and '58, fanning his way through her weeks and days to April 05th, 06th and 07th, Easter. He wanted to smash something. Her.

Saturday, April 05th, New York, John Anderson, Good Timing, Wedding Bells, Gratuitous.

Sunday, April 06th, Future Mrs. Him, Gratuitous.

Monday, April 07th, Future Mrs. Him, Gratuitous.

Friday, the 04th she had spent with some guy who might now be dead, another that same evening before she went home to pack. On the 07th she had a luncheon meeting with a Rex, possibly rested and cleansed by 8:00 PM for Max's turn at the trough economically priced at one-fifty.

He was gratuitous, his pages written with red ink. She'd written him off as a financial loss. He considered for a moment putting a bullet somewhere in her home. He didn't.

Too telling. Too stupid. She would not be a crime of passion. She was being killed because she deserved to be dead as payback. Then he could write her off, though he had decided to drown her to derive the most pleasure.

1959 was the year that most intrigued him, the 12th of January in particular telling him everything he wanted and didn't want to know.

Monday, January 12th, J-F. All Week, Decide about Brenda's, Too late for wedding, 1250$

The rest of the week was all about du Valois, Brend*a*'s, and twelve hundred tax-free dollars. What he had brought home in a month before Uncle Sam came calling.

He went to her cabinet in the living room. He poured two fingers of Glenfiddich that she wouldn't notice, returning to the source of his mounting curiosity: 1953.

Friday, September 25, Alejandro, Teacher, Mentor, Last Time, Will Miss Him, 50$

No shit. The Mexican made his way into her and into her books first. All those years, all the evenings he was invited to dinner, Garcia was part of what she was doing. Anderson shook his head.

He fanned his way through the decades tome by tome. Eight, nine, ten men each week in her early years before the wedding at two-fifty a pop into the sixties, curbing her appetite to five or six men each week he was at home and until his arrest. Twice that number when he wasn't.

She never stopped, never took a vacation without her agenda, many of the entries indicating a month or more of travel each year, celebrating the arrival of 1990 with Enrique in the south of France at the incredibly low price of seven-fifty. Bonne Année, putain,

He couldn't believe what he was reading thinking back to his frequent trips with or without her. He needed to do the math, using her calculator, giving her the weekends off, compensating for female issues with double duty the weeks following. Conservative estimate: Eleven, twelve thousand, give or take.

Staggering. The woman worked seven days a week, if one could consider fucking as work. He never did.

At her desk he found keys to her row of filing cabinets, most of which were related to Brenda's, her weekend job. He ignored them, more curious about the one marked "Freedom '95.

The drawer contained a single ledger, a folder for each of her years as a whore, a key to a safety deposit box, a strong box containing a bundle of hundred-dollar bills wrapped in plain paper with "June" scrawled in ink, and a folder marked "Côte d'Azur" with a series of floor plans stapled to the architect's business card. Seemed like a retirement plan. Good luck with that.

Removing the current year folder, sitting at her desk to scan the contents, he couldn't decide between dizzy or sick, happy he was seated and forcing himself not to vomit. Her European portfolio was worth 12.3 million.

Returning that folder he went through more file drawers. She had no mortgages, her three properties paid in full, that drawer containing a cluster of tagged keys to the home he was already in and the condos, the two Brenda's and the new Bentley. A new model each year that she paid for in cash. The lady was doing alright. Not only her life but her body was insured for another ten million. No wonder she wanted him in prison. She had to get rid of him somehow. He was a loving husband and, one would assume, one serious impediment to her success.

He freed the keys for Miami, squeezing them into a clenched fist. He really should have killed her that night.

He drained his glass, dropping half his weight onto the edge of the desk, allowing his mind to wander into the past, a creeping awareness emerging from a sickening notion. Du Valois was at his house all week, sleeping over, and would have been through to Friday when he was expected home. Maybe du Valois was complicit, though not likely. He was a smaller man in height and weight, an easy fifty pounds. Snapping his neck was incredibly easy, too easy; John still not certain whether he had murdered the man or had simply killed him because it happened so easily.

Brenda's was a front. That was a given because she couldn't fake teaching forever. Even the least amiable person had one friend somewhere. She had no one and she needed a reason not to be home many nights. That's why she married him. He was no less a front. Who would suspect a young married woman from Nebraska of being a high-priced prostitute, high in demand? Shit.

The fact that Brenda's came so soon after the wedding was proof that she had acted too quickly that Easter weekend. Talk about being rash. More like exemplary trash with a diamond ring. Excellent performance though. Very convincing. As believable as any true virgin.

Despite his travels he was in her way. Wednesday or Friday didn't matter. Du Valois was precisely where she needed him to serve a purpose. Divorce, John mused. Simple, easy, and guaranteed given her history. No bullshit about reconciliation. The murder, if that's what happened despite the appearance, was unexpected. She *was* truly surprised by that. Water under the bridge.

She kept good files; he gave her that much. Yet the Côte d'Azur thing, John didn't think so. She would have to understand. He also discovered that her home was regularly maintained by a full staff of maids, a pool boy and gardener Monday mornings. Her two condos each morning. No kidding. And that Mondays, Wednesdays and Fridays were her treatment days at the spa, John pausing to wonder if one of their specialities was pumping out cesspools.

He assumed the bundle of money was about seven grand, given her schedule. And he *was* tempted since his funds were running low with half a month remaining to free Billy.

He was thinking the 29th or 30th. Either way she had

nothing to do with Billy and by then she might possibly add weeks three and four to the pot. He didn't know. What he did know was that he was thirsty and went to the living room for a refill.

The time was 8:50. Dinner first with Dirk was probably coming to an end. The sun was.

He wondered what they might talk about, her other johns. Were these guys even aware of Brenda's? Not his problem. She was the problem. He assumed a minimum of three more hours for the man to get his money's worth, another hour for the drive home. He was good to go until midnight. His cut-off. Or hers if he misjudged.

Sitting again at her desk he reached for the phone, an appropriate hour to call Dwight Rigby to sincerely apologize and reschedule.

The woman's voice greeting him was neither feminine nor soft, more get-to-the-point.

"Good evening, ma'am. I truly regret disturbing you at this hour. Pat Fellows here for Dwight Rigby."

With his name came a shift in tone. "Mr. Fellows, good evening. I remember you, of course. My husband hasn't arrived home yet. May I take a message? I'm Eleanor. We and the Carltons are so looking forward to our luncheon with you and your wife."

"Which is the very reason I'm calling, Miss Eleanor. My wife has unexpectedly fallen ill. She's come down with some sort of flu-like condition. May I intrude upon your busy calendar to suggest the following Monday, the twenty-fourth? I do apologize, however to exclude her would cause me no small degree of marital malaise."

"How terrible for Brenda. Yes, by all means."

"And would you on my behalf postpone my meeting with Mr. Carlton to that same day and time?"

"I surely will, this very evening."

"Thank you. As for Mr. Rigby, I would like our meeting to go forward as scheduled. I'll stop by Rigby's Monday for the papers, leave them with my accountant while my time is taken up in New York, and be delighted to conclude the transaction when next we meet."

"He'll expect you, Mr. Fellows."

"Patrick, please, Miss Eleanor. Once again, excuse my intrusion into your evening."

"You are not an imposition, Patrick, and please give our best wishes to your wife."

The call ended. Monday would come soon enough. In the meantime he needed another scotch and a revitalizing soak in her Jacuzzi. He had a lot to remember, a lot to consider, not the least of which was not returning to Battle View or being hanged by the neck until dead as welcomed entertainment for Prescott who hadn't yet made the world a better place by leaving it.

Twenty-Six

1959 - 1965

What remained of the new Professor Anderson's January was mundane with John remaining at home with his bride throughout those two weeks of routine evenings. All he wanted to do was cook her fine meals, as she had no culinary talent whatsoever, take late-night strolls on the beach with her, and make love with her while Brenda made the best use of her time rearranging schedules, rebooking and creating elaborate excuses that would placate her disappointed clients and ensure their lasting devotion.

She was afraid they would find release elsewhere. South Beach and Miami were overrun with attractive and eager girls who would charge a lot less than she did.

She was more than a cheap one-nighter. She was Brenda Peters, increasingly by referral and highly sought after. In spite of which the first quarter of the year's forecast was in the red, a severe sixty percent downturn that would be impossible to reverse in the short term. His fault.

Her clients were men of quality, executives both foreign and local. Mornings for them were as much out of the question as was their prolonged and painful privation of her.

Her business was all about the fine lunches she would prepare and serve with their favourite wines, a leisurely few hours of seduction, recapturing their youth or making use of it before joining their own clients or peers for dinner. Or succulent dinners, often served by her for those gentlemen who, for as often as they could, desired the companionship and body of a younger, more beautiful and vibrant wife. The Europeans however preferred the ambiance of restaurants and the anticipation of what would follow.

Though giving less than her best, squeezing them in before rushing home for a late dinner because she had issues at school would mar her reputation. She wasn't into five-dollar street corner hand jobs. Neither were they. They paid for the best and expect no less.

February was somewhat improved, Brenda never certain when he would call to tell her too many times how much he loved her, until Friday the 13th when John arrived home with a bouquet of roses to begin a Valentine's weekend of effusive attention and marital sex.

She had a plan and she wanted his blessing. What he thought mattered. She was coming to the sad realization more each day that teaching was unfulfilling.
*

Jean-François had agreed with her. The time was right for change. He had what he believed was an interesting proposal, the ideal solution to her understandable dilemma, and a dear friend who owned a cabaret who would happily offer his advice.

And she knew someone as well who worked in a bar, whom she was certain would work with her, "but how would I be different, Jean-François? Miami is full of bars."

"You must be yourself, petite chérie. Sexy and charming and alluring. You must only and forever be Brenda, whatever you do, wherever you go. Nothing more. I hear how my dearest of friends call you, as I do. We breathe your name, Brenda. That is what you must do."

"I adore the way you say my name," she giggled, "the way you make the "a." You're right, like a breath. Brenda's, Jean-François, with a breath. That's what I want."

The next day Jean-François introduced his dear friend to Brenda who listened and took notes, by week's end deciding that she need not change her name to Professor Anderson. Instead she would own a cabaret and become Brend*a*.

A short month later she was ready.

*

She needed and wanted more from her life. She was paralyzed with fear that she would end her years and her career like so many of the others who simply read to their students what they themselves had repeatedly read from outdated books rather than teaching from life. As much as she did enjoy teaching, she felt stagnated. She felt endangered. She didn't want to end up like them.

Could he possibly understand how unfulfilled she was feeling? She had to know that he understood.

"What do you have in mind, a master's in another field, a new career? You've enjoyed a remarkable career the past few years, a strong base, which is a separate issue. Nothing's wrong with change. If you're not happy or fulfilled give your notice Monday. I fully agree. You're not good to anyone if you're not happy. However, I can't possibly imagine you ever becoming like them...stodgy Professor Anderson."

"Thank you, sweetheart. I think." She leaned forward, intent, the way Jean-François had taught her. "I want to open a bar, sweetheart. I want to call it Brend*a*'s, the way some of the Parisians said my name. You know, like a whisper. I've done some research. I wanted to convince you with solid information, not a girlish whim. I went behind your back. I'm sorry. And, sweetheart, when you were gone I met with an old friend. He was sort of my guardian angel when I first got here from there, a big brother. We sort of lost track, but I called him this week. We had dinner, sweetheart. I'm sorry. I needed to be fully prepared before telling you. He owns a very successful hotel bar and he likes the idea, sweetheart. He's willing to bankroll me with a ten-year loan for a quarter share. His name is Alejandro

Garcia. You'll absolutely be impressed with him."

"Then let's meet the man together next week. Quit school if you're that adamant. We don't need the extra income that badly." He chuckled. "What you will need, however, is an honest lawyer and a dishonest accountant."

She reached over and kissed him. He was the absolute best, and their special dinner wasn't until the next evening. She would go shopping for a gift in the morning.

*

Two weeks earlier she'd gone searching for her former mentor, advisor, and first paying customer.

He wasn't hard to find. He worked at the same hotel bar.

They kissed and hugged and brought each other up-to-date. Alejandro had never married; he enjoyed women too much. He saw no need to staunch an endless flow, nor had he ever given thought to which one might serve as the best possible plug. Nor did he have any great desire to follow the paths of his sisters and brothers who drove ancient cars and wore outdated clothes in order to put food into the mouths of their children.

Her proposal was simple. She would fund the venture entirely; she would meet his current salary in addition to a ten percent share of Brenda's for as long as he remained with her as manager. In return he would assist her with all facets of the business. He would hire a staff and a responsible replacement to take his place when needed and, at times, pretend to be more than he was.

They went shopping for a location the next day. The day after that they met with a designer and through the rest of the week with Alejandro's employer's current supplier. They met with a lawyer, an accountant, and placed recruitment ads. By the time Alejandro met John he was already actively interviewing young women.

John reviewed the various contracts not long after, impressed that his wife had so quickly and efficiently achieved her goal. The most important of those contracts

Brenda discarded through a shredder, signing instead the ones John had not seen.

Brenda owned Brenda's, a quaint bar that opened its doors in June and quickly became a popular lunch destination and a nightspot for casual encounters; Alejandro did the rest. He made Brenda's a thriving success, while she made almost daily appearances, interacting with guests, alternating between evenings and afternoons and on rare occasions with John.

Scarcely closing the books of her second year-end, Brenda bought the location outright. She expanded as well through the east wall into the adjoining available space, doing the same in the fourth year through the west wall.

Brenda's was the place to be seen for anyone under thirty or for anyone willing to pay the way for the willing woman who wasn't.

Throughout those years Brenda never once thought to invite Alejandro to her private apartment, nor did he ever think to propose a trip down memory lane. Not since the fifty dollars, the one time he had ever paid a woman for the use of her body.

She knew better than to lose a good thing. They were friends, and partners. As did he. Alejandro had moved into a more expensive home, he drove an import and owed everything to Brenda's. Not at all resentful that she seldom participated in the day to day operation. She was Brenda and, more importantly, Brenda.

Their patrons loved her and John was proud of her. His single insistence was that she was entirely his during their vacations.

She worked the nights John travelled, occasional Saturdays and Sunday afternoons with businessmen remaining in town a day longer or arriving a day early for the sole purpose of experiencing Brenda Peters, which helped to narrow the gap between her current and pre-marital revenues. A situation which would not change until her divorce.

She couldn't find any way of conceding to herself that she might love him. He was attentive and an ardent lover, if not as curious or deliberate as many of her other men, in particular the Europeans. He was a way to annul her professorship. She didn't love him; she had once needed him for a very brief time. Whereas now they were bound together by law, shackled, when he served no purpose other than causing her to misuse her time and her energy going to him at no cost the many times he wanted her.

Months into her sixth year as cabaret owner, September 1964, she celebrated her twenty-ninth birthday in Paris, welcoming John's idea with gleeful hugs and kisses.

They would extend their vacation with two weeks of his business that would leave their evenings free. Brenda could reacquaint herself with le Professeur du Valois, take day tours and shop for the latest fashions. She deserved. She'd been working too hard, putting too much of herself into Brenda's. Let Alejandro take over for a while, he told her. The man was a natural.

She was delighted. She loved Paris; she loved him. Paris, the most beautiful city in the world where they became man and wife. She absolutely adored him.

They departed September 04th, spending a week meandering through vineyards, spending their nights in quiet, family-run gîtes, eating their breakfasts and lunches at the plastic-draped tables of quaint bistros, their dinners in more animated auberges where Brenda was a hit each evening before nightfall.

She spent the days of her entire second week with Jean-François, the third week of pleasurable mornings and afternoons with his notable friends and associates who had welcomed the news of her French visit with wildly beating hearts.

En route to Miami she slept on her husband's shoulder, his hand held tightly in hers. How could she possibly exist without him? He knew her so well. No girl anywhere could have dreamed of a better vacation, birthday or man.

Christmas '64 came with gifts and guests from Nebraska, Brenda insisting that her parents would be more comfortable in a nearby three or four-star. A five star would make them uneasy.
She was only thinking of them.

Mr. and Mrs. Peters hadn't yet been invited to visit their daughter's Miami success, nor did John have to ask why.

Nebraska vs. Miami. She was ashamed, which John decided to correct without prior discussion. He took Folly to a spa, instructing her, admonishing her, to let things happen. Promising that her attendants would not ridicule her once she was gone. He ordered the million-dollar platter. The works, and he left her with strangers from eight until four when he took her shopping until their twelve-hour day ended in his living room where he presented the new Mrs. Peters to her husband and daughter.

The streaks of grey were gone, as was the bun. In their place was a neatly styled updo that was all the rage in New York. Her buckled shoes were history, in their place low-heeled pumps. Her paisley housedress was gone, replaced by a dress appropriate for a slightly plump lady of fashion that came to her knees.

Her husband was quite aghast and open-mouthed, insisting he would not stand for any shenanigans or wild notions from her, his wife telling him to shut up and serve her a drink. Vermouth on the rocks, or he wouldn't even see a peek of what was holding up her stockings.

Even Brenda had to admit that John had done well, whose guests they were that night first at Brenda's for a cocktail or two before dinner and dancing across the street with the loveliest lady from Nebraska.

For that Brenda wanted to stab him. The last man on earth she wanted to dance with was her father. She had always resented her parents for not leaving Nebraska to give her a better life in a place where kids didn't go to school smelling of cow shit. Instead she was forced to settle for Gomers mauling and sucking her tits in a barn as her sole escape until she could run, when she could have brought nice boys home to her bedroom in clean shirts and ties who would have fondled her gently and helped her to forget.

Then too quickly came their sixth anniversary in Miami, the parents ignored in Nebraska, Brenda's New Year's resolution an impossible dream while still trapped in her nightmare.

Divorce in Florida was impossible without him being charged with a crime, infidelity or abuse. Or her. Yet he had no criminal background, he didn't screw around and he hadn't once touched her in a way that wasn't a caress. And she was the respected owner of a popular nightspot. Her one possible alternative, several weeks in Reno to claim residency and get rid of him legally, would work against her. She was booked solidly into March with no intention of upsetting those well-established clients.

She was spending their two-week vacations confined to cruise ships and the Caribbean with little else to do except be on vacation. France and Spain were too much like work for him, though she loved France and two, three times each year she was accompanying him on trips to Paris that would ease the malaise of his being away from her so frequently.

She entertained Jean-François twice in January, once in Paris, once in Miami. He was infatuated with her, and not merely paying her. He was bringing her lavish gifts and promising to see her again in April.

More than a client, he had over time evolved into a devoted lover and confidant. During their frequent and heated liaisons they would speak mostly of their fantasies, their dreams and their futures which often included Brenda's that Brenda was beginning to outgrow.

She wanted something different, something new and sophisticated. She had to reinvent her brand. She wanted

Brenda's on everyone's lips.

Jean-François agreed. Very soon, that coming September, she would have nothing in common with those under thirty whose main quest was to conquer or be conquered by closing time. She had grown into a sophisticated woman and Brenda's should then and always reflect all that she was.

The week following du Valois' return to France the design phase began for what would very soon become Miami's foremost and raved about dinner club. Construction began the first of March with Brenda's and Alejandro's daily involvement. His ten percent share remained intact, his remuneration increasing in accordance with his new positions of maître d' and GM.

For his part John removed himself from the confusion, preoccupied with his own clients and schedules which pleased her no end since the same company was at the same time renovating and updating her more private place of business.

John, however, would be their first guest and thereafter their most frequent patron and vociferous promoter, he promised, leaving her on Sunday March 28th at the airport for a week on the West Coast from where he seldom called due to the four-hour time differential.

The more he refused, the more she insisted. She wanted to drive him to the airport, to have that extra time with him.

He always kissed her so passionately, holding her tightly in his arms, hating to leave her. This time was no different. He would think of her every moment until Friday.

He waved from the gate. She blew him a kiss, waiting until he was gone to dissolve her smile, twirling on her heels and strutting away. An hour later she greeted Air France flight 811 at the gate and went home with Jean-François du Valois, unconcerned by what the neighbours whom she seldom encountered or spoke with might think.

The Frenchman believed her when she told him of the

renovations of her second home, eager for his next visit. He also believed her when she told him that, with Brend*a*'s so close to completion and the contractor working sixteen-hour days, her home would be so much more convenient while allowing each of them familiar comfort, privacy, and the attentive devotion he had come to expect.

So much nicer than a hotel that after so many years would somehow seem improper.

Du Valois harboured no qualms about trespassing into another man's home. No more than he did about trespassing into Anderson's wife since his own wife had for years entertained, and continued to entertain, younger men at an expense no less than his. Flirtation was civilized. Divorce was not. The concept of one woman, one man for life conflicted blatantly with the human condition. The notion was ludicrous, had been for countless millennia since the first man and the first woman ever created came upon the second couple.

Truth be told, how anyone could reasonably presume upon the complete ownership of another's body for a lifetime, or swear to the devoted submission of their own, was as much a great American mystery as a great American lie. Brenda early on genuinely surprised to hear from a forthright du Valois that he regularly enjoyed the professional affections of another woman in Paris. Why would he not, when sadly Brenda was his a mere four times each year?

He was pleased and honoured that Brenda would share her home with him, not the least distracted by the presumption that *his* wife was quite probably at that hour similarly intertwined in one or another of their guestrooms.

Brenda prepared his dinner as usual while du Valois enjoyed John's Johnnie Walker Black on the rocks.

They made love through the evening until fatigue usurped their pleasure, each one honing their skill. That's what Brenda brought to her clients, erotic and expert love.

What du Valois brought home to his wife was a craving and heightened ardour equal to her own.

Monday and Tuesday they left for work, husband and wife to all but a few, Brenda greeting him at the early end of each day with a scotch as she had so many times before.

Wednesday he promised to arrive home not a moment later, to share time with her before dinner. Often, when in Miami, Brenda would accompany him to dinners with his clients as Miss Brenda Peters, owner of Brenda's and special friend. March 31st was no different, when they would again be a charming couple in public.

They would enjoy each other's warm and eager flesh, shower, and leave to greet their guests as a perfect host and companion.

*

American flight 1842 arrived from LAX on schedule.

His week was a complete disaster. Monday's client died Sunday evening; Tuesday's first was so late coming into the office owing to weather that John had rescheduled, the PM client cutting his meeting short due to the same weather. His Wednesday cancelled the entire day, caused by an in-house situation. His Thursday AM wanted Friday PM when John was hoping to be halfway home to Brenda.

He cancelled what remained of the week and flew home, stopping not far from the upscale love nest to buy her a dozen red roses. He had thought to surprise her at Brenda's, deciding not to crowd her. He remembered how distracted she was Sunday as he passed through the gate.

The renovation was a major project, her decision to refashion Brenda's no less daunting. He wanted to give her space.

Stepping from the elevator, however, and into their condo, hearing the music coming from the bedroom, he was elated. He would sneak up on her, surprise her, accept his deserved punishment for scaring her and take her to dinner.

His first thought was to kill. Then he saw the suitcases,

her clothes neatly draped over one arm of a chair crowned with her panties, the man's hanging from the other. He stepped back, shocked, deflated and furious. He felt weak, sickened.

She was under the man, her legs wrapped tightly around his waist, locked at her ankles, securing him in place. Her hands were digging and squeezing into his back, his body braced on taut arms, the muscles in his shoulders and back straining.

He was calling her petite chérie. John stood dazed, mesmerized, watching the stranger fuck his wife with mounting intensity until her soft moans became compelling whimpering that metamorphosed into urgent and guttural groans, rivulets of sweat dripping along his spine. Stranger? No. They knew each other. Petite chérie?

"Now, Jean-François. Now! Do it!" She practically screamed.

John gulped, or tried to. His mouth was too dry. He whispered an inaudible "What?"

Brenda anchored her feet onto the damp and dishevelled sheets, jerking, lifting du Valois' weight, grinding, pulling him in impossibly close with her hands digging hard into his buttocks. They shuddered in unison, their bodies visibly trembling, du Valois remaining perched on his arms.

Her voice spoke to him of utter exhaustion; the flowers fell from John's hands.

"Of all the men, Jean-François, who find their way into my bed, you are the most special."

"We have history, petite chérie. We are the most special to one another. Even when we are apart." His head sank between his shoulders, kissing one breast then the other. "It saddens me greatly when I must leave you, yet my heart reawakens when next we meet."

"Are you ever jealous, you know, when I'm with your friends or strangers?"

"Some things, petite chérie, are intended for all mankind

to share, to enjoy. You are one of these things. You can never be the possession of one man alone, while desired by so many. This would be...impossible, as impossible as me rising once again to the current desire I see in your eyes."

"That isn't what I'm feeling, sir."

"A gentleman's prerogative, I must insist."

"Then later. Not only am I the best, Jean-François, I also deserve and demand the best. That's you."

John took a deep breath. What the hell was he hearing? He was a reasonable and rational man. She was cheating on him. Okay. Shit happens. But what the hell was she saying? His head was ringing, his feet moving.

Brenda saw him first, genuinely startled. She hadn't expected him this way, not until Friday. She composed herself instantly, her mind clear. Now or never. It's what she wanted, what she had always wanted.

"Oh shit, sweetheart," she hunched her shoulders as best she could under du Valois' weight, "what are you doing home?" She was smirking, the glint in her eyes mischievous. She wasn't the least fearful of rage or embarrassed. "Sweetheart, this is Jean-François, my good friend from Paris. We weren't expecting you. I'm so sorry. You really should have called."

What was she doing? No! She was combing her fingers through the Frenchman's hair.

Paris seared his mind. He could feel the intense heat, electric jolts numbing his senses.

Du Valois did appear somewhat embarrassed, choosing to remain as he was atop the wife rather than possibly inciting the husband with his current condition.

"Sir, we must approach this truly awkward moment as civilized gentlemen. Neither Madame nor I anticipated your early arrival. I assure you, our discretion has always been of the highest...."

"Yes, sweetheart. That's true and we're almost finished here. We can talk about this in the morning, the three of us, like intelligent people. Right now though, sweetheart..."

He stopped listening. Madame? Always? Highest? Intelligent? In the morning? The man was calling his wife Madame? What the fuck!

John sought solace in another dimension of space and time. He needed to comprehend, to process. Admission denied. Deal with it.

The couple with him was naked. They were soaked, their bodies depleted; he mounted upon her, she completely unruffled. Her expression was coquettish, teasing him, the man's face oddly farcical. He could smell them. He could smell her. Blackness, bile rising in his throat. He needed to vomit, the iron fist of a fit, six-foot-three man slamming into the side of the naked man's head to dislodge him, to free her. The man was raping his wife, harming her.

John had size and the strength of blind rage on his side, du Valois helpless against the brutal impact rudely jolting him to one side.

Brenda yelped with pain, their bodies deeply conjoined. Du Valois was defenseless against the hands clamping his head, twisting him sideways, turning his frantic alarm into eternal peace. The crackling sound was sickening, the force of his last gasp a putrid wind on her face.

Jean-François du Valois lay dead, strewn across the woman whom he had paid for in advance.

Brenda was hysterical, her splayed body penetrated by a dead man. She was screaming, desperately trying to free herself, to push him away, wiggling and squirming, pushing and pulling her way free of the dead weight.

John stepped aside to watch her scramble from the bed to the floor to her feet, to study her. She was distressed; she was ranting on the verge of an apoplectic event.

He said nothing. What could he say? He'd just killed a man, a rapist; a vile and loathsome deviant who had come into *his* home from France with suitcases and a briefcase to drink *his* scotch and rape *his* wife. Not a problem.

"What?"

"He's dead!"

"I believe that's correct. Yes."

She was running in place, stamping her feet. "John, you killed him. He's dead!"

John glanced at the body. He was calm, reaching for the phone. "He was raping you. He was, wasn't he?"

She ran to the other side of the bed, pressing an open palm against du Valois' shoulder. The eyes were wide open, the mouth was open and twisted, the face expressing disbelief. She began blubbering, pulling at her hair. "Jesus, John, why couldn't you just leave? We were just having a good time together. You had no reason to kill him."

"Strange, how we all die with our mouths open and our eyes open. You should have told me, Brenda. And I would appreciate your telling the authorities otherwise. I believe that would be very helpful under the circumstances."

"Tell you what!" She was jumping up and down, hopping backward, stumbling into a wall. "He wasn't raping me, you idiot. He was a good friend. We were just having sex, having some fun. What's the big deal? You didn't have to kill him."

"The big deal is that killing a man for having a good time is murder. And I should kill you, Brenda. Really, I should considering your attitude. Problem is, then I *would* be a murderer and not simply a pissed-off husband. You do see the difference, don't you?" He raised a finger. "Good evening, operator. Miami Police, please. This is an emergency." His voice was even, unemotional. "Yes, good evening. This is John Anderson, fourteenth floor at Beach Towers. A few moments ago I apparently killed a man whom I mistakenly believed was raping my wife in my bed. I have no weapon and we'll buzz you in at your convenience. Thank you." He wasn't up to a drawn out conversation or premature questions. He replaced the receiver into the cradle. "I hope you realize that I won't be taking you to dinner…sweetheart." His smile was weak. "You should have told me. Or at least invited me to the party. Shit, Brenda, how long?"

She was snivelling, smearing her face with tears, make-up and mucous.

"How long, Brenda?"

"Since before you, you fool, long before you. I never loved you! Never!"

"Calm down. And please stop your blubbering. It's unbecoming."

"You're insane."

"So…are you a cheat, or a whore? What? Help me out here. Was this guy a freebie?" He scanned the room, the luggage. "Seemed to me more like you were fucking him. So I'm thinking whore."

"Shut up! I was not fucking him," she sobbed. "I'm not a fucking whore! I'm beautiful. Men love me. They adore me. Jean-François was my lover. Jesus, I thought you'd be gone until Friday. I wanted you to see us like this. I did, then, to finally get you out of my life. I wanted you out of my life, not him. God! I didn't think you'd actually kill him."

He snorted. "*Men* love you? Adore you? So you are a whore. Then you should really be the dead one, and I the insanely jealous husband."

"You are insane!"

"Upset, not insane. There's a clear distinction."

At most a minute had elapsed, sirens piercing Miami's still evening air. Brenda was turning tight circles, frantic, abruptly stopping. She was hugging herself, rubbing warmth into her arms, gaping at the dead Frenchman gaping at her.

John sat by the corpse, staring at her, nodding. "Yes, definitely. Now that you've told me, you do look very much like a whore, Brenda. I've never seen you so dishevelled and matted, dripping and glazed. You are a whore, and very repulsive. And, Brenda, you stink badly."

Her eyes flared open. She lunged at him, Anderson launching his weight from the bed he would never again sleep in, a single open palm striking her chest, landing her on the floor.

"Do not call me that!"

He sighed. "I suppose this is the last time I'll see you naked. Him too, which is truly unfortunate for each of you since even in his current condition he appears very at the ready to fuck you again. Somewhat of a bizarre compliment, I must say. I suppose you should be very honoured."

He moved around her to his night table, reaching in for a photograph of his wife, du Valois' whore, taken a year earlier in a scanty French bikini he'd brought home from Paris.

He peered from the window to the ocean, turning to face her. "A memento, Brenda, since I prefer not to remember you as I see you now. And I don't believe this will turn out very well for me." He sighed deeply. "Strange, how I'm feeling. I truly do regret not killing you for what you've done to me. Five minutes ago I was a devoted husband in love, now I'll be tried for murder. So let's make that a must-do sometime in the future. Killing you. Thing is, I can't figure out what's worse, trying to fathom that you're a whore, or that all these years I've been fucking your infested snatch while believing that I adored you." He stepped closer. He paused. "I will kill you for this one day, Brenda. You know I will if they don't hang me. So enjoy the interim. And please close your legs, the sight of it is repugnant."

She screamed, sucking in air. "Get out!"

"It's a bit too late for that. They're here. Besides, I would rather greet them in my home than in the lobby." He took in her body from her contorted face to her lacquered toes, pausing midway to snort as derisively as he could muster. "You might want to slide into your dainties to answer the door, Brenda. I do believe whores are illegal in Florida."

He saw her panic, partly amused, seeing her scramble to her feet, tripping her way into her panties, fumbling into a bra he'd never seen before. The thought striking him that he bought most of her lingerie, often returning home with little surprise gifts. This time he was the one surprised.

He didn't mean to chuckle, but a dead man lying on his bed with a hard-on was an unusual sight. "Goodbye, Brenda."

She scurried from the room, through the apartment, seeming not the least embarrassed that she was, except for a few strands of sheer fabric, naked. He shrugged. Not his problem. He heard the door crash into the wall, then nothing, her footsteps fading into the hall, then yelling and screaming, her voice, then pounding footsteps, then black revolvers pointing. Four of them, their feet braced apart, all smaller in stature, all threatening. Each one ready to piss himself.

"On your knees! On your knees! Hands behind your head! Now!"

John remained as he was. Were it not for the guns and their agitated mood, he might have chortled at the theatrics. He never did like cops, high school dropouts with guns and attitude.

Instead he slowly raised his open palms, turning to face the ocean, crossing his wrists behind his back. "I would rather not. Somewhat of an overreaction on your part, gentlemen, and too demeaning on mine. You understand, of course."

First came the handcuffs and the Miranda, then unreal questions better suited to television.

John never one for stupidity or bravado. He admitted his guilt, which he conceded far exceeded the guilt of his cheating wife, pointing out to the police how the grieving dead man's lover was standing so shamelessly amongst them in lingerie that was skimpy and sheer to the extent that she was in fact stark-naked. Who but a whore would be so brazen?

Each of the four offered Brenda momentary and particularly close scrutiny, none of them instructing her to dress. One of the four remaining with her as John was shuffled along unceremoniously from the apartment as though they had personally devised the sting operation and then captured public enemy number one.

He didn't say another word until the next morning.

*

John stood in her Jacuzzi, the warm water swirling around his hips. At least an hour remained before he would leave well ahead of Brenda walking through her door. He went to the bar, refilling his glass, letting his body dry in the warm evening air.

He chuckled softly, swirling the amber liquid in the glass. That was his lasting memory of her, his wife standing naked in a room with five men and a corpse with tiny strips of sheer colour accentuating her charms more than providing modesty. Damn right he should have killed her.

He dressed from force of habit, not that he had to. After so many years of being clothed twenty-four hours a day except for ten minutes on odd-number days, being undressed made him uncomfortable.

He had so much to think about: Her, Rigby, Carlton, the wives, Billy. And the time had come to leave. Staying longer would gain him nothing. He drained his glass, gloved his hands, returned it to its proper place ready for use another night, and left.

He flew home Saturday morning, refreshed.

Time was his until Monday when he would see Rigby before calling Brenda from his home.

After which Pat Fellows would fly to Miami. He would visit Brenda Peters' one-woman bordello, taking advantage of her hospitality while learning more about her. He would reserve a table for dinner at Brenda's, spend a few lazy hours each day on the beach studying and appreciating the female form, and fly home Thursday evening to prepare for Necessity on Friday, personally delivering his contract for five new vehicles to Rigby Saturday evening.

Life was good.

Twenty-Seven

1991

John Anderson left his apartment late Sunday afternoon for an unhurried drive to the airport outside the Necessity city limits where he rented a vehicle more in keeping with the image of a corporate executive than a ten-year-old Monte Carlo.

Monday morning Pat Fellows arrived at Rigby's Fine Motors on time, greeted by Eleanor who hoped Brenda was feeling better. Sadly she was not, though Fellows was optimistic that his wife would be completely herself by week's end.

Rigby had the prepared documentation in hand for his client. Five European imports priced to seal the deal, and not a single one that Anderson could afford. But Fellows could, confident that his CFO would agree. He always did despite his obsession with nickels and dimes. Rigby understood.

Would he like a coffee? No. He was expected in New York and he didn't believe the pilot would wait. They shook hands. Fellows would see himself out, passing by Rigby's wife to wish her a wonderful week and remind her not to forget their luncheon date. She promised with a practiced smile that she most certainly would not.

At 10:00 he drove past their home, two pink cars parked in the driveway, another two in Carlton's, blue script announcing to neighbours and would-be intruders alike that

Bonnie's Broom Brigade were inside cleaning the homes.

He went for an early lunch where Rigby or Carlton likely would not, formulating, doing his best to detect and repair the slightest fault with his plans.

At 1:00 he drove past the homes once again, parking on the next block for half an hour. Nothing. Bonnie and the girls were gone to polish and sweep in yet another spoiled and idle wife's home.

At 1:35 he walked with a purpose to the rear of the Rigby home. A few minutes later he was inside with his hands gloved. His single objective was the office where he opened the woman's agenda. He needed confirmation. Nothing had changed. Dinner Saturday was still on.

He poured two fingers of scotch into a glass he'd taken from the kitchen and toured the home. In their bedroom he went to the drawer he remembered was clustered with a myriad of her silk panties that he couldn't imagine serving any practical purpose except his. He put two into his left pocket. He would have put one of the porno flicks into what he now knew was a VCR, if he had the time, if he had known how. He didn't. Instead he borrowed one that he fully intended to return.

He replaced the empty and smudge-free glass to its appointed cupboard and left, crossing the property to the Carltons. Seconds later he was inside.

He had a suspicion where he might find the bedroom, congratulating himself. He also rightly assumed what he might find in their night table drawers. Nor was the closet a great surprise, Anderson taking a moment to rummage through the colourful mass of silky strings and patches, choosing the two smallest and brightest, pausing to ponder how Darlene might react to discover that he had her panties in his right pocket. Or Carlton for that matter.

He borrowed another video cassette, quickly toured the home, and left unimpressed. Too eclectic and too gaudy.

He returned the car to the airport and went home to

Charleston for a dinner at a seaside restaurant, anticipating a restful week. Tuesday he left early with a coffee and a box of doughnuts for breakfast, Pat Fellows checking-in to his Miami hotel room not far from her condo by early afternoon.

He needed to reconnoitre the building before walking in, not being reckless, not doing something stupid now that he was so near to achieving his life's ambition. Another day wouldn't matter.

*

He loved Miami, he always had. He loved the women whose most notable change in twenty-six years was how much more of them he could see. He loved the Cuban influence, the laisser-faire mindset and all things he was discovering. He loved being free to do what would come next, Black Boss leaping into his thoughts. Because of Cleaver's foresight and his cousin, because of Pat Fellows, he was essentially invisible.

Wednesday he stood outside the building sipping coffee at an outside makeshift terrace, waiting until the workday foot traffic dwindled from hectic to nothing. He lingered over another coffee before crossing the street.

The twenty-three storey building didn't have a doorman. Good thinking on her part.

How much would she have to bribe some old coot standing on his feet all day to keep a secret like hers? The entrance had double doors, each requiring a key. B. Peters was on the twenty-third with three others. All penthouses. No huge revelation there, and no doubt hers was facing the ocean. He dialled PH-4, waiting. Nine rings, ten rings. Nothing.

He went in. The lobby was designed with simple lines, well-appointed with posh furniture bolted to the marble floor and framed artwork behind Plexiglas shields bolted to the walls.

The elevator required the same key. He stepped in and

seconds later stepped out with his head down, his fedora and sunglasses his sole protection from he didn't know what. He was merely following the precautions of his more learned Battle View associates.

He had his pick set, in case, though he needn't have bothered, crossing his fingers that she didn't have a central alarm. She didn't. Good girl.

What he saw first was the blue horizon, too high and too far back to see South Beach.

The condo wasn't remotely like her home, designed for the comfort of men; including a collection of tasteful bronze and ceramic statues uniquely depicting the female nude in various stages of readiness and arousal.

He went first to the balcony, to what he called a balcony that extended thirty feet on either side of the floor-to-ceiling tinted glass doors. The concrete and Plexiglas patio was fully private. He was standing in a miniature Eden with exotic flowers and plants, cushioned lounge chairs, a Jacuzzi, a glass wall of cascading water behind it, and a retractable awning so that anyone working on the roof wouldn't accidently or on schedule see her grinding herself onto someone else's husband or playing kissy-touchy with someone's Denise.

One bedroom was hers, private, the closet brimming with designer fashions for any occasion and lingerie to satisfy a wide variety of client-tastes; her bathroom was scented, boasting a vanity and bidet which he assumed she must use every night in one or both directions. The other was well-appointed and masculine, the closet empty, the bathroom furnished with all manner of sundry items for her clients' convenience. Not a single can or bottle with a single splotch or drip.

The place was a home away from home, better than any five-star and equipped with a ready and willing wife for a mere seven-fifty a night. A true bargain.

The kitchen was professional, he assumed, with enough

gleaming knives to perform a crowd-pleasing fifties' circus act. The living and dining rooms shared views of the ocean. The dining room was simple and elegant. Behind its single door was a collection of fine wines, many bottled before he was arrested, and a wet bar boasting the most exclusive labels.

She was servicing the best, at the very least the wealthiest.

Perhaps the hour was a little too early for a cocktail but he was adamant about maintaining his training, teaching himself moderation, pouring a shallow Johnnie Walker Blue before completing his tour.

The living room was tasteful, not lived-in, more comfortable and inviting with hi-fis and radios of some sort that had complicated dials and knobs and metres he had come across in his previous home visits which he didn't trust not to give him away so he didn't touch them.

He retraced his steps. What she did not have was an office. No files. No agendas. Nothing. Nor in any of her drawers did he find a single toy or costume. She had standards, good for her. She was the toy. He liked that, though what he did find were Brenda Peters' business cards that had nothing to do with Brenda's. Simplicity. Her name and toll-free number in swirly script, Anderson quite amazed that she hadn't added *Florida's Premier Whore*.

He poured another scotch. He was beginning to hate the thought of returning again to his make-do apartment in Charleston. After Rigby, Carlton, West Palm Beach and now this, he felt like an indigent beggar despite his improved appearance and circumstances. He thought he would stay the night, sleeping on the sofa since the two beds were hotel-perfect that he could never recreate. Maybe watch a video. Maybe drink more scotch.

Screw it. He would, for no better reason than telling her one day soon. He could bathe the next day in the ocean, or shower at one of the rinse stations along the boardwalk.

Leave without a trace. Why not?

He left, removing his gloves before striding into the lobby.

From his hotel room he called Brenda's, reserving a table for one Thursday evening, leaving dressed for the beach with his luggage and a faint excuse they knew at the desk was a lie.

Not his problem.

On South Beach, with sufficient food and drink for what remained of the day, the first beer gone, sitting on his new mat in the sand while letting one image and thought usurp another, still curious about Denise, he changed his mind.

He was becoming over-confident. What he was thinking was too dangerous despite her schedule. After two days he would almost certainly leave behind careless traces: His imprint on the sofa, a dirty glass, an open drawer or sand from the beach on her immaculate floors…something so small, so stupid.

No. He would check-in to another hotel and not spend two sleepless nights worrying about ruining his one chance. That was her way, not his. He had accomplished too much to intentionally invite irreparable failure for the sake of ephemeral spite.

He dropped his head onto his forearms bridging his knees, sighing. Were it not for her seething spite so long ago, the deep loathing she alone created and nurtured, he would be elsewhere in the world with a far less jaded view of things. And in that better world she might well be in jail or prison or reduced to walking the streets with a soiled mouth for pennies on the dollar as deserved rewards for her crimes borne of a twisted mind against the wives of so many men. Something he imagined she would very much prefer to his reuniting with her in so few days.

Although he would drop in again the next day for a scotch and a memento of his visit. That, he most certainly would do.

He drained his last beer and fell asleep in the sand murmuring to Billy Rider to be patient. In as little as four days the shit would hit the fan. The judge and the DA and the detectives were still living. He'd called asking for each one in turn. He'd called Sally, and he might again. As for the Merriweathers, they hadn't moved from their home, no less guilty of condemning an innocent boy because a town's myopic and festering blame was easier to embrace than searching for difficult truths.

Pat Fellows was acclimating too easily to five-stars and fine meals. The housekeeping lady outside his room happily agreed to demonstrate the use of the VCR; she was even happier when she left a few moments later with twenty dollars tucked into her apron.

He ordered a light meal from Room Service and a bottle of wine that wouldn't make him appear as though he was sacrificing his dinner so that he might afford more luxurious accommodations. Image was important, dressing properly for the job at hand. He looked as though he belonged in a five-star; he wouldn't stand out.

With the meal laid out on the coffee table, the wine breathing, he followed the young woman's instructions. He'd never seen a porno flick, didn't really know what that was beyond the obvious. The front cover depicting a woman's bare ass framed in garters offered the most significant clue.

He sat back, then he leaned forward, his mouth filled with wine, gulping.

The opening scene was Eleanor Rigby pirouetting in her bedroom, soft music playing in the background. She stopped, standing still, pouting, her red lips pinching into an exaggerated kiss for the camera as she hugged herself.

First her blouse came away, what there was of it. She unknotted the bow, tugging each band in opposite directions, shrugging the sheer white fabric from her shoulders, dropping the thing to the floor.

Her smile was sensual, he supposed, for a suburban housewife touching on forty. Then went her bra, seductively, the front clasp undone, her breasts exposed enticingly as though drawing back the curtain of a theatre to an anxious audience. Her hands cupped the soft flesh he remembered from his early morning in her backyard, slender fingers kneading and pinching. Not bad, he conceded, with no past-her-prime slope, though better if they belonged to someone else.

One hand cupped over the other, converging at the hem of her short and pleated plaid skirt, pressing down, rubbing the fabric against her. John drank more wine, coming close to losing it through his nose, doing his best not to choke. She was moaning, oohing and aahing, coming close to locking her jaw. Once a schoolgirl slut...Well, we are what we are.

Her hands came away, deliberately, one deftly releasing a single hook, the other flinging the skirt into the air. The camera zoomed in, her panties remaining in place wherever she had put them because she wasn't wearing any.

Rigby's Fine Motors' very fine receptionist was standing naked in garters, stockings and high-heels four feet away and filling a screen beyond his reach.

The camera circled her, Eleanor imitating a B-rate actress, caressing herself as though her body were a finely sculpted figurine created for all to admire. That said, he hadn't seen a woman that naked since watching the whore strut around her patio and, before that, when the same whore sat sprawled on his bedroom floor with her dark brown pubic doormat glistening.

He wasn't complaining, feeling more like an honoured guest than a voyeur, following Eleanor to the bed he recognized. Perhaps she might even autograph his copy. Something to think about.

She eased onto the neatly folded-down sheets, reclining. She raised her feet into the air, kicking away one shoe then

284

the other. Sitting, her fingers teasingly worked at the garter. One clasp sprang free, Eleanor rolling the stocking to her knee, to her ankle and past her painted toes. Then the other leg, her body twisting away, crawling onto all fours, her ass perfectly white save for the tiniest tinge of pink the size of a fingertip. Apparently Mrs. Rigby did not enjoy the sun's cosmetic rays.

The camera jittered throughout a brief few flashes of the ceiling, the floor, Rigby's feet and glimpses of Eleanor playing intense touchy with herself, John postulating that Rigby was making the camera ready to record his grand entrance as her leading man.

Seeing Dwight Rigby naked was not part of the plan. He watched five or so minutes longer before pressing EJECT as Rigby flipped her onto her back and brought her legs up over his shoulders. He'd had enough of twisted faces, smacking sounds, grunts, groans, wide eyes and "oh, darling, oh, darling."

He went to bed, his mind working, formulating.

*

Thursday he woke refreshed, pleased with his decision.

He had roused himself from the beach the evening before as the sand was cooling, sun bunnies reluctantly surrendering their spaces to strolling couples, hopeful hobbyists or the desperately needy with Geiger counters skimming the sand for the billfolds or Rolexes they hoped to find before the clean-up crews frustrated their monotonous work.

Midmorning he returned to her Miami bordello. He went straight to her walk-in, to the drawer where he selected what he believed would instantly be familiar to her. He wanted her to know he had been there. He needed her uncertainty and disbelief to mature at a gradual and steady pace into panic and fear.

From her wine storage he chose a chilled Pouilly-Fuissé, which he remembered was her favourite. 1973. His eighth

285

year in prison. He uncorked the bottle, thanking her, putting the plug and the torn cap into his pockets. He filled a crystal goblet, sipping, relishing the explosion of flavours in his mouth, pleased with his choice.

He scanned the room once before closing the door behind him on his way to the patio where he planned to spend a pleasant few hours in the swirling water of her Jacuzzi and drinking her wine.

The coming few days were cemented in his mind. He no longer needed to plan. He was set. The final phase was two days away. He glanced at his watch, then at the Berretta resting innocently within reach: Fifty-three hours.

With the bottle empty and his glass half-full he made his way to the railing. He felt on top of the world. He was. He was eager and elated, not the least apprehensive, not certain whose evening he would enjoy most, the Rigby's dinner party or his more intimate setting with Brenda.

He dressed when he was dry, once again retracing his path through the condo, stopping at the wine storage for a Grand Cru de Pomerol, '81, certain she wouldn't miss one out of a few hundred.

He returned the clean glass with tender care and gloved hands. He bid her adieu, and left with the two bottles and her panties. The Pomerol he would save for later, for the next evening at home to savour with a pizza and a video which he believed might feature the talents of Mr. and Mrs. Jackson Carlton.

He showered at the hotel, dressing in a suit and tie and the weakest eyeglasses he could buy from a drugstore that didn't make him look like Clark Kent or John Anderson.

Peering into the mirror for long minutes, searching intently for a familiar face, a welcomed stranger stared back. He no longer resembled Mr. John Anderson, the young and aspiring, tall, dark and handsome marketing executive from the sixties. He was deeply tanned from years in the yard, his face and body chiselled and hard. His new clothes didn't disguise that. He was pleased, satisfied. When once he was gregarious and charming, now in the mirror he seemed cold and isolated from the world. Which he was. Not his fault. Hers. Most definitely hers.

No one would recognize him after so many years. Not possible. He doubted many if any remembered him at all.

He had killed a man, which wasn't good for anyone's future, particularly with Battle View then and forever headlining a once enviable résumé. However now he was Pat Fellows, a new and possible better man with some semblance of hope. He was coming to the irrefutable realization that John Anderson was better off dead and that Mr. Cleaver of New Orleans might necessarily be of future assistance to him.

She was the one who sentenced him to Battle View, not the judge. Her. So why was he so willing to let her condemn him once more to hell. He didn't yet know, struggling to resolve what he truly wanted as the battle waged in his mind. First things first.

Reserved for 8:00 at Brenda's, he arrived thirty minutes early. His table was ready. Others were drinking at the bar, being sophisticated.

"Buenas tardes, señor."

"Sí, buenas tardes."

"¡Ah, qué bueno! Bienvenido a Brenda's."

"Gracias. This is my first visit. My expectations are as high as the opinions my contacts in Miami share of you. Unfortunately this evening I dine alone."

"¡Claro! And I am most certain, señor, that you will also speak well of Brenda's and that this will not be your final evening with us."

"Is Señorita Brenda in-house this evening? I am told that she often speaks with her guests and that she is most charming. I would welcome an introduction to her."

"I regret that she is not."

"Another time perhaps."

The tuxedoed and white-gloved waiter went on to explain the menu, suggesting a suitable vintage to accompany Señor Fellows' selections. He left with the order, returning first with an old-fashioned of Johnnie Walker Blue, neat. All or nothing. The evening was too important, too significant. He hadn't yet come to the end of memory lane. Nor would he for another several days.

If his destiny truly was hell, then so be it. He was good with that, providing he would take with him fresh memories to sustain him.

Brenda's proposed an understated elegance to its guests, the blending of stylish décor, muted lighting, private tables, soft music and quiet Miami sophisticates unaffected by hundred-dollar bottles of wine. The waiters appeared more like guests, most of them Latino; the hostess who greeted him at the door, who led him to his table, was dressed in a sequined and form-fitting evening gown, the three ladies behind the bar fashionably alluring in shorter and décolleté party dresses.

Behind them on the wall was an enlarged portrait of a very demure and very self-adoring whore for all to admire or fantasize over.

The restaurant was full, yet one could hear a pin drop were it not for the plush carpeting, Anderson careful not to make direct eye contact with the major-domo himself, Alejandro Garcia. He would know the man anywhere despite the passage of so many privileged years engraved into his older face. Unlike Anderson whose body, mind and once outward grace remained imbued behind the grey taint of prison.

Garcia was as culpable as her. He knew everything, yet said nothing, Anderson undecided as to what he should do about that. He had to do something. The man had blatantly perjured himself. One simple word, whore, would have set Anderson free. That didn't happen.

He remembered most facets of his trial, the swiftness of

the proceedings most of all. Truth be told, he didn't have much to remember. He remembered his March 31st arrest, his lawyer coming to him on the first and his initial arraignment on the Friday when he heard the charges against him read, the post-indictment plea on the Monday when he at last pleaded his innocence asking for trial by judge.

The short-lived trial by judge commenced a week later, April 12th, his conviction and sentencing hearing, which he learned was in great part intended to appease the French Government, was convened that Friday, April 16th. His next conscious moment was his first sight of Battle View prison, Tuesday, April 20th, from which point his past had no meaning and, his lawyer, no interest since Anderson was penniless.

John Anderson was officially a guest of the Federal Corrections System in Battle View Tennessee and destitute.
*

March 31st was John's first night in jail, silent after requesting a lawyer that didn't depend on the state for the reimbursement of his dubious pro bono work. He was stripped of his possessions and made to exchange his clothes for theirs; he was fingerprinted, questioned without success and put in a cell featuring a toilet and a matted bench.

The lawyer arrived the next morning to hear John's version, later meeting with Brenda Anderson and the prosecutor's office before hiring a private detective.

What John told the cops in the lawyer's presence was the truth. He killed the man whom he believed was raping his wife, whom she then admitted was her lover amongst many others. They were married six years earlier when she was a professor and he a frequent business traveller, the brief and tragic tale of love and treachery lasting less than a morning as the determined cops scribbled their notes.

Friday afternoon during his first arraignment the charges

read against him were Aggravated Assault, First Degree Murder, Conjugal Abuse and Issuing Death Threats. When John stood to address the court his lawyer dragged him into his seat by the elbow, ordering him to shut his mouth,

Monday afternoon in court, during his post-indictment plea, John pleaded not guilty to the first charge; he was not aggravated, he told the judge. He was pissed-off. Not the same thing at all.

To the charge of First Degree Murder he pleaded not guilty, telling the judge that he hadn't stood in the hallway plucking a daisy and thinking "she loves me, she loves me not." He just went in and killed the man.

To the third charge read he pleaded not guilty. Conjugal Violence was a stretch. He was defending his person against what he believed at the time, and under extreme distress, might be the carrier of an infectious disease. She was entirely naked; her body was wet, and in certain parts leaking with fluids not her own, after having confessed moments earlier to wantonly being with countless other men over several years. What choice did have?

To the final charge he pleaded not guilty. What he told her should not be construed by anyone as a threat, more like precognition.

The trial date was set for the coming Monday. Until then John was too numbed by events to think ahead more than minutes at a time. He was more concerned about his crumpling present. He no longer had a job, his employers and co-workers instantly disowning him. He no longer had a car, or a home, or anyone's respect, his lawyer advising him that Brenda Anderson had sold his car, vacated their home and had relocated to an address in West Palm Beach.

"She isn't wasting time, John. Du Valois is still stateside and to no one's surprise she hasn't gone to console the wife."

"I could give a good shit. My bank accounts, are they safe?"

"No, which is on you. Joint accounts. A completely stupid idea, otherwise known as Blind Love Accounts. They're cute, just not very smart. A man of your experience should have known better. In your case, which I discovered this morning… closed on Friday. The good news, the judge issued an immediate court order making her entirely responsible for my current fees pertaining to this case. I'm not going anywhere. We're a team, and we're going to beat this thing."

His numbness of the past few days faded, John realizing without any doubt that his hatred of her would never diminish. He wouldn't allow it. Quite the contrary. He would nurture the sentiment, embrace her for as long as he had to in his dreams.

"The first degree is the worst you should worry about," his lawyer consoled him. "We'll get that reduced to second degree. There's no proof. Your word against hers. You'll be out in fifteen, tops, much less with good behavior. The other charges are salad dressing, something to enhance the DA's case and ego. They won't stand up in court, I promise you. A little jab in the chest, what's that? Self-defence. Not exactly wife-beating. That said, absolutely no more daisy shit, no more threats, and no more doing my job for me. I talk, you keep your mouth shut. That's how things work, and we will get through this."

"So…twelve years, ten? What?"

The lawyer nodded. "About that, and probably in medium security. Reasonable for killing a man. Really, John, you would have done better by killing her. He wasn't the guilty one. She was. Not for prostitution, even if I could prove that, rather for setting you up and setting you off." He stood. "I'll see you Friday. In the meantime you stay quiet."

"That's it, stay quiet?"

"Holding your hand is not my job. So let me do what is. Four days is insane. You fucked up big time by killing this guy. The French are pushing hard. We're in a battle here,

John, so you let me find out about Brenda Anderson and Brenda Peters. The more deep dirt we can prove she's standing in, the better for you."

John spent the week on his back, either on the floor or on his bunk in the Dade County Jail doing sit-ups, or doing push-ups. Anything to prevent going insane. He had no books or magazines, no television or radio. His single freedom from excruciating boredom and a cell open to the view of several other detainees was the not-too-private five-minute showers each morning.

The lawyer did return as promised late Friday, finding John discouraged and beginning to accept that he had been abandoned.

"John, good news first, or the bad?"

"The good, which I'm assuming will give you more time for the bad."

"Brenda Peters throughout high school was promiscuous beyond anything I ever experienced, if memory serves. My guy didn't interview a single man who didn't remember her in detail. He heard countless stories. Got to say, along with the federal boys stirring the same pot, we pretty well caused a major shit storm in Bubba, Nebraska." He lit a cigarette. "Gets better. When she worked at the nightclub, still well-known today for certain off-the-menu services…"

"No. She never worked in a restaurant. Her parents scrimped to put her through college. After graduation she accepted a post at Miami State, Professor."

"She was never a professor. They know nothing about her. She never went past Grade Eleven with average marks. Spent too many hours in barns doing the dirty with country oafs that haven't stopped drooling and, however she discovered the restaurant, the female staff was then and is now viewed as agreeably sociable. She was a two-bit street hawker cashing in on a body that didn't require a brain. Need I expound on her current prominence?"

"I have a feeling you will."

"She's a smart one, though. Smart enough to own a club and enjoy a high-priced, high-rise oceanfront apartment on South Beach...officially the head office of Brenda's. Hers for six years and currently under reconstruction."

Anderson heard the words, speechless, one rampant thought crashing into another inside his head. "Or the woman's whorehouse. That's why he was there, in my home. She wanted me to see them. Sick bitch."

"You were duped, and we have no right to enter the apartment. Even so, proving prostitution is highly unlikely. She would simply claim the place as a secondary and justifiable business location for Brenda's and there is no law against a wife seeking pleasure elsewhere unless the husband claims and proves injury, which, in this case, comes a little late in the game."

"Grade Eleven. So...le Professeur Jean-François du Valois was more of her bullshit?"

"That's the bad news, John, and lots more of it. However I wouldn't say bullshit, very far from it. Possibly her way of strengthening her deception for whatever reason."

"Me, the fool. She came with me often to Paris on business. Her days were free, mine weren't. Any thoughts on that one?"

"Du Valois was a highly regarded businessman and representative of The French Foreign Trade Mission responsible for the US. However you say deep shit in French, you are in it. Apparently they're very big on capital punishment over there and his wife wants your head in a basket, literally. This is international, John. It is not going away. The entire world wants to know about you."

"You're saying I'm screwed."

"No. Though a contingent of French envoys has arrived to officially make serious waves."

"So what now?"

"We do our best and we hope for the best. Really? I

think we're good. I know we are."

John felt nauseous. Being a city boy he could always smell bullshit before he stepped into it, despising himself for falling so deeply into Brenda's constant flow.

"Do what you have to. The French are pit-bulls. They're tenacious and don't give a good shit about anyone else." He raised his elbows to the table, crossed one hand over the other to rest his chin. "Think I'll hang?"

Twenty-Eight

1965

The waiter woke Anderson from his trance, excusing himself. John examined the plate, nodding his approval with a scant smile, waiting for the man to replenish his wine and leave before cutting into the delicately prepared filet mignon aux poivres and bright legumes, his appetite suddenly lost.

That entire week had been a waste of time. The French lynch mob and the DA wanted him dead; sure as hell she did. The trial was a sham, du Valois spoken of by his compatriots in heartwarming terms through the voice of the one elected to take the witness stand as though du Valois hadn't done anything despicably wrong and immoral for so long.

He was held in the highest regard by all who were fortunate enough to call him a friend or acquaintance, they declared. He was a devoted and loving husband and father. A husband and father now dead, thoughtlessly murdered for no reason but a madman's enflamed indignation and rage.

The judge allowed it. Anderson remembered the judge allowing everything the French had on their accented tongues to say, Anderson's lawyer arguing that loving husbands did not steal other men's wives.

Irrelevant.

*

Over the weekend John should have been making final

arrangements for a trip to Madrid, somewhere he'd never taken her. Now he understood why, or why not.

He scarcely slept, his mindset continuously interrupted by too many sordid and tormenting images of a naked whore leaping and skipping around a dead man's erection.

What would he do? What could he do? He didn't know. He had no script, no business plan; no history of standing in a box pleading for his life. Pleading. Why? Why would he now have to plead for his life when she was the guilty party? Who would not believe that?

Monday morning the lawyer arrived at the county facility with a freshly pressed suit, shirt, tie and accoutrements requisite for impressing a federal judge.

The courtroom was crowded, despite being closed to all but journalists and three select witnesses. This was big news, the French contingent commandeering the front row directly behind the DA, the ADA and Brenda Anderson who followed the prisoner's unblinking cold eyes from the marshal's entrance to the side of the Defence Attorney where they seated him.

They secured his hands to an iron ring fixed to the desk noticeably uncluttered by papers or files, a single notebook opened to blank pages filled the space in front of him that John cared not to think about.

Nor was the DA's desk the usual chaotic mess of papers, though for appearance sake a neatly stacked and staggered pile of thin folders filled with widely-spaced notes and photographs filled his space.

The court was in session, the judge reiterating to the defendant that he, the district attorney, and defence counsel under protest that went unheeded, had agreed to forego the testimony of character witnesses pertaining to either lifetime prior to their marriage including that of the Peters of Nebraska who were at present, in the court's view, estranged from their daughter.

What Mrs. Anderson may have done as a teenager bore

no relevance. Nor would the judge consider testimony pitting the outcome of his decision against the fact that Mrs. Anderson had not graduated from college or that she had never worked as a professor at Miami State.

Those were domestic questions of no concern to the court. Nor would he consider speculative hearsay regarding her previous work as a restaurant greeter since too many years had elapsed.

Although Mrs. Anderson may have concealed one past life while fabricating another with the intention of luring the defendant John Anderson into an unhappy marriage, she was not on trial. That speculative evidence was irrelevant to the case and beyond the current concern of the defendant or the court.

John made no attempt to acknowledge the remarks.

*

The first witness called to take the stand on behalf of du Valois and his widow who declined the prosecution's suggestion due to the frailty of her English, faced defence counsel with the enthusiasm and vigor instilled in him by the prosecution's arrogance.

"No! This man, monsieur, he killed a beloved father and caring husband of a loving wife who now wallows in such deep sorrow as she waits for his body to return home. And for this, of course, he must pay as dearly."

"A caring husband, really? If he hadn't been in my client's bed fornicating with my client's wife he would by now be home safe and sound with his own wife. So let's not feel too sorry for the grieving widow. If du Valois thought so little of his wife with such frequency and ardour with her carnal substitute, why should we?"

"Monsieur, you are American and less open about such natural matters. Such is our culture in France. This has been our way since many generations before the revolution." He snickered. "Vive la France! Vive la différence! No?"

"No. That difference got your man killed because he

was foolishly in my client's bed being entertained by a very devious woman." The DA objected. The judge agreed, counsel for the defence admonished. "And no, sir, to continue, because in this country we choose as a culture of decent people, not lecherous opportunists and adulterers, not to import the incontestably corrupt social mores of yours."

John interrupted the testimony to say in a strong voice and in French to the instant bewilderment of the judge, "his wife no longer has a husband because your *Frenchman* died for fucking my wife in my bed. So beware of whose wives you will fuck tonight. And fuck your French culture."

The court stenographer froze into a catatonic state.

Shocked heads jerked in the French row. An incredible and diplomatic insult. Heads turned this way and that, puzzled expressions facing other puzzled expressions. The French journalists alone scribbled, the Americans sat clueless.

When the judge requested the open-mouthed witness to translate the outburst, the man paled. "Sir, with great respect, I cannot. Decency and civility forbid me to offend this court. I will say, however, that his terrible words were not those of a gentleman and very much a grave insult to Madame du Valois."

When the judge ordered John to translate what he had said, John obliged without the slightest hesitation, his lawyer sharing the judicial ire and condemnation. However contempt of court would have seemed ridiculous from any intellectual perspective.

The time was right to adjourn.

John's company had sent the CEO who spoke Tuesday of his character as unassuming and gracious, not the kind of man who would ever contemplate violently ending another's life.

He was successful and respected by the corporation, by European and American clients alike for constantly being the best at what he did. He was unquestionably destined for partnership in the firm one day…Was."

"You fired him, in essence prejudging him."

"He killed a man, an important man…and a French citizen. A country of extreme importance to the firm. Yes, I fired him, in absentia. And I would make it understood by everyone here that we do not share the sentiments of his outburst yesterday."

"What would you have done in his place?"

The executive replied, "In the case of assault, the very same without question. Or so I would hope. In the case presented to all of us present yesterday during your opening remarks and theirs…Well, how do the fees of criminal attorneys differ from those specialized in divorce? No woman, no matter how lovely or seemingly pure, is that lovely or pure. Not a single one is worth whatever grief Mr. Anderson is now, or will later, endure. I would have walked out, as he should have. We will miss him without question, as a friend, as a pillar of the firm, and we grieve for him. That said, he should have walked out."

"And what would you have done, sir, had your wife…" The lawyer caught himself, theatrically. "A question I will consider putting to you later in the week." He faced the French delegation. "Perhaps I'll ask you Frenchmen as well as you obviously sympathize with and condone this man's disagreeable view of womankind."

Wednesday Alejandro Garcia was called to the stand.

The DA made him appear as the Andersons' best friend, as Brenda Anderson's savior, mentor and caring guardian when first she arrived in Miami. He adored her as a younger sister.

He had always considered John as an honest and well-intentioned man. However he was undeniably and frequently neglectful of his wife's emotional needs, putting himself and his business first. Brenda was often lonely, delving into the club's business, often seven days a week to assuage her despair.

"Were you aware of Mr. du Valois and of his occasional interactions with Mrs. Anderson?"

"Yes, to the extent that he dined with her and brought a much needed balance to her life."

"Balance? You were aware they were lovers?"

"I was, as her confidant and friend. Yes. However, who in this room can blame her? Look at her. She is divine. Who in this room could find fault with her need for warmth and attention? She deserved more than he gave her."

The prosecutor sat, feeling good about himself, first acknowledging each grim expression of the French delegation.

Defence counsel stood.

"Mr. Garcia, you were her guardian and mentor in Miami, were you not, her first friend? In fact the only friend of a girl already familiar with the eager hands of boys crouched behind bales of hay."

The prosecutor sprang to his feet, outraged at the breach. The judge concurred, defence counsel once again scolded, once again demonstratively servile in his apology.

"How fortunate. You must have felt blessed. Exceptionally generous of you, I would venture to say, befriending a farm girl lost, making her way into a big city. In what way, precisely, did you guide then Brenda Peters and for how long?"

"In her career, until she was comfortable."

"Yes, her career as a sidewalk lounge greeter, when you were employed as a barman in one of Miami's least respectable hotels, where then Brenda Peters remained for a fleeting few weeks before moving on to more luxurious quarters without you."

"No. We remained friends, just friends."

"Her only friend, as we have established. When questioned by me, Mrs. Anderson could not produce the name of a single man or woman as a friend from those pre-marital former years. Bizarre, don't you think, for a woman so divine, who, shall we agree for the sake of argument is worth a second casual glance? Then out of the blue she's married, for reasons known only to her, suddenly in desperate need of a husband while maintaining and preferring illicit relations with a foreign adulterer amongst others from who knows where."

"You insult her, and you insult me. For some, a single friend is sufficient."

"Friends apart, since you were then separated for six years until she hired you as a barman at Brenda's when, for the first time in their fourteen months together she mentioned your name to Mr. Anderson who recalls clearly that your first reunion was more catching up than nostalgic."

"She remembered that I would always be there for her."

"And she could rely on your discretion since she was seldom present at the club. She was entertaining men like Mr. du Valois and now you are to be her maître d' in her new and magnificent Brenda's and Mrs. Anderson, Brenda Peters, has an upscale apartment in which to receive her," he paused for affect, "before and after-hours patrons."

"She owns the club. She is better suited to business than serving drinks or waiting tables. Such work is beneath her."

"From the meagre beginnings as a modest barman to maître d' in this city's arguably most enviable nightspot. Did you ever sleep with her, Mr. Garcia? Aren't you, in fact, the carnal instructor of a young girl then recently turned eighteen who never envisioned college in favour of a more adventurous and lucrative life in Miami laying with men such as du Valois for profit?"

"On my honour, I never slept with Mrs. Anderson. The suggestion that I would think of such a thing, or that she is such a woman as you describe, is distasteful to me."

"Yet you were aware of her intrigues with du Valois?"

"I know nothing of intrigues. He was gentleman and a

comfort to her, a good friend, as I am.

"Indeed, all the while sharing the hospitality and friendship of both husband and wife in their home."

"Yes."

"And decidedly two-faced, which I find distasteful."

Garcia shrugged. "You're allowed."

"Yes, I am. I am also allowed to believe that Brenda Peters became Mrs. Anderson with ill-intent, that you were complicit in her scheme and that you remain so. I suggest to you, and to the court, that any woman discussed in such debasing terms, though truly innocent in her mind and in her body of such lewd, immoral and possibly illegal behavior, would scream out her virtue and purity in justifiable rage." He twirled, facing the prosecutor's desk. "Yet she sits there so calmly and unaffected." The lawyer faced the judge. "I'm done, Your Honour."

Each day the gavel struck at noon, adjourning for the day, the judge retiring to his chambers to reflect on testimony that was for the most part circumstantial. In truth, the trial might have taken a single day if not for requisite protocol and the weight upon the shoulders of a single man, who was not a jury of John Anderson's peers, to pass judgement.

The defendant had confessed to the police; he was guilty. To what extent? His wife had substantiated with minute and emotive details the sequence of events as confessed by her husband.

Brenda Anderson was not guilty of committing a heinous crime, rather of engineering one that for one man or the other would have dire consequences.

Thursday would certainly prove longer, more arduous when the protagonists themselves would be called to the stand.

Twenty-Nine

1965

Anderson's waiter removed the plate without asking whether his patron had finished. John was in another world, sensing his mood deteriorating from eager to assuage his curiosity about her, about Garcia, to sombre.

He was so close. His single greatest and mounting fear was failure, the fear of Billy Rider no longer believing.

The waiter refilled the wine goblet with what was left in the bottle and left.

*

The prosecutor called Mrs. Brenda Anderson to the stand, who strutted across the courtroom in low-heeled pumps and a simple yet exclusive pantsuit with her hair styled into a girl-next-door ponytail.

"Mrs. Anderson, Brenda, take your time. You are not on trial here"

"Thank you. I am a little nervous." She inhaled a deep breath, composing herself, glancing timidly at her husband who wanted to snap her neck.

"Tell the court what inspired you to invent, in fact create, the false characterization of a professor."

"Yes. I had no future in Nebraska, as much as I hated leaving my parents. Because I do love them so much. I knew I had to go to Miami, to become like the women I would read about in magazines. I fabricated the story for my parents' sake, to make them proud of me."

"And once in Miami you discovered Mr. Garcia who assisted you in finding employment."

"Yes. He was, and is, a good friend. I could never work in an office. That was never my dream. I wanted to be part of Miami, not simply live here. I was hired to greet patrons at the restaurant where I did very well, earning in a single week more than what office girls would in a month. I was young. I was living a dream."

"You were successful, and then you met Mr. Anderson and you fell in love."

"That's correct. I don't make friends easily. Most girls don't like me because I'm a threat, and men, well…you know, here today, gone tomorrow. He wasn't like that. He was different. He was honest and sincere. Those first months were a fantasy."

"He thought you were a professor, teaching history."

"He did until the wedding, which I wasn't expecting. I couldn't lie to him anymore, not to a man I loved so deeply. That's when I began imagining my own place, Brend*a*'s, my club. Then gradually things turned bad. I began feeling as though I had made a terrible mistake. Soon after the wedding it seemed as though he was no different from all the others. Gone…all the time. I began suspecting that he no longer loved me."

"Indeed. You thinking solely of him while entertaining such horrible thoughts, enduring such painful solitude, ironically of his doing. And then, at some point, you met the elegant and charming Jean-François du Valois. When exactly?"

"Two years ago, at Brend*a*'s, when our marriage truly began suffering…at least for me. I was lonely, more convinced each week alone that he was travelling to avoid being with me. I felt hurt. I was vulnerable."

"Allowing yourself to become a willing victim of an eloquent and persuasive manner?"

"Yes. I hated John for making me sink to such a low

point. I wanted to hurt him the way he was hurting me."

"However Mr. du Valois became a good friend over time, not merely an ardent lover?"

"Very good friends." Brenda Anderson glanced over to Madame du Valois, lowering her head. "I would say soul mates. We needed each other for the very same reasons. As much as I longed for his visits, for his kindness and attention, he also yearned for mine. More than once Jean-François suggested that we should marry."

Madame du Valois screamed to her feet, her tone scathing and accusing, her outrage directed at the witness, her body twisting violently away from the man beside her, her face a dark mask of pure hatred.

The gavel crashing repeatedly onto its base was scarcely noticed, the judge standing, leaning over his bench to terminate the unintelligible tirade.

He pointed a threatening finger to the most senior of the Frenchmen beside her. "Sir, I order you to tell this court what that woman said."

"Sir, I cannot." The Frenchman raised his hands in supplication. "I cannot possibly express such words or sentiments. They are beyond my ability."

"Mr. Anderson," the judge practically screamed himself, "did you understand her? And remove that goddamned smirk from you face!"

"Apparently my wife, Mrs. Anderson, the current witness, is a despicable whore and a common street slut not worth a single franc let alone a marriage." Anderson snickered. "I believe Madame du Valois possesses an insightful understanding of the situation, Your Honour." He acknowledged the Frenchwoman. "Je vous remerice profondément, Madame du Valois. Sachez que je regrette la mort de votre époux. Croyez-m'en. Je concède ouvertement que j'ai en effet tué la mauvaise personne." He did regret killing the wrong person, du Valois and not the whore, reinforcing his compunction towards the agitated woman with a kind smile, tilting his head in a gentlemanly salute before facing the judge. "I thanked her for her understanding."

"Madam, take your seat," the judge instructed harshly. "As for you, Mr. Anderson, a murder trial is no place for glibness, particularly when *you* are the one on trial." He pointed to the prosecutor. "Get on with it."

"Yet despite your evolving relationship you never brought Mr. du Valois into your home, or to your secondary workplace as owner of Brend*a*'s?"

"Not once. Not until this time, and I don't know why. I knew John wouldn't be home for a few nights. I hadn't felt special in my own home or in my bed for so long a time, and Jean-François made me feel very special. I suppose I wanted to imagine for one romantic night that we were married."

"And he alone. You never once sought comfort from other men, men you might have met at your establishment?"

"Never. How could I do such a horrible thing to myself or to Jean-François? No!"

"And the rest is sorrowful history. Mr. Anderson arrived home unannounced, he saw you with your lover in a heated moment, and brutally murdered Mr. du Valois before beating you and threatening *you* with murder as well."

Her eyes began to well with tears. "It was terrible. I still can't believe he's gone."

The prosecutor passed her his pocket hanky. "Compose yourself, Brenda. Take your time."

He waited, the court waited; John wanted to vomit.

"He wanted to kill me. I saw the pure hatred in his eyes. Then he stared at poor Jean-François and laughed like a madman. That's when he called the police and I ran out, terrified that he would kill me."

"And now we are here, aren't we, to see a murderer appropriately punished for a heinous crime? Thank you, Mrs. Anderson."

The prosecutor returned to his seat, reaching for his pen, prepared to scribble notes.

Counsel for the defense approached the witness. He stood quietly studying her, piercing her eyes with his, the smooth skin at her throat articulating with each dry swallow. She was nervous, with good reason. She was a liar, one leg crossed over the other, her hands clasped together to prevent inadvertent lapses in her composure. Nicely prepped. Well done.

"I believe the district attorney ignored certain facts, Mrs. Anderson. Unintentionally, I'm sure. How does one make one's parents proud by commissioning the production of a fraudulent university diploma in Tallahassee where those same parents believed you resided...and not Miami?"

"A piece of paper, one that I never used. So what?'

"One that you used to ensure that your new husband would never question your credentials or your professorial activities while your actual profession, job, was luring passers-by into one or the other of your places of work by distributing menus in questionably provocative attire. A preview of succulent temptations as it were."

"I never did anything wrong. My restaurant job was honest work."

"Possibly so. Yet not quite worthy of a man of such character as Mr. Anderson whose real credentials are impressive, enviable to most of us. He could hardly be expected to pursue a future with a woman of so little ambition, a woman believing that passing out menus on a street corner for hours at a time in a revealing costume was her dream."

"Like I said, the money was good. I'm not ashamed."

"The now deceased Mr. du Valois, you met him two years ago?"

"Yes."

"And you fell in love."

"That came later. Yes."

"Yes, as your marriage was crumpling because your husband paid you little or no attention."

"Correct."

"Please tell the court when and where you met Mr. Anderson, your husband."

"October 1957, in-flight. I was returning home from Paris."

"Ah, Paris, the City of Lights. Another dream, Mrs. Anderson?"

"Yes."

"You were at once enamoured of your future husband, accepting his proposal of an evening of dinner and dancing that coming week. This from a girl who doesn't easily trust men or make friends."

"That's correct. He was different. He was a gentleman."

"Please tell the court how different, Mrs. Anderson, from your French colleague in Paris whom you conferred with while deserting your parents whom you love so dearly to find their way around Paris each day on their own."

Brenda Anderson, abruptly and visibly taken aback, paled. "Excuse me?"

"One Professeur Jean-François du Valois who, according to you, was quite eminent in his field. Which was what, Mrs. Anderson, since you are the one person seemingly aware that he was in fact a scholar and not a high-ranking businessman whom you mentioned to your husband some six years prior to the date of your previous testimony and well over a year prior to your marriage."

"That was the last time I saw him, until we met by accident. I am not a liar."

"Well the fact that you absently did not employ the use of a contraction in that denial indicates that you may well be. Shame on the prosecutor for not forewarning you. Were you intimate on that first occasion?"

"Yes." She glanced at Madame du Valois. "Very intimate."

"Let's for the moment believe you," he faced the judge, "with clear misgivings. Tell the court why you chose to marry Mr. Anderson."

"Simple. I was tired of my restaurant job. I wanted more, I deserved more. As John became increasingly interested in me, finally proposing, I realized I could have something better. So I quit a few days before the wedding."

"In point of fact you did not quit. You were fired almost a year earlier for thinking too highly of yourself, for constantly making demands for time off. So now tell the court what you did with all that free time between mid-February '58 and your wedding night as your groom-to-be believed you were a professor, an intellectual, and not an unemployed street hawker."

"I was planning Brenda's. I had enough money in the bank to live well until he married me, when I knew he would help me with the financing."

"And did you plan to repay him at some point, the way you repaid your parents for their selfless contribution to your invented university education?"

"No. I did not."

"So you didn't love him."

"No."

"You married him for gain."

"I married him for convenience. He got me, I got Brenda's. We both did well."

"Did he also finance your oceanfront hideaway which you rented several months prior to opening the club, and purchased, paying in cash and in full four years ago?"

"That was mine. Like I said, before quitting I made good money. I didn't need him for everything."

"Yet your romantic life was quite adequate, wouldn't you say, until that ill-fated evening."

"Frequent, not adequate. My feelings of romance were reserved for Jean-François."

"Who was to be with you for the entire fatal week, is

that correct?"

"No. That one night only, for which I will never forgive myself."

"The man travelled widely. He favoured five-star hotels and fine restaurants, yet he came to you, into your husband's home and into his bed with a week's worth of luggage."

She shrugged. "He didn't tell me why. And I didn't ask."

"Do you remember the actual event? Not du Valois' unfortunate end, rather what emotions you felt: Fear, elation, sexual arousal at being watched by one man while sexually engaged with another? Dare I suggest shock, Mrs. Anderson, possibly regret, remorse…anything?"

Her mouth curved into a sneer. "Why would I?"

"For inadvertently contributing to a man's death."

"I didn't do that. I felt relief. I was finally going to be rid of him."

"I believe that's the one truthful thing you've said this morning. In fact you mocked him, sneering as you are now, seeing fit to remain feverishly entwined as one with Mr. du Valois as you casually introduced him to your husband's profound disbelief." He turned to face the spectators, staring down John's ex-boss. "How, sir, I wonder, would you react to that, to see the wife you love so profoundly firmly embedded onto her lover and scornfully telling you that she wasn't expecting you? Would you care to tell the court?" He paused for affect. "No? Nothing?" He faced the witness. "Furthermore, Mrs. Anderson, I soundly believe that only a woman accustomed to the frequent display of her body on a professional level would possess that degree of composure."

"I'm not a whore."

"Ah! The use of a contraction. You learn quickly, Mrs. Anderson, despite which certain of us would disagree with that personal assessment. At which juncture Mr. du Valois was not yet lying dead on top of you. He did, in point of fact, bring that condition upon himself in somewhat of a cavalier manner by declaring to your husband that he and you were frequently treacherous in each other's loving arms or mutually rewarding embrace." He addressed the judge. "We can imagine the ensuing drama, Your Honour. I have nothing further for this witness. The rest, as noted, is history."

The witness was excused. Defence counsel returned to his seat, scribbling notes more for affect than need as the familiar gavel commenced a two-hour recess for lunch.

The courtroom emptied, all conversation held in check until the surge of bodies crushing together through the open doors and into the corridor subsided and quiet prevailed. The prisoner was the last to leave.

When once again the judge appeared through the door of his chambers, court was again in session, the DA calling his next and last witness.

He waited by the judge's bench as John was unshackled from his desk, escorted by marshals to the witness box and once again secured.

"Let us assume, Mr. Anderson, that Mrs. Anderson must share part of the blame insofar as she was a dissatisfied wife searching to fill a loveless void. That said, you must have suspected the slightest possibility of her adultery, the faintest glimmer of a clue. A beautiful young woman so frequently left to her own devices by a husband that she herself might understandably have suspected of adulterous treason."

"Assume what you wish. I was as blind as I was faithful. The woman's a consummate and habitual liar. The better question is, why don't *you* see that? She's lied about absolutely everything and incredibly you people believe her."

"Mrs. Anderson has no reason to lie. She's not on trial. You are."

"Compulsive liars always have every reason to lie. It's a

pathological continuum. I should think you would know that. Or are you new at this?"

The prosecutor ignored the barb. "Is that why you arrived home unexpectedly and unannounced, because you didn't trust her?"

"That's right, very intuitive of you. I arrived home with a dozen red roses because I believed she was a cheating whore, or didn't you read that in the report?"

"You thought she was being raped."

"No! I believed she was being raped. What would you think or believe? Of course I did. I ran in believing the worst. Until I saw her grinning, stroking his hair, staring straight at me. Then he spoke. That's the instant my mind went blank. Yes, in my mind he was raping her. That's when I struck him. Then I heard her scream, and then he was dead."

"At which point, your heated rage increasingly out of control, you beat her."

"There was no rage, no anger. Like I said, she's a liar."

"Her body was bruised."

"Not her body, her upper chest. Get your facts straight. She ran around the room, hysterical, charging at me when I called her a whore, which she is. We know that now. Don't we? I pushed her away, once, which does not constitute a beating in anyone's book."

"Who could blame her? She was frantic, trapped in a room with a crazed murderer. You were ranting at her, calling her a whore, an offensive abuse in itself, and threatening to kill her."

"I wasn't ranting. I was calm. As for her, we are what we are. You wouldn't take offense to me calling you a district attorney, because that's what you are…and she's a whore. Ask Madame du Valois."

"An unlikely issue not before this court, though very much a young and vulnerable woman you threatened to kill."

Anderson smirked, his eyes fixed on his wife. "Yes, for an instant. I didn't see that killing her could make matters worse. Then she was gone, and here we are."

The prosecutor addressed the judge. "No further questions."

Defence counsel took his place.

"John, why did you insist on trial by judge against my advice?"

"Demographics. She's white, middle-class, young and beautiful…on the outside. On the inside, not so much. The typical girl next door, the envy of all those who aren't. I didn't want shocked mothers or horrified grandmothers, or women her age whom the DA would lead to believe could well be potential victims of men like me. Nor did I want angry or potentially biased fathers, or men my age sitting in a jury box fantasizing about screwing her brains out at my expense. I chose in favour of professional rationale, not emotion."

"Your wife is a practiced liar."

"Very much so."

"Tell us what we don't know about her from the time of that now historical flight, in your own words."

John twisted in his seat, facing the judge. "Seven and a half years, in my own words, is that right?"

"The court will tolerate a reasonable degree personal opinion and latitude, Mr. Anderson, since this entire case is one of emotional conflict. That said, I caution you to measure yourself."

"I knew then that I wanted to marry her. The first six months were somewhat reserved to say the least, which then I believed was cute, refreshing. Our dates were always planned in advance due mostly to her teaching schedule, which I never thought to question. I couldn't imagine for a moment that so many others were taking my place, filling my coveted space as it were. She says she loves her parents, she doesn't. That's a lie. They embarrass her. Prior to that flight they were lost in Paris while she was with le Professeur Jean-François du Valois, six months before she first yelped for me as my virgin fiancée in a New York hotel room. Another lie, that one embellished with remarkable acting skills as you can well imagine. Soon after we moved in together, to a place we really could not then afford. That was one of her better lies, a compound-lie because she rented one equally upscale for herself on South Beach eight months before word one was mentioned about her cherished Brenda's, eight months before I met her parents for the first time in Paris for our wedding. Like I said, she was ashamed of them. So much so that during that first flight together she practically dragged me from the plane to prevent my meeting them." Anderson paused, musing. "Anyone keeping track of this?"

"Why a secret nest of her own, do you suppose?"

"I don't suppose. No one should. She was entertaining; she didn't want to chance hotels. Very likely because she had outdone her welcome. I say entertaining because no one here seems to believe that a stunning twenty-nine-year-old female who chose to have herself spayed at eighteen when just off the farm could possibly be a prostitute. Well, she was then and she is now. What other explanation is there? There isn't one. Let's all understand that. That South Beach apartment is owned by Brenda Peters, not Anderson." He chortled, staring at her. "If not a paid whore, and I suspect well-paid, she always did want and expect the best. At the very least she's a discerning nymphomaniac who intentionally placed a man in harm's way to serve her selfish needs. Another lie, this time directed at du Valois...and, regrettably, his wife."

"Adding insult to injury, John, by placing your condo on the market this week prior to her relocation in West Palm Beach, once again as Brenda Peters."

"You mean destroying evidence of her prostitution by renovating, knowing she would do this, before setting up shop in Palm Beach when all this blows over. She's not a victim here. I am, Madame du Valois is. I stand accused of killing her husband, I accept that, for initially misconstruing the situation, stung for an instant by an unfortunate blind rage. However Brenda Peters is equally guilty. She orchestrated the event whose outcome she predicted, playing me as well as she played du Valois. The way she's playing this court. Then one day, for some reason in her twisted mind, divorce wasn't enough, deliberately enflaming the situation with a smile I can still see her wearing behind that theatrical expression the rest of you see."

"I can't imagine your distress, believing the centre of your universe rudely violated by another man, then to discover her euphoric and cunning participation in his arms."

"I felt too sick to vomit. At the wedding I believed I was the happiest man in the world, despite her less than modest attire. In retrospect I suppose she was too accustomed to standing half-naked on a city sidewalk. Go figure."

"Her mother thought her quite vulgar at the wedding, did she not?"

"She did. Nice folks her parents, anxious for grandkids, which would never happen, not since the tubal ligation that your detective recently discovered. She planned this life from the start. So you tell me, another lie? I believe so. She told me the night of Monsieur du Valois' passing that she'd been with him and other men for a very long time. Now we know how long. Don't we? We know how she occupied herself during that second week in Paris as the new Mrs. Anderson with Monsieur du Valois while I was working. Another lie. All lies."

"Until her most creative invention."

"Teaching didn't satisfy her, she needed a change. When, in fact, she was fired from the restaurant. Two lies. Then came Brenda's, the ultimate cover for a lady, so-called, of the night."

"She no longer needed you, John."

"She discovered too late in the game that she never did. She should have asked for an annulment. Du Valois would be alive and she'd be working him on her back instead of sitting in court nailing me to a cross. Brenda's was an afterthought. She needed a cover to replace her teaching position since she no longer had her sidewalk job. Let's face it. She had the money. She certainly had enough to maintain the teaching ruse from the time we moved in until we married. Had Brenda's come first, which didn't happen despite what she claims, we wouldn't be here today. With the money she was once earning from the restaurant, and with what du Valois and her others were paying her, obviously top money, she must have had more than enough to fund a small club."

"And so life went until two weeks ago, each night in bed another lie, each trip to Paris another lie, a once beautiful wife lying repulsive and vile under a naked and cavalier stranger, mocking you."

"Two people know what happened that night, for the rest of you it's a question of your vivid imaginations and interpretation. Imagine her smiling at me, stroking his hair, telling me in a guttural purr that we should all talk about it the next morning. Imagine that, Judge, and tell me she's not a despicable whore. What followed happened in a blink, as though in a netherworld. I may have killed du Valois, but she pulled the trigger. That smile killed him, though what I will always vividly remember is how repugnant she was to me, how pungently rotten she smelled. That will be my lasting memory of her." He leered straight at her. "Her stench."

Thirty

1965

John wasn't ready to lock himself into his hotel room, his cell. That would come soon enough. He swirled what little remained of his cognac, signalling his waiter for another, pleased that the man wasn't bothersome with effusive attention.

He didn't regret visiting the restaurant he had originally financed. He didn't feel resentment. Those days were over. Being there was something he had to do, seeing Alejandro Garcia was something he had to do.

What would Garcia do, John wondered, to know that a guest in his restaurant was deliberating on his deserved punishment? He was no better than her, possibly worse. She had a motive; Garcia merely had a good job and a whore for a boss.

John didn't have to read lips to understand how the man had metamorphosed from being no better than a pimp to an arrogant and effusive Latino asshole in a tux, charming to any woman who wasn't Latina. Latinas, they all had one defining attribute in common: Piercing eyes that could see through shit.

Likely as not the man had completely erased the trial from his memory; not so for John. He remembered the shared glance, the intensity of the sparkle in their eyes, the glee. Why they hadn't jumped up and down and clapped their hands remained a mystery.

That he would never forgive. He'd never forgotten that cruel exchange. Nor had he forgotten the she'd smiled in his bed, the shrug or the odour she gave off. Remembering had kept him alive; gave him hope, gave him a mission.

He glanced at his watch. Thursday: Nine-forty. Not far from the hour of his final meeting with his lawyer that last Thursday of his relative freedom, the evening they conspired to lawfully violate the judge's court order.

The judge had refused John any direct communication with the outside world, placing a gag order as well on the media throughout the week until the verdict was read. He said nothing about John's defence counsel placing a call to the Peters in Nebraska through a speaker box.

He hadn't thought about them since the trial, wondering how they might have heard or how they might have reacted with horror to the sentence handed down. He wondered whether they were living and whether they had ever forgiven her. He didn't think so. They were too decent, too devastated.

He traded snifters with the waiter, putting his nose to the rim, inhaling the intense aroma, sipping, savouring the prickly heat, pondering how the Peters would react to news of their daughter's death and who would tell them. Possibly he would.

*

John shared his lawyer's confidence. At most he would get ten to twelve. Even the French contingent was shocked to a man at what they had heard, if not forgiving of his outburst.

Madame du Valois as well was visibly horrified that her husband could intentionally find himself in the company of such a contemptible woman.

The Peters were unaware of the trial, despite their town of a few thousand being all abuzz with supposition and innuendo regarding the private detective who knocked on so many doors including the Peters', yet answered no one's questions. And the FBI. What could possibly be the matter?

Why were the police so interested in Brenda Peters?

"It's not good, Polly. You'd better get Walter to the phone. You'll need him nearby."

Mrs. Peters yelled for her husband, screaming out his name much louder a second time. The old man came running.

"John, we're both here. What happened, dear boy?" Mrs. Peters asked. "What has Brenda done?"

"The fuss is all about a murder trial, Polly, Walter. My trial. I killed a man a while ago for fornicating with Brenda. I walked in on them. I had a bad reaction."

"My Lord, John. No!" she gasped.

"We knew something was terribly wrong, John, but the police refused to say anything. Our phone hasn't stopped ringing. We must have left you and Brenda a hundred messages. We've been beside ourselves with worry."

"Polly, Walter...this is not good. Brenda was never a teacher. She never went to school in Tallahassee. Her entire life since leaving your home has been a lie. She found a job in Miami that allowed her to meet men, men who paid for her favours."

John went on to acquaint the tearful couple with their real daughter.

Walter took over the call. Polly was too distraught to speak, barely able to breath between sobs.

"I'll be damned to hell if I'll ever set eyes on her again, John. I knew she would come to no good, always flirting with the boys. Not surprised at all to hear she's a lowlife trollop. I will never, never in my life say or think enough bad things about her."

"I'm very sorry, Walter."

"She's the sorry one. All these many years telling her mother outright lies, never coming home, making us sick with worry till she found you."

John chortled. "Honestly, Walter, I'm even sorrier about that."

"You're a good one, John. Nothing bad about you, son. Me and Polly, we always speak kindly of you. Never a mean word. Always will. You did what was right, what a man should do. Would have done the same myself. More's the pity you came home to her too soon. Terrible when a man's heart can't express the shame he feels. We gave her what we could, taught her what was right, what wasn't. Now to hear she's a full out tramp. Rotten to the core, that girl."

"Be strong for Polly, Walter. You two don't deserve this. I hope you understand I had to call before she does with another lie."

"What's to become of you, John? What's she gone and done to you, son?"

"My lawyer says I won't hang. That's the good news, I suppose, though I'm facing ten, more like twelve years of easy time. I won't know until Monday. But I won't be calling you, Walter, not for a few years anyway."

"Good Lord, John." Walter's sobs were melding with his wife's. "Would have killed her with my own hands twelve years past if I'd even thought for a second. Sure as hell's filled with fire. Would have dragged her to the barn and put a knife to her gut. I swear. Would have spared me and Polly the one that's twisting in ours."

John forced a weak chuckle that didn't work. "You get that jug from under the sink, Walter. Not too much for Polly, mind. You'll get through this. We all will."

"You did the right thing, John. You stand tall. You're a young man. You'll get through this. Me and Polly, we'll find where you are. We'll come visit often as we can. That's the God's honest truth, son."

John knew that. He believed that, ending the call.

His lawyer went home. They wouldn't see each other until Monday morning. Neither had a reason. Waiting was the final phase, John pondering continuously over his long weekend why the judge had ordered his suicide watch.

Monday morning John sat in his cell staring up at his lawyer as his wrists were chained to his waist and his feet were shackled to a twelve-inch chain. No one said a word. No one had to or wanted to.

Led through the marshal's portal into the courtroom John felt ridiculous shimmying his way across the full width of the room like a medieval geisha wrapped too tightly in a binding kimono. He was a joke, something to laugh at; the entire assembly of spectators was absorbed by the amusing spectacle. He, the once dignified Mr. John Anderson, reduced a comedic character in a courtroom drama.

He ignored her; he ignored Garcia. The reality of what was about to take place was seeping into his mind, spreading like wildfire, John realizing that he was shackled so that he wouldn't leap over the DA's desk and snap the bitch's neck the way he had rid the world of du Valois' charismatic charm.

Serious shit was going down. They wouldn't chain a man like a wild beast simply to entertain and delight the crowd or for a mere ten to twelve years.

The room was still, John turning to penetrate his wife's mind with his. She was so beautiful and innocent, angelic. To all but him. How could she do that? All that was missing to complete the imagery was the golden glow of her halo; her chocolate-brown eyes unblinking, her expression…immune. She wanted the day to be over.

Garcia was another matter, sitting behind the Frenchmen, gazing into his lap.

To Madame du Valois he let his eyes tell the truth of his deep regret. He could do no more.

A sudden hush permeated the courtroom as the judge entered unceremoniously to take his place behind the bench, raising and smashing the gavel matter-of-factly against its base.

Court was in session.

He cautioned everyone to remain completely silent or face immediate contempt of court and arrest. No exceptions.

He would first offer Madame du Valois the opportunity to confront the accused, who would then be permitted to make his statement before hearing the charges against him read as a preface to sentencing.

He, the judge, would then deliver the verdict and the sentence to John Anderson without further delay, reminding the defendant and his defence counsel that trial by judge was agreed upon at their behest. There would be no appeal.

"Mrs. du Valois, do you wish at this time to address the accused or the court?"

Madame du Valois stood, aided by the men on either side of her, composing herself before speaking to John as though they were alone.

The stenographer thought to stop typing, her fingers scurrying to catch up.

"Monsieur Anderson, my children and I are the innocent victims of your extreme violence. I should not be here. We should not be here, you and I. In France, you know, you would have simply felt anger and left them alone to their dalliance. Not more. You know this. You know our culture. This, however, is not your American way and my family must now pay dearly for Jean-François disregarding this embedded and eternal dissimilarity in our cultures. He was wrong, as you were wrong. He was wrong allowing himself to be so easily deceived and enamoured of that woman, as you were to believe that she might love anyone. She has love for no one. I believe she has no heart. Clearly she does not. You should have walked away from her, Monsieur Anderson, from them. Yet, what is done is done. I forgive you, and I forgive Jean-François who must share his guilt with her, the one I will never forgive."

She sat composed, acknowledging the judge, disregarding his obvious displeasure with her previous deception.

"Mr. Anderson," the judge prompted.

John twisted in his seat, facing Madame du Valois. Standing was impossible. "I believe Madame is fully aware of my sincerest regrets and my heartfelt sentiments. N'est pas, Madame du Valois?"

Madame du Valois tilted her head in acknowledgement, her expression grim.

"Very well, Mr. Anderson, I will now restate the charges against you, make known my judgements, and pass sentence. Do you understand?"

"I do."

"Very well. You, sir, heretofore have led a very privileged life. You are well-travelled and educated, successful in business and level-headed. Or you were. You should indeed have known better than to be deceived for so many years by a woman decidedly your social subordinate in immeasurable ways."

"Her possible involvement with prostitution, which is of no interest to this court, is impossible to establish. Mrs. Anderson is in the midst of renovating her Miami apartment, which may or may not have served as a convenience for that sordid business, and has relocated her residence to West Palm Beach in what I am certain is a pristine dwelling. She fooled you, Mr. Anderson. Whether you were blinded by love-struck emotion or you chose to ignore obvious signs of either her discontent or her insatiability is a matter of your own reflection and remorse."

"Women, even in this era of emerging equality, still must answer in many ways to their husbands. In that you failed."

"I find myself concurring with the wisdom of your ex-employer. You should indeed have walked out. No woman culpable of extra-marital fornication with one or more strangers is not worth risking the death penalty."

John Anderson stopped breathing.

"I am dismissing the charge of Aggravated Assault since the more serious charge of murder obviates the need. On the charge of Conjugal Violence I find you not guilty since Mrs. Anderson clearly precipitated the event within an already explosive situation."

"The charge of First Degree Murder is reduced to that of Second Degree. The verdict: Guilty. It is the court's opinion that you could not have stood by and observed the folly of Mrs. Anderson and Mr. du Valois together and that you did, in fact, believe your wife was being attacked. That said, you did in fact strike him with sufficient force to control the situation, after which, as an intelligent man, you should have taken a breath and regrouped elsewhere. You didn't do that. Instead you chose to brutally end his life."

"On the charge of Issuing Death Threats, I find you guilty. Such words are often spoken in the heat of the moment, meant to convey one's emotional distress and not our actual intent to do harm. In your case, Mr. Anderson, I believed you. I believe Mrs. Anderson has very real cause to fear for her life as retribution for her persistent crime of adultery."

"It is the court's decision that you be confined to Battle View Prison in the State of Tennessee commencing tomorrow, the twentieth of April, for a term of twenty-five years without chance of parole. I would hope that by then your anger and resentment will have subsided, Mr. Anderson."

John felt a deep heat surge through his body, his breathing accelerating. He felt his lawyer's hand grasp his arm. His head pivoted deliberately to the right, his blank eyes staring past the DA to his wife, to Alejandro Garcia.

His mouth went instantly dry. They were sitting calmly, exchanging glances, their eyes rejoicing.

"This tragedy might well have been avoided. What is clear to me is that Mrs. Anderson is very likely other than what she appears and that she is amongst the most despicable women I have come across in this court. She is not blameless here. To contemplate such an appalling scheme for no better reason than to procure a divorce, she is decidedly and contentedly bereft of decency and propriety. She is clearly the architect of this entire misadventure and one might conclude that she has gotten away with murder. However, she is not on trial and this court forbids the present and future use of her name, or names, in any such context including the suspicion of prostitution, whether here or abroad."

The gavel crashed down.

John Anderson was frozen in time and space. He hadn't moved, hadn't stopped staring at her. The judge's condemnation of her made no impression at all. She was impervious. If he had wanted to kill her that first night, arriving home with flowers, or felt the urge in court during her testimony, he particularly did at that very moment as she stood catching his eye.

Her shrug was imperceptible to all but him, her smile more caustic than anything she might have said.

*

The rest was history. Black Boss and a deaf kid who was far from dumb. The smile and the shrug kept alive all those year by a wallet-size photo his lawyer had somehow managed to acquire from the correctional guards at County and John somehow managed to keep in Battle View, possibly in lieu of a tattoo that might have read "Whore."

He owed Billy Rider a lot, his sanity for one thing And Black Boss for thinking decisively into the future.

The waiter came with the bill. No wonder the whore could afford a sprawling home, two bordellos and a frigging Bentley.

John left the restaurant, crestfallen. He'd never paid so much to eat so little, which wasn't the issue. He was. He wasn't where he should be. He didn't belong. He was surrounded by pretty girls and attractive women sauntering along without a care, arm in arm with handsome and tanned men. Everyone content inside exclusive dream worlds.

Those who weren't were noticing him, which made him uneasy; he wasn't ready, the air too filled with gaiety and romance. He felt conspicuous, as though they might suspect everything about him.

He needed solitude; he needed the quiet of the ocean.

He ambled past patio bars and quaint shops, stopping from time to time to peer through windows at even more things he had no idea about, things not yet invented when he was sent away, like the man walking towards and past him talking on a phone whose coiled wire fed into a leather case hanging from his shoulder. Or Rigby questioning whether or not he wanted phones and air conditioning installed in his cars. Naturally he said yes. Why would he intentionally appear more disconnected than he was?

At the beach he removed his shoes and socks, meandering his way closer to the dark water lapping the shore, dropping his weight onto the cool sand when walking farther seemed pointless. Where was he going? He was already there, wondering why anyone would need or want a phone in their car, or in a shoulder bag. Besides, a man with a shoulder bag, really?

All those missed years without someone who might have loved a tall, dark and handsome man divorced from a whore, once sanitized. All those Christmases and birthdays, starlit nights and romantic strolls by the sea. He had not seen stars or a night sky once in all those years. Cells in Battle View didn't have windows, the first glimpse of sundown to Whites, Blacks and Latinos alike was the much hated precursor to wailing sirens clearing out the yard, enforcing yet another evening of segregated confinement and lockdown.

The shortest days of fall and winter were no exception, grey and cloistered evenings that much longer. So why was he now taking both for granted? He didn't know, promising he never would again. He hadn't felt rain on his skin once in those twenty-six years either, yard time on wet days disallowed by the ever despotic Warden Prescott.

The prison laundry wouldn't bear the extra load of wet coveralls.

He would do that also, walk in the rain. He would relearn being human, first becoming a man, then a gentleman if that was even remotely possible.

Women? He didn't know, not convinced he had the time. Not convinced he had the desire. Women had always told him he was a superb lover, a fabulous lover in fact. Mostly French and Spanish girls who generally held their lovers to higher standards and expectations than American women whose single motive was either conceiving a family or trapping a man.

He didn't know. Perhaps they were all more in love with his open-ended expense account. Worse, he couldn't clearly remember a single one.

He never would understand why she married him, particularly since he had recently acquired a far better appreciation of the extent of her pre-marital resources. Four times other girls, he mused, somewhat of an understatement. Another lie. All those years in prison because she needed a smokescreen, then telling the court he was a lousy lover when he couldn't tell them she was a whore.

Haughty bitch.

He sat for a long while staring into the glittering sky, across the field of ominously silent water to his past. Perhaps Pat Fellows might enjoy Europe. He certainly would far more than John Anderson would once again enjoy Battle View. He knew that much. However Pat's finances were quickly depleting, better spent locally as his smokescreen to achieve his goals.

His current undertaking was of far greater importance to him than a fanciful escape to a better life because his life would never be better. The coming week would be the best he could hope for.

Live for the moment. And he would.

Driving a beat up Monte Carlo that smelled of smoke and squeaked and rattled on bumpy roads was one thing. A woman? That was something else. No one but a whore would want him, until his money ran out. No one serious at any rate who would be what, fifty, fifty-five, scarred by time and motherhood? Or could he settle for a discarded or jaded divorcée or a single mother on the prowl, a cheat, the wife of a globe-trotting account executive, when his last woman was twenty-nine and flawless? He didn't believe that he would.

The dilemma didn't merit further thought. He didn't need frivolous questions robbing him of the exhilaration he deserved. He had enough on his mind. Time to leave. The coming two days would require an energy he felt waning. He could not allow that to happen. He would not. He would not let her ruin his moment.

At the hotel he steeled himself against the temptation of wasting the Pomerol on his dark mood. And Darlene Carlton, whatever she was doing behind the cover image of a woman running naked in the rain, could run for Pat Fellows Saturday afternoon in a Necessity hotel room.

What he needed was sleep. He needed to stop thinking, to begin a new day refreshed.

His melancholy, he was realizing, had nothing to do with them. They had forty-three hours, give or take. Or Florida's State Whore.

Black Boss was right. He did not want to return to Battle View. He chuckled softly, or fight Billy Rider for the upper bunk.

Thirty-One

June 22nd

Early Friday morning was bright and warm and sunny in Miami, sloppily dressed tourists very much out of place on wide city sidewalks teeming with fashionably attired businessmen and women who clearly had succeeded in life beyond the middle range.

Motorists in a panic on the perpetually congested A1A were agitated by the ones who were not. Most likely, he believed, because they were amongst the city's failures in life or the please-the-boss wannabes who were running late. Suck-ups.

John was not one of them, never was. He was relaxed, laid back; he was at peace with himself. His high spirits had reignited and were stronger than ever, the road trip north on the I-95 a constant seventy-five MPH on cruise.

By Georgia conditions had worsened to the far end of the weather spectrum. A dark grey mass of rumbling clouds was threatening to burst apart and by Charleston he had driven the last hundred miles in a cacophonous deluge, his temporary laid-back disposition graduating by the mile into heart-pounding fear. He was afraid. Driving wasn't a requisite skill in prison and eight weeks of freedom and fine weather hadn't prepared him for a biblical flood and light show. His knuckles were white, his jaw aching from gritting and grinding his teeth.

At last parked at his apartment he slouched behind the

wheel, rubbing his hands hard against his face to dispel the exhaustion, the choreography of swirling winds acting against phantasmal steam wafting from the car's heated hood amidst a ballet of a million crystal raindrops was mesmerizing.

He smeared the thickening fog from his side window, hesitating. The former Mr. John Anderson had always enjoyed the luxury of indoor parking, this Anderson was faced with a field of uneven asphalt puddled with heavy rain. Despite which he had made a promise. He inhaled a deep breath, rationality at once usurping whimsy.

He was promptly and utterly drenched from head to toe, at first bounding from his car to the building, leaping over some puddles and landing in others before finally surrendering to the day, slowing to a more dignified pace. He looked ridiculous. Besides, what the hell! Why not? He was walking in the rain, precisely as he had promised.

In his apartment he stripped on his way to the bathroom, shuddering with a chill, feeling good, feeling alive, discarding his sopping clothes onto the floor, stepping into the tub and into pulsating streams of steaming water which he freely admitted to his ears alone was in no way as luxurious as the whore's whirlpool.

By the time the tempest outside had abated, a low ceiling of ponderous clouds lingering over the city refusing to dissipate over the Atlantic, the air became thick with a tangible and eerie mist hovering over sidewalks and streets.

He didn't want to go out. He wanted to remain fresh. He had things to do, things he was constantly relearning or learning anew from hotel televisions, thinking he should at least rent one of his own.

He went with his laundry to the basement, sitting first on the washer, then atop the dryer as he killed time outlining his Saturday agenda, ignoring the stack of mutilated magazines that appeared as though they'd been used to mop up a spill of something sticky or unpleasant or both.

Later he prepared a dinner of baked lamb chops, oven-roasted potatoes, steamed vegetables and two-fingers of Johnnie Walker Black. He dressed for the occasion in slacks and a sweater, feeling civilized, feeling more so with his second scotch accompanied by week-old chocolate cake. He doubted he would ever eat beans or wieners or grits or white bread or stewed prunes again. He believed now that he would rather die. He believed that he might.

He didn't have a VCR. Instead he pressed and laid out his clothes for his Saturday drive, his afternoon with Darlene running in the rain, and his evening with the Rigbys and Carltons.

He was ready. In the morning he would leave home shortly after breakfast and arrive at the hotel in time for a quiet lunch by the hotel pool. He would enjoy a dip, take a nap after her run, and knock on their door at a respectable time after 7:00. Perhaps he would be invited in to share an aperitif and congenial conversation before they would sit down to dinner without him. Of course he would. They were high on social graces, though by no means was he expecting an invitation to dinner with such short notice. Certainly not.

Naturally, being a gentleman, once upon a time, he wouldn't consider impolitely interrupting their evening empty-handed. He would arrive at their doorstep bearing gifts as well as with documents signed by Pat Fellows.

He'd bought decorative little boxes with bows for the ladies and expensive wrapping paper for the men's gifts. Understandably, their biggest surprise could not be wrapped. He had prepared for that also, filling his black satchel with all manner of appropriate goodies.

He was set, his checklist completed and verified before disappearing in tiny pieces into a whirling vortex somewhere beyond his toilet. Everything he required was sitting by the door.

He went to bed with a JWB neat, thinking to let his

mind wander. Instead he drifted into a deep sleep, waking in the morning to the untouched glass on the night table. He left it there. Any contact with booze that early in the day, tactile or olfactory, was somehow offensive to the senses. There was a time and a place for drinking alone, which was any time after noon and anywhere outside the walls of Battle View.

The day was again bright and warm, well-trained and expert meteorologists guessing that the entire East Coast could possibly expect to take advantage of a beautiful weekend.

"Twelve hours, Billy. Twelve hours."

*

Pat Fellows did not like Necessity. Not in the least. He supposed, he knew, not because he didn't like the people, which he had no particular reason to, or their homes and cars sponsored by the Carlton Bank and Rigby's Fine Motors. He didn't like the town of bible belt bigots for what they had done to Billy Rider.

John didn't swear, not very often. Neither did Pat who mimicked most of what John did or said. Swearing diminished a man. Yet that afternoon, finding his way to a gas bar that wasn't Rigby's, then to the hotel, he hated every fucking one of them. All of them so fucking pious; subservient housewives and mothers pushing strollers, breadwinning fathers pitching ball in the streets with their progeny who, like their good old dads, were destined to hate and to think and to believe whatever their neighbours thought or believed.

That's why Sally Cutter no longer lived in Necessity. Trouble is she waited years too long to leave, though what he truly and visibly abhorred were the dozen or more kids screaming and, he knew, pissing in the pool.

With that part of his day ruined he ordered a pizza to his room, a glass goblet and a corkscrew because a fine Pomerol warranted more than a contaminated paper cup from the bathroom.

Pouring his first glass he swirled the deep ruby elixir, examining the colour, breathing in the intense aromas. He thanked her, and he would again one day soon in person.

He paced himself, savouring the wine's smoothness and flavours for several minutes before degrading the grand cru with a mouthful of all-dressed on a thin crust. The VCR was set to go.

He pressed PLAY, increasing the volume.

Darlene Carlton drove up to the curb in a red SUV, the wipers working lazily to sweep away a constant drizzle. Whoever was filming her was already in place recording her parking by a walkway or a path and killing the lights.

She was smiling, waiting with her hands on the wheel. She leaned forward into the windshield, craning her neck to see beyond the cars parked ahead of her. She peered into her side mirrors, and then she nodded. She was ready, apparently, for something, which John presumed would involve her ass being bare.

Whenever the day was, whatever time, for John's money they'd chosen a spring weekend, probably a Sunday, and very early in the day. Not a creature was stirring except Darlene Carlton and, he assumed, Jake the cameraman.

The backdrop was a deserted corridor of high-rise buildings, tall structures of tinted glass and steel lining either side of a tree-lined boulevard like towering and humourless sentinels.

The camera came around to the driver's side. She stepped out wearing a flimsy white skirt and tee-shirt, white bobby socks and sneakers, sauntering like a girl half her age to the tailgate, the delicate material plastered to her skin. Raising the door she stood under the canopy dangling her keys, talking to the camera, her face radiating excitement. She was ready, she told the camera, her voice husky and even. As was John, dropping his first arc of crust into the box.

The wet tee-shirt came away first, though not easily, pulled and stretched over her head and tossed blindly over her shoulders. The camera zoomed in. Nice titties, he thought. And primed. Nicer than Eleanor's from what he could see. Fuller. No middle-age slope. The woman worked-out; he supposed as much for old Jake as for his lesbian sister.

Then came the skirt, easily, John thinking he had once had bigger pocket hankies. Hello Darlene, naked, very naked, slamming the gate closed and posing. Standing calm and collected on the sidewalk as though she were fully clothed and waiting for a bus.

"Oh, darling, this will be so much fun. I'm so glad you agreed." She twirled, her arms outstretched. "I so hope somebody sees me. I feel so incredibly sexy."

"You are sexy, darling, and beautiful. All the more reason for us not to linger another moment. Your eager audience awaits you. Run along. Enjoy yourself."

She took a deep breath, her tanned body glistening with a thick coating of oil beaded with rain trickling down every inch of her. She was a sight. She was prancing from the camera, gleefully, spinning, waving him closer. Seems like Jake or Jackson or darling was on roller skates keeping pace. Whatever the case, John needed more Pomerol.

She was, from his perspective, shapelier than Eleanor. Not that Eleanor as a body wasn't appealing. A question of taste. He had to admit seeing a woman jogging along a residential sidewalk naked in the rain was a compelling scene for a man so long deprived. For any man.

Nothing was moving in a way that it shouldn't, the scene jerking slightly as she skipped into the middle of an intersection indicating a dead-end, running in place. She held out a palm, halting him, telling her darling in a pant to stay as she ran at full tilt alone along the car-lined alley, leaping to a stop, swinging herself in circles with both hands around a lamp standard and leapfrogging over a row of cast-iron posts meant to protect pedestrians at the far end.

Skipping back in the middle of the street, she leaned forward catching her breath.

"Darling," he admonished, "that was not planned. We must stay to the script."

"That's why I did it, darling. Bye-bye."

Off she went, her skin lustrous and wet. At the next intersection she crossed over, twirling, skipping back to the corner and running in place, waiting for the camera, blowing a Marylyn Monroe kiss as he rolled closer. She wasn't the least inhibited or concerned about possible traffic or passers-by. She was on a high, getting off.

And then she was gone, romping along another side alley lined with sleeping cars, halting midway to wait for the camera.

She took her time, her legs apart, teasing, bending and stretching, choosing a late model that was polished and beaded, dragging her body enticingly and nimbly onto the hood, leaning back. She crisscrossed her legs in the air, sitting to let the camera capture her smearing raindrops into a sheen from her shoulders to her bobby socks.

Pivoting, rolling onto her front, she let her body slip from the hood over the grill, easing to the ground where she paused.

She combed her hair into a single thick strand, waving goodbye, jogging to the end and to the right, disappearing onto a narrow path bordered by a flowing river. When he found her she was cupping her breasts with one hand, facing the water, bending, caressing her ass with the other for her darling that, John had to agree with Carlton, was very fine.

The pathway meandered behind the eastern-most row of high-rises from which a few hundred eyes may or may not have seen her. This was her second chance at stardom, albeit with a more intimate, more privileged audience. She was closer to their windows than she had been from their street vantage.

Her body was glistening, her eyes sparkling, her hair matted into a cloche.

"Darling, I'm breathless and excited... so absolutely turned-on. We should have done this before. And we definitely will again. We have to." She took a deep breath. "But let's walk for a while. Please? This is exhausting."

"Yes, darling. How can we not do this again? We will very, very soon, somewhere else."

Good old Jake, John was thinking, would agree to anything. He remembered Billy saying how he was as much Rigby's lapdog as Eleanor was hers.

Jake was skating circles around her, at times slowing to film her passing by, other times skating well past her when he would lose her for an instant before recapturing her sauntering towards him.

Until she stopped midway along the block, scanning the high-rises. "Darling, how many do you think are seeing me, jealous of me or wanting me? Many do you think?"

"I have no idea, darling. I hope for your sake there are many. Who would not want to see or be with such an incredible vision?"

"Ooh, I do hope so. This is so...I don't know. Eleanor would hate me if she saw me like this."

She was gone, unexpectedly bolting from the path, adlibbing once again. The camera zoomed in to follow her scurrying across the manicured lawn, zigzagging her way towards the wall of tinted windows where she stopped short of them, spinning in elliptical circles, making herself dizzy. She stood for a moment, wobbling, facing the windows, another moment spent facing away so that they might see all of her before she was prancing past Jake whose pursuit was instant.

Again at the cast-iron posts she leapfrogged, pausing, telling him to wait where he was. She wanted to run alone between the buildings to the boulevard. She would be gone two minutes, three at the most. She really wanted to, for him. She would run quickly, she promised.

"No, darling. Much too risky. They have seen you already…and possibly waiting. I must forbid you."

She was gone.

John heard Carlton's breath blowing into the recorder. Still, he obeyed her and stayed as any good puppy would. He let her grow smaller into the distance, groaning as she scampered across the intersection on a red light, skipping across the green to the corner where she stopped to wait and look to the left, the right, and behind her. Unworried. She waved her arms high in the air, growing larger on the screen as she waited for the light to change. On green she sauntered across four lanes, bursting into an all-out run towards the camera that captured her slumping out of breath onto a park bench.

"That was very unwise, darling."

"No, darling, that was thrilling. I don't want this day to end."

Carlton reached out a hand. "And we don't want to catch our deaths either. We want the rain, not pneumonia. Come."

She shook her head. "Not yet, darling. Bye-bye."

She was off, prancing and skipping, slowing to a saunter. John was impressed. Nothing was bouncing, nothing was jiggling. This was much better than watching Rigby fuck his wife and decidedly more creative. He glanced at his watch. Twenty-one minutes. He couldn't believe it.

She was bending forward, her hands clutching her knees, glancing behind her. Her smile devious, or cunning, or sensual. John leaned closer, unable to discern which. He didn't care. What now?

Straightening, her legs apart, her hands on her hips, she said, "darling, I see a nice table."

She was pointing to a private picnic table coated with beads and dripping very near to another wall of tinted windows.

"That would be daring, darling. They would be very close to you. They would see all of you."

"Do you mind, darling? Do you?"

Old Jake was thinking. John certain the man was afraid of being confronted. How would he explain cavorting in the rain on skates with a video camera and a naked wife a mile from their car?

"You know I don't. You really should. We've come this far."

Again she ran across a lawn, glancing over her shoulder, beaming. She was ecstatic. John thinking, too bad that she'd be dead in a few hours.

She was walking tightrope one way on the narrow bench with her arms stretched out, twirling, then the other, leaping to the ground and blowing Carlton and John a kiss before leaning against the table with her hands flat on the surface until Carlton was ready for her to continue. When he was, she was, pulling herself onto the beaded planks, one leg dangling over one edge, her other leg at ninety degrees.

Carlton blew air into the microphone, John reached for more wine.

She leaned back on one hand, her hair and body dripping. With her other hand she gently squeezed her breasts, unhurried, adoringly. She was losing herself in a dream world and taking John with her.

An open palm absently smeared a gleaming path to her belly, coming to rest over her neatly trimmed V of crimson red hair where she deftly parted the soft folds to teasingly strum a silent concert between them at the apex of taut and tanned legs left wide-open to a few hundred windows.

Carlton immediately urged her not to stop, to go all the way. "If you don't, darling, you'll be sorry. As will I. You may never be able to again. Make this the best ever. Who knows how many you may be delighting?"

She squealed, delirious with excitement. She had

crossed over the threshold from naughty and risqué to incredibly daring. "Yes, darling, yes. I will. Watch me."

The camera closed in. John glanced at his watch, forgetting his wine, presupposing that anyone seeing her wouldn't be stupid enough to waste time waiting for an elevator. Twenty-five minutes and counting down, everyone involved on the edge of their seats or pressed against windows. At least John was. Then, three, two, one and…Houston, we have liftoff at fifty-three seconds.

She shuddered and shrieked, launching her body from the table. Composing herself, letting her heart rate settle, she combed her fingers through tangled hair and wiped her face. "Darling, I did it. How sexy was that?"

"Absolutely incredible. You were erotic, darling." The camera scanned the building, zooming into the windows. "We can see later who saw you, but we should go. I have to believe we were an attraction to at least a few."

She shook her head, hopping backward onto the table, reclining onto her elbows. "No, darling. Please. Caress me. Caress me first, then we'll go."

Carlton didn't waste time. His breathing was hard. His hand travelled deliberately from one ankle to her hips, to her breasts, fondling each one, completing its journey at her pubic hair blistered with beads of rain, urgently doing his best under difficult conditions to bring on the slightest tremor.

He pleaded with her to cooperate, the much awaited spasm and her sudden yelp triggering instant camera jitter, flashes of grey sky and wet grass until Carlton managed his way to the path giving John time to appreciate his wine and to critique Carlton's work which produced a failing grade.

Carlton's shock was audible at seeing his wife still poised at the table and completely unruffled. John waiting patiently as she came into focus sitting serenely with her feet planted apart on the bench, smiling and waving, waiting for his signal. She wasn't ready to leave. Neither was John.

"Very sexy. Delicious." he yelled. "Let's go, darling. And you might want to hurry."

She groaned her disappoint, pouting, arching her back, pivoting on her ass to face the tall stack of condos for all to admire every inch of her one last time before she hurled her body into the air, landing with both feet and sauntering gaily towards the camera.

Thirty minutes and she wasn't ready to end her turn-on, spurred on by his "Go! You fabulously naughty girl."

She started at a trot, building to a jog, a minute later turning right into her final leg, slowing once more to an arousing prance, to an idle stroll. A minute after that the SUV's taillights were flashing ahead of her, Carlton stopping, letting the camera follow as though right behind her.

At the vehicle she raised the tailgate, sheltering her body from the rain, probably hoping, John mused, for anyone who might have missed her earlier, or for those who waited with bated breath for more, to see her radiant beauty glowing amidst a bleak and rainy day. Very possibly.

She towelled and tousled her hair into a tangle of damp strands, toweling her body dry with measured strokes as though in the privacy of her en suite bathroom. Sitting into the cargo space she pulled away her sneakers and socks, drying her feet and pulling on red rubber boots, smiling for the camera and swinging her feet.

"Darling, you are completely brash…and very beautiful."

"Thank you, darling. How long?"

The camera didn't budge. "Thirty-five minutes, and counting."

"I should drive home like this, you know. I really should." she insisted, sliding from her seat.

"No, you should not. We'll find you a place. Don't worry."

She stepped onto the sidewalk, pirouetting a final time,

firmly planting her feet wide apart, waiting with her hands defiantly on her hips.

Carlton stood firm. No.

Pouting, she squeezed her breasts hoping that he might change his mind. He didn't. Then she was smiling, reaching into the SUV, wiggling her way into a very short and shiny red poncho.

She had a much better idea. One he could not refuse.

John coughed a laugh. She wanted to go shopping. No shit. Most likely for underwear, no doubt.

From the street Carlton's hand was waving adieu to her. He would see her at the mall, he agreed.

"And please hurry, darling. Or I won't have anything to wear. Will I?"

Darlene Carlton pulled away her poncho in a single swift motion like a matador's red cape teasing a bull, flinging it into the airspace between them, climbing into her seat and driving off dressed in red rubber boots.

THE END. Although apparently not their day.

A minute shy of forty. Incredible that anyone could do that, and good for her. Why not, John allowed? Life is too short, especially hers.

John rewound the tape to a drizzly and daring Darlene getting herself off on a picnic table for hubby and countless unseen others who would talk about her for years. Then to the beginning. Why not, indeed? He was merely acquiescing to her fondest desire, the thirty-inch hotel screen no different than a high-rise window.

He had enough pizza and wine for another forty minutes around two suburban blocks, one and a half orgasms that he was aware of and a wardrobe change...sort of, thinking he might have to borrow more Darlene tapes. Her performance was without question superior to Mr. and Mrs. Rigby's. Kudos.

Problem was, they weren't a couple out for a spontaneous once in a lifetime sexy thrill that was a little over the top. He was a killer and she was no better. After all, that was the reason he was going to dinner.

Thirty-Two

1991

By 7:00 the pizza and Darlene's second scamper around the block were history, the empty wine bottle standing atop the crust-filled box outside his door for pick-up. He did, however, save one glass for a special occasion: 7:00 PM.

Pat Fellows was dressed in a black suit, a bright fuchsia button-down shirt, brushed gold links, polished black loafers and a nine millimetre chrome-plated Berretta. No tie. A tie was too formal for such an impromptu visit.

He stared at his satchel by the door. Everything was ready. He was ready.

Peering into the mirror he smirked. He was impressed with his work. Pat Fellows was even more handsome than John Anderson. He raised the glass, his expression solemn.

"This is it, Billy, like I promised years ago. Was always careful about what I was thinking around you. I half believe you read minds too. That you doubted me doesn't matter. Not now. You just be ready, like I told you. Though I suspect you won't hear until tomorrow or Monday that tonight you're igniting a whirlwind of shit. I sincerely hope that you believe I was the one. I told you, didn't I? Do not ever give up hope kid. I told you that and I know you'll keep it to yourself being the quiet guy that you are. I doubt we'll be talking after this evening. No point. I enjoyed your company. You helped get me through this, but life goes on. Doesn't matter what we might want. So for that, best

343

wishes, Billy. Happy Birthday a few days early with my best regards to Miss Sally."

He drained the glass in a toast, adjusted his collar, and walked out to free Billy Rider.

Pat Fellows was a quick study, taking over from what John Anderson had never forgotten: Time was money. Do not waste either. He arrived on time, as planned at 7:15, counting down as he retreated a few feet. Never stand in another man's space.

The door opened wide seconds later. The smile was immediate and practiced. Do something often enough, seek perfection, and our second nature confuses who we are.

"Pat, what the hey! This is a marvelous surprise." Rigby peered into the street for a car, for any sign of Mrs. Fellows. "No Brenda?"

"Dwight, please forgive my ungracious interruption of your private time with Eleanor. I won't steal more than a fleeting moment from your evening. Thing is, my schedule is completely skewed...for the good, I hasten to add. I need those cars ASAP. I have the signed documents with me. We're good to go. My crew is hired and they're biting at the bit." He chuckled. "You know sales guys. I thought that perhaps by dropping over this evening you could have them road-ready before our luncheon this Monday. At least the three."

"Well, I sure as hell can. Now get yourself in here. Meet the Carltons. They're dinner guests this evening." He waved a finger. "Not bankers. Let's not aggravate the females of the clan."

Eleanor wiggled her way to her foyer too effusively to greet him. He didn't believe any woman could properly disguise when she was royally pissed-off. And she was. Big time.

Pat was actually somewhat shocked, chiding himself for his naïveté. Her white on white dress was too short, displaying too much leg, the white panties underneath too obvious. Good quality, he could see, if not a little over the top.

"Miss Eleanor, I promise, five minutes and I am gone with a thousand sincere apologies as my evening's legacy."

"Don't be silly, Pat. Won't you join us for a cocktail," she countered? "We won't be sitting at the table for a while yet."

"I will, thank you." He tilted his head in a genteel Southern bow. "Brenda sends her regards. She's much better. In fact we have dinner plans in town," he checked his watch, "at eight with our new hires."

"Scotch?"

"The smallest splash, Eleanor. Thank you."

"Jake," Rigby cut in, "meet your newest account."

Carlton stood. "Good meeting you, Pat. Dwight's had a lot of good things to say about you. Eagerly awaiting Monday, I must say."

"Monday," Darlene reproached.

"And you must be Miss Darlene," Pat chanced.

He wanted to ask her why she bothered wearing a blouse when his peripheral vision instantly taunted him, testing his resolve. Or the skirt for the very little she was concealing, particularly since their intimate afternoon runs together. A male peculiarity which he had no doubt about: See a pretty woman at the beach all day in practically nothing, or very naked on a picnic table, and most men would definitely want to peek under her dress. Go figure. And sheer blouses high-lighting push-up bras were no less enthralling.

"Indeed. Excuse my rudeness. This is my wife, Darlene."

Pat smiled widely. "A pleasure, Miss Darlene. Strangely, I feel as though we've met."

Eleanor passed him an old-fashioned, waving him into a seat. He chose another, one less comfortable, less engulfing, making mention of his chronic back pain. He raised his glass. "If I may, to two lovely ladies."

The husbands concurred, raising theirs.

He wasn't one for idle chatter, never had been. Get in and get out was his constant MO in business. Friends in business were liabilities. Certain trouble held in check, biding its time for the appropriate moment to reveal itself.

"You have a lovely home, Miss Eleanor." He noticed the photographs. "And lovely children, I see."

"Lindsay and Bart. Thank you. We're very proud of them."

"You must be." He sipped his drink. "Oh, I'm forgetting my manners. Please forgive me. I brought you each a small gift. I do hope I chose well."

"Oh, how thoughtful," Darlene gasped with delight, clapping her hands.

He reached into his satchel. "Nothing much, I assure you. You might say a declaration of my goodwill and intentions." He passed the women their packages, standing to pass Rigby and Carlton theirs, retreating into safe space. "However, before you open them, let me say that, Darlene, your gift are the panties I took from Eleanor's closet upstairs; yours, Eleanor, come from her closet. One I'm sure you are intimately familiar with. Your gift Jake is a video of Rigby here fucking your sister on all fours upstairs, and yours Dwight is a video of sexy Darlene here running buck-ass naked in the streets of somewhere for close to an hour and doing herself on a picnic table in the rain, which I found absolutely fascinating. Excellent work, Darlene. You, Carlton, not so much. Some things should never be hurried. Shame on you, disappointing all those people. Though you must tell me later what happened as a sequel at the mall and where I might expect to find a copy for my library." He stood straight, sipping the scotch. "Go ahead, open them. I borrowed the underwear to make a point, ladies, which I believe I have. The videos, gentlemen, were strictly for my personal entertainment. I applaud you all, especially Miss Darlene."

The scene was a tragic comedy, four gaping mouths; the women emptying theirs into their laps, gasping for air, clutching their chests, the men tearing at the paper, staring stupidly at the cover images of their sisters.

"Tell me, Darlene, are Loraine and Brad up there in Boston going to imitate you four, you know, marrying little Lindsay and big brother Bart?" He grinned, putting down the glass. "Yes, I know. I know about the vodka and scotch in the desk drawers downstairs as well, Eleanor. And you really should not stand at your bedroom window undressed in the morning sunlight for anyone, me, to see. Yet...very delightful."

Rigby lurched forward, halted by Pat's open palm, which Pat believed spoke volumes about the man.

"What is this, Fellows, a kidnapping?" Carlton demanded. "A ransom demand? Who the hell are you?"

Pat reached into his jacket for the gun. "No. Your kids are fine, for the time being. I expect they'll be home next week as planned. This is a simple robbery folks. Let's not get frazzled. So please, Mr. and Mrs. Carlton, your cash and ATM cards with your PINs. Believe me, I don't need much." He reached into his satchel, dropping a notepad and pen onto the coffee table. "I did say please, didn't I?"

Rigby and Carlton stared at each other, dumbfounded; the two horrified women pleading with them to do something, anything.

Carlton said, "Do it, Darlene, goddammit" digging into his pants for his wallet. "The man's got a silencer on his gun."

They put the cards with an assortment of bills on the table, Darlene jotting their codes onto the pad.

Rigby said, "Ours are upstairs."

"Thank you. We'll get to them later. First I want to explain what will happen next. Please do not disappoint me. I need the men to stand in the corner." He waved the gun, not waiting long. "Darlene, Eleanor, I need you to clear the dining room table. Return everything to the cupboards, everything." He waved them into a dither as well. "Now, please."

They did as he instructed, slowed by dishes and cutlery dropping from shaking hands as the men looked on. With that done he stepped with them into the kitchen, instructing Eleanor to empty her soup and the water ready to boil into the sink. Darlene he ordered to remove whatever was in the oven, passing her a double reinforced garbage bag, adding the empty pots, vegetables and bread to the mix. Dinner was over.

He instructed Darlene to gather the gifts and wrappings, to put everything in the plastic bag with the meal. Everything except the videos as he widened the distance between them, putting on his gloves before reaching to deposit the money into his satchel. The cards he ordered Rigby to take.

"Ladies, gentlemen, let's all have another drink and find our way upstairs when and where I will describe what remains of your evening and say something to you that will convince you to take me seriously. A secret code, you might say."

"Shortly after, when I have all four cards, Rigby and I will proceed to the bank. I will remove a few dollars, enough to get by, and I'll be gone as he returns home as a hero to free you. No police, or no Rigby. Your choice." He turned to Rigby, adding his old-fashioned to the litter. "Your drinks, sir, if you please. I believe doubles are appropriate for the occasion, more as required, and take the bottles with you. Darlene, bring your purse."

Rigby filled each of their glasses halfway, passing Carlton a bottle. At the stairs Pat ordered them ahead of the women.

In the bedroom he ordered Rigby to set up his video camera and tripod, and to disable the sound, time and date functions. Then he asked Eleanor to address the ATM and cash issues, telling the four to finish and replenish their drinks. He didn't want to rush the evening, however he was somewhat pressed for time. They did.

He ordered the men to sit on the floor with their glasses in their left hands and their legs stretched out. They did that also.

"So Fellows, what is this secret code? And why the mystery?" Carlton demanded. "You've got what you came for."

"In a moment." Pat closed the door. He walked over to the television, inserting Darlene, grinning when she shrieked.

"Darlene, that is my favourite scene by far. A very nice body. Very nice indeed. And this one." He ejected her, inserting Rigby and Eleanor. "I hear on very good authority, Eleanor, that you like this doggie thing. You do seem to. Yes, you do. Mind you, as lovely as you are, having seen Darlene alone, Rigby here was a disappointing distraction."

"You're disgusting. We don't even know you,' she hissed. "How dare you?"

"I'm curious, ladies. I might have been too hasty in my choice. Should I check your drawers now? Did you two ever film yourselves together?" He waved the gun. "Now don't lie to me. I'm well aware how fascinated you are with each other. In a word, lesbians, and very much into each other. So to speak...since high school."

Rigby cried out, "You're foul."

"Gentlemen, let me tell you a story as we watch Miss Darlene playing in the rain." The machine spit out Eleanor; seconds later Darlene was rewound, pulling off her clothes at her SUV where he froze her on the sidewalk. "My tale begins on a beautiful spring day in 1965 when I killed a man for quite personal reasons. And now, because of that, I have to kill someone else in a week or so. At least that s the plan." He feigned thoughtfulness. "Forgive me, I digress. Much to my regret, as I was not entirely culpable, I was found guilty and sent to a very bad place where a few years later I met...who? That's right, Mr. Billy Rider. Battle View, people. Ring a bell...anyone?"

He chortled, their faces as frozen as Darlene's screen persona.

"That's what this is about," Rigby cut in, "a deaf and dumb deviant? Whatever bullshit he told you Fellows, it's a damned lie."

Carlton tried to chuckle, coughing instead. "What did he do, write you notes?"

"Something like that. Twenty years, Carlton. A man can write a lot in twenty years. I daresay when Billy gets out, and he will very soon, he'll have quite a story to tell."

"He's a mindless idiot. No one's interested. And he is not getting out."

"Wrong on both counts, Rigby. I would think you and your friend here are very interested. Or should be. You see, that evening, gentlemen, which I am certain you recall vividly, your sisters, your wives, were performing for Billy. They were putting on quite an exotic show for him before they tore apart from each other's nubile and naked embrace to take turns fucking him. Your wife, Carlton, wanted him a second time, eagerly participating from the sidelines to accentuate Eleanor's pleasure with him, if I may say so, while Miss Eleanor was getting abundantly serviced down and dirty on her knees. But, to be fair, she had to wait until after Darlene here expertly and very enthusiastically demonstrated with Eleanor how Billy was to proceed for maximum results."

"Filthy lies, which prove he's an idiot with a sick imagination," Rigby retorted.

Pat glanced at Darlene. "Unfortunately Darlene here didn't get her wish for seconds because Eleanor, shall we say, was in a state of memorable disrepair. She'd had enough, despite telling Billy breathlessly that he had a dick like a horse." He turned his attention to Eleanor. "Too much of a good thing, I suppose. How sad that you deprived your friend who, despite arguing that Billy was hung more like a donkey, wanted and needed more. Not very nice of you, since you weren't exactly complaining. Were you? No, and neither was Billy."

"That is not true. Dwight, he's lying. I would never do such a filthy thing. You know that."

"No. I'm not. You see, Eleanor, the dummy reads lips fluently. He understood every word you two spoke as you ridiculed him to his face. But hell, he didn't care. Hell, no. He wasn't fucking one pretty girl. No way. He was fucking two, big time, and, as a bonus, to make very sure he was primed and wouldn't disappoint you, you performed a little lesbian theatre for him."

"Jake, darling, what he's saying is an absolute lie. I swear."

He turned to the men. "Gentlemen, it is true. Every word. They had quite an appetite for each other. They still do have a serious thing for each other as you'll see later. Hell, if I were you I'd be curious about how they spend their Friday afternoons. Something, to my deepest regret, I was unable to document. And, yes, they were indeed well-serviced by Billy who was no less voracious himself."

"Even so, who says we care?" retorted Carlton. "Two women, it's hot."

"And no one's business," Rigby added.

Pat shrugged. "Hot when you're included, gentlemen, not when you're personas non grata or in second place behind a deaf dummy. You weren't then and you aren't now being invited to their parties. Imagine, all these years Billy's had fond and vivid memories of your best fantasies." He chortled. "Now that is fucking hilarious. But don't despair. Ladies, would you please stand by the bed. Please." They hesitated, jerking backwards at the poof sound coming from the gun and the splintered hole in the floor between their feet. "Please, do as I ask. Now. And finish your cocktails."

They did, gulping and coughing.

"Jesus, Fellows, you have the money," Carlton said. "There's no need for such violence."

"My story isn't finished, Carlton." Pat went to the women, refilling their glasses two-fingers deep. "Ladies, drink up, though I don't believe you require the extra euphoria." He paused. "It's not a request, ladies. Do it. At least tonight you're not drinking from a bottle on a dirt road."

They did, retching, glaring at their husbands, following instructions to place their glasses each on a different night table.

"And now, ladies, would you please undress? Then redo your lipstick, draw back the covers and lie on the bed for me."

Fear exploded onto their faces.

"No! Jake, for Christ's sake..."

"Darlene, Eleanor, I have fourteen more in the clip and many more in my suit. Please do as I say. Come on, Darlene," he looked at the screen, "you're amongst friends here. Don't be shy. Besides, I've seen you at your finest...twice in fact. Which I very much enjoyed. This should be a dream come true for you. You too, Eleanor. Let's go, ladies. And everything neatly folded and placed wherever you normally would when you're together."

Pat Fellows eased into an armchair. The least he could do was give them his undivided attention.

The two desperate women searched each other's eyes. No help was coming from their husbands who were spread on the floor like abandoned puppets, their shoulders hunched and their glasses empty. Darlene began first with her blouse and skirt; Eleanor nervously following her lead, waiting for Darlene to finish her pragmatic striptease before pushing her own panties to the floor.

Darlene gathered her clothes first, placing them on a

love seat, Eleanor went with her. When they were done Pat tossed each woman her purse, waiting until the requisite touch-ups were complete and the bed ready.

"Excellent, ladies. Very nice. And please understand that there is a reason for everything, even this. Trust me. Now lie on the bed and do something lesbian while I talk to the men. Cuddle and kiss. You know, that sort of thing. Do not disappoint me, or Carlton. He's expecting something hot."

He began the tape, waiting until Darlene was sprinting from the camera. "Good. Very good. You see, gentlemen, your sisters were particularly lustful in high school. You weren't their first, you were their last. Together they did every kid in the tenth grade, everyone but the dummy. And when that wasn't sufficient they played with each other as they will for you now."

He paused, excusing himself, dragging the lounge chair closer to the bed yet remaining behind the camera. "So that fatal night, as you went your merry way from the prom, they were at the now historic cul-de-sac doing exactly this for the dummy. Though not because he was so handsome. No. Because they wanted to get back at Lucy Merriweather for childishly girlish reasons." He turned his attention to the women. "Ladies, please, a little bit of smearing. This may be your last time together. Please, do your best for us. Pretend we're not here. The way you did for Billy before you fucked him dry and left him in the dark to walk home."

He shot another round into the night table closest to Darlene, her mouth crushing instantly against Eleanor's, muffling her yelp. Eleanor reacting in kind, fondling her friend's breasts.

Though far from enough smearing was happening, he admonished; he wanted lipstick everywhere, their breasts and shoulders quickly streaked, for which he thanked them.

"But he didn't walk home. He went to the River Watch to meet Lucy Merriweather who wasn't there to greet him because you, Rigby, and Carlton here, decided that evening to rape and kill her."

Darlene sprang apart from her lover, screaming "What!"

"That's right, Darlene. Your husbands raped and killed Lucy Merriweather, not Billy."

"That's completely ludicrous." Rigby yelled. "Rider's insane. He always was. He always will be."

"That's a damned lie, Darlene." Carlton yelled. "Rider killed the girl. He raped her. He panicked and he killed her. Cased closed. Goddammit, we heard every word in court. You know that."

"No, Carlton. She doesn't. You killed her, or Rigby did. Either way you both raped her. And so did Billy hear everything in court. Do you possibly remember this? I somehow believe you do. Rigby, you were shaking your head in court. Listen up, ladies... Eleanor!" She pushed herself onto an elbow, leaning into Darlene. "Good. Thank you. Because this is the best part." Pat leaned forward. "Holy shit, Battle View. That could have been us. I've heard about that place. It's a bitch and he's got you to thank for it. Hey, I'm not the one who smashed in her head. Let's not get too righteous. Can't say I even remember how she felt. Can't say I'll do it again. Too much like work. Anyway, what's he got to lose? We've probably done him a favour."

Pat turned his attention to the women, making his way to Darlene's night table, pouring more vodka into her glass, then Eleanor's. "It is all true, ladies. That's who you married. Two killers. Now, drink up. Believe me, I am doing you ladies a really big favour here. As I said, Billy reads lips. I wrote those very words on the back of a photograph and read them each night for years. I had to, and I still have the photo." He reached into his pocket. "Meet my wife Brenda, taken years ago. Truth be told, she makes you two seem like angels."

The drinks were taking affect; the last two-fingers were

a kindness. "This is unreal."

"I agree that your evening certainly has taken a turn, hasn't it?" He took Darlene's glass, then Eleanor's. "However this is very real, Darlene. So, comfort each other while I talk more with the men. Enjoy the movie, especially you Eleanor. It gets a whole lot better."

He returned to his seat. "He read yours too late, Rigby. You got off because he was afraid. He was afraid he would be charged with raping under aged girls, these two high school sluts; the very same girls who could have come forth to save him. But they did not, and Billy Rider sits in the nation's hellhole for a crime he did not commit. And the worst part is, Lucy's murder would probably have gone unsolved."

"None of this is true," Rigby tried. "You accepted the word of a madman, because who else would do such a terrible thing? And now you're here blaming us and humiliating us in front of our wives."

"Of course it isn't," Carlton injected. "Complete lies, all of it. Everything you've said here is ludicrous. Won't you please just go and leave us? You've done your damage."

A hole appeared in the wall between Rigby and Carlton.

"No, I cannot. And nothing I've said is a lie, Carlton." He turned to the television where Darlene was walking alongside her husband.

In bed she was consoling Eleanor with tender strokes and kisses, oblivious. "So why am I here? Well, to make things right, and I need your full cooperation. Mr. Rigby, would you please lie on your back with your hands in your pockets. And Mr. Carlton, would you please join the ladies?" Carlton's eyes were glued to the screen. "Mr. Carlton, you may watch your porno flick if you want, after you strip and drape your clothes with the ladies'. Then please join them in bed, centre stage if you will. And ladies, I need a little more realism, a little more enthusiasm. Please do not ignore your more exciting attributes and yearnings.

I'm sure your husbands would welcome seeing your faces glistening with pungent fervour. Billy did, very much so. I believe that even now he drifts to sleep each night reliving the scene. Darlene, top or bottom? Your choice."

Carlton stood, making his way to the loveseat where he stripped. "This is so incredibly sick. What now?" he asked.

Pat went to the camera, checking the functions which he thought seemed fine.

"Stand quietly, Mr. Carlton, by the camera as we film them. Ladies, I caution you, be very convincing. And smile. I need lots of happy. This is for Billy. Do your best. Camera! Action!"

Darlene pulled away from her friend, prompting Eleanor to slide down, crossing over her body, straddling her chest, pushing her legs apart and burying her face into her thighs.

Pat commended her, directing Eleanor not to surface for air until one or both of them recreated the climatic beginning of that long ago evening, urging Carlton to take more of an interest as Rigby craned his neck to see what he could.

Pat took his seat, checking his watch. Darlene was fourteen minutes into her run. Incredibly the two women were driving each other into a frenzy. Eleanor's legs flailed first, Darlene's body twitching seconds later, squirming to sit on her friend's hips, Pat silently directing Carlton to stop filming.

"Thank you, ladies. A fine performance, which I am certain your husbands will agree was not improvised, adding to my credibility. Thank you. Excellent indeed. Bravo. Now…"

He directed the women to manoeuvre onto their hands and knees away from the camera. They were to glance over their shoulders at Carlton, coquettishly, inviting him, teasing him, who would then walk to them facing away from the lens since Pat didn't believe he could act very convincingly.

Eleanor was the weaker of the two, she was drift_ng. He knew that. Darlene, not entirely drunk, though not fit to drive, seemed to be adapting beyond expectation to his improv theatre. She helped position her friend with an affection he could see visibly shocked the husbands. Well done.

He thanked her, begging her indulgence. Everything had a reason, he insisted. She ignored him, smiling into the camera.

He directed her to remain as she was for a moment, and for Eleanor to slide forward onto her side. They obeyed, Darlene taking the initiative to caress her friend's hips and side. Excellent.

"Mr. Carlton, your presence is again requested. Would you please, hmm, how shall I ask this of you… join the ladies and fuck your wife? Darlene, your ass or your legs in the air, please. Your choice. Remember, we're friends now. So whichever is the best for you. Drama here is not required, although as you currently are may be of assistance to your husband under the circumstances. You are very captivating to the male of the species, as you well know. As for you, Carlton, take as little or as much time as you need or wish. Darlene's gratification is of no great importance."

Carlton refused. "No, I will not. You're a despicable animal, Fellows. I refuse."

"Yes, you will." Pat recited two phone numbers and the addresses in Boston. "Yes, you will.
Believe me. Lindsay and Loraine, Brad and Bart want you to as much as I do."

Darlene realized what she was hearing. Her brow furrowed, raising herself upright from her knees, twisting sideways to glare at her husband. "Do it, goddammit! What is your fucking problem?"

Pat checked his watch as Carlton clambered behind her. He wasn't interested, watching the screen as Darlene was approaching twenty minutes into her run. He paused the

Darlene video, instructing them not to stop. They'd been there, done that. "Eleanor, helping them is optional. Be my guest. Your choice. But first this is for you." He pressed PLAY, increasing the volume.

Darlene said, "Eleanor would hate me if she saw me like this."

"Would you, Eleanor, hate her?" Pat asked.

"No. I wouldn't ever."

"And there you have it, gentlemen." He lowered the volume. "I believe you, Eleanor, and please keep watching. This is special, which I truly believe she did for you."

At twenty-six minutes Darlene's body jolted from the picnic table, shuddering, unexpectedly grunting in unison with her video image as though on cue for everyone in real time, pulling free of her husband and diving forward onto the sheets.

"This is so fucking sick," she murmured.

"Smile people. I need smiley faces. I really do. And so is fucking the entire tenth grade sick, Darlene. So is fucking a naïve boy and raping an innocent girl." He glared at Carlton. "Mr. Carlton, do not look back. Do not, or I will be the last thing you see. I promise you that. Now, mosey over and do her. Do the other one."

"What! No! She's my sister for Christ's sake."

"Your adopted sister. Humour me. I'm sure Rigby here won't mind. You'll notice he's not saying much. Might have a fantasy thing going on. So, go ahead. Eleanor, same choice. Your ass or your knees? Or do I need to repeat those numbers?"

She shimmied forward, reaching for Darlene's hand, squeezing her eyes shut. "Do it, Jake. Get this over with."

Darlene was jumping from the picnic table, skipping and jogging, rounding the corner to the finish line. She was walking, waving her arms. The SUV was in sight with no need to hurry. In real time she was fascinated watching her husband with Eleanor whose gasps were genuine from fear or pleasure. He couldn't tell which and he didn't care.

Carlton was done, pulling free from his sister, inching backwards, directed to remain facing away, face down between her thighs and at least pretend to enjoy their finale. He obeyed.

Darlene's expression was priceless. She was transfixed, visibly rapt and completely oblivious to her brother and Pat. Sick bitch.

He snapped his fingers.

"Darlene, listen very carefully. Focus on Eleanor. Put your face over hers. Kiss, don't kiss. Don't care. You could have saved Billy Rider. You know that. No one would have cared that you and Eleanor here were hot for each other. The boy was innocent. Carlton, you and Rigby killed that poor girl. You know you did. And I know. This video and the others when found will tell the entire world what kind of depraved people you truly are. You are guilty, all of you."

He turned to see Darlene standing in the screen, waiting determinedly in her red boots for Carlton to give in, to let her drive home naked.

"Strange how a woman can be so flawlessly carved on the outside," he froze the image, "chiselled so delicately in places, sculpted with such fine care in others; while on the inside she decays."

"Fuck you, Fellows, whoever you are. That's my wife, goddammit."

"Be quiet, Jake. Keep snacking."

Darlene followed Pat's gaze with her head bowed. Her voice was clear and calm. "I am beautiful. Are you blind, or what? So is Eleanor. We get off on each other. What's the big deal? Really? You were right. I did want her to see this. I wanted her to run with me. That doesn't make me rotten and if you think I'm embarrassed by this, or us, I'm not. Neither is she. And you watched me twice. Did you puke?"

"Precisely my point, Darlene. No one would have cared. But rotten? Yes. Very."

"We never hurt anyone."

"You were spiteful, mean-spirited girls, way beyond servicing an entire school for kicks, or each other. You precipitated a murder. You left Billy behind and drunk. If you hadn't he would have found Lucy at the river in time. She would be alive, you wouldn't be married to a killer, and Billy wouldn't be sitting in prison with his back terribly mutilated by a few hundred lacerations that required years of agony to heal."

"But he did heal."

"I don't believe you said that. But yes, he did."

Eleanor was sobbing. Her stomach was heaving. Good. Very good. She wanted to go home, Pat agreeing that was a good idea. The evening had gone on too long. He told Darlene to kiss her eyes, to smudge the tears, telling Eleanor to focus on the screen where Darlene was performing at her very best. She did, straining to see over her brother's head.

Pat pressed PLAY.

"Darlene you really need a drink and I'm leaving now with Rigby. I've had enough of you Bible Belt freaks. Isn't that what *you* called *him*? And you three need some serious alone time. But first get on your knees, take your glass and gawk at Eleanor as though…well, you know…the way you do. Put a bright smile on your face, very bright, then turn quickly to the door and call your brother's name. Do it. Now!"

Darlene scrambled onto her knees, hunched slightly forward, unbalanced. She was definitely exhausted. She spilled vodka into her glass an inch deep, gulping, putting her fingertips to Eleanor's cheek. Her smile was weary, yet truly believable. "Dwight…!"

At that precise moment Pat crashed the camera to the floor. The Beretta came up instantly. Triggers and shutter releases had one thing in common: Each one would freeze a subject's expression. He needed to keep her smile real. The first bullet went into Darlene's forehead, slamming her against the cushioned board at the very moment she was slipping into her red poncho.

Her husband didn't notice.

"You're right, Carlton. Fuck me. I guess I never will know what you did with her at the mall. Too bad. Like I said, nice body."

The second round exploded the back of Carlton's skull.

The third went between Eleanor's breasts who scarcely realized, before she died gazing at Darlene in red boots clambering into her red SUV.

Thirty-Three

June 22nd

Pat gave his attention to Rigby who was sprawled on the floor gaping at the corpses, propped onto his elbows, the back of his head and shoulders pressed into the wall. He was moaning. Not quite the man he was.

"You killed them? You actually killed them, just like that? Fuck!"

"You look stupid, Rigby. Sit up properly." He waited. "I suppose you realize I won't really be needing those cars."

Rigby was chalk white, his tan obliterated. "Listen, Fellows, take the money. We'll go to the bank and…"

"Whoa, Trigger. This is not a movie. You do not get to walk away from this." Pat squatted in safe space. "Ah, shit. No way! You pissed yourself?" He stood. "That is not cool, not cool at all. Carlton over there, he's allowed. And the ladies. Things happen. But not you."

"What do you expect?" he choked. "You just murdered my family."

"Tell me, did you piss yourself when you killed Lucy?" No reply. "I'll take that as a yes."

"Carlton killed her. Like Rider, he wanted seconds. He got greedy. That's when she ripped off his mask. That's when he killed her. Not me. I wasn't anywhere near them. I was finished with her, ready to leave."

"Finished with her? Is that right?" Pat fired a round into the wall a few inches from Rigby's head. "Just so you know, this is the first time I've handled a gun. The guy I killed, I snapped his neck. He was about your size. So heed the warning. As for Lucy, you'll be apologizing soon enough for that sick remark. In the meantime keep it clean. Which of you killed her is not an issue. He's dead, you're not. That makes you the killer. That's how these things work."

"Okay, so I killed her. Says you." He nodded to the bed. "You've got your own problems. That's not my gun. I don't even own one. So now what. Me?"

"No. Nothing as quick and easy that. No need to piss yourself again. I am not killing you. However you are going to hell for murder, eventually. That's the plan. You're going to Battle View, Rigby. As fate would have it, I might even walk in with you. We can be buddies."

"I don't understand. You're not killing me?"

"Not unless you fucked me up with the video. Then, yes."

Pat went to the television, rewinding Darlene to where she was standing at her SUV in her red boots, pouting until her shopping epiphany made her eyes sparkle when she smiled so gleefully into the lens. He ejected her. The video of Rigby and his former wife he dropped into his satchel.

He ordered Rigby to stand, to insert the evening's performances into the VCR, intrigued by the process. Together they watched the ladies' initial and silent love scene, fast-forwarding to Darlene's final word. Satisfied, Pat replaced the cassette into the camera. He put the empty cartridge shell into the satchel, instructing Rigby to re-insert his sister.

Rigby closely studied the theatrical Darlene as Pat busied himself, then the one atop the bed staring back at him.

"So it's true? They did fuck that freak?"

"Hot and heavy. And that freak is a good friend of mine, for which reason you would be smart to remember this gun of mine."

"I can't believe they were lovers all these years. Shit."

Pat coughed a laugh. "No. What you mean is, more sick Bible Belt shit you and Carlton missed out on. Personally, I don't think brother dear was having a rough time down there. Could have been you and your sister, I suppose, the way you're gaping at her. Sorry about that. Luck of the draw."

Pat reached for Carlton's glass, placing it by the armchair, ordering Rigby to change from his wet slacks and underwear and to leave what was soiled on the floor where he stood. He took the ATM cards, sliding them into his shirt pocket, dropping the cash into the satchel.

"Do you remember what Lucy was wearing that night? Don't lie to me."

"How could I forget? Shit, every kid in that entire school wanted to fuck that girl. She was the hottest thing with two legs. We just got to her first."

Pat crashed a fist into Rigby's jaw, landing him on the floor. "First. Yeah, before you started fucking each other's sisters." He waved Rigby to his feet. "The facts."

"A white skirt, short, and a blue blouse. Her underwear was black or blue. Something like that, and fancy."

They were done in the room for the time being, leaving the setting undisturbed.

Downstairs he instructed Rigby to the far end of the living room, instructing him to say something, anything, and silently. "Be creative."

Rigby thought for a moment. "What was the point of the video, yours, the three of them doing each other?"

Pat repeated each word to a stunned Rigby. The point was made: Keep your mouth shut. He answered, "Disgrace: Payback for the Cutters. And public humiliation: Payback for Lucy. You'll understand more in due course. Now get your keys."

From the backdoor he walked behind Rigby to the

Mercedes. With no traffic the drive to the bank lasted under ten minutes. Pat had previously tested the weapon, as much as he did his eyes. He trusted both. He was confident he could kill Rigby from diagonally across the street, if need be.

Rigby was to stand sideways and not say anything into the ATM's camera, Pat reminding him that children, four in particular, should never pay for the parents' sins or foolishness. Despite which unfortunate things did happen. Nor was this a time to agonize over the high cost of requisite living expenses.

That much Rigby did understand. He started high, working his way through the other three accounts in small downward increments until hitting pay dirt. The transactions were time-consuming, though produced a higher yield than expected. Yet despite Pat's concerns all went well to the tune of seven grand in fifties and hundreds, not far from eight with what he had reaped from the wallets and purses. He was pleased, returning to the homes in silence.

From the driveway they went into Carlton's home, to the office where Pat took the agenda from Darlene's desk and searched Carlton's briefcase where Pat Fellows was pencilled into his for 11:00 on Monday. Both went into the satchel. Photo albums were opened and flung onto the floor, boxes of photo slides opened and scattered into the air.

In the bedroom Pat opened the drawer of each night table, tossing Darlene's toys helter-skelter onto the bed and the floor. Searching the other he rummaged through the video cases as a crazed man might, finding one he believed was a good choice.

Once again he slid Darlene into a VCR. She was sunning in the backyard, getting that all-over tan, fast-forwarded to a racy and self-absorbed shower scene on the patio where he left her, shooting her through the screen to add a sense of emotion before leaving.

Crossing the lawn to Rigby's home they went to the bedroom. Nothing had changed.

Rigby packed a suitcase with enough casual clothing and a freshly dry-cleaned suit to last a week. Meanwhile Pat searched through Eleanor's drawer to select toys he believed the ladies might have enjoyed that evening, or more likely already had, dropping them between the bodies. The others he put into his satchel along with all the Rigby and Wife Creative Productions taken from Rigby's drawer, who, as a decent and church-going Christian in Baptist Necessity, would not possibly think of fucking his wife for someone else's viewing pleasure.

Rigby left without paying his last respects. Pat trailed behind, glancing once over his shoulder at Darlene's debut performance, thinking what a tragedy. No one would have cared.

The suitcase was put by the kitchen door with the garbage bag.

What he needed he would find in the office where he retrieved the old-fashioned from his satchel, telling Rigby that two-fingers would be about right. With his first gulp of scotch he ordered the man to discard the ATM cards and receipts into a waste basket while he occupied himself with rifling through photo albums and slides as though searching for evidence of home-made porno as Rigby looked on. Nothing. Because of their snooping kids, he supposed.

He coughed a laugh at the irony. A completely wasted effort. Those same kids were mere days away from a total brain-fuck.

Satisfied with the mess he'd made, he confiscated Rigby's and Eleanor's agendas, searching Rigby's briefcase and desk for anything additional relating to Pat Fellows, not for a moment believing the man.

Again, nothing. Good.

"You should have kept your mouth shut in court that day, Rigby. Billy knew about the girls. Of course he did. He knew they had a thing going on. He used to read everyone's lips at school. Seems he had a lot of time on his hands. He knew who they screwed and who was next, all the while playing prim and proper for their loving mommies and daddies and you two. Too bad he never saw you talking about Lucy. Too bad for everyone."

"The kid was a…"

"That kid has two degrees and got your buddies upstairs expunged, making the world a much cleaner place. He's also putting you in prison for their murders and Lucy's. You see, this *is* your gun, or will be when I'm finished with it."

"Thanks. But somehow I don't think so."

"More to the point, I do. So sit." He pushed over his glass. "One more, then throw what's left against the wall, hard. Make it very real. Make believe you killed your best friend in a rage for fucking your wife, which I half suspect you enjoyed as much as your sister's on-screen and live performances. You did, didn't you? You may have pissed yourself, yet I didn't see you puking."

He hit a nerve. The bottle smashed a framed photo of the happy couple, ricocheting onto the floor.

"Thanks for that. Guess I really didn't want that drink. Good work though. Now it's time to compose a letter. I dictate, you write. And make it legible. Die here or die in prison, I could give a shit. Your decision. However your kids will each see those videos before lights out. Special delivery. Believe it. Comprendes, amigo?" He waited as Rigby reached for his pen and a lined pad. "Good choice."
*

Tonight I have willfully shot and killed my wife, my sister, and a man I believed for years was my trusted friend.
I acted with just cause and a clear mind, exclusive of insanity. I could not bear to witness their animated obscenities, or hear of their secret and long enduring

adultery, the incest and the debauchery that I happened upon by the purest of coincidences.

To my stunned and speechless disbelief, standing before them dumbfounded, their initial amazement at seeing me transmuted quickly to their shameless confessions and welcoming arms. They invited me to join them, my wife and my sister confessing with girlish giggles and fervent kisses that they had for years been each other's truest and most ardent lover, that I was but a convenient social fixture.

When I refused they mocked me, telling me to leave. Can anyone imagine the sickened state of my heart?

Good Lord, Carlton was having the most abominable sex with his own sister, my wife, where he now lies in purgatory between her wide-open legs; my own sister turning her back on me, freely and brazenly participating with each of them.

I was devastated by so vile an act of betrayal after these many years of love and devotion to both these women whom I once cherished so deeply, and Carlton. The three colluding against me, mocking me in such a loathsome and repulsive manner when since our youth we have shared the deepest and the darkest of secrets. How dare they betray me this way?

On May 22, 1971, I and Jackson Carlton together raped and murdered Lucy Merriweather by design. The act was intentional, devised well in advance. Our sole error was in not binding her hands. For which reason we killed her when, by her own misfortune, she discovered our names due solely to Carlton's insatiable greed for her.

Her skirt, I recall, was white; her blouse was blue. Her underclothing was darker, black or blue. I have no doubt that her parents will vividly remember those intimate details kept from the public.

She was found near the clearing and undressed, the extent of her failed escape and another fact not previously made public. Her clothes and her purse we disposed of into the river.

Billy Rider is innocent of those two crimes. He was, in point of fact, the innocent victim of my wife's and my sister's whimsical and thorough seduction of him, thereby satisfying their mutual desire to ridicule him and cause Lucy the anguish of teenage jealousy.

Question Rider yourself. He alone knows of the cul-de-sac and their most intimate details. You can see for yourselves their bodies' particular features, proof alone of his innocence, which he may not have dispelled from his mind with so little else to ponder.

I am not fleeing from these crimes I have committed. I merely intend to fulfill a lifelong desire which I have denied myself all these faithful years since long ago forgiving my wife's sordid evening with Rider, believing in her renewed purity. For who was I to judge?

Now to discover her treason. More the fool am I.

When I feel the time is right, when I feel properly and fully recompensed for her wickedness against me, I will willingly and happily surrender to justice and the scorn of my children.

Lastly, to ensure Rider's release from prison by reason of his innocence, I am forwarding copies of this confession to the following:

Cc: The Necessity News, the State District Attorney, (Capital) Judge Allison Stillsworth, the Merriweathers, and to his mother, Miss Sally, who will soon greet her son with her first breath of joy in so many years. I trust this letter strengthens her heart.

As well, I am leaving one at the gates of purgatory where they lie.

June 22ᵗʰ, 1991,

Yours, Dwight Rigby

*

Pat read the letter, producing five pre-stamped envelopes. He dictated the addresses, telling Rigby to make five copies and sign each one, which he verified before stuffing the envelopes and sliding them into his jacket.

Together they went again to the bedroom where he taped the original to the television, taking care not to obscure Darlene from future adoring eyes, sprinkling the bed and bodies with scotch and vodka as an after-thought to help properly convey the enchanted mood.

Replacing the scotch bottle on the table by Eleanor, he said, "I can't imagine what your proud parents will say when they see all this, and read the letter. Or theirs for that matter. Collateral damage, I suppose. Unavoidable. Like Sally Cutter who was driven from town and lost her husband because of you. I can't imagine they'll like you very much." Replacing the vodka bottle by Darlene, he said, "I'm curious, Rigby."

"About what?"

"Your wife, here...no tears for her? We've got a few minutes if you want to sit by her side, to say goodbye, to touch her one last time while she's still warm."

"She fucked Billy Rider. A brainless zombie. How sick is that? And who knows what she did with my sister all these years? No, I don't think so."

"Then what about your twin sister? Even with a hole in her head she is quite the beauty. A little brotherly embrace, an affectionate squeeze? I have to believe she'd like that."

"Thanks, I'll pass. So, what now if you're not going to kill me? What's this lifelong desire of mine?"

"We're going to West Palm Beach. Think of it as a working vacation, at the very least extending your freedom. Believe me, you are going to enjoy yourself."

"I don't understand."

"You will. You see, the person I have to kill, well, she's my wife. Actually she's a prostitute," he shrugged. "She is, a real one. Very high-end. Gets paid for it big time and I want you to fuck her because I can't. I won't swim in a sewer, whereas you can. You have for years in Eleanor. And I presume in a few others. Consider Brenda as my compensation to you for excluding you from the festivities this evening. I do get the sense you wanted in." He grinned. "I couldn't help noticing your very clear interest in your sister. Can't say as I blame you, though. Sure you don't want a personal moment?"

"You're sick."

"Anyway, I want to see Brenda perform, like these notable stars of screen and stage. I want to humiliate her the way she humiliated me. Then I'll kill her and you're on your own with a smile on your face to live free as long as you can, by which time Billy Rider should be a free man."

"That won't happen."

Pat signalled Rigby to bring his glass, pointing to the door. Rigby preceded him, listening to further directives as they went for the last time to the office where he sat reaching for his phone. The moment John Andrews had waited impatiently for all evening was now his crowning glory.

Rigby knew what to say, understanding that his suicide would be an unhappy alternative.

The phone rang three times.

"Hello?"

"Am I speaking with Mrs. Sally Cutter?"

"Yes, you are."

"Mrs. Cutter, in a few days' time you will receive a letter from me. My name doesn't matter. What does, however, is that I am the one who murdered Lucy Merriweather. Your son Billy is innocent. My letter is a signed confession to you and several significant others named in that letter which I believe will suffice to free Billy Rider, possibly before my letter arrives at your door. I sincerely hope so. Goodbye."

Pat could hear Sally's loud wail seconds before the line went dead.

"I need a drink."

"Later, when the job's done. Dial."

He gave Rigby another number, Rigby inhaling a deep breath, wishing for an answering machine.

"Yes? The Merriweathers here."

"Mr. Merriweather, my name is not important at the moment. You will discover who I am soon enough, when you receive a letter I am forwarding to you this evening. It's a confession. I am the man who, with another, hurt and killed your daughter. Billy Rider is innocent. He did not kill Lucy. He happened across her by accident. She was already dead."

Merriweather screamed for his wife. "What! That cannot be possible."

"Very possible. We didn't intend to kill her, not until she saw our faces. I am truly sorry, but Billy Rider is innocent. I would suggest that you call Sally Cutter immediately. You will find her in Seattle. I believe you owe her and Billy an apology and, if it's any comfort to either of you, my accomplice was killed this evening…by me."

Pat drew a hand sharply across his throat. The call ended.

"What now?"

"You'll smash your glass on the living room wall, we'll mail the letters, and we'll get the hell out of Dodge." Pat checked his watch: 9:55. "This actually lasted longer than I anticipated. And you know what? I feel good. I kept a promise."

"You killed three people, degrading them like animals."

"Notice my tears. Carlton was an animal. So are you. And everything done here this evening did have a purpose."

"What possible purpose could be served by him fucking my sister and my wife, other than your own depravity?"

"Very simple. An autopsy. Or, better said, creative realism. The proof in the pudding, so to speak. Your bisexual wife was cheating on you with her own brother. You said so yourself. Why else would you have murdered them? And let's get this straight, you did murder them.

That's what your mortified parents will believe when they see Carlton burrowing his way into his sister whose lipstick is everywhere on yours, particularly when they replay the evening's feature film. As will the police and whoever else is required to free Billy. Essentially, Mr. Rigby, you are screwed."

"Why so much effort for a deaf and dumb kid? You talk about Eleanor and Darlene, what about you?"

Pat chuckled. "He was a good friend. We had each other's back. That's all we had." Pat stepped aside. "Shall we go?"

The crystal old-fashioned shattered against a living room wall. Good. Convincing.

Leaving through the kitchen door a quiet Rigby pulled his suitcase, the garbage bag rattling over his shoulder. Pat's hands were full with his burgeoning satchel and his gun.

With everything stored on the Monte Carlo's rear seat, Rigby drove to the nearest mailbox and from there to the I-95 South, driving five MPH under the posted seventy-five.

Rigby had nothing to say that Pat wanted to hear. Conversely, Pat felt obliged to explain in detail what was in store for a new arrival in prison, particularly Battle View, convicted for his particular crimes against a young girl.

He explained the dehumanizing first few hours. He explained how the lash rips apart a man's back, describing the varied expressions a man's face undergoes as he chokes to death hanging from a railing, the gagging, the bawling, his feet wildly kicking the air, his hands tearing at his throat too late as a second thought. Which, in Battle View, was entertainment.

They stopped for gas every forty miles, foregoing coffee, each time depositing spoiled videos and the ingredients of a spoiled dinner into frequently used and frequently emptied garbage cans.

Arriving at the Charleston apartment's parking lot near

2:00 AM Rigby walked ahead, stopping at the waste company's bins where Pat discarded the knotted plastic bag containing little boxes, gift wrapping and panties. His souvenir glass he took with him into his home where he let Rigby urinate before strapping his ankles together with duct tape and offering him a Johnnie Walker Black, as promised.

Rigby clearly did not like how the other half lived.

"We could have worked something out, Fellows. A good job with me, a no-interest and forgivable bank loan from Jake. We could have done something a lot better than this. You didn't have to kill them." He drained his glass, holding out his hand for another. "For that matter, shit, given the choice, you could have fucked each of them instead of Carlton. Like you said, who would have cared? And when was the last time you saw two that good-looking and willing?"

Pat filled the glass three-fingers deep. He wanted and needed Rigby to sleep.

"Like I said, I don't swim in sewers, not even pretty ones. And, yes, I did have to kill them.
Believe me, once you feel that whip, you'll wish I'd put you in bed with them. If they don't hang you. For my money, Rigby, you should be contemplating a very long vacation in Cuba."

Rigby inhaled deeply, expelling the breath through pursed lips. "I have to say, I never had a clue. Thinking about it, they always had a reason to spend time together." He savoured the scotch, examining the glass. "You know what, neither of us would have had a problem with it. Live once, right?"

"Wrong. Some of us have a second chance, like me and Billy."

"Don't be so sure. You know they're going to block the highways, the ninety-five first and foremost. That tells me you're screwed, not me."

"You're forgetting about Lucy."

"And you're forgetting about murder and coercion."

"No, I'm not. Either way, you won't be missed at church tomorrow. Even if you are, after all the handshaking, kissing and social blah-blah you might get a call midafternoon. By which time we'll be in Florida driving in a shitbox from Charleston. What's more likely? They'll be found Monday when the four of you don't show up like clockwork. Rigby's may call the bank, or the inverse, though I don't believe either will. They'll phone your homes and leave messages, maybe drop by on their lunch breaks. They'll find your backdoor open, smell the roses, and a few steps later shit themselves. Which we don't care about because we're in West Palm Beach drinking expensive booze by a pool with an ocean view." He stood. "Drain your glass. We're done."

Pat taped Rigby's hands, then taped his chest and feet to a kitchen chair before switching off the lights and laying on his couch.

Six hours later he showered and shaved. He put his soiled clothes into a plastic bag for laundering once they arrived and packed a suitcase with more casual attire and a suit for the week. Rigby did not shower or shave. Part of the plan. Though he was permitted to change, dropping the clothes he'd been wearing into the garbage. They left near 10:00, Pat tossing the shoes he'd worn to Necessity separately into the garbage bin.

Battle View: 101.

They arrived at Peters Lane at 5:30, Rigby much more acquainted with prison life than he deemed necessary and decidedly less confident. More importantly, no Bentley was sitting in the driveway.

After an hour on the beach, Pat's right hand concealed in his straw shoulder bag, they strolled the lane to the front. Excellent. Still no Bentley. A few minutes later Pat was as deftly and quickly through the gate as though he'd used a key, the garden doors no challenge at all.

The first order of business was personal, the second was taping Rigby's left hand to a chair that would be his constant companion most hours of each day. The third was two-fingers of Johnnie Walker Blue.

Thirty-Four

June 27th

Sunday in Necessity came and went. The day was exceptionally lovely without summer's usually blistering heat, luring more parishioners to the beach and family picnics than the Carltons and Darlene for whom time was standing still.

Monday morning no one noticed Dwight and Eleanor missing. The newest salesgirl routinely filled in as receptionist whenever Mrs. Rigby was frequently absent with or without her husband who also routinely exploited his rank. Nor did anyone at the Carlton Bank question the uncommon absence of the more dependable Mr. Carlton and his wife. Not until early afternoon when a matter of some urgency arose requiring his immediate attention and his steadfast secretary was unable to reach him anywhere.

Her phone calls to the house and car went unanswered, the woman informed minutes later that the Rigbys had taken the day off as well. They were close friends after all.

Tuesday, the 25th, by 9:30, Carlton's secretary left her desk. She wasn't worried; she was ruffled by his lack of consideration. She was stiff and no-nonsense, seldom caught smiling, paid for doing what had to be done. She drove to the lavish home she had been invited to many times and, seeing both cars in both driveways, she went first to her boss' front door, crossing over to Rigby's when she felt frustrated and foolish standing alone on the porch.

No less exasperated there, she removed her heels and padded cautiously between the homes, calling out their four names. Nothing, urging herself first towards Carlton's patio, to the open backdoor, again calling out then shouting their names through the screen without any reply.

Inside she found nothing untoward in the kitchen. The first chaotic mess that shocked her was in the office, and again she called out their names. Marching up the staircase more than climbing, she peered first into a front guestroom before coming to the master suite.

She saw the disturbing array on the bed, gawking in disbelief as her mind autonomously catalogued the colourful obscenities piece by piece, her face scrunching into a tight grimace at the mess on the floor and the imploded television.

Inching slowly backwards into the hallway, puzzled, she called down the stairwell to the lower level from the main floor. Silence. Alone in a deserted house.

Outside she went midway into the lawn, intently scanning each home before plodding a straight course to a midway point in the Rigbys' yard, again seeing an open door that she hurried towards in stocking feet to call all their names. Where she hesitated. She wasn't at all certain.

She was acquainted with the Rigbys. She had dined with them as a guest of the Carltons on rare occasions and she drove a Fine Motors mid-range sedan, convincing herself they would understand her concern. Reason enough, she determined, to be discovered lurking inside their home.

She didn't see the shattered glass or damaged wall. She went immediately to the catastrophe in the office, pausing in the doorway, curious more than frightened. Like her boss and his wife, the Rigbys were always good-natured with never an angry word or hateful glare between them. They were decent and kind people, both of them loving couples. She didn't understand what she was seeing.

Making her way up the stairway she went directly to

their master suite without pausing, driven by purpose, sniffing the air that became more fetid with each footfall.

Striding through the doorway she halted so abruptly that she stumbled forward, screaming. She stared at the gruesome bodies, too horrified to move. Her heart was beating wildly, her breathing erratic. She was gasping hysterically for the very air that threatened to suffocate her. She wanted to run, frozen where she stood.

She saw the television, Darlene smiling at her, and the paper. The fetid air was gagging her. Her throat and her chest were constricting, her stomach churning. She went rigid. Her mind was reeling. She was trembling. She felt her legs on the verge of collapse, devastated by sight of vomit spewing from her mouth across the armchair and floor.

She lurched from the room, sobbing, her eyes flooded. Her stocking feet slipped from under her on the first polished step, her body tumbling uncontrolled past thirty more where she dragged herself upright by the banister, clutching her stomach. Her head was spinning, her body teetering. Everything around her was swaying.

She had to collect herself. She knew what was required of her. She wiped the spittle from her mouth, inhaled a fresher breath and cleared her eyes. She stepped cautiously from the first step to the floor where she paused for a moment before hobbling to the office where she trampled heedlessly over the debris to sit at the desk and struggle with the phone

Some three minutes later, an eternity alone to the stricken woman, a horde of uniformed cops burst onto the scene through an open door brandishing their weapons. She wasn't impressed with the excessively theatrical bravado. She had indicated to them precisely who she was and what to expect.

She was seated in the living room, poised, gulping from a full glass of whiskey. Her skirt and her blouse were dishevelled, stained with her vomit.

When the detectives arrived they reprimanded her for tampering with evidence at a crime scene. Was that so, she challenged? She drained the glass and poured another, suggesting they refrain from acting as such blatant idiots.

Naturally they had the last word as arrogant cops are wont to do. Barking instead of listening. They were detectives and they were not finished with her. They posted a guard to make their point and, not very long after, pale and distressed, both men were drinking from the same bottle.

Necessity would never be the same. Nor would two aging fathers who were called to witness their daughters and a son so shamelessly exposed.

The bodies had begun their decay, the smell of rot and the bodies' secretions impossible to bear without hankies heavily scented with liquor found in the room.

Dwight had not thought to close his sister's eyes. Once bright green and clear, they were dull and dry, leering at the fathers unrepentantly, a thin trickle of brown blood parting her like a closed zipper from her wound to her crimson pubic hair that seemed as artificial against her greyish-blue hue as the once lustrous curls cascading in careless strands over her shoulders.

Eleanor lay serenely. She was reaching out for her lover's hand, her chest wound buried under a thick plaster of dried blood, her belly and legs coated with much of what heretofore had been contained inside her brother's head.

He lay with his calves suspended above the floor, his hands clutching at the legs he lay sprawled between. His badly damaged skull was all anyone could see, a palette of gruesome colours and textures, as though hiding his shame or hadn't yet finished with the most unthinkable incest.

What would the fathers say to their wives? What could they say? They had no comment for the press, nor Mr. Rigby any appeal for his outlawed son. The letter was devastating enough, what little they could bear to watch of

Darlene's video inexplicably worse. Yet their grief was instantly and completely purged once viewing what Jackson Carlton had filmed of their daughters' voracious depravity minutes before being murdered.

Mr. Carlton refused to enter his son's home. Instead he drove his son's secretary to her home. He waited by her side until her family arrived to console her, calling from his car as they drove to instruct the bank to close its doors at once and that anyone who might seek an ephemeral fifteen minutes of fame with the press would be immediately terminated. Carlton senior never explained or repeated himself.

He then went home to his wife as a much older man, soon after calling Sally Cutter with a clear head, weeping at her words of forgiveness, asking that she speak with Mr. Rigby who would contact her later that evening. He then called Lucy's mother and they wept together. He called his grandchildren in Boston, insisting they come home without delay.

The school year was over. They need not be concerned. With the families' combined annual congratulations and gratitude to the teachers and tutors, their passing grades were assured. Lastly he called his lawyer. After which, sending his beloved wife of forty-two years to bed, he got very and uncharacteristically drunk.

Mr. Rigby called his lawyer first from behind the closed door of his home office. Moments later all doors to the Rigby Empire were closed until further notice with the same threat of dismissal imposed on the staff.

He called Sally Cutter. He told her, as his lifelong friend had, that she would have whatever she and Billy would need to make their lives whole. They spoke a long while and they would speak again soon, he promised. Then he called Lucy's mother to confirm that the Rigbys and Carltons would together, as soon as possible, and with their help, make very certain that Lucy Merriweather would always be remembered.

He called his grandchildren, ordering them home. Depleted, he went tearfully to his wife who had waited so stoically to share his strength and her grief with quiet sobs and unspoken questions until he settled her into their bed. Then, like Carlton, he went with a full bottle of scotch into his office.

That evening the six o'clock news had nothing to go on, excepting the quickly spreading rumours based on the willing conjecture of neighbours. The letter was not made public, the Necessity News claiming they had not yet received their copy. In spite of which an unscheduled Wednesday morning edition proclaimed on the front page and from every street corner:

Lucy's Killer Confesses
Declares Billy Rider Innocent

The byline went on:
Dwight Rigby of Rigby's Fine Motors confessed in writing this Saturday, June 22, to the 1971 savage rape and murder of Necessity's Lucy Merriweather. This before fleeing from the triple homicide of his wife Eleanor, his sister Darlene, and Jackson Carlton of the Carlton Bank whom he allegedly happened upon in a sordid sex triangle described in his letter as a lifetime of debauchery; the details of which this paper deems unsuitable for print.
He currently remains at large.
The Rigby and Carlton families, Judge Allison Stillsworth, the Merriweathers and Mr. Rider's mother are all unavailable for comment at this time, in addition to which this paper's attempts to contact Mr. Rider himself were refused by Battle View Prison's Chief Warden.
Billy Rider…
*

Wednesday evening, the 26th, Billy sat in his cell five days from his twenty-first year as a guest of the State of Tennessee.

He stared at the note Black Boss had scribbled for him days earlier. A historic event to say the least: Black Boss mingling with a white boy. *Your man John. He kept that promise he made you. He good. He real good. You soon be good too.*

John did call his mom, the way he promised, Billy spending all that day wondering what they said to each other and for how long. The rest made no sense, though he chose not to question Black Boss' communication skills. He missed John. He missed their animated conversations, hurtled into a soundless solitude the very moment John walked free.

He didn't really believe John would, or had, killed his wife. That wasn't him. He was too decent a man, once sent to Battle View because of a single and fleeting moment in time out of how many tens of millions.

He couldn't start over. He didn't want to, teaching the new guy who was at least as dumb as everyone had once thought he was. Even when sleeping with his eyes closed the guy didn't seem bright enough to knot a shoelace.

Nor did he feel any great sense of hope. He would die in Battle View. He harboured no illusions about that, and hopefully before his 114th birthday. Because what would he do then with all his education?

From almost day one John had taken care of him, protected him, practically forcing him, if not threatening him, to get smart, to learn and be ready to become someone who could make a difference. Why? Why bother?

Well that was a question Billy was never allowed to ask, John constantly reminding him to never give up hope.

Why John was particularly insistent throughout his last few weeks that he should have hope, Billy had no idea. In a way the constant lecturing was hurtful. John was going, he wasn't. Yet Billy hadn't wanted to injure his friend's feelings or take away from John's own mounting elation at finally being set free.

He wondered what John might be doing. He wondered because he couldn't imagine.

Billy had never driven a car. He'd never been to a fine restaurant or worn the fine clothes that John had often told him about. Nor had he ever travelled farther than from Charity to Necessity to Battle View. His knowledge came from what he read, from what John had imparted to him. He had no visual or tactile memories other than in his worst nightmares, and now the little good he did have was gone from his life.

Curious, though, the way John ignored him that last day, deserting him with not so much as a wave. That, at times, when his mood was often darker, was difficult to forgive.

Then real darkness engulfed him that no longer came as a surprise, not in years. Ten PM.

He slid onto his back, closing his eyes. Tomorrow was another day, shower day, another day of bench-pressing in the yard, if it didn't rain, and shaving heads to repay what remained owing on his textbooks. He never knew, no one did, not until each new day when the doors into the yard would either be open or closed.

That was the greatest hope anyone had: Time in the yard.

He harboured no doubt that one day soon John's memory of him would fade; not so for Billy who had very little else to remember. He was good with that. He understood and was happy for his friend who had done so much for him.

He mouthed goodnight to his mother and father, to his brothers and John, remembering Lucy before sleep engulfed him, transporting him to where he could speak and hear and was free.

Thursday, the 27th, at 7:00 the grating vibration of cell door 312 sliding open woke him in unison with his cellmate's head crashing into his ass. Dumb. Really dumb.

At 8:00 he went to the mess for breakfast where his and other writing pads remained as permanent fixtures. Then he went to the showers to wash away two days of sweat.

On his way into the yard through the doors that were open, he was halted by a hand on his shoulder. The guard showed Billy a note, talking despite his words falling on deaf ears. The warden wanted to see him, pronto.

No one had ever discovered his and John's secret.

Once inside the office he realized Prescott was ill-tempered, and with good reason Billy was about to discover.

He was aware of Billy's academic and social achievements, of how well-regarded he was by all three blocks. But this life-altering event Prescott had never anticipated, hadn't once given credence to as he heartlessly and contentedly watched as Billy suffered through six vicious whippings so many years ago, whippings that were abolished by federal legislation less than a year into the boy's sentence. Word of that getting out would sink him into the deepest quagmire of shit.

No time was left to him to quietly disappear, to retire from the service, to begin collecting his federal pension free of any repercussion.

He'd whipped Rider simply because he didn't like the kid. Never would. His embossed name on fancy paper didn't mean he wasn't still dumber than spit.

He ordered the guard from the office, pointing to a chair. "Sit down, Rider."

Billy did. Inmates, not even Black Boss or El Jefe fucked with the warden.

"Sure would help if you weren't dumb as an ox, Rider. I've got a shitload to say and not enough paper."

Billy shrugged, because he was dumb. He wrote: *What, Warden?*

Prescott tossed him a folded copy of Wednesday's

special late edition.
*

Judge Allison Stillsworth to Visit Battle View, Thursday
Rider Conviction is Under Review: Certain Freedom Pending
Dwight Rigby Remains at Large

Billy took his time, reading the byline, turning to page two.
Jackson and Darlene Carlton, with his sister Eleanor Rigby, will be buried tomorrow afternoon in a private ceremony attended by their fathers...
Their killer, and self-confessed murderer of Lucy Merriweather, is believed by police to be...
Mrs. Sally Cutter, desperate mother of Mr. Rider, is hopeful of seeing her son Billy by week's end in...
Judge Allison Stillsworth remains silent on '71 verdict.
*

"Seems like you're going home, Rider." He pounded his desk. "Said, seems like you're going home, Rider."

Billy stood, walking to the chalkboard without permission. He wrote: *When do I see my parents?*

The warden began writing, startled by Billy bashing his fist against the black slate.

In a day or two, I expect. But your father, he's dead. Died some twelve, fourteen years back.

The colour drained from Billy's face. His breathing was laboured, his mind racing to comprehend. *When will Stillsworth be here?* The warden began writing, Billy banging the slate, scribbling: *Tell me!!!*

"Three, four hours...with the DA and someone who can talk for you."

Billy answered: *Good. Good.*

The warden reclined his seat. "You understood all that, everything I said?"

Billy ignored the question. He wrote: *What happens now?*

"You're in protective custody until she gets here If she gives the go-ahead, that's where you stay until you're released. Anything happening to you now would cause a shitstorm I don't need."

Billy pointed to: *Good. Good.*

He was taken from the office to a room with a cot more comfortable than his bunk, a private bathroom with a shower stall and two guards posted outside his door. When asked what he wanted for lunch, he wrote: *Hamburger. Coke. Fries. Ice cream and pizza.* And a beer. He wanted a beer.

He got it all, the beer premeasured into a four-ounce glass. He saved that for last, the gentle effect completely foreign. He was delirious, too excited, too anxious and too afraid of dozing off, of waking.

He ate standing, pacing in circles, jumping and skipping, punching the air to stay awake. Too afraid, in fact, that he *was* sleeping.

Don't give up hope. Don't ever give up hope. This wasn't happening. How did John know? How did he know! Billy wanted to scream out the words. How did John know this would happen? Would he have read the papers? Would he have heard the news?

At 3:00 PM Billy was a nervous wreck. No one was bringing him news. His eyes were glued to the door, searching through the sliver of reinforced glass panelling for any movement or shadow. So intent was he, and so wound up, that he sprang back as the door swung open. The two guards motioned him into the hall with cupped hands.

Entering the warden's office with his wrists uncuffed, his feet unshackled, he recognized her immediately.

She didn't stand. No one stood. Instead, he sat before being told.

Judge Stillsworth began. "Mr. Rider, with me here today

are the DA, a non-partisan interpreter fluent in signing and legal counsel on your behalf paid for by the Rigby and Carlton families. We are here for one simple reason: To hear what you chose not to tell us two decades ago. Please do so now. But first, please read this." She proffered a copy of Dwight Rigby's confession. "Take your time. Your freedom depends heavily on what you tell us."

Billy Rider read the letter twice. He signed to the interpreter, *Miss, do you lip-read as well as signing?*

She spoke, "Yes, sir, I do. I'm a specialist in both."

"Good, then we shall forego entertaining our disadvantaged audience."

He turned his attention to the judge. "Is this true? Rigby wrote this?"

Stillsworth replied, "Yes. We have confirmed his handwriting and he is currently on the run. He was also videoed at an ATM removing substantial amounts from all four accounts."

He glanced at the interpreter. "What's ATM? What's video?"

The two legal men exchanged curious glances, their brows furrowed; the judge remained unmoved.

"He was caught on camera stealing from their bank accounts," the interpreter answered.

Billy's lawyer said, "Billy, get to the story, whatever you remember. So I can get you out of here. Your mother isn't far from here in Memphis. She's waiting for you and she's fretful that things won't go right. So let's not let disappoint her a second time. Tell us what you remember, in detail."

To all but the interpreter, seeing Billy talk without a single whisper of sound was unnerving.

"I did not kill Lucy. I loved her, as a friend. I didn't want to attend the dance. I did so for my mom. Our plan was to meet at the River Watch near eleven because Lucy's parents were invited somewhere and my mom and dad

388

expected me home a little later. Silly, really. They actually believed someone might want to dance with me. Naturally, because I was deaf and dumb, no one did."

"About ten, as I recall, Darlene and Eleanor offered to drive me home, after they made a stop which they believed I might like." He snorted. "No kidding. Anyway, I didn't care. I hoped I might have more time with Lucy. She was fluent in signing. Well, almost, and we always had so much to talk about. But that never happened."

"We drove to the end of what all the kids called the cul-de-sac, a long dirt road leading nowhere with tall grass on either side. I was in the backseat, so I only understood them once I got out. They were drinking vodka and had a blanket for the ground, which I thought was strange because of the hour."

"Very soon after they began undressing each other, everything. What they did after was pretty explicit. So, yeah, at eighteen and, shall we agree, unpopular, I was mesmerized by two very popular and naked girls squirming on a blanket completely oblivious to me. They were in another place and I wasn't with them, which I didn't care about. I believe ten minutes would be about right, give or take. I was a little drunk and more than a little too preoccupied to check my watch."

"I believed that was it, sort of a turn-on for them, but not quite. I was next. They stripped me to my socks. Did I run away? No. Did I object? No. I had sex with each of them and, as I recall, I very much enjoyed myself."

He snorted, grinning, shaking his head. "When Eleanor's turn came she needed Darlene to demonstrate what she wanted from me. That spectacle I could have watched all night, catching on pretty quickly, taking over as Darlene sat beside us to watch us and do her own thing. She was pretty wild."

"And when we finished the show wasn't over. They weren't in a hurry, drinking from the bottle, cleaning their bodies in front of me under bright lights with water and a cloth from the car. They weren't hurrying to dress either, helping each other. But when they were finished they were gone without me. I was left alone in the dark."

"No water was left in the bottle, and not much vodka. The little bit that was I drank while searching for my clothes and dressing. I started walking to the River Watch, pretty certain Lucy would hate me, convinced she would know why I smelled the way I did. You see, Lucy was a virgin. She wasn't like the other girls, like Darlene and Eleanor. Those days, in school, reading lips was like reading everyone's diaries. Darlene and Eleanor were pretty popular."

"So, you see, they knew I didn't kill Lucy. The timing was all wrong. I got to the river late. Too late. She was already dead." He stared at the judge. "I said nothing in court because I was afraid of being charged with their rapes. The same penalty, my lawyer explained, as second degree murder with guaranteed parole after serving fifteen. That's the reason I'm here. I wasn't expecting your decision. No one was. But primarily because I wanted to spare my mother the shame of what I did do and because my mother knows I did not kill Lucy."

"Only once the sentencing was read out, did I read what Rigby and Carlton were saying. They killed Lucy, somewhat pleased with themselves that I happened along when I did."

Billy's lawyer asked, "Can you describe the Rigby or Carlton girls, as you recall them?"

"Eleanor had a faint mark, possibly a birthmark on her right buttock. Not a very big one."

"You're sure about that?" the DA questioned. "All this happened at night, in the dark."

"On a dark night, yes, under glaring high beams. That's why I reeked so badly. Between the night, them, and the car's lights, I was pretty spicy. Besides which, when a geek is that close to a cute girl's bare butt, he lives for the moment. Cause it ain't gonna happen again anytime soon." He smiled. "And you know what? It hasn't."

"And the other one…anything?"

"Darlene had a pale scar from sutures on her lower abdomen, which I wouldn't have noticed were it not for the particularly intense pleasure Eleanor was deriving while on the blanket from that particular region. Apart from which Darlene was perfect…physically anyway."

"You left, you found Lucy and…what?" Billy's lawyer queried.

"I covered her. I spoke with her to comfort her and I was arrested. The rest is history." He met the judge's eyes. "Do you remember, Judge Stillsworth? Happy birthday, Mr. Rider. My single disappointment in this trial is that I am unable to impose the death penalty since premeditation could not clearly be established. More's the pity. You are a despicable being and I profoundly wish that the earliest stages of your physical punishment at Battle View will prove as effective as any noose."

"You see, I read your lips the same way I read theirs. That's when my hell began, three years of medieval torture imposed by you. Would you like to see my back, my shoulders, or run your judicious hands over the two hundred and seventy raised welts that I will never explain away?"

She retorted, "I delivered a sentence I believed was in keeping with the crimes against Lucy. I don't apologize for my judgement or my comments. My judgements are severe because I judge the most severe crimes. However, Mr. Rider, that form of punishment was abolished in the earliest part of 1972, as was yours. You may want to recant your statement. We are not here for theatrics or implausible untruths."

"Implausible? Is that a fact? August, 1971; February and August, 1972; February and August, 1973; Valentine's, 1974…Your Honour." He leaned closer to her. "But I didn't scream. There was no point." His laugh was caustic, the sound unsettling. "No one would have heard me…Judge."

She stood. "Then, yes, by all means show me your back."

He did, manoeuvering from the top of his coveralls, tugging his tee-shirt over his head.

Her abrupt shriek and grief-stricken expression coming close to making her appear half human. The interpreter gasped, covering her mouth.

Stillsworth turned to Prescott. "Care to explain yourself, Warden?"

He remained seated. "There was a mix-up in communication. I was not aware of the abolition until much later, years for whatever reason. I am not responsible for this. I discharged my duties as precisely mandated by you. Whatever went wrong is not my responsibility. I am not at fault here."

"I suppose throughout those two years you didn't read your correspondence, or perhaps a newspaper, or listen to the news," the DA interjected, reaching for the phone, calling the head of the Federal Bureau of Prisons. Several minutes later, with everyone present privy to the conversation, Warden Prescott was relieved of his duties pending an investigation. He was ordered to leave his office and to leave the prison, escorted to the parking lot by his own men.

Judge Stillsworth spoke next, her composure fully regained following a brief sidebar with the DA.

"Mr. Rider, you are going home, wherever home is. I see no reason for you to remain here another minute. The paperwork will take most of tomorrow, however as of now you are a free man. That said, you are not rid of Battle View entirely. You will be called as a witness against Mr. Prescott and your legal counsel here will guide you through a process of compensation for your time served as well as the illegal punishment you endured, during which time your interpreter will be retained at no cost to you. Also, you may derive some modicum of solace from my assurance to you that Dwight Rigby, when found, will occupy your cell, 312." She extended an open hand. "Good luck to you "

He accepted the gesture, taking her hand in his. Then he signed with a smirk.

"What did he say?" she asked the interpreter.

The young woman giggled, she liked him. "No hard feelings…Miss Allison."

That was John Anderson: 101.

*

Billy had his books from the library to take with him, nothing more, the interim warden forgiving the outstanding debt. He had no other possessions.

Word of his release spread quickly through the blocks and the yard. Battle View Prison no longer had a barber.

He went with his elite entourage from the office to freedom, past the fenced-in yard from where several hundred stunned faces watched him stride towards the silent gates.

Unlike John Anderson, he stopped to face them. He placed a hand over his heart; he smiled, bowing ever so slightly. If he didn't have friends inside, he had respect. He hadn't once been threatened, abused, or had the shit kicked out of him. He was grateful for that, and no less respectful.

Black Boss was predominant, a centrepiece, his pink lips curved into an amicable sneer that was the best he could manage. He knew. Damned straight he knew. John-boy had done good for the quiet white boy.

Once through the gates Billy saw only what lay ahead of him. He had seen Battle View Prison from outside its grey walls once before. That one time was enough.

The lawyer didn't have to ask what was on Billy's mind. He was all too familiar with cons and ex-cons. The smart ones all wanted the same thing: To forget. And he didn't think new jeans and a sweater was what Mr. Rigby meant by "you do things right."

When they arrived at the Memphis hotel several hours later, Billy Rider appeared to the staff more like a Mr. Billy Rider in oxblood loafers, a dark blue suit, white shirt and dark blue tie which he had asked the sales clerk to knot. In fact they had no idea at all who he was.

The lawyer and the interpreter went to dinner feeling good as Billy went nervously to his mother who wasn't expecting him until sometime Friday at the earliest when Billy's brothers would join them. The lawyer, not wanting to cause Sally traumatic shock, first called her suite to give her a heads-up as the interpreter introduced Billy to an elevator. Back in the seventies no such convenience existed in any Small Town, North Carolina.

Stepping from the cubicle that he didn't like one bit, seeing Sally's agitated arms and hands scrawling the air, Billy opened his arms, ignoring the foreign tears trickling from his eyes. He had nothing to say, or too much. An hour later a fine meal was delivered to Sally's suite. The lawyer was following his instructions to the letter with the greatest pleasure.

Slowly the evening took shape, mother and son parting reluctantly near midnight when Sally wound up sufficient courage to ask.

"His name is John Anderson, mom. He's a good man, a good friend." Billy paused, clasping his hands, gazing between his knees. "He's the best."

"How could he possibly have known to assure me with such powerful conviction, darling? He left me very much beside myself that day. And then to discover that he did somehow foresee your return to me. How could he possibly have foretold the terrible events revealed to us in Dwight Rigby's confession?"

"John is a very powerful man. He somehow knows what is right. How else would he mould a strong and educated man from a skinny deaf and dumb idiot?"

She smacked his cheek gently and sent him away. She hadn't slept in forty-eight hours. Conversely, Billy stayed up all night flipping through channels, though his mind roamed elsewhere until the 6:00 AM local news.

They weren't telling him anything about himself that he didn't know. He was more interested in Prescott, smiling, nodding his approval. An appropriate payback, albeit years too late. The man was found early Thursday evening by his wife who went running to their bedroom at the sound of an explosion to discover her husband's lifeless body nursing a shotgun by an empty bottle of bourbon.

The police were not releasing any more details until their investigation was concluded. He chuckled. Preston was concluded, that's what truly mattered.

John Anderson was indeed a powerful man. Anyone who could command the respect of a thousand of the country's worst criminals was that and more. How he managed Rigby's confession, Billy couldn't for an instant imagine. Yet somehow he did. He sure as hell did, while unwittingly orchestrating Prescott's suicide, Billy's gut telling him that somehow Stillsworth was wrong. Dwight Rigby would never see Battle View. He would not spend the remainder of his life in Cell 312. John would, and very soon a past or present Florida whore whom Billy had seen once in a photograph posing in a tiny yellow bikini would become front page news.

Friday, the 28th, Billy Rider dressed in new slacks and a sweater that would have taken him years to afford from his prison income, this after the protracted luxury of his second shower alone without the company of forty or fifty other men.

He dined privately at breakfast with his mother who was also registered at the hotel under the lawyer's name. The media as yet had no idea where to hunt for falsely convicted Billy Rider, although he and Sally had consented the evening before to meet privately with their luncheon guests.

At 11:30 the lawyer asked if they were ready, if they were certain, counselling them to expect a flood of emotions. They were ready, fortified with the warmth of each other's hands, and the four went into the reserved salon together to greet the Rigbys, the Carltons and Merriweathers, the lawyer having greatly underestimated the magnitude of the heart-wrenching tsunami.

Their guests were made aware in advance of Billy's academic success, that they should not expect a simple-minded boy in a man's body. What they did not expect was Mr. Billy Rider who strode into the room confident and straight with Sally by his side, his expression not at all aggressive or resentful.

He first acknowledged the ladies, stoically, his sympathy towards the mothers of Eleanor and Darlene sincere, shocking them. To Mrs. Merriweather he apologized for failing his best friend when she most needed him, which did nothing to stem the flow of tears. In spite of which civility was the most he could give them.

His face and his hands were darkly tanned; his grip was strong. He shook the hand of each man firmly, thanking them for coming, assuring them there was nothing for him to forgive. Though Mr. Merriweather clearly sensed the truth.

Throughout lunch no mention was made of the cul-de-sac or the River Watch, nor of the triple homicide, the confession or Dwight Rigby.

The Carlton Bank was in the process of becoming a City & District, a move Mr. Carlton had resisted for years. Rigby's Fine Motors was in the process of a complete takeover, transitioning to Outer Banks Imports.

The families were moving out of state, together as friends rather than living out their remaining years in deep shame and possibly ruin whatever the future might bring to their grandchildren, which in no way negated their promised intentions to make things right. To the extent that they could. They fully understood that money alone could never heal the deepest wounds

Mr. Carlton passed Billy an envelope, the interpreter taking it upon herself to explain the function of a bank card. Mr. Billy Rider, temporarily residing in Seattle, was that city's City & District newest customer with two and a half million dollars in his account. A deposit, he explained, which was shared by the Rigbys. He handed another envelope containing a cheque for the same amount to Mrs. Merriweather who, nineteen years earlier, had created The Lucy Foundation to assist young girls in trouble.

Billy at once refused. They should not have to pay for their son's crimes, he insisted. To which Mr. Rigby replied, "We disagree with you on two levels, Mr. Rider. Firstly, we have no sons living or deceased. Nor do we consider that we ever brought daughters into this world. Two critical points on which our wives concur. Secondly, this money is derived directly from the ill-gained success of those responsible for your incarceration and misery, which we four consider appropriate. We are simply the humble and remorseful couriers. This matter is closed."

When the time came to leave, when civility and remorse had reached their inevitable saturation points in concert, goodbyes and best wishes were exchanged with expeditious decorum. Neither Sally nor Billy would see the three couples again.

As much as he continued loving Lucy, and wanted so badly to sit with her where she lay, he could not bring himself to forgive her mother or father for not letting her go with him to the dance.

Friday evening Billy flew First-Class with Sally into Raleigh, North Carolina with the lawyer and interpreter who would meet with them again on Monday. Sally's ability to interpret for her son was not considered sufficiently professional by Stillsworth.

He had never flown, never soared into clouds at 400

miles per hour or felt such nerve-wracking vibration, pretty certain that John hadn't described the experience as well as he might have.

John did this. He did; Billy creating possible and impossible scenarios in his mind. Though he kept that imagery from Sally not wanting to upset her when what she wanted most, now that her son had come home, was to find John and wrap her arms around her son's savior.

Billy wanted to find John also. He had a debt to repay. He figured he owed his friend one and a quarter million dollars, and more.

Sally touched his arm. "Darling, I feel I must tell you something that may greatly disturb you. Forgive me. I have not been forthcoming with you."

"Yes, of course, mom...anything."

"Her first breath of the joy. I trust this letter strengthens her heart, that's what Dwight Rigby wrote in his confession."

"Yes, a peculiar sentiment for a killer."

She shook her head. "No, darling. Not from a killer, from our John. I spoke those very words to him when he first called me. 'I will tell him with my first breath of the joy of the hope you have brought me this very day. You have strengthened my heart as I believe you once strengthened my son.' John was sending you a message through me, darling. He wants you to know that somehow he kept his word." She grasped his arm firmly with both hands, her eyes glistening with distress. "Whatever will become of him?"

Thirty-Five

June 28ᵗʰ

John naturally assumed that Brenda would remain at her South Beach Condo throughout the week. He was confident that she would; he wanted to kill her on the weekend but he wasn't taking anything for granted. He had no reason whatsoever to trust her.

The cities were only about an hour apart, and anyone with the stamina to be a whore with her untiring schedule at age fifty-four would undoubtedly have the energy to drive home after work. With that in mind, if push came to shove, anytime would be a good time. Y vaya con Dios, puta.

Monday morning the men woke early, leaving through the beach entrance, spending a quiet few hours as Pat observed the pool boy and gardener doing their thing through his Bushnells. By noon the workers were gone with the maid, which for Pat was far from good enough. He wasn't taking chances, waiting until two.

The first forty-eight hours since the Necessity killings were monotonous, Pat truly disappointed by the lack of news throughout the day Monday, telling Rigby to take heart. His celebrity status would surely be recognized the next day.

True to his word, news of the triple homicides did come with Tuesday's 6:00 PM broadcast, cause indeed for celebration. Mr. Dwight Rigby was a fugitive, considered armed and dangerous, Pat tipping his glass out of respect to his houseguest. But that wasn't the news he wanted. He was in the loop more than anyone else. He wanted an update on Billy, which didn't happen until Thursday when he learned that Billy Rider had been released from prison late that afternoon with his whereabouts currently undisclosed.

That announcement called for another bottle of Pomerol '81, which Pat chose not to share. Then he heard about the pious Mr. Prescott, ex-warden of Battle View Prison and spent the next hour bent over in fits of raucous laughter.

The week had been mostly a dry one for Rigby. Pat needed him in the best possible shape for his encounter with the whore, limiting himself to a hit or two each night for the same reason and the fact that he had a dangerous fugitive in custody. He wanted his final memory of her to be vivid and everlasting. He deserved that much.

Friday, the 28th, was a day of preparation. Rigby had spent the entire week with a wrist taped to a chair, save for a half-hour reprieve each morning in a bathroom whose window Anderson had nailed shut. Friday was different.

Pat vacuumed and dusted the entire home, wearing his gloves that were fast becoming a second skin. He sprayed and wiped her tables, the stereo and television he was becoming adept at using. He washed and put away the day's dishes after a late lunch that would sustain them, exchanging his leather gloves with her rubber gloves. He repaired the bathroom window and made certain her pool area was pristine. He was set to go, Rigby asking whether all cons were that paranoid, Pat replying that he shouldn't worry. He would find out for himself soon enough.

Rigby hadn't shaved for a week, though Pat had allowed him to shower until early Thursday for selfish reasons, nothing more. And throughout Friday he wore the clothes he'd worn Thursday and had slept in because everything Pat Fellows had learned from John Anderson had meaningful purpose. Including that near 5:00 PM Pat sprayed him with the beer from a few shaken cans before making him roll several times in the already damp sand outside the patio gate.

Pat showered twice on Friday, as late in the day as he deemed wise. Finished, he flushed the ceramic stall with the handset until he was satisfied, dropping the soap bottle and towels into a plastic bag that he put in the pantry with another containing the week's empty bottles, food wrappings, scrapings and duct-tape handcuffs.

The evening would be unforgettable for both men, memorable to each one for different reasons, Pat dressing for the occasion in a suit and tie. He felt he needed to make a favourable impression, reminding Rigby of his commitment not to fuck-up, that a hole in his polo shirt would spoil his chest and ruin the evening.

He assumed Brenda's Denise might be on any of the three flights departing Miami between 6:30 and 8:15 to Montreal, Paris or Brussels, his curiosity about her undiminished, which could put Brenda at her home any time between those timeframes.

At 6:30 he poured a Johnnie Walker Blue, a Black for Rigby who was now free to use either hand.

For two hours Pat stood back from the window, peering at the gated entrance, exhilaration fending off tedium. At 9:00 the sun was quickly disappearing behind neighbouring homes, an amber glow from her front entrance lamps taking over to illuminate her driveway and garden.

He ordered Rigby to refill their glasses, then to stand in the hall and to stay put.

The glare from her car's lights lit up the room closer to 10:00. The Bentley scarcely made a sound, Pat thinking that he should take the thing for a ride in the morning if she didn't mind.

Seeing her strut from her car to the door reminded him of his childhood Christmases with Sally and Sam, waiting for Santa Claus to eat the cookies, drink the milk, and get the hell out of his house so that he could open his gifts.

Each step she took seemed to carry her farther away, Pat forcing himself to leave her to join Rigby in the hall which he hoped would heighten her surprise. He always was all about her. Nothing, and no one, was ever more important to him than Brenda. And that hadn't changed since the day she screwed him over.

Rigby had to admit he was curious about the woman. He pretty much knew the entire story, not doubting for a moment that she would be dead within a few hours, not certain how far he could make it in her car. He hoped as far as Key West, the way Fellows suggested. There he could hire or steal a boat that would get him to Cuba, a destination he believed made sense. Fifty-fifty was better than no chance, and he knew not to fuck with Fellows.

At the clicking sound of the key working the lock, Pat stopped breathing. He wanted to absorb every audible detail: Her keys rattling onto the table, her footfalls, her purse dropping to the floor, her sigh after a hard day's work squirming in her bed with Denise… her scream. He wanted to savour every precious moment.

She flicked the light switch. The keys did rattle, her purse did drop, and she did sigh. Pat musing that Denise must have worked her frigging hard for a grand. Good girl.

He waited, strangely composed. For better or worse, Battle View had a way of supplanting fear. He felt not the slightest trepidation. He couldn't see her, nor did he want to. Not yet. He needed her away from the door. He didn't mind that she might scream. In fact he wanted her to, a melody to his ears, as long as she wasn't running hysterically into the middle of the street.

Countdown: Three, two, one…Pat jerked his head. The stage was set.

"Good evening, Miss Peters," Rigby said, stepping from the shadows.

Pat was elated, on a high. The fright he saw etched into face, her violent halt as though he had punched her in the chest again, her terrified squeal, all that fulfilled his greatest expectations.

She shrieked on cue, stumbling backwards, terrified. He was filthy and he reeked; his clothing was stained and crumpled. He was one of the beach's homeless who constantly harassed residents and tourists for money. "There's no money in the house. I swear. Take what's in my purse, then leave. Please."

"I'm not a vagrant, Miss Peters. Very much the opposite. You might possibly have heard about me recently. I'm Dwight Rigby...the North Carolina killer."

"I swear, I don't keep money in the house."

"We're not here for money. We're here for you, Miss Peters. You."

The fear in her eyes fixed on the other man stepping into view, stopping inches behind Rigby. Then on his gun.

"Please don't hurt me. Take my purse and my car. Take anything you want. Please."

"Thank you for acquiescing. We intend to."

"Good evening, Brenda."

She stood frozen. "How do you know me? How did you get in?"

"We've been enjoying your hospitality for a week, not quite certain when to expect you. Although we did allow your maintenance staff the privacy and time they required. As to your first question, a reasonable one, you and I were married once upon a time. I'm the Anderson in Brenda Anderson." He chuckled. "Have I changed that much...sweetheart?"

Her hands clutched her throat. "You!"

"Yes, me, John, one of a few thousand according to your vast array of history books. Very interesting reading. Tell me, what does a man get for seven-fifty these days? Or, better yet, what did du Valois get for his two-fifty back in the day?"

Rigby interjected, puzzled, "John...?"

"Shut up, Rigby."

"This cannot be real, John. Why now? Why after an entire year?"

"Not a year, a few weeks. I did extra time for shit-kicking some guy. That's Battle View talk."

She glared at Rigby, disgusted. "You both killed those people? And now you want money to escape? Is that it?"

She straightened, foolishly more confident.

"No, and no," replied Pat. "I brought along Rigby here to lend me a hand."

"With what?"

"With you. You see, I never got to see you finish with the Frenchman. I've felt cheated all these years. I need that closure and Rigby here has happily volunteered to assist you with the re-enactment." He stepped forward. "I have a present for you, which should help you to understand that we are serious." He gave her the gift box, waiting. "I apologize for skimping on the giftwrapping. I haven't worked for some time."

She lifted the lid, pausing, removing the silk thongs.

"You bastard."

"I really do prefer the Miami condo, sweetheart. May I call you that? The one up the road, not so much. You've done well for yourself…dinner clubs, a fine home, a couple of exclusive high-rise whorehouses and a Swiss bank account. Good for you. I mean it. And, oh, thank you for the Pomerol. Absolutely divine. And the JW Blue…well, delicious doesn't say enough. You certainly have come up in the world."

Her mind was struggling to process what she was seeing, what she was hearing. "This stupidity stops right here. Get out. Now."

"Tell me, have you spoken with Polly and Walter lately, your parents in Nebraska? Do you even know if they're well, or even alive?"

"No, I don't."

"Like I told you, Rigby, a loving and caring daughter. You know, Brenda, I spoke with them before my sentencing and daddy didn't like his little girl being a whore. He wanted to gut you. That's what he said."

"I need you to get out. I have no cash in the house and I am certainly not letting your killer friend touch me."

He took a moment, giving her concerns due consideration. "No, that doesn't work for me. I don't need your money and yes, you are. You see, I promised Rigby here that you would. I told him all about you. He's been as excited as a Nebraska farm boy all week. He's never been with a real whore, since his wife doesn't count. Thing is, you'll have to do him pro bono, and no time like the present. He doesn't have money of his own and not much time before he's captured. And, on that note, how was Denise today? A grand? Really?"

"Better than you ever were."

"Ouch, sweetheart. You know, I'm thinking you should talk about her first, about what you did with her. You know, to get Rigby up and running."

"Yeah, right. Good luck with that."

Brenda Peters was wearing a simple skirt and a raglan sweater. Even close up and in person she didn't appear older than mid-forties…for the time being. Her skin was tight, her complexion smooth, her brown eyes as dark as he remembered them.

"I somehow thought you might be a tad indisposed, given his current financial and social status and his somewhat scruffy condition. I'm good with that. I understand your reluctance. It's a quality thing with you, keeping your standards high. Clothes make the man…particularly when he has seven-fifty in his pants. In spite of which I took the liberty of laying out your clothes for the evening." His mouth and cheeks twisted into a mocking sneer. "You'll find everything on our bed, sweetheart. Thank you. I haven't slept that well in years."

Her reaction was so convulsive, her face such a scarred mask, that he believed with visible amusement that she might vomit.

The jeer curdled in her throat. "Good for you. As long as he didn't disappoint you. A taste you acquired in prison, John?"

"Not exactly. You're the taste I acquired a greater appreciation for in prison." He went to the bar, adding a splash of Blue to his glass. "For which reason I need you to change into your work clothes, sweetheart."

"That will not happen."

"Au contraire. Because I've made very clear to Rigby here that, if you do not play nice, I *will* kill him instead of giving him your car keys. Since I can't kill you. That would be too obvious, counterproductive in the extreme. I mean, really, more than a few curious minds out there must be wondering why you're not dead already." He turned to Rigby. "Tell her. Who really killed those people in your family?"

"You did."

"That's right. I did. And how did that make me feel?"

"You felt good."

"Yes, payback for a friend and I did feel good. Getting the idea, Brenda?"

"Fuck you, John. Not a chance I'm fucking this guy. Not for you, not for any amount."

"A freebie. We're not paying. Instead I've given Rigby here Carte Blanche to get things done, short of killing you. However you may, at your discretion, attempt to make things appear real. Fight back, get some skin under your nails. Kick and scream. You know, the way I believed the Frenchman was raping you. And really? He's not that tough."

"Do you actually believe I'll keep my mouth shut about this? They'll come for you again. You know they will."

"I appreciate your concern. I've got that covered,

particularly since I have proof that you're a talented and well-paid whore with a Swiss bank account."

She was shaking her head. "No! You will not do this."

Pat glanced at his watch. "Rigby, do not be gentle. Not now, not later. This whore put me away for twenty-six years for no good reason. She could have saved me, yet she chose not to. Sound familiar? So you get her stripped and have a good time with her. No time-frame. You deserve each other. And, Rigby, your lives depend on it. That's right, Brenda. Yours too. I simply want to refresh a faded memory, nothing more, to remember you more vividly as a treacherous whore. So help me here, people."

Rigby stepped in closer to her, slapping her face, the impact jerking her head hard to one side, knocking her breathless to the floor. Her shock was real.

"John, this is not who you are. Do not do this."

"That John died his first day in Battle View," he countered, unmoved.

Rigby extended a hand to her. "Here's the deal, Brenda," he said. "So please listen. You will change and you will spend a little time with me. He'll get to see you in action and I get a fresh start early in the morning. I don't imagine he'll stick around much longer either. Think of me as a surrogate. Then you can get on with your day. That doesn't sound so terrible to me. What do you say, shall go into the bedroom? I've seen the books. It's not like you haven't done this a few times before."

She kicked out at his legs, missing. "Don't touch me!"

"Listen, if not his surrogate, think of me as a referral who's doing his best right now to save our lives. Do you really have a problem with that?"

Pat sank onto the arm of a sofa. "Grow a pair, Rigby. She's not a moody housewife, she's a whore. Treat her like one. Or do you need a rock?"

She stood on her own, unsteadily. "I am not a whore, John. I'm not. Stop calling me that!"

"Frankly, I expected tears by now. You're doing very well under the circumstances. I'll give you each a few moments to friendly-up and change. Then I'll join you."

She remained adamant, her breathing laboured, "No. This is not happening, John. This pig is not raping me."

The next blow sprawled her more violently onto the floor, Rigby rubbing the back of his hand. "I'm a businessman, lady, not a pig. And get this straight, I am not raping you. I'm saving your frigging life for Christ's sake. So get involved here."

Pat savoured his Blue. Delicious. "Better him than me, sweetheart. That shit-kicking I mentioned. He and I were evenly matched, which didn't prevent me from shattering his jaw. Now get your tight ass up because I don't particularly view you as a vulnerable woman."

She did, uneasily, staggering. Her face stung from the smack, her cut lips beginning to swell under a glossy mahogany coating. Her legs were weak, shaky; her mind was spinning. She bent forward, inhaling a deep breath, her eyes fixed on the floor. She bolted for the entrance, instantly shrieking, flailing head over heels in the air, crashing the side of her head and her shoulder hard onto the floor.

"Rigby, I *am* impressed. You might survive Battle View after all. Good man. Now get up, sweetheart. Accept what's going on here. We are not leaving. This is my dream. So, come on. Help me out here."

"You are sick, John. You really are. Feel proud of yourself beating on a woman? Asshole."

She waited seconds too long.

Pat drained his glass, pushing himself upright, impatient, tucking the weapon into his belt. He was on the clock and she wasn't cooperating.

He grabbed one of her arms, jerking her upright, bending to meet her as she continued in an arc over his shoulder.

He ordered Rigby to follow. In the bedroom he tumbled her onto the bed, with one sharp tug at the waistband ripping away her skirt, evoking a helpless high-pitched squeal. Jerking her into a sitting position like an unstuffed doll he tore away her sweater, jostling her, jolting her rudely from the covers. He tore at her bra, tossing the ruined thing over his shoulders, leaving her naked with her tattered panties gripped in a gloved hand.

"Yeah, sweetheart, this is happening." He turned to Rigby. "Get her dressed. Call me when she's ready. Brenda, ten minutes. Do not challenge me and do not waste my time fixing your make-up. He's not interested in your face or your mouth, not unless you want him there. Whatever makes you happy. You're the pro. Just get it done."

He strode into the living room, adding to his glass and Rigby's, finding a suitable Bordeaux that might help to calm her.

He heard Rigby call out a few seconds shy of her deadline.

He passed Rigby a Black with a gloved hand, offering Brenda the wine. She wasn't interested. She wanted them gone, her tone somewhat less demanding. Instead he placed the crystal goblet on a night table and made a toast to the evening before removing his jacket and tie and ensconcing his weight into a comfortable armchair.

Brenda Peters was dressed in a strapless, slim-fitting black cocktail dress, stockings and heels; Rigby hadn't wasted any time stripping-off and sliding under the covers. Pat assuming he was timid.

"Brenda, sweetheart, be convincing."

She ignored him, unfeeling. She unzipped her dress, pushing the top to her waist and to the floor.

Rigby was anxious. He first saw her not thirty minutes earlier, an incredibly attractive woman in a skirt and sweater, far lovelier than he'd ever seen his wife. He'd seen her dishevelled and bruised by his hands, exhilarated. He'd seen her stripped naked and sat gaping as she mechanically dressed for him. Now she was altering the visual dynamic for Rigby from all that to a glamorous and alluring body he was about to ravage. And, he sensed, she was more than aware. Disappointing Fellows, whoever he was, was not an issue. He was more than ready and very willing.

She draped the dress across her leather and chrome récamier, standing for them in sheer stockings; Pat musing that her bronze-coloured garter, high-rise backless panties and strapless bra came almost close to making her seem desirable. Close, but failing the grade.

 She kicked one stiletto away, and the other, planting one foot on the récamier where both men could see her. She unhooked the silk clasps matter-of-factly, leaning forward, pushing the stocking to her ankles and past her toes, the second following mere seconds later to rest by her dress. Facing Rigby she freed her waist of her satin belt; that too dropped to the récamier, the fingers of one hand freeing her breasts while her other hand halted its descent by cupping a delicate hand over a perfectly tanned breast. She added that piece to her short-lived costume as well, her panties seconds later, wasting no time raising one leg, and her other, to complete the striptease which Anderson commented was somewhat lacklustre.

She wasn't at all recapturing their once enchanted evenings he fondly remembered. He required a little more effort, a little more enthusiasm.

She didn't care, crawling in beside Rigby who was draining his glass. She left hers untouched.

Pat let them get started. He wasn't interested in high school hand jobs or Rigby apparently believing that grunting louder would get him harder faster. No wonder Eleanor didn't complain all that much when her brother was fucking her. She had a clown for a lover.

Pushing himself upright he went to the bed, throwing back the sheet, chiding them.

Rigby was a star in his own right. Pat had seen the uncut version of the movie. Now Rigby was in bed with Florida's most sought-after whore and this was the best he could manage?

"And Brenda, sweetheart, you might be pricing yourself out of a job. I expect much more from you. Think back. Think Frenchman."

They needed direction. He wanted a heated performance, he reminded them. He wanted sweaty realism, as though he had paid big bucks for her, which he had for years, not some aging mom and pop searching blindly for wilted parts under a quilted blanket.

From that much needed intervention he wasn't certain whether Brenda wasn't having a change of heart. She seemed to be having a better time, either from a prostitute's street-sense of survival or at last remembering that she was a certifiable nymphomaniac beginning to lose herself in the moment. Or possibly she was experiencing difficulty staying in the stirrups because Rigby was bucking and jerking and twisting as though racked by a grand mal seizure.

His hands were all over her. He was fondling her breasts, craning his neck to kiss them. He was rubbing her thighs, stroking her back, pulling her closer, pulling her hair, grabbing her ass, spending most of his limitless time there until he emitted disturbingly loud sounds like a car engine dying, sputtering, groaning and gasping. All the while Brenda was sitting spread in the saddle with her hands on her hips or on the bed, succeeding in not touching him.

With his final grunt she dismounted in a quick half-spin onto the space beside him without uttering her usual and professionally believable whimper. She felt nauseous. Not much better than Pat felt.

"That's it? You're done?" Pat queried, disappointed. "Hell, I seem to recall when…"

"You wanted a whore. You got a whore. That's what whores do. Seven-fifty gets you a whole lot more, including what you're drinking. Now get the fuck out and take this preemie jerk-off with you. I did what you wanted."

Pat stood, putting his glass aside. "Sorry. My fault. I thought he was better than that, from what I knew of him. He misled me, and for that I truly apologize. I would have done you myself but, you know, the sewer thing."

"Fuck you. Do I look like a sewer?"

"Yes, you do." He paused midway between his seat and the bed. "Brenda, you know what? I'm thinking, why not? Why the hell not, for old-time sake? You and me." He dug a hand into a pocket, counting out seven hundreds and a fifty, laying the crisp bills on the night table. "No favours though. No family consideration. I want the whole nine yards. So, what *does* this buy?"

"You're serious? You want me?"

He nodded. "Rigby, off the bed. And get your ass into that towel. I've seen all I care to, and stay put while I'm gone."

Rigby obeyed. He slid from the bed as Pat took his glass, returning with it brimming with Black. Brenda hadn't touched her wine, she was preoccupied staring at the money; she wasn't certain. John would never do any woman so quickly after another man. Not even her.

He ordered Rigby onto the récamier, passing him the glass. "Drink up. Enjoy. Since I can't let you out of my sight, and since I have no more duct tape, you get to see how this is really done."

Rigby swallowed several quick gulps, sitting. He was partly exhilarated, partly unsure, not at all willing to upset a man with a gun and very little compunction.

"You cannot be serious," she blurted, "after all these years? In front of this creep? No!"

"I am very serious, sweetheart. I'm also curious. With all the hours I've spent here and at your condos, I haven't yet come across a single divorce document. You are still Mrs. Anderson, aren't you? Or am I missing something?"

"Don't flatter yourself. I'm Brenda Peters. Your name is all about business, about Brenda's and this place, not you. Never you. You were a joke then and even more of a joke now."

"Let me see if I have this straight. What you're proposing to your clients is Mrs. Anderson for a great meal, and Miss Peters for some great pussy? Is that about right?" He beamed. "Was this another of Garcia's brainwaves? You know, something like take a lady to dinner, but take a whore to bed? Good thinking. Separate profit centres."

She hurled her wine glass at him, missing, splashing herself, the bed, him, and the floor in a deep ruby red.

"You never thought of me, Brenda? Not once?"

"You were a bad mistake. I got on with life. Why don't you?"

"Apparently not enough of a mistake to disown. What I did find interesting, what I did come across, is your will. And, more importantly, your beneficiary. You have none. How about that? Too old to remarry, sweetheart, or too busy fucking for money to date?"

His still current wife blanched; her cut lips gaped apart. He could practically see the tickertape running across her furrowed brow. She'd fucked up big time, taken too much for granted. She had never expected polished and refined Mr. John Anderson to survive the demons of Battle View Prison that the DA had described to her in vividly colourful language.

"I wouldn't be that stupid. That document is obsolete, predating any last thought of you. So you can stop dreaming. Like I said, you were a huge mistake. Not one I care to repeat. So do what you have to do. Rape me and get the fuck out. And take your dirty friend with you."

"Thank you for the clarification and the request." He went to the récamier. "Rigby...here, put your feet up. Make yourself at home. Behave yourself and you'll have her again while I disinfect myself or until the seven-fifty runs out, whichever comes first. Because that's what whores do. Hell, for that matter, once I'm gone, take her as often as you want. Hell, take her to Cuba. She's paid for."

"Fuck you, John!" she seethed. "Not even for a hundred times that much."

Rigby did as he was told, bringing up his feet, paying no attention to her designer clothes. "Perhaps I will. I can't say she's not tempting."

"Tell you what, Brenda. Rigby here, he likes the doggie thing. Or at least his wife did. Guess they never had much to talk about. Anyway, sweetheart, get on your knees." He waited. "Your knees, Brenda, or do you really want Rigby here all night, all ways, instead of me? Your choice."

Brenda crawled onto her hands and knees, each movement deliberate. He could tell she wanted to kill him, something about her eyes. Though he also sensed relief, that somehow she believed he was the stupid one. His mind perhaps dulled by all those years in prison.

He circled the bed examining her while removing his shirt. He couldn't resist chuckling at her expression. Yes, he had changed, because of her, and not simply his physique.

His shoes, socks, and slacks were next.

She was gawking, clearly taken aback. Many of her best clients were in their thirties and forties, all of them satisfied, eager for more. Many others had reached their fifties and into their sixties, not a single one anywhere close to resembling the unfamiliar man leering at her.

What shocked her was the tan, how slim he was, and his tone. He'd become more than the confident, handsome man she had so quickly and easily forgotten. He was intimidating, his eyes and his oddly casual manner threatening beyond the gun held in his hand. He was dangerous.

Precisely the reaction he had hoped for, the one he was

savouring. She was ridiculous on all fours, staring at him as though waiting for yet another willing and hungry male to mount her.

"So, Rigby, you all set up, comfy? Ready for the grand finale and your great escape?"

Rigby was halfway through his Black and very relaxed. "I am. Not that I have much of a choice." He raised his glass in a salute to Brenda, smiling stupidly. "But, yes, I am. For this and for a lot more."

"Well, you did have a choice... once. But you fucked-up, amigo, big time. You all did. Give my best to the ladies."

Pat pressed the muzzle of the Berretta quickly and firmly against Dwight Rigby's temple from the side in a single smooth motion. He had practiced the proper trajectory for days.

An imperceptible click discharged a nine-millimetre round into his skull, spraying a good portion of his grey matter through the exploded exit wound and across much of the room, intentionally missing the bed and a horrified whore that was flung backwards by some imagined shockwave slamming into her. Déjà vu.

She was terrified by Pat's serene smirk, his smug and contented expression. She was gasping for air and sobbing, her legs and feet thrashing wildly against the sheets, slipping, her body jammed against the unyielding headboard.

"Remind you of anything, Brenda? Anything at all, sweetheart?"

"John leave. Get out. Please. I'll say he broke in, that he raped me. I swear I will. He did rape me, John, and you cannot do this again. I'm begging you."

"Oh! So now you'll say that, that he raped you? You're a bit late, Mrs. Anderson. Don't ya think? However I do agree with you. I do. They will certainly believe he raped you. Seems to me that he emptied a full clip into you, sweetheart. And I have to presume Denise didn't leave much behind."

She nodded frantically. "Yes, John. Yes, they will."

He dropped the weapon, reaching out with open arms. "One hug for old-time sake, that's all I want. All I came for. Then I'm out of here and you can either report him or practice on him. The gun's clean. Come here, sweetheart."

She crawled closer, crying, raising herself onto her knees to face him. She was expert at reading men's thoughts, her shoulders slumping in defeat. She wasn't seeing a burning anger borne of her ancient betrayal. She wasn't seeing hurt or resentment. Brenda Anderson was peering into a dark and pitiless void.

"Please don't hurt me, John," she pleaded in a desperate whisper. "Please."

"That's right, Brenda. You always could read what I was thinking."

She glanced over to Rigby. "John, please. That did not happen. We can take care of that, you and me. We can do that. You can have a good life. I can do that for you. I can, and I will. Please."

He shook his head. "No, sweetheart. I'm pretty sure that did happen. Here's why. Rigby was a fugitive with nothing to lose, convinced he would hang. Or at the very least spend his life in prison. He felt cheated and betrayed by his wife for what she had done throughout their marriage. You know, pretty much how I felt. That's why he ostensibly killed her and the others before running with nowhere to hide. Then he saw you from the beach. The same way I did, on your deck in your little orange eye patchy thing. You were a vision, a beautiful and naked woman climbing the steps of her pool. You were his last chance at love, his last chance to feel like a man. Too bad the gate was left unlocked. Really too bad about that. Anyway, you fought him off. Good girl. You did your best, struggling to survive against his maniacal and superior strength. You got a little messed up and, yeah, he raped you. Then he got nervous. You knew who he was. That's when he killed you and you can see for yourself what happened next."

What!" She clutched his forearms, digging her nails into the hardened flesh "No! John, no!"

"You have a choice, Brenda. His way is fast, my way is euphoric."

She was blubbering, her pride and dignity obliterated. "John, I am begging you. Anything. Please do not do this."

"Listen to me. The Côte d'Azur thing at sixty, that's not going to happen for you. Tomorrow, the beautiful sunrise…is not going to happen. You were as guilty as me, Brenda. If not for you du Valois would not have happened. He would be alive. You drove me to murder a man you were fucking for money and then you gave me up. So, yeah. This payback time, like I promised. You really shouldn't be surprised. And I really don't feel the need to see you uglier than you are to me right now, which is good news for you."

An instant later he spun her around as easily as fluffing a pillow, a gloved hand clamping over her mouth. A few seconds later, bounding into her closet, her body pinned against his, he dropped her to the floor, stunning her, grabbing a fist full of her hair, snapping back her head and stuffing her mouth with a rainbow of silk thongs. He needed her fullest assurance of quiet.

She was limp, sobbing, screaming a muffled whimper as he swept her into the air like a little child and into his arms. She was too weak to struggle, focusing all her energy on clearing her mind. She knew John. She did. He was always a good man. He could forgive her; he would forgive her once she could make him listen. He'd always listened to her, always loved her voice.

Pat ran with her through the home, through the garden doors and onto the darkened patio, Brenda firmly locked in place. One arm and hand trapped her torso and arms, his other hand intent on muting her hysterical whines and guttural groans.

At the pool he twirled her again, as though she were weightless, planting his feet wide apart, for an instant freeing her mouth to trap her arms behind her, waiting, staring into her eyes that were panic-stricken and pleading. She was shaking her head maniacally from side to side, her hair wild, silk strings drooling from her mouth. She was whimpering, her face a horrible mask drenched with tears and stained with make-up.

He said "here we go, sweetheart," taking an exaggerated stride that carried them over the contoured edge.

They crashed into the water, her legs trapped between his. He wasn't counting, holding her under for five, ten seconds before letting her resurface.

He wiped her face, swept back her hair and cleared her mouth of the silk. Her youthfulness was gone; her dark eyes were wild with fear, her once beautiful face bruised and cut.

"I haven't once failed to keep a promise, Brenda. You know that. This one taking a good while longer, I grant you. All the same, you knew tonight was coming. I should have killed you that night. You can't imagine how many sleepless nights I sat awake in my cell regretting that I did not. I would have saved myself a lot of trouble and pain…and this."

She was sputtering and coughing. "No, John. Please. Please do not do this. We can talk."

"No, we cannot. A bit too late."

She went under again. One, two, three. He couldn't tell whether she was gasping for air or snivelling for mercy, tiny bubbles bursting into the night air. Not his problem.

She resurfaced.

"You sent me to the worst hell, Brenda. I could have gotten over you being a whore, if you had given me the chance. But not Battle View with nothing to do each day but remember you and Garcia smirking in court, mocking me, and my constant dream of this moment. And here we are, man and wife united. Don't be afraid. I'm told this way is painless and euphoric. I'm sure they're right. Just let it happen. Goodbye, Miss Brenda. Regards to Monsieur du Valois."

Brenda Peters lost consciousness in under a minute, the dark and hectic water veiling and distorting her face. When her convulsing ended he released her, inverting her, propelling her towards the deep end before climbing to the deck to watch her aimlessly drift face down around the pool like a robotic pool girl.

When he was certain Brenda Peters was no longer an issue, not that evening, not another day or night in his lifetime, he stripped away his Lycra boxers to let his body dry in the warm night air.

Once inside, with no reason to hurry, he wiped the always pristine weapon free of doubt. He pressed Rigby's fingertips along the barrel, then helped him to squeeze the barrel in a tight fist before securing the grip into his right hand. When he let the hand drop the gun fell to the floor.

He put a few tens and twenties into Rigby's otherwise wallet. Apparently the man had gone on a spending spree. He retrieved his seven-fifty, self-serving another two-fingers of Blue and making his way to the patio and Jacuzzi to ponder why on earth Dwight Rigby would rape and murder Brenda Peters, much sought after owner of Brenda's dinner clubs. He was devastated. Was no one safe in the world?

He had no idea. Who would, unless he waited too long to leave?

He glanced at his watch: 00:05. He had five hours to kill. Leaving too early might find his nocturnal stroll on a dark beach leading him into the arms of some gung-ho cop; whereas too late might prompt curious neighbours to err on the side of caution. Or bring forth passers-by who later might remember seeing a 6'3" man leaving her home. However a businessman in a suit leaving home with a suitcase for an early flight out was no one's issue.

He wouldn't dare to sleep, or to mess up by turning on more lights than her bedroom before 1:00 when he would do what he could to further help set the stage. He had much left to do.

He started with the bedroom where he dressed into his suit after stripping away Rigby's towel and dripping believable amounts of pool water over his shoulders, his chest, along and between his legs. Rigby's glass had fallen to the floor, hers was pretty well everywhere, delivering better drama than he could have hoped for. He left her tattered clothes where they lay.

He accounted for each piece of his week's clothing, soiled or unused, putting each piece into a plastic bag. He pulled each item of her more elegant costume from under the lifeless legs, adding them as well. He did the same with Rigby's wardrobe, leaving behind what he'd worn to the beach that afternoon and had scattered on the floor before raping her, adding the wet thongs that he'd taken from her mouth.

When he was done, when he was certain, he put everything by the gate leading to the beach.

He took Rigby's towel and a fresh bikini bottom from her drawer to the patio. He tossed the towel into the water; the thong he tied, soaked, ripped apart, and left by the steps.

He arranged the deck furniture to provide an adequate privacy screen between the pool and the beach and again he went inside to pour a healthy measure of Blue. He was on a high with every reason to celebrate.

He took Rigby's suitcase into her office, filling it with the whore's agendas dating back to 1953. No reason for anyone to discover that his wife was a consummate slut, particularly since she'd been thoughtful enough never to divorce him. No reason to publicly disparage the woman, though he wasn't raising his hopes or thinking beyond his capture that was a real possibility despite his best efforts until those efforts made him absolutely free. Before leaving he slipped the bundle of hundreds from her strongbox into his jacket.

From her walk-in he wheeled a designer suitcase to her wine storage where he selected a few dozen of her finest vintages she would want him to have as recompense for not destroying her lovely head with a nine-millimetre round.

Lastly he selected her favourite shade of lipstick from her vanity, keeping the message he scrawled with his left hand simple before dropping the ruined tube where he stood.

His work was done, further anticlimax unwarranted and foolish.

He left once at 4:30 with two bags of clothing, and a suitcase filled with her history.

The sun was barely peeking over the horizon, no one yet strolling the beach or searching beneath the sand for lost treasures. Not fifteen minutes later he returned through an unlocked gate to retrieve the two garbage bags, deciding the wine would perforce require a third trip. The suitcase was too heavy, awkward to drag in the sand. He would appear suspicious to anyone seeing him, not to mention leaving an unwanted trail if someone prematurely discovered her.

He completed his last inspection at 4:55, ensuring that she was peacefully afloat.

She was, drifting carefree.

Know when it's time to leave: The difference between success and failure. Precisely what he did, through the beach entrance the pool boy had forgotten to securely lock several days earlier.

Thirty-Six

July

The unofficial time of death was sometime after midnight, June 29th, two days ahead of schedule. The official time was uncertain, the coroner noting sometime between late Friday evening and early Saturday morning.

The pool boy was the first to discover Ms. Brenda Peters early Monday morning, the police blaming Sunday's heavy downpour for lack of exterior evidence, when the most crucial evidence, her killer, lay somewhat crooked on the victim's bedroom lounger with what they would later discover was a blood alcohol level of 1.2.

The dinnertime news from West Palm Beach would tell the country that Dwight Rigby, self-confessed killer of Lucy Merriweather, his sister, his wife and best friend, had taken his own life after the savage beating, rape and murder of that city's Brenda Peters, age fifty-four and owner of the popular Brenda's dinner clubs.

In his final moments Rigby wrote a thick and illegible "im sory," on a mirror before cravenly bringing an end to a string of his past and present violent crimes.

As was expected, Rigby's parents were not available for comment.

Mr. Alejandro Garcia, her distraught business associate, met with police earlier in the day. To the best of his knowledge Ms. Peters, an only child, and single businesswoman, leaves behind no living relative. In a brief and tearful interview he assured the people of West Palm Beach and Miami that Ms. Peters, his loyal friend and business partner, would, until his own heart ceased to beat, breathe life into Brenda's.

Four hours later, across the country, Billy Rider was finishing his last wedge of homemade birthday cake, sitting with his mother and brothers in her Seattle home. His lawyer and interpreter were absent by design. Sally wanted the special day alone with her family. Tomorrow would come soon enough.

"What is the matter, darling?"

"Rigby, killing that woman." Billy put down his plate. "Why didn't he kill himself instead?"

"He was a terrible man, darling. He killed poor little Lucy and now his family for which I feel not the slightest sorrow. Nor will I ever forgive him for the suffering he caused you to endure. He is best off where he is. All I can ask and hope for is that, wherever he is, his suffering will never cease. The least he deserves for his senseless crimes. And that poor Brenda Peters, so young and beautiful with so many years ahead of her to enjoy. Terrible, just terrible." She saw her son smiling, curious. "I can scarcely imagine the tumult of your emotions, darling."

Billy Rider sat shaking his head. Not so terrible. He at last knew her name. Brenda Peters was dead. The whore was dead, sent to her destiny by a man who always kept his word.

Billy leaned closer, his grin widening as he read the newswoman's lips. He said, "No, mom. Wherever he is, he is in a much better place than where he might be. Believe me. I've been there. My most fervent wish is that he remains wherever he is."

"Whatever do you mean, Billy?"

"He's free, mom. No more worries, no more running. Listen to her, the case is closed. Let's hope it remains that way."

Sally wasn't sure she understood, or even that she should, patting his knee. Her son would require a long while to sort out his emotions.

Billy said no more. He squeezed his eyes shut. He was worried for his friend. John was a thorough man, very possibly too thorough. He didn't believe for a moment the case was closed, not from John's perspective.

*

Early Monday evening, still in West Palm Beach, free of clutter and a wardrobe he no longer desired to wear through another season, Pat Fellows sat on the veranda of his rented beach villa gazing out to sea. He was wearing one of several new outfits, ruminating, contemplating life as he lingered over the richness and aroma of a delicious Margaux '78. Life was good.

He'd remained in town to hear. The case was closed. He could go home. John Anderson hadn't once been mentioned, which he hoped was a good thing and not a ruse that would backfire on him. Although he wasn't anxious to call Polly and Walter. He thought he might wait a few days.

More importantly he'd lived a dream, fulfilled a promise. His friend Billy Rider had his life and his family back, and would soon have a whole lot more, which he knew Billy understood would be far too little to forgive or forget two decades in Battle View.

He wasn't in a hurry. A full month paid in advance remained on his Charleston lease, money he didn't want to waste. He hadn't spent any of the eight grand garnered from his evening with the Rigbys and Carltons, with a few grand more left over from his 401K that she'd never gotten her hands on. Enough money to get on with life somewhere.

Where exactly, he wasn't certain. Cuba would be the best idea, the easiest. Or possibly Québec where an entrenched sense of culture made them as distinct as Latinos.

Europe would bankrupt him in a month. Nor could he

imagine himself in black pants and shirt with a white apron strung to his waist and serving wine or expressos to a narcissistic in-crowd or, much worse, young lovers.

He had time and he went to sleep that night for the first time since his arrest and conviction without thinking of her. He was free, and he was free of her. At least his mind was, fairly certain that his body wasn't far behind. He'd been neglecting the physical, too intent on succeeding.

He left for Charleston on Tuesday before sunrise, travelling alone without Billy Rider or John Anderson beside him. He arrived at the apartment at noon with a new wardrobe to unpack, a supply of wine to store and a designer suitcase to toss in the garbage bin.

The last several weeks had taken a physical and mental toll. He felt he needed to recondition his body while resting his brain. He was tired of mundane sit-ups and crunches and thinking. He needed a yard to workout in.

Tuesday afternoon he bought a membership at a gym he'd heard about that did not cater to upwardly mobile anyone, or spoiled housewives, or old men who could use their purple balls for a game of croquet, or brain-dead hunks sniffing around to track females in heat.

He went religiously each day for a week, each day feeling more himself, each day embracing more of Pat Fellows and less of John Anderson. He spent his evenings walking alone in bare feet on cool sand, breathing the sea's fresh air, watching late-day skies evolve from blue to red-gold to a black littered with specks of silver. Life was good and getting better.

So he wasn't wealthy, when a quarter-century earlier he was pulling in 100K. So what? He had enough to live on until he figured things out.

Not an evening went by that a dozen or more attractive and viable ladies wouldn't smile warmly at him, emitting equally warm and encouraging signals. He was honoured, his male ego sufficiently pleased that women could find him attractive at sixty. So what? He wasn't interested. How could he be? He had no job, no real money, and he lived in a dump where he kept a drawer filled with wine worth six months' rent.

The woman upstairs who somehow managed to fit her hooves into shoes, seemed never to sleep; the woman on one side of him seemed to want him to be aware that she was getting seriously laid each and every night on a bed well past its best days; and the hearing impaired welfare case on the other side wasn't much better with daytime soap operas blaring through his wall and her year-old brat screaming through the same wall each night that it was pissed-off being born to a loser.

A murderer and ex-con with no money, a ten-year-old Monte Carlo, and living in a tenement: The ideal man. What every woman longed for. Or not. He went with not. He didn't need the hassle. Besides, that they hadn't yet knocked on his door didn't mean they wouldn't one day soon. He was taking a gamble, a huge risk, when newly born Pat Fellows needn't have returned to Charleston or stay a moment longer.

Yet he felt more confident each day.

Nothing was different on the ninth. They meandered past him, smiling, some in short skirts, some in shorts, some with girlfriends, some alone, all of them worth the second glance he didn't give them. Most of them currently residing somewhere between forty and fifty. He figured.

He stayed out as late as he could without sleeping on the beach. He cherished the tranquility. Hell, the 378 other men in his block, excluding Billy, were quieter than her and that damned kid.

The tenth began at 7:00. His mornings always would.

The girl next door had sprung from her bed and was gone with enough love swimming inside her to last until dinner. The hog-woman upstairs was plodding her way across the parking lot to a bus stop with a girth and angle of sway that would ensure her the right of way anywhere, while the brat next door was heralding a new day of privation and hunger because at seventeen its mom had a long-term, workable plan. She had run away from home, fucking her way into a two-bit job she no longer had, and her mommy and daddy had closed the family door. Good plan.

Not his problem.

He arrived home from the gym as rush-hour was in its infant stage. He strode through the main entrance with his gym bag slung over his shoulder, taking the steps two at a time to his landing and ready for a long, hot, and private shower. Those other times were gone, history. The next naked body to stand beside him in a shower, whenever that might be, if that would ever be, would come equipped with soft skin and smooth curves at no cost other than a fine dinner.

Fuck!

John Anderson had never run from a problem, neither would Pat Fellows. The men stationed on either side of his apartment door were all about business, their heads pivoting in unison when his intimidating physique abruptly filled much of the dark and dank corridor.

They weren't smiling, which he could understand. The building was a cacophony of unbearable sounds, the smells worse than Battle View's latrine.

"Help you gentlemen?"

They pushed themselves from the wall. Stereotypes in striped grey suits, black ties, cotton shirts and laced shoes: Clones of one greater and all-knowing. And briefcases. These guys were not cops. One was older and more experienced, visibly jaded; his buddy, Pat mused, anxious for his chance at becoming old and cynical.

"Are you Mr. Anderson, Mr. John Anderson, formerly of Miami, Florida and more recently of Battle View, Tennessee?"

"I am. And you understand, I'm sure, that I am not on parole. I did my time, gents. So what is this about?"

"Not about that, we assure you, Mr. Anderson. May we come in, to talk more privately?"

John Anderson opened the door stepping in first, dropping his bag, not certain that Pat Fellows had any good reason to follow. He needed a drink. Shit did he need a drink.

"Take whatever seat you can find. We're sort of casual here. I would excuse the mess, but that would extend to the entire building. I'm having a JW Black. Been a rough day. You gentlemen? Scotch, red? I wouldn't trust the water if I were you."

They declined, opening their briefcases for something to do, sorting papers as they waited.

The senior man began. "We are here, Mr. Anderson, representing Mrs. Brenda Anderson as the executors of her estate."

His brow furrowed. "I don't understand."

""Then may I assume that since your release you have had no contact with Mrs. Anderson?"

"That's correct, as much as I wanted to see her. I suppose I was afraid to reopen old wounds."

"Mr. Anderson, your wife was murdered some eleven days ago." He forewent condolences. "We apologize for the delay in meeting with you to deliver such unfortunate news. However we were required to follow certain protocols and employ the most stringent due diligence."

"You might have to check your facts, gentlemen. I believe I'm divorced. Isn't that the natural order of things after hubby kills the boyfriend and goes missing for twenty-six years?"

"Apparently not in Mrs. Anderson's case, for whatever her motives might have been. That said, your dossier was made somewhat more complex given your previous years and, as you suggest, the natural order of things which your wife chose to disregard. You are, sir, her sole beneficiary, which we have verified innumerable times as her sole provider of insurance and financial services."

Pat blew a stream of air through pursed lips. "She never remarried."

"No, sir. She was, in fact, the owner of two very successful dinner clubs in Miami and West Palm Beach. For whatever reason choosing to remain single. I presume to the dismay of many eligible gentlemen. I had the privilege of meeting with her on several occasions. She was very attractive indeed."

Not so much when I left her. "She had no children?"

"She did not."

Lucky kids. Pat sipped his scotch. "What did she leave me, her cat and dog, a few bills? I'm not living the high life here, gentlemen."

"I believe your situation may soon metamorphose into a more privileged one, sir, as a result of your wife's tragic passing. We never know, do we? Perhaps Mrs. Anderson was, for reasons she kept private, wishful of a reconciliation of sorts. We are, of course, privy to the court case, Mr. Anderson, which played no small part in our extensive investigation prior to this meeting."

"I can honestly tell you that not one night in Battle View did I fall asleep not thinking of her, wanting to see her one last time. How was she killed? Did she suffer?" Was she floating?

"I believe she did, sir. An intruder attacked her inside her home, a man accused of murdering his family. He took his own life after needlessly killing Mrs. Anderson."

I beg to differ, not needlessly. Not by a long shot.

The man opened a file. "I would prefer that you contact the police for more precise details."

I believe I'll pass on that one, thank you. "I will definitely do that. The least I can do. What happened between us was a long time ago. Time heals all wounds when we learn to forgive."

"Indeed sir. I believe so." The age-old problem of blending banal conversation with formal business diminishes with experience and jadedness. Get to the point and get out. "Mrs. Anderson's estate is quite extensive, Mr. Anderson, bequeathed to you in its entirety as her husband who legally constitutes first and foremost her beneficiary named as Estate. This encompasses her West Palm Beach oceanfront home, two high-rise income properties in Miami and West Palm Beach, as well as her dining establishments in each of those cities. She also carried a life insurance policy which necessarily nullifies the clause covering any permanent physical incapacity or disfigurement she might have suffered in her lifetime."

And twelve million in a Swiss bank account you know nothing about. "Gentlemen, are you sure? Scotch, a glass of red? Not the very best, nevertheless very drinkable."

They refused, their blood alcohol most likely already at .04 or one shot higher, he guessed. Not everyone gets to sit in a slum with a Battle View graduate.

Pat stood for a refill, taking his time. His mind wasn't racing. He'd been expecting them. Better said, he was hoping they would come first.

"What we need, Mr. Anderson, is to establish that you are indeed you. After which the process is quite expeditious. Two, three days at most."

Pat produced John's driver's permit, his payslips from the cartage company, his car purchase agreement, and his release signed by the dearly departed Warden Prescott.

They spent the next half-hour signing documents and resolving the issue of what should be done with her ashes, neither Pat nor the two corporate clones thinking to embellish the meeting with handshakes or good wishes. They wanted out and were gone. Not that he blamed them.

Pat saw no need to enquire beyond his first quip, he didn't want to appear ungracious or avaricious. Besides, he had a pretty good idea.

Two days later the older man returned with an arm full of documents which included Brenda Peters' birth and marriage certificates and her will. The younger man carried the urn. John Anderson was now the indisputable owner of what was once Brenda Anderson's and Brenda Peters' life past and present.

That same day he received a call from his bank manager, advising him of the ten million dollar deposit made by the insurance company; the same banker who a few weeks earlier had refused Anderson a credit card. That afternoon Anderson converted the entire amount into bearer bonds and deposited them into a safety deposit box in another bank where Patrick Fellows had recently opened an account.

That evening John Anderson paid his landlord in full, gave the man his wine, left the keys in his car with the windows down and flew to West Palm Beach where he booked into another beachfront villa for the remainder of July.

On the morning of the thirteenth he hired a realtor, putting the condo and Brenda's on the market. In the afternoon he drove to Miami in a Bentley, checked-in to a five-star because he wouldn't sleep in a whorehouse and went to dinner at Brenda's without a reservation.

Big surprise. No seating available, until Pat told the man who he was, that the restaurant would be put up for sale the next day, and that he was there to speak "with Garcia. Unless you would prefer to lose your job also."

Brenda Peters' table was always set for two, the staff never certain when she would arrive or with whom. Which was no longer an issue.

Pat ordered a JW Blue to start, telling the waiter whom he remembered that Garcia was to serve the drink.

"Buenas noches, Juan. ¡Cuánto tiempo sin verte!"

"Not long enough, Garcia."

Garcia snapped his fingers for a drink. "You are here, I must believe, to gain in some way from this most horrible news. I cannot help you. The insurance people, they tell me nothing."

"No. The whore's dead, which is quite fine with me. And don't bother sitting. Fact is, I'm more interested in you, why you let me hang when you knew what she was."

"Brenda was the finest of women. Never speak of her that way in my presence."

"She was the finest of whores, and she didn't come cheap. I've seen her books, her rates. But you know that, don't you, since she gave you first dips into the pool? She kept very good notes. So, yeah, she was whore and you come pretty close to being her pimp in a tux."

"I will not listen to this. Leave. Now. Or I…"

"¡Cállate la boca! Hijo de puta."

"You dare to call me this?"

"As of yesterday this place is mine." Pat sipped his Blue. "As of tomorrow it's up for sale. Interested? Six million."

Garcia chortled. "I am interested in my ten percent of whatever you get. This would be one and a half millions, Anderson, since I am a partner in both."

"Actually you're a partner nowhere, not legally. So I was thinking more like get the fuck out, right now. You're done. The accountant, when I find him, will mail you a cheque. I believe a half-day's pay for each year I spent in prison because of you and your whore is a fair severance."

"You insult me. This place is mine as much as hers. My life is in this place, my blood is in the walls."

"It could be, Garcia." He sipped more Blue, unblinking. "Adios, amigo."

Garcia hesitated. "I cannot tell you, Anderson, how many times at this table we laughed at you. She wanted you to see her that way with the Frenchman, you know, to have you out of her life. What you did gave her even more freedom than you can ever believe. As for me, you will hear from my lawyers on this matter."

He whirled, storming out in a Latin huff.

Pat signalled the waiter, asking the man to send over the person next in charge. The Latina who had led him to his table, who already knew about him, came over. He stood to greet her, inviting her to sit with him. She was now the new maître d', he informed her, and for the next hour they spoke. He had a plan.

The next morning he met with a realtor, instructing that lady, as he had done in West Palm Beach for those properties, to post the condo below market value. He wanted a quick sale.

He spent the next few hours filling garbage bags with her clothes and personal sundries, disposing of them, leaving the condo as empty as a hotel room and the sympathetic concierge with a fine array of wines.

On the fifteenth he woke early. He went for a long walk along the shoreline, changed and drove to the sprawling home which the police had vacated.

He placed two calls before setting to work sorting through her papers he might need in the short term and shredding everything else. He removed all traces of her in countless bags until the three waste management trucks arrived. He instructed the crews to empty the entire house and deck, to crush and compact whatever was not fixed to the structure, which included the contents of the drawers, the closets, and garbage bags.

All this while Pat was emptying the wines and liquor into the Bentley, waiting until the crews at last finished...when he could toss his wife in with the compressed debris with the greatest heartfelt satisfaction since marrying her. She was at last where she needed to be.

The next day the painters arrived and a week later the house was sold for 3.6 million, during which time Pat flew to Nebraska.

Walter and Polly recognized him instantly, hugging and kissing him. When he informed them that their daughter had passed away as the result of a home invasion, Walter asked how *he* was doing. Nor was Polly the grieving mother. Her regret was that he had been kept from them for so many years. Now he was home, where he stayed just one night.

When he asked them during supper whether they still dreamed of living out their lives on the quiet shores of the Florida Panhandle, they smiled sadly. They did, but...

But nothing. He gave them the name of a good realtor and a personal cheque for two million dollars, explaining simply that while in prison his personal portfolio that was beyond Brenda's grasp had continuously performed beyond expectations. They were his family, enough said.

Before leaving them the next afternoon he helped put the farm up for sale for next to nothing, leaving a teary Polly with a warm embrace and Walter with a handshake and a suggestion that he might want to lose the coveralls before migrating to the sandy South.

The problem was Brend*a*'s. He wanted that concluded by the thirty-first. He was on a tight schedule and he wanted out. Taking the first offer that came in at four million for two restaurants doing three times that in sales. He wasn't cutting his losses. He was being smart, providing they would also take the condos off his hands for an additional two-point-five.

They did, John Anderson adding another six and a half million to his account which he immediately converted to bonds and carried with him to Pat Fellows' bank, whose net worth was now over seventeen million dollars.

Thirty-Seven

August

August 01st Pat Fellows stood on the corner of New Orleans' Canal Street and Bourbon.

For the past several days as John Anderson, preoccupied with expeditiously finalizing his affairs, Pat spent his evenings pondering the coming months as much as he reflected on the previous three.

Several days earlier he had confirmed by the evening news that Billy Rider was currently in Seattle, and that the federal folks in Washington had quickly agreed to compensate him in the amounts of fifty-thousand for each year of his incarceration, one million for each illegal whipping he endured, and an additional three million for twenty years of pain, suffering, and mental anguish. In addition to which, the news reported, Billy Rider would soon undergo corrective surgery that would restore his physical appearance and the promise of a normal life.

Nine million, Pat mused. The kid would do alright. He would have a life, and possibly one day soon be able to trust a woman.

An errant glimpse of Rigby flashed across his mind. He wasn't dead because he had raped and killed Lucy Merriweather. He was dead because he and Carlton were inherently debauched. That doesn't leave a person with the passage of time, a good job, or the subterfuge of old-family money. Evil that deeply embedded does not correct itself, it propagates with a single and proven remedy.

Their women were no better. They were worse. Their lives were never on the line. They cruelly and coldly placed their meaningless schoolgirl reputations that no one would later give a shit about ahead of a young boy's journey into hell that would continue to catapult Billy over the walls of Battle View Prison and into Cellblock Three with each fitful night's sleep for the rest of his life.

They were gone, sent swiftly into their own deserved hells and best forgotten. As was the whore, her ashes thoughtfully interred by him in a way that he believed would appropriately honour her life.

The gleaming black Cadillac slowed to a stop, the passenger window lowered for the men to acknowledge one another.

"Mr. Fellows, dare I presume?" Cleaver ventured.

Pat chuckled, reaching for the door's lever. "Getting used to him is a work in progress, Mr. Cleaver."

Cleaver waited until Pat was settled and buckled in. He hadn't yet acclimated to shoulder restraints, any restraint. He almost hated using cufflinks.

"You appear to have experienced certain successes since we last met, Mr. Fellows. I applaud you."

"I've had a busy few weeks to say the least. And yes, a good deal more than I expected."

Cleaver drove off. "I must admit that I was somewhat surprised to hear from you. I assume however that your once requisite utensils served you well and are no longer of use to anyone."

"You assume correctly, Mr. Cleaver. Unfortunately, as often is the case in business, I was unable to complete my strategy by reason of an unexpected yet welcomed adjustment in my thinking which prompted an unforeseen need to protract its scope. I came across unfavourable evidence that was more comprehensive than I had previously thought to consider. However, going forth at this juncture would cause me serious personal injury which I am no longer willing to suffer. And for that reason I would like to employ your services once more, which I clearly recall you once cautioned me was your most delicate and your most costly service."

"Mr. Fellows, what is the current condition of John Anderson?"

"He's lost in a crowd and he is not re-emerging." Pat snickered. "Along with a brand new Bentley at a very unreasonable price."

Cleaver lost his strangely endearing smile, pulling to the curb. He scanned Pat's thousand-dollar suit, loafers which he knew were imported, the French cuffs and the Rolex. 'Certain success' may have under understated Fellows' current situation. "Then you must also recall the cost."

"I do. Thirty-five thousand. Will you accept the fee in hundreds?" Pat retrieved a bundle of bills tightly wrapped from inside his silk-lined suit jacket. "His name is Alejandro Garcia. This is a current photo taken recently in front of his home. He lives alone in Little Havana and, without theatrics or endangering your people, I would very much appreciate that realizes from whom the message comes." Pat reached for the lever, pausing. "I'll get out here. First, however, please manage this on my behalf for Black Boss. Ten grand. Cigarette money. Tell him thanks, from a friend."

"I did, Mr. Fellows, as you requested. As I will again, this time in person. I understand that certain good changes have happened since Prescott's self-inflicted demise. Battle View is no longer a remnant of the Dark Ages. A new warden, monthly visits and television… all manner of changes. You must remember a certain Billy Rider from your tenure with them."

Pat nodded. "Vaguely."

"Well it would appear that when Mr. Rider regained his freedom he had quite a story to tell. From what I hear, he is very much the hero to those he left behind." Cleaver accepted the smaller bundle. "Thank you, from a friend, though I do have to admit that I am somewhat nervous about seeing my cousin, about what to expect. Do you have any suggestions that may assist me, Mr. Fellows?"

"Yeah, I do. Do not piss him off."

Cleaver nodded, grinning. "Good advice, indeed. Once was quite enough. And, Mr. Fellows, put your mind at rest. My associates will meet with Garcia within the coming week, which I believe now concludes our current and future business."

The men shook hands and Cleaver was gone.

From there Pat Fellows hailed a cab and went to his hotel. After an early dinner he went to the Louis Armstrong Airport where he boarded a flight to Chicago in time for a late connection to Paris where he remained a day before continuing on to Geneva with letters from his bank, Brenda Peters' original will, and certain other documents that made him 12.3 million dollars wealthier when added to the seventeen million in bonds he carried as work-related documents in a fine leather attaché case.

*

The evening of August 08th was exceptionally humid. Without slightest breeze all day the air was thick and stale.

Alejandro Garcia was assuaging his misery and hate in his living room, oblivious to the comfort of the cooler air when his doorbell chimed. The well-dressed and attractive Latino couple was interested in purchasing a home a few doors over and simply wanted to ask a few questions about the neighbourhood. They excused themselves for interrupting his evening. However it would be their first home and they were nervous.

He empathized, not surprisingly, particularly since the young lady's dress was incredibly flimsy and short with nothing much left to challenge the imagination, Garcia graciously suggesting they stand inside his foyer to shelter themselves from the oppressive heat. Though if not for the woman he would have told them flat out to ¡vete a la chingada! Or just fuck off.

They thanked him profusely, stepping inside timidly as he closed the door.

"We will not take much of your time, Señor Garcia." The young man assured him. "Thank you for accommodating us in this way. You are so kind to help us."

"You know my name?"

"We do. Señor John Anderson sends you his best regards." The gun was a ten-millimetre black Glock, and menacing. "He sent us here to set things right between you. Please step back several feet." He waved the weapon. "Several feet, Señor Garcia. This gun, it makes a terrible mess, and I have promised my lady a fine dinner when our work is done."

Garcia obeyed, trembling. "There is nothing between us. I swear to you on my mother's grave. What does he want with me? What more harm can he do?"

The young woman answered. "He wants you killed. señor…in five minutes. His wish is that you will have time to properly remember him. Please stay as you are. Five minutes is better than nothing."

His panic set in quickly, his Latino glow draining to a pasty white, his rapid gasping making his pleas pathetic and difficult to understand. "He cannot do this. His wife did everything to him, cheated on him. She is the one who told such terrible lies, not me. This I swear to you. She was a whore. Yes. Yes she was, who could not keep her legs together while I did everything to conceal what she was. No! He cannot do this. Please do not do this to me."

The couple glanced downward, unaffected. They were pros, hired by Cleaver because they were the best.

The legs of Garcia's white summer-weight slacks were staining and wet, each leg a conduit for his urine that was spreading across the tiles at his feet. He appeared ready to collapse, tears flooding from his eyes.

"Stand straight, Señor Garcia. And do not beg. You will die as quickly on your feet as on your knees, and with dignity. When they find you, they will know this." The man glanced at his watch. "This is your choice, of course."

Garcia was snivelling, wanting to flee before his knees gave out.

The young woman cautioned him. "Señor, to run would be much worse for you, and instant. Enjoy the time you have left." She raised her wrist. "Almost two minutes," that passed as two seconds as the couple waited patiently, listening dispassionately to Garcia begging through the spit and dribble blubbing from his distorted mouth, clutching the sides of his face, pulling at his hair.

"Señor, this should be your final moment of prayer," the man offered. "Señor Anderson is very generous to allow you this unusual kindness. Do not waste what little is left to you."

Garcia collapsed.

Disgust spewed from the woman's mouth. "Señor, you add dishonour to your shame."

The first round went through the top of Garcia's head, the second into his temple the instant his body came to rest.
*

The corpse was discovered several days later when a neighbour called the police, suspicious after seeing Garcia's car parked for so long in the driveway and the lack of response to his several phone calls.

By the evening of the fourteenth he was national news, the police at a loss to understand or create any link between his death and the Rigby-Peters murder-suicide.

Nothing made sense and John Anderson, a person of interest solely out of their desperation months after his release from prison, was nowhere to be found. Nor were the several million dollars he had removed from his bank as bearer bonds shortly after the deposits were made.

*

Several million, and missing, Billy Rider mused. Good for John. He'd been worried that his friend would screw-up somehow. He should have known better than to doubt the man who had engineered his freedom. John would be alright. He would find his way and do well. Billy believed that now.

That night Billy went to bed early, for once not thinking of John, partly because he was heavily sedated in preparation for his first of several surgeries the next day which the doctors had assured him would be a piece of cake compared to the infliction of the injury itself. He wasn't worried. He'd learned to never to give up hope.

His next conscious thought was that he was awake, lying on his front with his wrists tied to the bed which he didn't much like. He cried out for help, believing his freedom had been a horrible dream, twisting and straining until his mother's warm and gentle hand pressed against his cheek. A moment later he returned to peaceful slumber.

The procedure went as expected, as did the week-long recovery period. He was doing well. Everyone was encouraged, despite which he could tell that Sally was doing her best all through the week to disguise her worry and the heaviness of her troubled heart.

When he asked several times what the matter was she clasped her hands and smiled weakly, telling him she was being a foolish mother.

Once settled at home she sat with him. Her mood was solemn, her hands folded in her lap.

"Darling, I fear that I might truly have the worst possible news to give you. I cannot tell you how sorry I am." She passed him a sealed envelope. "This came for you the day of your operation. "I could not bear to distress you with what I believe you might now come to learn."

Billy took the envelope addressed to him, a faint gasp

escaping his mouth upon seeing the return address that was: Cellblock Three, Suite 312. His heart sank. How could that be possible?

He mindlessly mouthed "What the fuck!" Then, "Mom, this cannot be happening. I cannot read this. How can I be free when John is not? I was so convinced he was free."

Sally forgave the emotive expletive. "You will, darling. Because John made you capable. He made you strong. He would not have written to you had he not something important to impart."

His mother was right. She always was. He tore open the top edge, his fingers trembling. He had so many good feelings, now lost; so many hopes for John to live a good and happy life. Those hopes now shattered.

Seeing her son's eyes glass over, Sally dreaded the worst possible news.

Inside the card was a photograph of a well-dressed and debonair gentleman relaxed and smiling. He was standing at the portico of a white-stuccoed villa on a bright summer's day with a vast and beautiful body of blue glistening water in the distance.

A tear dropped onto the parchment as Billy read the words.

Hey, kid, a belated Happy Birthday. Been keeping a close eye on you. Glad to learn you've done okay for yourself. We both have.

Pork and beans in the mess at Christmas won't be the same without you this year. Then again, we must never give up hope. I believe you know that now.

My best regards to you and Miss Sally.

Your friend, Patrick Fellows.

Other Mystery – Suspense - Thriller Novels

By Doug Booth:

Split Verdict

The 4th Man

The Madam

Family Lies

Mother of Pearl

From Inside Her Bedroom

The Feast of Tombola

Deferred Prejudice

The Hunt for Gilligan Rose

The Fatal Diners' Club

Silent Conviction

A Christmas Killer, Comfort and Joy

Pariah In the Mirror

***

No One to Tell (Creative Non-fiction)